GULF

GULF

At last the real story of Arabia
as it truly is in the eighties.

A NOVEL BY
JOHN BURROWES

MAINSTREAM
PUBLISHING

Copyright © John Burrowes, 1988
All rights reserved.
First published in Great Britain in 1988 by
MAINSTREAM PUBLISHING COMPANY (EDINBURGH) LTD
7 Albany Street
Edinburgh EH1 3UG
ISBN I 85158 161 8   .

British Library Cataloguing in Publication Data

Burrowes, John
        Gulf.
        I. Title
        823'.914[F]

        ISBN 1-85158-161-8

Typeset in 11 on 12 Times Modern by Capital Letters, Edinburgh
Printed in Great Britain by Billings & Sons, Worcester

"Ambition is so powerful a passion in the human breast, that however high we reach we are never satisfied."

Niccolò Machiavelli

"The Martyrs glory in the fact
That on them is no fear
Nor have they cause to grieve"

Sura III, the Koran

Acknowledgement

The majority of those who helped me with GULF did so without knowing the precise nature of the book that it was to be. Nevertheless, so many acquaintances and colleagues, Arab and non-Arab, answered interminable questions with immense patience and politeness and made my journey through the intricacies of Islam one of memorable pleasure. I am deeply indebted to them all as I am to M and C for helping me, among other things, know a Stechkin from a Makarov.

Contents

AUTHOR'S NOTE

There are many prisons in Arabia about which little is known and about which there is no documentation. Zamakh, the prison in which part of this story takes place, is one of them. Zamakh is not its real name. Nevertheless it does exist and the account of life there as portrayed in this novel is a unique and first-hand description of the harsh régime that is experienced by the prisoners of many nationalities who are incarcerated there.

Similarly, there was an attack by Fundamentalists of a Hussein Martyr Squad in a particular country of the Southern Gulf, as described in this story. No details were ever published in the Western world of this occurrence. This book is based on the incident.

While much of this story is founded on real events in the Southern Gulf of the 1980s and every effort has been made to adhere to true historical facts and happenings, all of the characters depicted are of the author's creation and bear no similarity to people living today.

List of Characters

P. Carl Sabamontes, expatriate Indian worker and Soviet recruit.
Oleg Gurinovich and *Vasily Burenkov,* U.S.S.R. Government men in India.
Yaqoob Jaffar, expatriate Pakistani worker and inmate of Zamakh Prison.
Gordon Watson, expatriate Scot.
Brian Bria, Australian photographer from London.
Said and Yousuf, two of the men from Razak.

Jock Carlin
Bill French
Geoff Melmouth } members of the Thursday-Night Club.
Arthur Marsh
Steve Powers

David Anthony, the Major and Arabist.
Colonel Billy Bainbridge, M.C., head of Red Alert.
Saby, bar manager at the Rani Hotel.
Arie Van Est, "Dutchman" and Spetsnaz platoon commander.
Esther, a nurse from Manila.
Amar, a domestic from Baguio.
Tony Mills (Major Antony), Emirate Army officer.
Mustafa Ali Abdullah, the Minister of Public Buildings.
Haider Barjani, souk trader.
Issa, a former rebel leader and elder.
Mohsin, a Khoja from Turkey.
Mr Chanov, Soviet Trade Mission employee.
Pavel Bessonov, of the Soviet Embassy.

The Recruiting of Boris One

P. CARL SABAMONTES would be the very man, they thought. An Indian living in Bombay, he could easily be placed as a "sleeper" in one of the Gulf countries. He would be the kind of man who would have the patience to wait without contact from them, even for years should it be necessary. Their only acknowledgement to him that he was still required would be the small envelope which would be delivered regularly to his family, and which contained a sum of money that would be roughly the same as he would earn in the front job they would arrange for him as an expatriate worker in the Gulf.

He would be loyal to their cause; he had already proved that over the years as a faithful and active member of the Communist Party in Bombay until, that is, police harassment forced him to quit in the interests of his family. And even though he was a man of peace, he had often proclaimed that he would kill if necessary, if he was convinced it would hasten the day of world Communism, particularly if that Communism were to come to his own country. As he had so often preached, Communism was the only hope that India had to free it of the plague they called poverty.

Men like P. Carl Sabamontes had already proved their usefulness in the Arabian Peninsula, in places like Aden and later in Sana'a in the two Yemens. Now they were needed in the countries of the Gulf itself, much coveted by the Soviets as an area where they hoped to extend their sphere of influence. The country they had earmarked for the new man they were to recruit was Emirate, in the southern part of the Gulf. He would be based in the administrative and commercial centre there, known simply as Capital Area.

The function of the "sleeper" varies according to the specific needs of the countries which use them. Republican Irish have them planted in England for years, waiting on the call to go into action, usually in their case the planting of bombs. Some are still there . . . waiting. Islamic Fundamentalists have their own "sleepers" in countries where their cause is repressed, quietly organising and biding their time till the day when there is a political or theological change of climate, whereupon they can emerge and manifest their movement. They have operated like that in Egypt for decades.

The Soviet "sleeper" in the Gulf had to be of an acceptable nationality so that he could easily disappear among the polyglot communities of the region. His function was not that of a spy. A role such as that required much more sophistication. Nor was he there as *agent provocateur* or gatherer of information or for any active daily duty. His only purpose was to act as a contact man when and if the day came he could be of service to others who may be sent there, whether from the K.G.B. or from a small detachment of Spetsnaz, the squads of Soviet Special Forces which carry out a variety of clandestine operations throughout the world. Perhaps a safe house might be required, maybe on-the-spot data, such as current jargon, gossip, local habits, prices and other familiarisation facilities, minor but so vital information for others on a mission.

There was no lack of suitable candidates in India for such functionaries. The K.G.B. section at the Embassy of the USSR in New Delhi had files of such men ready should the word come from Moscow that one had to be placed in a particular country. And when it was decided that one should be placed in Emirate, P. Carl Sabamontes topped the list.

The file statistics detailed him as being aged 31 and married. Father a Goan Catholic, deceased. Mother a Keralite Baptist, alive. Active Party worker in Bombay for many years. Favours the radical Naxalite philosophy of overthrow by force. Ceased his Party activities in 1985 following Bombay Police clampdown on the movement. Bombay Consular staff check reveals no convictions. Categorised as "responsive" to appropriate overtures. The file only told a fraction of the story.

P. Carl Sabamontes was born in Bombay in 1955. His father worked as a loom hand in one of the cotton mills. The family lived in a single room, as did other families whose men worked in the mills or the chemical factories or one of the other labour-intensive industries which ringed suburban Bombay. Their house, together with hundreds of other single-roomed houses, was in an old low-rise block of flats in Parel. It was one of the smallest rooms in the crowded building, a crudely rendered concrete block which, because the contractor had skimped on his building materials and had used cheap, high-salt content sand, was visibly crumbling, appearing as if it had some kind of structural impetigo. Other buildings around, for one reason or another, had a similar dilapidated appearance.

Carl's mother gave birth to six children in their little house, but only three had lived. Young Carl Sabamontes was five when his father died of tuberculosis. There was a younger brother of three, a sister of two. Although she cleaned Parsee houses in the Colaba district, Mrs Sabamontes didn't earn enough to pay the rent of their room in Parel. They were evicted. Destitute and homeless, there was only one alternative. The pavements of Dharavi.

Anyone in Bombay will point you in the direction of Dharavi. But no one goes there, except those who live or make a living from it. For Dharavi is for the downtrodden. The downtrodden of the downtrodden. It's known as the biggest slum in Asia. That means the biggest slum in the world.

Dharavi lies on the eastern side of the Western Railway tracks near the fetid tidal creek of the Mahim Causeway and close by a stinking river called the Mithi which brims with foul waste. The lucky ones in Dharavi live in hutments made from oil drums and petrol containers laboriously hammered into metal sheets then wired together to form a crude tin shed. Other dwelling-places are pieced together from an assortment of tin cans and look like metallic patch quilts, the parts that aren't rusted being begrimed by the atmospheric pollution, a permanent and noisome mix of the fumes of dense traffic joined with the rancid stench of nearby leather and tanning factories.

The not-so-lucky live in lesser shacks of cardboard and industrial waste of all sorts scavenged from rubbish tips. The joins and corners of their make-do shelters are stuffed with rags and paper, which at best offer their occupants the most basic protection from the searing Indian sun and a modicum of privacy.

Those even less lucky live in the open on the pavements where they have to perform every human function in public. At the last attempted census in Dharavi, one estimate was that there were about half a million living in the densest and most despicable conditions to be found anywhere on earth. The area was measured at 432 acres. That's about the size of an average dairy farm in Britain. In the most populous sections, the areas where they lived on the pavements, the density was between 8,000 and 10,000 people per acre. An acre is roughly the size of a soccer pitch. An animal farm — for people.

P. Carl Sabamontes became a man on the pavements of Dharavi. A man of five years of age. For when his mother left her young family early in the mornings for the long walk to her work in Colaba in South Bombay, he was left in charge of his younger brother and sister and had to guard the family's meagre possessions . . . three blankets, a small charcoal stove, two pots, two bags of clothing, and a small purse his mother had tied round his neck and which he was to let no one touch for it contained her most valuable possessions, a wedding ring, a lock of her husband's hair and a small brooch he had given her before they had married.

Carl spent his formative years on the pavements of Dharavi. When his family arrived there at first they had to stay on one of the most exposed sites, where at no time of the day was there any shade from the merciless summer sun, apart from the putrid gauze of thick pollution that hung heavily in the air. The exposed pavements, such as these, were the cheapest to rent . . . yes, not even the near-destitute in what they term the world's biggest democracy, are allowed to squat free of charge in a place like Dharavi. Deposit money they call *pugree* and weekly rents have to be paid for the privilege of living in the shacks. "But we will protect you," say the men who collect the rents on behalf of the slumlords who have carved up the district. On the pavements too they make them pay, the rents varying according to what they consider the amenity of the site. In India there is always someone with an outstretched hand ready to grasp what coins he can from the miserable poor.

In Dharavi the slumlords, men whose own lives had been moulded by the dictat that if you didn't take it, it would be taken from you, were in control. The protection that they spoke about to their customers was no ruse for there were marauders ready to pounce on the Dharavites for their meagre rupees.

The men who took the rent and protection money from the pavement dwellers were at the bottom of a monstrous parasitic pyramid, paying a share of their blatant opportunism to ones who looked after a bigger section, who paid to ones who "owned" a street or streets. They, in turn, paid others who ran a district and who, in turn, paid their tribute to one who ruled over an entire *nagar,* as they would call a township. Then the ones who lorded over the *nagars* paid their percentage to the man who presided over the entire community, the Slumlord of Slumlords, the head of one of the world's most wretched gangster operations which, by comparison, made the Mafia seem like some benign benevolent society.

From her daily wage of 18 rupees — less than one British pound — Mrs Sabamontes would save a little for the day when she hoped they would have sufficient for their fares to Punalur in Kerala, three days away by train in the deep south of India, where her parents still lived on the small farm on which she had been raised. It was to take her four years to save the money, four years in which the family grew and Carl's younger brother became old enough to be left on the pavements on his own, in charge of his little sister, in order to let Carl earn some money.

He worked first of all as a lookout, or watchboy, guarding the possessions of other working families who had no one to tend their belongings. Then he raked in the garbage dumps for old batteries from which they extracted the powder needed by Dharavi's illicit distilleries to use together with other chemicals for speeding the fermentation process. From the same dumps he would also gather the rotten fruit which made the mash for the highly intoxicating drink they made called Country Liquor. Later, when he was bigger and stronger, he delivered cases of the hooch to vendors in Indira Gandhi and Kamala Raman Nagars, two of the townships of Dharavi in which the men for whom he worked had the sales rights. "That's how the great Vardarajan started off in life," they would tell him. "And look at him now . . . he's the greatest of the slumlords. The greatest ever. So great he can send to Madras for men should anyone try to organise a bigger army than his."

Indeed, great he was — great being in the sense of power. So great was Vardarajan in Dharavi he could ordain instant justice anywhere in the suburb. If two parties had a dispute of any kind they would never consider going to the courts. That would have taken years to settle through the labyrinthian Indian legal system. Instead they would let Vardarajan decide. He would listen to their pleas then decree who he considered was in the right, at the same time collecting a fee from each of the parties for his service. With his service there was also enforcement, meaning the verdicts of his jurisdiction had to be carried out, quickly and without argument. There was no court of appeal.

But even at the age of nine, young Carl Sabamontes was doubtful about the merits of being another Vardarajan and there was no one happier than he on that great day when his mother announced that they had enough money for the long journey to Punalur.

It was the P from Punalur from which Carl, as was the custom, was to take the first initial of his name. The little property on which his grandparents lived was called a small farm. A small farm in a place like Kerala was about the size of a market garden in Britain. It was just four acres. A little more than half the acreage was planted with rubber trees, the rest in rice, banana and coconut trees. It was an extra burden for Carl's grandfather and two uncles to take on more mouths to support but they were part of the family and therefore there was no questioning that they had to be looked after.

By comparison to the pavements and later the cardboard and tin shack in which they had lived in Dharavi, life on the little farm was a joy, even though their accommodation was a frail lean-to shed of wood and calico at the rear of the humble house in which Carl's grandparents and two uncles lived with their families. Carrying the heavy cases of liquor around the narrow and noxious alleyways of the Bombay shanty town had helped his physical development and although he had just turned ten he was strong enough to tackle many of the vital jobs that were required to keep up production on their smallholding. He learned how to plant the rice in the watery paddyfields in June then harvest the crop in September, planting it once again in the October for another harvest in January. He learned too how to collect the milky sap from their small rubber plantation and to shinny up the slender coconut trees to shake down the ripe fruit, most of which they would take to the market in Punalur.

As a young man he would walk with his grandfather and uncles once a week to that market town where they would sit with the other small farmers. The menfolk would drink the robust Country Liquor, real liquor made locally, and legally, from jaggery, bananas and grapes fermented together then buried in huge pots in special pits until it was ready for drinking. Just as men of the land the world over, they would talk together about their crops and the weather, invariably complaining and bemoaning the lateness of the rains and the poor prices they were being paid by the co-operative for their produce. That, in turn, would lead them to talk about the Government and invariably, as the liquor flowed, there would be some hot words about the lack of help which they got from the State administrators.

Farmers like themselves were looked after much better in other lands, one would say, and the others would acknowledge their agreement. They should be getting subsidies for their little tractors and other essential equipment, said another. They would signal their agreement to that too. And usually there would be those, and there was a fast-growing number of them, who would extol the virtues of Communism. The farmers in the Soviet Union had benefited greatly under Communism, why couldn't they? They would all shake their heads from side to side in that gentle rocking motion the Keralites would use when they were answering in the positive. As the months and the years progressed, the political consensus of the farmers who met like that every week in Punalur and in the other rural towns of the State, became more and more in favour of Communism until eventually in a State election they gave the majority vote to ENS Naamboodripad of the Communist Party — the first-ever democratically elected Communist Party in power anywhere in the world, they would quietly boast.

But Communist Party or no, there was to be no room on the family farm for Carl when he was a grown youth. When his grandfather died his two uncles inherited the farm and each of them had big families with sons to whom the farm would pass one day. Even at that the uncles would have to find part-time work as well because the farm was too small to keep all of them. Carl was faced with the prospect of leaving home but that was the way of it in the small rural communities of the Indian countryside, particularly in Kerala, the densest state in all India, the populace of which was known to be the most upwardly mobile work force in the country. When Carl was 16 his mother and her brothers pooled their resources in order to give him the fare back to Bombay where he would find work of some description in the booming factories that were mushrooming in the sprawling suburbs of India's biggest industrial city. Through a family friend, also from Punalur, accommodation was arranged in Parel, the suburb in which he was born. There he would share a room with six other young boys who had also come in from Kerala to work.

It was one of them who said he would introduce him to the foreman at the tyre factory where he worked, which proved sufficient for him to get a job there. A week later he got himself a second job, working as a helper on a roadside tea and samosa stall. The vendor suddenly disappeared after a fortnight, however, without having paid him any wages. It turned out he had refused to pay protection money which the gangs extorted from such small businessmen and he had to make a hurried departure from the locality. But there were other vendors and other jobs with them. From the roadside stalls, his evening work progressed to a small cafeteria then as a waiter in a small restaurant and later as a barman. Between the two jobs he was able to repay the money he had been loaned by his family as well as send regular sums to keep his mother and his brother and sister.

It was to take him three years to get away from the filthy work as a vulcaniser in the tyre factory, a job at which many men had become sick with the black dust in which they laboured without any form of protective gear. During that time he had leanred to drive and another of his friends who shared his room had got his name on the list for a vacancy with the taxi firm for whom he worked. He patiently waited the year it was to take to get to the top of the list.

The taxi drivers rented their cars from the owners. The going rates was 160 rupees for every 100 km registered on their clock. That was the equivalent of about £8. After they had paid that to the owner they would be left with almost the same amount, out of which they had to pay for fuel and maintenance. But because of the number of taxis in the city and the fact that most fares were only for a short distance, it could take a long time to log a mere 100 km. So long, in fact, that many drivers would spend their time in the long queues of cabs out at the International Airport at Andheri.

There they would wait up to a full day for a fare, if they were lucky that is. Often they would wait two, sometimes three days, sleeping in their cab and living off tea and snacks from the vendors, in the hope there would be a substantial fare when they got to the head of the queue. There was never easy money to be earned in Bombay.

Carl considered himself luckier than some of the other drivers who had much bigger commitments than he had. One he knew could only afford to live in the Dharavi shacks with his wife who was in ill-health, their six children, and his elderly parents. His daily routine would be to rise at dawn and, with money borrowed from a moneylender, hire a cart to go to the market and buy sufficient produce to keep his big family for the day. After he delivered the provisions he would go to work in his taxi, driving anything from 15 to 18 hours, at the end of which he would have enough profit to pay back, with interest, the moneylender from whom he had borrowed that morning. He might also have just enough left to buy the following day's food. But rarely did he have enough to hire a cart as well, so he would begin the next day as he had the day before with another visit to the moneylender. He was just a part of the Bombay rut.

"What kind of society are we that allows a man to be treated like that?" Carl would ask his driver colleagues as they waited the interminable hours between fares. "The world's greatest democracy," he would laugh, "and we have countless thousands living on the pavements every night and paying thugs to protect them from other thugs. I lived on the pavements at Dharavi, you know. I'll never forget the terror. There was a madman going about at the time and do you know what his practice was? He would prowl about in the middle of the night when everyone was sleeping, then he would select a victim. With the biggest piece of concrete or boulder he could lift he would let it smash down on the victim's head. He killed about 30 before they caught him. Another killed even more. He went about at night with a spear and would silently stab people to death. When they caught him he said he was merely putting people out of their misery. And that's just some of the things you have to put up with when you are a pavement dweller. Then you have people like the Phatak Dada, the Gangster of the Tracks. They even voted him into the Assembly. Know how he got his votes? He used to run some of the illicit distilleries in Dharavi and when the people were voting he set up some liquor stalls just outside the polling stations. If you voted for him you got free drink. He had both the quick-kick stuff and slow-kick brew. I think half of Dharavi was drunk that day and Phatak Dada laughed all the way into the Assembly. And we call this a democracy!"

But the other drivers had little time for his thoughts. They would tell him it had always been the way and always would be the way in their country. Radicalism would only bring them strife. Strife only meant suffering, and when people suffered in India, the poorest always suffered worst. So why try to change things?

Their apathy didn't deter P. Carl Sabamontes. The few hours free time he had every week he would spend mostly between the Asiatic Library, where he studied the works of Engels and Marx as well as Shakespeare and Shaw to improve his English, and the Communist Party headquarters in the Dalwi Building, between Parel and Lalbag, not far from where he lived. They thought a lot of him there, both as an enthusiastic organiser and as a public speaker. Some were even saying he could be a future leader of the Party in the city.

The Party badly needed men of his calibre in Bombay. It had lacked the intellectual mix which they enjoyed in places like Kerala and West Bengal. It had also suffered from the harassment of the city police who had paid extra vigilance to Communist activities in Bombay since the outbreak of the Naxalite movement there in the late 'sixties. RAW, the Research and Analysis Wing, the Indian counter-intelligence agency, had noted the newcomer in the Party and his eloquent speeches which were drawing bigger and bigger crowds wherever he went. When they discovered him working full-time in one of the big city hotels, they tipped off the Marawari owners about the political leanings of their new employee. Communism was anathema to the rich Marawari traders who owned many of Bombay's leading business houses. After only a month in his new job, which paid him a steady income that was much higher than what he could earn on the taxis, he was sacked.

It was nearly six months before he was to get another taxi, a lean period which couldn't have come at a worse time in his life. Now married and with a first child on its way and still having to send money to his mother in Kerala, it took his considerable resources in order to stave off eviction from the small, single-roomed flat in which he and his wife lived.

When he eventually did get back to taxi driving he conceded to the other drivers that perhaps they were right after all. There seemed little likelihood that India would ever change. Gandhi may have led them to their freedom, but it would take an even greater man to free them of their serfdom. And P. Carl Sabamontes certainly wasn't going to do it, not even in Bombay. He had other things to do . . . like looking after a wife and, soon, a child. He would devote the rest of his life to that.

But there were others with plans for the future of P. Carl Sabamontes, for not only RAW and the Intelligence Wing of Bombay City Police had noted that the handsome and intelligent young Keralite with the persuasive and engaging use of speech was no longer to be seen around the Dalwi Building. They had been watching him with more than the customary interest and were among the first to make enquiries about why he had ceased being active in the Party. They began discreetly to enquire where they could find him.

"He's gone just like so many others," one of the officials told them. "More interested in his own welfare than the future of the movement." They smiled quietly to themselves as they took the details of his address.

A week later two men met for the first time at Bombay International Airport. One of them, a man in his mid-fifties with a tired, sombre face, had been one of the men who had made inquiries about Carl Sabamontes at the Party HQ building. He was a member of the USSR Consular Staff based in Bombay. His name was Vasily Burenkov. The other one, a smart, athletic man in his mid-thirties, had just come off the short, one-hour 50-minutes Air India flight from Delhi, the capital. He worked in the KGB section of the Soviet Embassy there. His name was Oleg Gurinovich. Despite never having made each other's acquaintance before, they recognised each other immediately when they met at a prearranged spot in the terminal building.

"Well, is your man ready to see us?" enquired the one who had just arrived from Delhi.

"I was at his home last night but he was out working. I left a note with his wife and am expecting him to call for us later today at our hotel. Oberoi Towers," he commanded the driver of the consular car which was waiting for them.

Gurinovich, the younger man, gasped visibly as the car took the long winding route towards the city, first of all through Parle then Santa Cruz, with its busy airport, used for domestic-only flights, then on through the dreary and crowded southern suburbs of Khar, Bandra, Mahim, Dadar, Parel and Bhaiculla on the way to the Back Bay Reclamation area where the Oberoi Towers, one of the city's tallest buildings was situated.

"I've never seen such slums," he said. "Delhi's not like this."

"No. There's nothing anywhere like Bombay, except Calcutta, of course. This your first time away from Delhi?"

"Yes. I've only been there for four months . . ." Gurinovich suddenly stopped speaking as the car came to a halt by a small piece of waste ground at a road junction. A look of utter disgust crossed his face. Right beside the car, one of them only about six feet away, two men were defecating.

"Oh, you'll get used to that," said Burenkov as he saw the look of horror on his countryman's face. "Happens all over the place. One must be careful where one walks, particularly at night. But that's Bombay. The poverty of the place subjects its people to the ultimate in human degradation. There's no place for the poor wretches to perform their toilet. So they do it right there in front of you. They show no shame, they just feel it. Everything they do in life is done like that in public, whether it's to wash, to make love or to dispose of the waste from their guts. They even have to die in public."

"I've never seen such filth," said Gurinovich, an angry note in his voice. "If ever a country was ready for Socialism."

"It's not Socialism this country needs most, comrade friend. It's condoms. Millions and millions of condoms. That's what the poor beggars need. Then maybe later we could give them Socialism. This is my fifth year in Bombay and even though I'm accustomed to all its horrors, I still get a bit of a shock when I return to it after leave. I keep reminding my superiors of the saying here that two monsoons are the life of a man in Bombay. Maybe next year my new posting will come through."

"Tell me about Sabamontes," said the KGB man, changing the subject. "Do you think he will accept what we have to put to him?"

"He'll be delirious at the prospect of becoming a Gulfie."

"Gulfie! What is that?"

"Oh, that's local jargon for those who go to work in the Gulf, like our friend will be doing."

"Why did he stop working for the Party?"

"Oh, the usual reasons. Police harassment. Lost his job. That sort of thing."

"How active was he?"

"Oh, as good as they come. He's very bright, well read, good command of the language, very persuasive in his speeches and latterly seemed drawn to the Naxalites."

"They're the Maoists, aren't they?"

"Yes. They originated in West Bengal in the late 'sixties. Take their name from the town there called Naxalbari. They made a very big mark with their direct action philosophy. It was the prospect of that happening here in Bombay that made the police clamp down the way they did."

"Won't that cause him problems getting to the Gulf . . . you know how fanatic these Gulf sheikhs are about Socialism?"

"I've gone into that. He's got no convictions, therefore will have no problems getting a passport. Emirate also demands a police clearance certificate, but he'll get that all right."

Carl Sabamontes had been puzzled by the message the man had left with his wife the previous day. It was merely a name penned on a small scrap of paper stating, "Please call personally to the Oberoi Towers Hotel tomorrow at 4 p.m. Ask for Mr Vasily Burenkov, room 406". All the man had said to his wife was that her husband should be told the meeting would "be to his advantage" and that he should be there.

Just before 4 p.m. reception informed room 406 that a taxi driver had called and his name was Sabamontes. "It's much better we take a ride in your cab," smiled the one who said his name was Burenkov. "And with your meter running, of course," he added. "My friend here has just arrived from New Delhi. What about a nice run to the Pherozeshah Mehta Gardens? I'd like him to see something pleasant about Bombay, something nicer than that terrible run in from the airport. You get the best view of all from the car park at the top of the hill up there. It's about the only view of Bombay I know that manages to make it look enchanting."

The two men sat in the rear of Carl's Indian-made Fiat Premier taxi and began speaking in a language which he didn't understand. He thought perhaps they might be German. It wasn't until he had stopped his cab in the car park of the gardens that the man who had spoken to him earlier reverted to English again. "You must be curious, Mr Sabamontes, about why I wanted to see you today . . . and, oh, don't switch off your engine. We appreciate the air-conditioning."

Sabamontes merely shook his head from side to side, indicating his agreement about his curiosity and the Russian thought how deferential he was by comparison to someone from his own country who would have asked long before they had even begun the journey about the purpose of their meeting.

"We noted," said the man, speaking very slowly, "that for a time you were a very active member of the Party here in Bombay."

Sabamontes turned round sharply at that and there was a look of fear, bordering almost on panic, on his face. "Who are you?" he asked loudly.

"It's all right, Carl. You are with friends."

"Friends! What kind of friends?"

"The kind of friends who could help you."

"I don't need any help. But who are you? Where are you from?"

"Mr Sabamontes . . . please. Relax. We are what I say we are. My name is Vasily Burenkov and I'm a First Secretary in the Consulate of the USSR here in Bombay. My comrade here is Mr Oleg Gurinovich from our Embassy in New Delhi. And we are here to put a proposition to you . . . a proposition that will be to the benefit of yourself and your family."

The younger man broke in at that point. "You really mustn't be alarmed, Carl. We are what my comrade here says we are . . . friends. Your work with the Party did not go unnoticed by our people. Nor did the fact that you are no longer active with them."

"You have nothing to do with the police?"

The men smiled at that. "Why do you think we are speaking to you here? No, we have no connection whatsoever with the Bombay or the Indian police."

"But I don't want to go back to the Party again. The Intelligence Wing of the police were making it difficult for me. I lost my good job in the hotel."

"Yes, we know about that. But we have an even better job in mind for you."

"But I don't want to work for the Party any more. My family comes first."

"Carl," said the one called Oleg, "the job we have in mind is not working for the Party. It is coming to work for us. Work which entails you having to do nothing, absolutely nothing, except wait for the day when you may get a call from some of our people asking for whatever help you may be able to give them. The call may never ever come. Our agents or our people may never have a use for you. But still we want you and need you to be prepared for them."

"Here in Bombay?"

"No. In the Gulf. We will arrange work for you through one of the reputable agents here in Bombay. It will be a job with accommodation."

"But why me?"

"Because we believe in your heart the fire still burns in the cause of world Socialism. Is that not the case?"

"Of course it does. I said in my speeches many times that we should go out and fight for Socialism, that we should be willing to die for it. I still believe that in my heart."

"But your head says something different?" said the older man.

"Yes. It says I could never leave my wife and child to the pavements of Dharavi like I was left as a child."

"What your head says is perfectly understandable," Burenkov replied. "I've seen them there at Dharavi. What a hellish place. I must show it to you, Oleg, before you return to Delhi."

"But the job in the Gulf you speak about?" said Carl. "Can you tell me more?"

Taking it in turn, the two men went into detail about the role of the "sleeper" and how they had other Indians like Carl working for them in the Gulf where they constituted such a large part of the work force.

"I cannot believe my ears that I will be going to work in the Gulf. The wages there are three times what we earn here in Bombay. I know many who have gone and they have come back rich enough to buy their own small house. I would have gone years ago but could never afford the money for the agent's fees."

"As we said, that will all be taken care of . . . and there will also be a regular retainer fee. A sort of bonus, as it were, to show our appreciation."

"How will I know your people if they call on me?"

"You will be given a code name. And that name will only be given by us to people we might be sending to the country in which you are placed."

"Which country is it?"

"You will be based in the Capital Area of Emirate."

"And how do I keep in contact you?"

"You don't. We keep in contact with you. Never at any time will you have a need to call us. But when and if our people contact you when you are in Emirate, you will be at their disposal for whatever they want."

"What would that be?"

"We have no specific answer to that. Maybe they will want to use your house. Maybe they will want to know where a certain place is, where they can buy certain goods. It could be for anything. You are there as a friend in need, a friend who says nothing, does nothing, until the day he is approached by someone with your code name."

"And what is my code name?"

The younger man had the answer to that. "You will be known as Boris One. Your code name and what took place between us today must never be repeated to anyone, not even your wife or anyone else in your family."

Sabamontes shook his head from side to side as the man spoke. The message was clearly understood.

"I am returning to New Delhi tomorrow, but Mr Burenkov here will make all the necessary arrangements about your work in Emirate. You will also be given a brief but intensive course on radio communications and firearms, neither of which need alarm you in any way. We are not sending you to the Gulf to shoot people or to be a spy. But we feel a knowledge of such things is important for our contact people. I am sure you will understand that."

Sabamontes shook his head.

"Let me stress once again that you are merely a contact man for us in Emirate, a link for any of our people who may one day visit the country. Neither Mr Burenkov nor myself will be in touch with you again after you leave Bombay. The only person who will ever contact you will be one of our own people, if and when we send one, in Emirate."

"Accha," said Sabamontes softly, shaking his head once more.

"Pardon?"

"Haven't you learned that one yet?" said Burenkov to the younger man. "It's the local way of saying okay, or everything's all right."

In the weeks that followed Sabamontes was to be informed through the Consulate that a job in a hotel had been arranged for him, as well as an apartment. After successfully completing the short course on radio and the use of selected firearms, he received his first brown envelope with cash. "A sort of signing-on fee," Burenkov had said. With the money he had moved his wife and baby son out of their small flat in the crowded and dilapidated block in which they lived in Parel to a house in nearby Dadar with a bedroom separate from the main room and a kitchen as well. Life had never been so good.

On Tuesday, 3 June 1986, three months to the day after he had first met the two Russians, P. Carl Sabamontes was on a Gulf Air Tri-Star for the relatively short flight from Bombay to Emirate. Just like the others carrying out a similar function for Moscow, he melted in with the thousands of his fellow countrymen working in the Gulf, a mere name and code name with a location point logged in the storage bin of a computer that would keep his secret till the day someone had the need for the action file listed under the subject heading of Gulf and the sub-heading of Emirate.

Zamakh — Arabia's Hell Jail

THE FOUNDATIONS of the long chain of events which were planned to change the course of history in the Southern Gulf State of Emirate were well established before news of developments reached a Soviet outpost in the region. Details were immediately relayed to the Headquarters of the KGB in Moscow and the Chief Directorate of Intelligence of the General Staff, known simple as the GRU Within minutes, high-ranking officials were studying computer print-outs of the relevant and most up-to-date information they had about the country.

The plans had begun with the desires of one man, the designs of another. The hand of fate, with its fickle ways, was also to play its part.

The story really had its origins in a place called Jilida. Jilida had been a household name in Emirate, but it was not the sort of place associated with the beginning of events. On the contrary, events normally ended there. For Jilida had once been Fort Jilida, the Alcatraz-Lubianka of Emirate, perched on its islet pinnacles in the Capital's harbour, a Zinderneuf by the sea. When the evening mists gathered after the sun had plummeted into the clutches of the jagged jebels which were the town's backdrop, it took on an eerie, forbidding air. It might even have been the place at the top of the storybook beanstalk.

But like everything else in the great Renaissance of the country which began in 1970, Jilida itself was reborn. The inmates from the prison fort where once murderers were strapped to the muzzles of cannons and blasted in pieces into the sea, were transported to a new Jilida 62 kilometres away, along a gracious six-lane highway with flyovers and gardened roundabouts that had automatic sprinklers, past fine houses and wedding cake palaces and magnificent mosques with golden domes. Along this highway, at every 30 paces on the central reservation, was a tall lamp standard, bearing a picture frame; 2,108 frames on 2,108 standards, each displaying the picture of the most special person in all the land: The Emir.

He was the man around whom everything revolved, everything evolved, in the country. He was the instigator of the bloodless revolution that had awakened his land from its centuries of sleep. He was the man who had used his wisdom to mould his country into the most progressive, and certainly the most stable, in all Arabia. He was also the man for whom they were making plans in the new Jilida, one of the three wings of the nation's new central prison, the place known as Zamakh.

The new jail at Zamakh marks the end of the splendid highway which runs
north-west from the Capital towards the Gulf Coast, past the main
international airport. After Zamakh and the end of the highway the road
continues parallel to an uninterrupted 200-mile beach, past Garden-of-Eden
villages where sweet water flows, fat dates hang in huge clusters from palms,
where tall alfalfa and clover are fed to sheep to make their meat the sweetest
and most tender of all, and where the sardine shoals can be netted from the
very water's edge of the tranquil waters of the Gulf.

Unlike the old Jilida, there is nothing storybook about the new prison at
Zamakh. It is constructed along the lines of that contemporary school of
design — modern anonymous. You see it and you forget it. Tall Australian
gums and thick palm groves hide most of the complex. The outstanding
feature is perhaps the sand-coloured high security fence topped by several
coils of barbed wire. If you drive slowly enough along the highway which
passes the main gate, what buildings you can see are squat and sprawling with
sleek watchtowers and staring cameras at vital junctions — the 1980s high-
tech penitentiary. No signs proclaim the new prison and if you want to direct
someone to it you have to tell them that it is on that part of the highway to
the Gulf Coast, just past a village called Mabraa, where a series of red and
white striped poles mark the areas where wadi waters flood in the winter
rains. There is a sign pointing the way to the Palace Guards School, followed
by an even bigger sign in green and white proclaiming Directorate General of
Palace Guard Stables Polo Grounds, topped by the Emir's emblem of crossed
swords, Crescent and Star. The sign immediately after that in blue and white
police colours announces "Restricted Area. No Admittance Without
Authority." That is Zamakh.

Inside there are three wings, each like a prison within a prison. Jilida is for
long-term prisoners, those serving at least a year. Hazz is for short-term
sentences of under a year. The third wing is for women.

That there is such a prison complex at all was one of the paradoxes of
modern Emirate which in every outward appearance is the idyllic society. In
the Capital Area, it is unknown for anyone to be mugged or robbed. Women
don't get raped and little girls and innocent boys don't get interfered with.
Grandmothers sleep soundly behind doors they needn't lock. Traders in
bustling souk markets can leave mountains of merchandise piled unattended,
for no one shoplifts. Cars can be left unlocked. Fishermen leave their boats,
even on the most popular beaches, with no more protection for their
expensive Yamaha and Evinrude outboard engines than a plastic sheet to
keep out the damp. Swimmers and windsurfers leave cameras and binoculars
and other personal belongings dotted along beaches without a second thought
about their safety. Vandals are unknown.

Yet, while you may never see or hear of a crime and while you can enjoy
the kind of personal freedom and security that was once known in the West,
there are offenders. There are people who break the rules of normal society as

it is known in the West, and who contradict the laws and the ways that are known in the East. The numbers who do so are never revealed, for crimes are never reported except on the occasions when the authorities waylay a liquor-smuggling gang and some of its members get shot in the process. They like events such as that to be known. The Emirate Police are the main custodians of law and order, as well as of moral behaviour dictated by the Koran. No crime or misdemeanour may be spoken of or written about without their permission, a permission that is never asked for because it is never granted, by an authority that is beyond challenge.

A Pakistani called Yaqoob Jaffar first heard about what was happening inside Jilida. Yaqoob was a big and powerful man, the kind of man the polite gentlemen in the Pakistani Embassy were always ready to speak of as being "worth three of those Indians as labourers, I'm telling you. Ask any of the big contractors, they will tell you the same thing." Indeed, many of them would. Yaqoob was even bigger and more muscular than the kind of men those envoys would speak about. He had a trimmed beard and a cruel twist to his mouth which, they said, had been a result of the time he had spent trying to make a living as a wrestler in the Old City of Lahore in the Punjab.

Yaqoob had lived in the Mochi Gate area of the Old City where life even today is little changed from the days when Genghis Khan and his hordes battered at the very entrance of the district which was his home. In the mid-'seventies Yaqoob and thousands of his countrymen from Sind and Baluchistan, and from the land that was once East Pakistan and is now Bangladesh, and from India all the way from Gujerat to Kerala and Tamil Nadu and south of there from Sri Lanka, flooded to the countries that needed them in the area they called simply the Gulf — countries which overnight were dramatically bypassing the centuries with wealth beyond belief from their oil discoveries. Where Saudi, Bahrain and Kuwait had been the developing pioneers, the others were quick to follow once their oil had been tapped. A cluster of sheikhdoms became the United Arab Emirates and spectacular new cities took the place of the humble fishing villages of Dubai and Abu Dhabi. Qatar followed suit. And finally Oman and Emirate.

Yaqoob was a worldly man, mainly because of his time as a wrestler, and because of his excellent English he was quick to rise from labourer to boss ganger, first with Wimpey, the big British contractor, then later with a big Greek-Cypriot company. When he had been working with the latter company on a road project at Razak, the oasis town in the Jebel Ahmar mountain range, he had got himself an even better, and easier job . . . as the local bus driver.

Razak, once the capital of Emirate, lay on the northern slopes of the Jebel Ahmar, the red mountain — red for its rock colouring, and a mountain about which there were many legends, many mysteries, many mysterious people. The mountain itself was one of the highest in all Arabia, nearly 10,000 feet.

On its man-made terraces, where green ribbons of land perched precariously on vertiginous slopes, the region's inhabitants grew peaches and figs, walnuts and maize, and it is said the shiraz grape too, for because of the cold winters on the high slopes they had been given dispensation to drink its wine. At least, so it is said. Many other things were said, and some of them were true, about the people who came from the mountainous region, people to whom intrigue had been the custom for centuries. Still fresh in many minds was the war they had fought and lost in the late 1950s against the Emir, in favour of their spiritual leader, and the terrible price they had paid for that.

Yaqoob had got the job as the local bus driver when the owner had come to his labourers' camp one day asking if someone could fix the seized engine of one of his buses. There was no problem in a job like that for Yaqoob, a man of many such talents, for he had served with the pavement motor mechanics who operated from the roadside "shops" on the MacLeod Road in Lahore, among boys and men who were masters of their trade, particularly in the art of improvisation. Because of the great heat and the habit of skimping on oil, seized engines were commonplace to them.

After Yaqoob had repaired the engine the bus owner had asked him if he could also drive buses. Of course he could. In the Old City where he came from young boys had to learn everything. Into the bargain, he told the Arab, he could cook as good as a master chef, he could speak Arabic and English as well as he could Urdu and Punjabi, and should there be any physical problems, had he not also been called King Khan in the wrestling ring?

Alas, such are the quirks of life, the job was also to be Yaqoob's downfall. What he didn't tell his new employer was that he was also an expert . . . as a lover. Among the regular passengers on his daily runs in and around Razak were the three daughters of the bus owner. The eldest and the youngest of them were married. The middle one, called Ahwa, a girl of 20, had rejected the man to whom she had been promised as a young child, which was something of a facesaver to the man for he couldn't afford the dowry money her father had been demanding. Because of her beauty, the bus owner wanted 4,000 dinar dowry money, much more than he had got for his other two girls. Her great beauty made her worth that, he maintained. He would boast that she was the loveliest girl this side of the Jebel Ahmar, ignoring the growing opprobrium of the dowry system, which even the Emir himself had criticised, saying it was a system foreign to his people and recommending that no man should pay more than 2,000 dinar for a bride.

Unmarried, Ahwa was not to go unloved. She would flirt with the big Pakistani when the other passengers had left the bus and when he offered her the key of his little house so that they could rendezvous there, she willingly accepted it. And after Yaqoob made love to her for the first time she said no Arab could satisfy her like he did. "The sheep make better love than the Arab man," Yaqoob had told her. "The woman should be treated gently and fondly . . . especially one as beautiful as you". After that first time, she returned to the little house many more times and she would weep in the ecstasy of their long hours of love.

When Yaqoob returned from his leave in the summer of 1987 he discovered the news about Ahwa. She was pregnant. And when she confessed to her father that Yaqoob had been the lover, the police were told. On his first night back in Razak he was arrested and two days later he was on his way, handcuffed to a group of other prisoners, to start a six months' sentence at Zamakh for fathering a child to a woman out of wedlock.

The other five prisoners with whom he travelled from Razak were all nationals. When he made to speak to the one nearest him to whom he was handcuffed, there was a sharp crack on his knee from the butt of the automatic rifle of the policeman accompanying them in the rear of the long wheelbase Land Rover.

Zamakh Prison is never mentioned in any publication about Emirate. It is not marked on any maps. It is not signposted. Nor is it ever reported that men and women are sentenced to terms of incarceration there. It is as if the country with the cleanest face in the Arab world wished it to be known it had no transgressors. But although nothing was ever written about Zamakh, its name and reputation were known throughout the Gulf. Most of the expatriate workers, like Yaqoob, knew about it for there was always someone who knew someone who had been there. They said if you went there you would never be seen again, which to some extent was true, for many prisoners were deported back to their country of origin at the end of sentence. Apart from that, little else was known about the jail.

Yaqoob was to learn most of the details. He remembered the roundabout with the signpost that said "The Capital 62km" and where, if you were travelling south, the highway with the big lamp standards began. About three or four hundred metres after that the Land Rover began to slow, then pulled off the road to the left. There were two cantilever blue and white striped security gates, one lifting from the right, the other from the left, overlooked by a big watchtower, sandbagged from its base to the canopied observation platform occupied by a policeman with a rifle. Then there was a high, wired entrance gate, in order to pass through which the driver had to hand over a bundle of documents.

Yaqoob smiled wryly to himself at the neat and tidy appearance of everything once they had gone through the gate. Just like an army camp anywhere, he thought, recalling the ones in which he had worked in Pakistan at the cantonments, or cants as they called them, near Lahore and further north at Sialkot, and how unlike they were to the dilapidated contractors' camps which had been their billets in Emirate.

His reflections were brought to an abrupt end when the vehicle drew up at a building and a policeman yelled at them in Arabic to be quick about getting out and through the door to which he was pointing. There the handcuffs were unlocked and a rough canvas bag was thrown at the feet of each of the six men. "All of your clothes and footwear off," snapped the policeman, "and into the bag with them."

When they had done that they were marched naked to another room where there was a counter and more policemen. As they walked along the counter, items they were ordered to collect were placed in front of them . . . two dhotis, the sarong-like undergarment of the Middle East, two vests, a pair of sandals, a white cotton cap, one toothbrush, a slab of rough soap, hard and crudely cut, a small hessian towel, one plate, three blankets and two yellow tabs which he was told had to be sewn to his vests. When they had collected the items another policeman had more instructions. "These will be the only possessions you will have, apart from your cigarette ration, during your stay in Hazz Wing here at Zamakh. If you are found with any other possessions, they will be confiscated and you will be punished."

That night, after he had found a countryman who had a needle and thread, he learned about the significance of the coloured tabs. They represented the categories of offences for which the men were imprisoned. His own yellow tab indicated simply "woman problems". The green tabs given to the five from Razak who had accompanied him in the Land Rover meant they had been assailants of some kind. The other main colours were orange, for motoring offenders, of which there seemed to be no shortage, there being mandatory sentences, he was told, if an accident resulted in a death, six months at least if a national had been the victim, less if it was an expatriate. A black tab meant you were a thief, and perhaps they were the most despised for only the lowly stooped to that in a society where one's possessions were virtually sacrosanct. The violet-coloured tab was for forgery and he was surprised at the number of them but as the man who explained the colour system observed, "Why shouldn't there be? Think of all the documents and passes and certificates and passports and everything that you require here . . . liquor permits so that you can buy drink, hotel cards for those who want to have a drink at a hotel bar, passport replacement cards, labour cards, and there are others. And there are always people willing to make them for you. I've seen some of them. Very good they are too. But not good enough — that's why there are so many here with the violet tab." Blue stood for drugs offences and there were two which were similar in colour, one a mocha-coffee colour which was for liquor offences, the other a lighter khaki colour which meant you were a homosexual offender.

A prisoner with a blue cap, which he was to learn indicated a privileged prisoner, or a trusty, appeared and told the six new men where they should sleep. He was a small, thin Indian who spoke to them at first in Urdu but when he saw the five men with Yaqoob didn't understand he changed to Arabic. Bad Arabic.

Towering over the little man issuing the orders, Yaqoob asked, "Are you a policeman, small one?"

"No," he replied. "I am the leader in this cell and you must do what I say or else I will report you and you will be punished."

"And how do they punish us, little man?" asked Yaqoob, much to the annoyance of the Indian, whom the Pakistani took to be a Gujerati by his stature and accent.

"Just you look over there at these two men," he replied in an excited voice.

Yaqoob could see two men making their way to a corner of the building, but having great difficulty in walking. Then he noticed their feet. They were shackled. Between each of their feet was a heavy object, like a concrete block, and in order to take a step they had to lift up the block with a piece of rope they had tied to it.

The little man smiled when he saw the look of shock on Yaqoob's face at the sight of the prisoners in the leg irons. "That happens to anyone who is caught breaking any of the rules or disobeys the orders," said the trusty, adding, "That space against the wall there. There is enough room for the six of you. And you must sleep in the same place every night."

"Where are the litters, the beds?" asked Yaqoob.

The little man laughed, his thin lips parting sufficiently to show a mouth that had half of its teeth missing. "This is not a hospital," he replied. "Your blankets are your beds and your bedding."

On their way to the cell block, Yaqoob had noticed that they were housed in a complex of their own and surrounding them was the same high, buff-coloured fence topped by the barbed wire which constituted the outer fence of the sprawling prison. The wing they called Hazz consisted of one main building divided into eight cell rooms, each of which accommodated 66 prisoners. A narrow corridor ran between the four cells on one side of the building and the four on the other side.

The first five feet of the outer walls of the building were of concrete slabs and from there to the roof heavy duty wire netting gave the buildings an identical appearance to a factory farm. There was no air-conditioning, no punkah fans, and despite the airiness of the long rooms with their open wire walls, the first thing to strike him, apart from how crowded they were, was the stench. Not only did it look like a factory farm, he thought, it stank like one. There used to be a smell like that in the construction camps when all the men returned from labouring in the sun all day. But no matter how primitive these camps had been, there had always been water available and the men had always washed. The dreadful odour of the building indicated that was not the case here.

The five men from Razak and Yaqoob each laid out their blankets on the bare concrete floor in the spaces they had been allotted and the trusty prisoner left the cell.

"What was the trouble in Razak, then?" Yaqoob said to one of the five, the one nearest him.

"Trouble?" he replied quizzically.

"Yes . . . trouble," he said pointing to his green tab. "Were you in a disturbance? A fight?"

"No. Nothing like that," the Arab replied. Then another of the men gave him a sharp tap on the ankle and he turned his back to Yaqoob to go into a huddled conversation with the others.

It was, as he later discovered, 3.30 the following morning when there was a harsh rattle, a sort of tinkle which he couldn't define and which awakened him with a startle. The neon strip lights, which had been lit when he had fallen asleep, were still burning and there were men all round him hurrying up from their sleeping positions, quickly wrapping on their dhotis and running out of the unlocked cell door, then turning right and disappearing down the corridor.

"What is it?" he asked one man hurrying past him carrying his plate. "It's the breakfast. You better come quick . . . sometimes they run out of bread."

The food was brought from the kitchens to a serving area outside the main cell block building but inside the high security fence which surrounded the wing. There were two long lines of prisoners waiting to be served. The stench from the men seemed even worse than it had the night before, particularly when they were herded so close to one another in the long queues.

When he eventually got to the head of the queue Yaqoob held out his plate to a fat bearded man who stood behind an enormous pan. He poured a ladle of runny, mud-coloured dhal gruel into the plate and another man handed him two large chapatis. Then Yaqoob followed the others again as they walked back to the cell building.

"No canteen tables . . . or mess?" he enquired from one of the prisoners walking beside him.

The man smiled before replying. "No. We eat where we sleep."

After tearing the brittle pieces from the hard chapati bread, all that was left were two small pancake-sized portions soft enough to help him sup, Indian-fashion, the gruel substance in his plate which was a dhal made of the coarsest of lentils. He spat out with every mouthful the multitude of little stones the unrefined lentils contained. The other prisoners were doing the same, filling the room with the noise of their spitting between sups. The smell of the food mixed with the sweat from the unwashed men heightened the horrific odour of the big cell and he was thankful to lie down again when he had finished the meal. It seemed the smell wasn't quite so overpowering the nearer he got to the floor.

"What's the time, friend?" he asked one of the prisoners on the opposite side of the Razak men.

"It will be just after four o'clock. You've got two and a half hours to the next call."

"But why are we up so early?"

"Because you're in prison, that's why. And they want to remind you that you're in prison. That's why you have no bed. That's why there are just eight doorless toilet cubicles and eight wash-basins for all the men in this wing, about 500 in all and you're lucky to get a wash. That's why the dhal tastes like muck. That's why we all stink like we do. You're in a Gulf Arab prison and they don't want you to forget it."

Despite the smell and the heat and the lights that never went out, he was able to fall asleep again until that same loud rattle roused him again. This time he discovered the noise was made by a policeman pulling a big cell key over the mesh wire of the hut as he ran past. The prisoners reacted much as they had the previous time, sitting up quickly, wrapping on their loincloths, then running towards the top of the room with their small towels and soap. By the time Yaqoob and the other new prisoners readied themselves there was a long queue stretching back from the ablutions and into the room. When they got near to the washing area they could see other queues from the other cell huts, all of which used the one set of toilets and ablutions. Despite the crush, the men were remarkably disciplined, although it was doubtless the presence of the police guards which ensured that. By the time Yaqoob got to the head of the queue, however, the policemen were starting to shout "no more, no more" and there was some pushing and scrambling to get at the wash-bowls, with the guards pushing them roughly away again. Yaqoob vowed he wouldn't be near the end of the line in future.

Looking around at the other prisoners as he had waited in the washing queue, Yaqoob had thought how alike they all were in their dhotis. He could still pick out the southern Indians with their jet-black wavy hair and wide, staring eyes, the round heads of the Baluchis, and the nationals, a good proportion of whom had their origins in Africa, and the rest mainly Bedu. Others had come from the Interior with their gaunt faces so different from their coastal cousins, the classical Arab division between Bedu and Hadhr, the latter being that rich mixture of the dozen and more races which formed their ancestry, ranging from the peoples of the Holy Books to those of the subcontinent. There were Filipinos, soft-faced ones with the khaki homosexual tab, and there was a sprinkling of white men there too but, like they said of them, they all looked alike and he couldn't have told whether they were English or Dutch or French. He reflected on how the common degradation imposed on Zamakh detainees was a great leveller.

White Man in a Dhoti

PRISONERS CAME and went all the time as some sentences finished and others began. He had been there for about two months when a new group of six men arrived one day, three of whom he took to be Indian. Another two were probably Arab and one was white. They were allotted their bed spaces by the privileged prisoner, the same little Indian man who Yaqoob had discovered was a homosexual and who prostituted himself for cigarettes which he paid to the cookhouse staff for better food. Five of the men were shown a space where they had to sleep together on the opposite side of the cell. Then the Indian spoke to the white man and pointed in the direction of Yaqoob where there was room, but just barely, for one man.

It always seemed strange to see white men dressed in the dhoti, as this one was. Yaqoob watched him as the little Indian issued his orders. The man was obviously talking back to the Indian and waved an arm in anger at him a couple of times. He was a middle-aged man, Yaqoob reckoned, although he had quite a trim figure, with a high forehead and fairish, thin hair. His body wasn't as white as some of the white men he had seen, so white that Yaqoob thought at first they must have some kind of illness, until someone explained to him that they could be that way and be quite healthy.

"There. There, beside that man," rasped the little Indian, who was obviously enjoying giving orders to a white man.

"Aye, all right, pal. Got your message," replied the white man in a fashion which showed his obvious contempt for the Indian, although Yaqoob didn't quite understand what he meant by "pal" and "message".

He had his issue of blankets, towel, plate, soap, and so on with him and Yaqoob noticed a set of mocha-coffee coloured tabs on top of the blankets he was carrying. A liquor offender. Without looking up, the man kept on talking loudly to himself. "Jesus Christ, what a bloody liberty. Talk about bloody sardines." Then he laughed to himself and Yaqoob thought how strange these English people could be. But then this wasn't the first time he had thought that. He remembered them as tourists in Lahore, walking around in the hottest part of the day when everyone else rested. And there were the ones he used to see when he was with the contractor building the Inter-Continental Hotel, lying in bathing costumes on the Qurat beach in temperatures well over 100 degrees. A man had to be really strange to do things like that, he had thought.

He was still smiling when his eyes met Yaqoob's. "Hello there," he said in a friendly tone. "I don't know why I was laughing there. I should be crying at this mess I'm in. Do you speak English, mate?"

Yaqoob nodded.

"Thank Christ. My Arabic's good, but not that good. My name is Gordon. Gordon Watson. I get called everything by the locals. Jordan, Ordon, el Ordon. And your name?"

"Jaffar . . . Yaqoob."

"Which comes first?"

"Yaqoob."

"You're a national then?"

"No. Pakistani."

"I know a few locals who are called Yaqoob, so I thought . . .."

"We have similar names. You are English?"

"Aye. Sort of. I'm from a place called Glasgow."

"But that's in Scotland."

Watson looked surprised at that. "How did you know that?"

"My brother is there. He has a shop and says he is rich. Maybe you know him?"

"Is he a grocer and his shop is on a corner?"

"So you do know him," Yaqoob beamed.

"Yaqoob . . . it used to be that every corner in Glasgow had a pub . . . a place to drink that is. You know, alcohol? Now every corner in the city has a Pakistani grocer."

"Why are you here?" the Pakistani asked. "Selling liquor?"

"No . . . drinking it." At that his mood changed and he looked down shaking his head. "Christ, Yaqoob, you made me forget there the state that I'm in. I am shocked right out of my mind, if you know what that means. I can't believe it, honestly, I just can't believe what has happened to me since the other night. It's like I'm dreaming this."

He sat down with his back to the wall in the space Yaqoob had made next to him. "Ever heard of the Rani Hotel?"

"Of course."

"That's where I was. In the Tie Bar. I'm a member of the bar Facility Club there. I pop in a couple of nights a week but always on the Thursday with the day off on the Friday and that. All I had was beer . . . never touch the spirits. I was drinking half pints to make the night spin out a bit longer. At the most I would have had about ten of them, five pints in all. I can remember everything . . . everything. That's how little I had to drink. There were a bunch of newcomers in the bar and they were telling me some great stories about my mate, a fellow called Brian. They knew him during his days in London. I left just after they did at about half-past ten. Got into the car. All right . . . I know. Drink and drive and all that. But I was all right. Really. Don't say it. You're not supposed to. But I did. I had just got to the Rani roundabout right by the hotel, you know, when some silly bugger rammed me from the back. And does the silly bugger not turn out to be a cop? He was in uniform but not in a police car. It was his own car. Next thing a patrol car is there and I'm whizzed off to hospital for a blood test. Then overnight in the police station. Then to court where it's just been asumed you're guilty. And now I'm here. They gave me two months. Yaqoob, I don't believe it. I've never been in a jail in my life. I've been in the Gulf now about ten years. Kuwait, Doha in Qatar, then here. Christ, it's got to be a dream. Look at the place! And these guys with the shackles on their legs. What the hell is that all about?" He didn't wait for an answer. "Yaqoob. This is like something out of the Dark Ages."

Yaqoob looked at him with compassion, thinking for a minute the man was going to break down, for there was a disturbed, shocked look about him. Then he laughed again.

"Oh God, Yaqoob. You've got to keep a sense of humour. Know what I was thinking? I'm dressed here like Bob Hope in *The Road to Bali.* If only my old mother could see me. Her Gordon with a sarong and a coolie's vest."

Yaqoob didn't understand that but his cheerfulness was infectious and he smiled with him as he laughed at his own misfortune. He picked up the tabs from his blankets and Yaqoob told him he knew a man who would sew them on for him. The white man asked about the significance of them and he explained about the various colours and what they meant.

"So you had trouble with a woman, then? Rape?"

Yaqoob shook his head with a frown. "No, no. Nothing like that." And he told him the story.

"You got six months for that! God! What about your friends?" he asked, indicating the men alongside him. "Are they Pakistanis too?"

"No. They're local johnnies. But I don't know much about them. We came in the same police jeep from Razak where I had been living. These johnnies are from Razak too. They were involved in some kind of trouble there, but they don't say much. They're strange men. I don't understand them or what they are about."

"God, it's warm in here, Yaqoob. You forget what it's like without air-conditioners. They broke down one night at the house and I thought I'd never see the morning. How the hell will I survive this? And the stench! What on earth is that stink, Yaqoob? The drains or something?"

"That, my friend, is the smell of men . . . men who are lucky if they get one wash a day. And you put 66 men together like this in the same one big room and you get a stink like that. But soon you will not notice it. For you too will have the same rotten smell as the rest of us." Then he explained to him about the morning routine, the 3.30 a.m. breakfast, then the long queue for the washroom and how you had to be quick if you wanted to get that one wash of the day.

"Breakfast at 3.30. Three-thirty! Is that right, Yaqoob?"

"That's right."

"Well, I'll miss it then."

"Better not. It is bad food, but you need it just the same. You will lose a lot of energy here with the sweating so you must replace it."

"So when do we eat next?"

"At 6.30 this evening. You missed lunch. That's the main meal. It's at 11.30 every morning."

"Good menu?" Watson asked with a smile. He knew Yaqoob hadn't understood the remark. "What do we get?"

"A ladle of rice, but it's only half boiled. On top they pour what they call curry sauce but it's not really curry sauce. It's chilli powder mixed with hot water. One day you get a piece of fish, but it is not cleaned and the scales and everything are there and you have to spit half out. Another day a piece of boiled chicken, another day some sheep . . . you know, mutton? Twice a week they give us a ball of dates. We call them zoological dates because they've got more animals inside them than the zoo."

"And what about dinner?"

"One mug of tea and one chapati three nights a week, one mug of tea and one sweet chapati for another three nights and on Friday it's a special night because of the holy day. You get what they call fried rice, but it's boiled rice into which they put colouring, one piece of meat, the piece like the chicken or the fish depending on how many cigarettes you have paid to the cookhouse staff, and one orange or one sour apple."

"So tonight it's a cup of tea and a chapati for dinner."

"That's right . . . but it's sweet chapati tonight." Watson shook his head again. "They call that dinner! Yaqoob. I still can't believe it . . . that I'm here and talking to you and dressed like this. Normally at this time I would be just finishing my work. Smart collar and tie. Nice light pants. Driving the new Honda Prelude, listening to a Frank Sinatra tape and wondering whether I should go to the Golden Falcon for their mother-and-baby shrimp sweet and sour or else to the Sheraton for the Turkish belly dancer floor show. Good God! Now look at me! Yaqoob, I don't know where you've been in your life before, but I've only met scenes like this in the films. *Bridge on the River Kwai* . . . *Spartacus* . . . *Papillon* . . . that kind of thing. I know you don't really know what I'm talking about, Yaqoob, but this is what they were like. These films, that is. I can joke just now, Yaqoob, but I'm telling you something . . . I doubt if I will make it here."

"What do you mean . . . make it?"

"Survive. Finish two months of this. I could die in a place like this. Look at the sweat on me, Yaqoob. It's gushing out of me. Look at you . . . not a drop on you."

"It *is* warm."

"Warm. Yaqoob, I'm roasting."

"You'll be all right. There are others . . . Englishmen like you. I have seen them come and go."

"Well, I hope you see me come and go. When do you get out anyway?"

"We have only been here for two months. Another four to go."

"And then back to your bus in Razak . . . no, I forgot about your girlfriend there. You won't want to be near her father or brothers, will you?"

"I don't mind. I would marry the girl. I am a good Muslim and we are allowed a second wife."

"You're married already?"

"Yes, I have a wife and four big sons in Lahore. And what about you? Where was your job?"

"I work for International, the big tobacco company. Our office is in Rani, not far from the hotel in one of the insurance buildings. Our brands are the market leaders. Bet you don't get issued with them in here."

"It is Pakistani cigarettes for the issue . . . but they are not like any other Pakistani cigarettes I have smoked before. You hear everyone coughing here when they smoke them. It is because they are old and dried. Do you have a wife, Gordon?"

"Yes, Yaqoob. One wife, two children, boy and a girl. They were too young to bring here when I came at first. Now they're at that age where it could be wrong to take them away from school. We bought a house that I could never have afforded on the wages at home and that was me right into the Gulf trap. Now I've got to stay here to pay the mortgage. The family couldn't keep up the lifestyle I've created for them if I didn't work here. Crazy, isn't it! The family come out here for the two months' school holidays, I go home for Christmas . . . and that's it. They've got uncles they see more of than their old man . . . but I better not think too much about that! God . . . Yaqoob. The heat! Honest, I don't even have the energy to talk."

The heat of the Arabian midsummer in and around the Capital was an experience. It was of an intensity that defied the appreciation of thermometer statistics, except perhaps the recorded daily *minimum* reading which would often be near 100 degrees, sometimes more. It was such that no metal could be touched, lest the skin would be scorched. Taxi drivers lined their car doors and dashboards and rear window sills with thick wool carpeting to reduce the hotplate proportions other materials would become. It was such that no longer could you get cold or even luke-warm water from cold taps, for the pipes and the earth or the building or whatever was around them would have absorbed the heat and so would the water have, to the extent that the liquid from the cold tap could be so fiercely hot it could scald. It could be of such an intensity that it would often seem that your eyes were about to succumb, just as they would smart and make you turn away when a furnace door was opened. It made routine life one of permanent perspiration, of sticky flesh and clammy hands that felt forever unwashed. It burned the very air, making the reward for any exertion an extra breathful which seared the throat and the lungs. Only the ubiquitous air-conditioning was a relief. And for the prisoners in the big cell blocks at Zamakh there was no air-conditioning.

"Just take it easy, friend. Lie flat on the bare concrete. It's the coolest place," said Yaqoob soothingly to his new companion, who looked pale and distressed, sweating profusely.

He was sound asleep when the dinner call came and Yaqoob let him lie on, telling the other prisoners not to disturb him. Later in the night he wakened with a sort of whimper. He felt something cool on his forehead. "Where . . . what . . . who is that?"

"It's all right," he heard the comforting voice saying. "It's Yaqoob. Remember? This wet cloth will help you cool down a little. And I've a mug of cold tea here for you. You'll need to drink it for you've lost a lot of sweat. Eat the chapati too. There's some salt and energy in it. Your body needs everything here."

"Thanks, mate," he replied softly. "Thanks a lot."

After that first night when he had been badly dehydrated because of the heat, Yaqoob took his new friend, whom he always referred to as "the Englishman", under his care. He had built up enough tobacco credit with some of the privileged prisoners in order to get Watson off the field duties to which most of the inmates were assigned during the day, tasks like cutting paddocks of grass with small blunt sickles or labouring in the open at the block-making plant where the prisoners mixed the dry sand and cement.

The best jobs in the Hazz wing of Zamakh, after that of the privileged prisoners who acted as house boys to police staff, were allotted to those who were tradesmen, like plumbers, joiners and electricians. They composed the maintenance squads who worked at keeping the establishment in good running order. Through his influence, as well as through some tobacco bribes, Yaqoob had got his new friend a job as a helper with one of the maintenance teams. And by using the remainder of their tobacco allowance, he was able to persuade one of the guards, a policeman he had known when he was working as a foreman during the building of the Ministries' offices in Al Mushrif, to get him a job in the cookhouse as a cook's assistant.

"You wait now," he had told Gordon that night. "Nothing but the best of food for us two."

"About time, Yaqoob. After that fish we had last night my stomach will never be the same again." He shook his head in disgust. "What a mess. Bones, heads, tails, scales, skin. Yeugh!"

In the evenings after they were locked into their big 66-man cells at 6.30, the usual time of sunset, some of the prisoners would play games. A group of Filipinos regularly organised a dice school and gambled for cigarette stakes. Some Indians played endless rounds of bridge. Groups of nationals, with others watching in fascination, had their own ethnic games to pass the long hours of evening under the insect-besieged perpetual neons.

The most popular of these games was huwayliys, which Watson had remembered seeing the taxi drivers play at their main stance at Rani. There had also been another group of men that seemed to play a never-ending game of it behind a wall near the last building on the Khudra Corniche, just by the Purshottam Kanji Exchange and the Bank of Baroda. They played with sea shells as pieces, moving them at a hectic pace in and out of a series of small bunkers in the sand. On the concrete floor of the cell hut they had to improvise by marking out circles as substitutes for the bunkers and using small stones in place of sea shells.

Some Bedu, sitting in twos, played one of their games — baswafafiy. "It's a sort of war game," explained a national in faultless English. He was obviously not a Bedu, more the kind some prisoners would refer to as a "Mercedes Arab", meaning one of the numerous affluent types from the Capital Area. He went on to explain how they played the game. "One line represents a ridge, and the spaces represent gaps through which you can take your soldiers, just like you would take them through a pass in the mountains. Some of the pieces represent soldiers, one represents a sheikh and another an officer. The object is to flick a man across the board in order to hit one of the men on the opposite side. And the game goes on until one player has failed to hit any of his enemy's men. It's quite fascinating really."

Other prisoners would seek out compatriots from their towns and villages back in the subcontinent and exchange gossip from letters. And when he wasn't watching the others playing their various games, Gordon Watson would sit with Yaqoob having long conversations on a whole variety of subjects.

"You wouldn't believe the story I heard today," said Watson one night as they sat together. "It was this Bangladeshi that I met. We were doing some maintenance work at the block factory and he was one of the squad mixing cement. God, how can they stand it out in that blazing sun? Anyway, they had a smoke break and we got speaking when he had come over to the shade for some water. God . . . his story would break your heart. He told me that just to get here many of the Indians and Bangladeshis are paying a fortune to agents in India. One group he said he knew took their life savings with them to Bombay, paid them to an agent who then made them pay more money to him for the next three months . . . and the week before they were told they would be going to the Gulf the agent and all the staff from the office disappeared. Just like that. Off with all their money. But the Bangladeshi had even worse happen to him. He sold his family home and little farm . . .."

Yaqoob interrupted him. "But do you know what that would be in Bangladesh? A palm frond hut and half a hectare if he was lucky."

"But that doesn't matter, Yaqoob. It was his family home and he and his wife and kids lived off it. Anyway, he gave all the money to an agent, about 140 US dollars. That represented half of the year's salary he was to expect here . . . 60 dinar a month. That's about 100 British pounds. After half a year he would have made up the money it cost to pay the agent to come here and after that the £100 a month would have given him a better living than ever he had. Well, that was his plan. But do you know what happened? He got sent to the Interior and every month when he asked for his wages the boss, I think he was Bedu, would just say 'We'll see'. He also made him sign a form which, he said, would be the wages he'd get. His accommodation was a hut and for food the boss made him take it from his store, with everything marked down to come off the wages . . . the wages he had never been paid. Eventually he went to the police. And what did they say? They told him the boss had already made complaints about him absconding from his work and that he would be arrested if he didn't get back to his job quickly. So he worked for another couple of months and still got no wages, so he went to the police again. This time they showed him the forms he had signed and they said that meant he had been paid wages and that he should make no more complaints. Then he told the boss he would report the matter to the Labour Court. But the boss moved first. He went to the police again and this time told them that he'd been stealing. So he was arrested for absconding and for stealing . . . and now he's here for three months. The man broke me up telling me that Yaqoob."

"Haven't you heard stories like that before? I could tell you dozens of them. Most of us have to pay agents in order to come here. With some it's just two or three months' advance salary. Others make you pay a lot more. I was lucky for I went to one of the big agencies, the kind that you know will be there when you go back to them. When I came to the Gulf it was for the big companies who pay you what they promise they will. But we all have to work for two years before we get our first leave. It is a long time for the men. We work six days a week, many of us seven days. Some get a little overtime money for the seventh day, but just a few baisas. And the food! Some camps are not much better than this. That is why this place is not easy on you English johnnies and the others who do not know the hard way of life that we know. For us the Gulf is the big chance in our lives. The chance to make much more money than we ever could in our own countries, even although all most of us get is 60 dinar a month."

"A hundred quid, eh . . . for a seven-day week and no leave for two years."

Yaqoob looked round for a moment as Watson spoke then turned to him and said, "Did you notice they are away again?"

"Who?"

"The Arab johnnies. The Razak ones. You know, the five men who sleep alongside me?"

"Yes. I've noticed them being taken away before and coming back again but just thought it was to do some work or the like. Do you think there is something unusual about them?"

"Yes. Very unusual. Notice how they never mix with the others . . . not even the other nationals. They never play any of the games, the huwayliys and that. And if they think I am listening they talk together in code."

"Talk in code!" exclaimed Watson incredulously. "Come on, Yaqoob. You are making fun of me. None of them look like James Bond to me. I don't suppose you've heard of him?"

"Of course, he was always in the picture houses in Lahore. But they do. They do talk in code."

"What do you mean, Yaqoob? How do you mean *talk* in code? Code is something you write."

"No . . . it is true. Some Arabs can speak in code. They call it speaking in Lahaja. It has been a tradition with them in the Interior for centuries. Sometimes it is used by children just like in games, other times in the house if they want to say something they don't want anyone else to know about. These men, these five, they are from the Jebali mountain people. I worked in their area for a long time. That's where I really learned my Arabic. And I used to hear them from time to time speaking this strange way when I was around . . . things they didn't want me to hear . . . gossip and that. I got an old man to explain it to me. What they do is use a combination of two letters and put them in front of all the sounds like 'ah' . . . and 'oh' . . . and 'eh'."

"You mean the vowels?"

"I don't know what you call them. But all these sounds anyway. So, if your two code letters are 'i' and 'g', and the old man told me they were the popular ones, a word like Abdullah would become Abdigulligah. It only takes a few hours practice to learn it. But what takes you a lot longer is trying to find out which two letters they are using together."

"God, you're some man, Yaqoob, knowing all these things. But what's the connection with that and thinking that they are up to something?"

"Have you noticed one of them is a bit simple? Notice the way he keeps fidgeting with his blankets, folding them and unfolding them."

"Is that the one with the slight limp?"

"So you've seen him."

"Yes, I wondered about the blanket folding bit."

"Well, two or three times they have been away and he has been left on his own. I asked him one day where they had gone and he replied . . . Jilida. Another time he was left on his own and we started speaking about Razak and about various characters and places in the town there. Then I asked why they were in Zamakh and he said it was . . . the shooting. I asked him what shooting, and the reply was the shooting at 'our enemy'. Then he got frightened and wouldn't say any more."

"So what do you make of that, then, Yaqoob?"

"I don't know. They're Shia and Fundamentalists and that sometimes can mean things."

"He told you that too?"

"No. I can tell. You see, when we pray the Sunni and the Shia do slightly different things. In the first part of our prayer we stand to face Mecca and ask Allah to help us to pray correctly, then we raise our hands to our ears and say that Allah is great and after that we put our hands down and cross them, the right one over the left before reciting the first prayer."

Watson listened intently to the explanation.

"It is at that point that you can tell the difference. The Shia do not cross their hands, but hold them straight down by their sides with their fists closed. Of course they could have been from the same sect of Sunni which they have in this country and who pray in the same fashion as the ones of the Shia. But they stand apart from them too at prayer times so that's how I knew they would be Shia. Then there were things about their appearance. The Fundamentalists wear their dishdashas shorter than the others. To wear it long is vain, they say. And their dishdashas were that short way when I first saw them in the cells at Razak and when we travelled together here in the police jeep. Another thing is their beards. The Fundamentalists don't trim theirs or have them neat like the people you see on the coast or in the Capital Area and you never see them with the moustache only. That too is vain, they think. These are just little things but they are the kind of things we know and understand about life here in the Gulf. So, you ask me how I know . . . that's how I know."

"Yaqoob, I've been living in the Gulf for nearly ten years now, but I never knew any of that. It's funny the different things we know about life, yet we live here in the one country. For instance, I can tell you when the Happy Hour is at the Inter-Con, the Al Rawda or the Rani hotels and the best place to take your liquor permit for a cut off the price of a case of beer. And you definitely don't understand a word of that Yaqoob . . . do you?"

The Pakistani shook his head.

"But getting back to this Fundamentalist business. What difference does that make? Isn't that just like being an orthodox Jew? Oh, sorry about the Jew bit, but you know what I mean?"

"I don't know about them. But the nationals here don't want the Fundamentalists. You'll see pictures of the Khomeini in many Arab countries, but you'll never see one here. They don't want any problems in this part of the Gulf. So they don't want Fundamentalists. Same with Palestinians. You get Egyptians, Jordanians and others from the Gulf coming here but did you ever meet a Palestinian? Do you know what my brother told me in his last letter? They have the Fundamentalists in your Glasgow."

Watson laughed loudly at that. "I don't think they would do well at Ibrox, Yaqoob," he said, still laughing. Then he added, "That was what you call a Glasgow joke, Yaqoob. But tell me. These Fundamentalists. Are they that bad?"

"No. They don't act in badness. They act in the way that they see our religion. They want things to be as they were in the beginning. They want the purity and simplicity of life as it was in the time of Mohammed, peace be upon him, and to be free of any influence of the Western way. It is goodness that they want. But the way that they go about it is where the badness that you speak of happens. To them America is the Great Satan and not to be tolerated. They believe so much in their cause that the greatest thing for them in life is to die for it. It is the quickest route to heaven, they say."

"Funny. I got taught about people like that when I was at school. They called them the Crusaders. They thought that everyone should be Christians like them or else be done away with. I'm glad I'm an atheist, Yaqoob."

"That means?"

"I don't believe in religion."

"You have no God!"

"None."

"But a man must have a God. He must believe. What about when you die? Where do you think you will go?"

"I know, Yaqoob. The crematorium . . . and that's the end of the story."

"I feel sorry for you, Gordon."

"Please don't, Yaqoob. I'll make out. Anyway, you say our friends next to you are Shias, they're Fundamentalists, and they were involved in some kind of shooting at Razak. What could that have been?"

"Could be anything. Lots of them have guns there. Maybe a dispute over water rights, or some date palm, or a woman . . ."

"Not your lady?"

He smiled. "No, Gordon. Not my lady."

It was to be a month before Gordon Watson had his first visitor to the prison at Zamakh and it was his best friend in the Gulf, Brian Bria. Bria was a tall laconic Australian in his late forties but looked much younger because of his athletic figure. He hadn't lived in Australia since leaving to go and work in London in the early 1960s. He was now a photographer with the Ministry of Public Buildings and had been contracted by them to compile a book on the mosques of the country. He had been a photographer in Britain "just doing the usual run of things a photographer does". And that's all he would normally say about his previous work. But there were the occasional nights at the Rani Bar when his reticence would disappear and he would regale the company, the same group of friends with whom Watson regularly met, with amusing tales about fashion models and his travels to some very remote spots for his photographic work.

Prisoners met their visitors in a building outside the main compound of Hazz, to which they were escorted. Each visitor was called forward when the name of the prisoner was announced and they sat, in the most up-to-date penitentiary style, on either side of a bulletproof glass screen and used a telephone to speak to each other. Bria looked concerned when he saw his friend dressed in dhoti and vest and being ushered over to the seat on the opposite side of the glass. Watson smiled at him and he managed an anxious smile back as they both picked up the telephone.

"John Dillinger here," said Watson, and Bria broke into a wide, relieved grin.

"Christ, mate, I've been really worried about you. I made inquiries about this place and I'm told it's no joy ride. How are you making out?"

"I'll be all right . . . The worst's over . . . and that was right at the start. Brian, that was really something. The conditions! Oh my God! And the smell . . . the heat . . . the food! I couldn't believe it. But I met a mate, thank God, and he helped me. In fact, I think I could have snuffed it the first night had it not been for him. And that's no kidding."

"A Brit?"

"No," he laughed. "He's a Paki. Yaqoob's his name. Swell guy. Has good English and tough as they come. He's even got a brother living in Glasgow. He made things really easy for me. Sort of took me under his wing. But what about my job? Do you think it will be okay? And Jean? Does she know?"

"You've not to worry. I went over to International and saw Tommy, your boss. He was really concerned but understands everything. He knows you're not a booze artist. He wrote to Jean and explained everything and I phoned her and she seemed quite relieved when I assured her everything was okay . . . so you've no problems there. He's also spoken to the police about you and they've told him you won't be deported."

"How did you all get to know?"

"Well, the police told your boss first of all because he's your sponsor. That was the day after you were arrested. Then one of your workmates came over and told us at the Rani. But how did it all happen? It's not like you to drive if you've had too much. Did you go on a binge or something?"

"No. No binge or anything. I remember every single drink I had, for I was watching it. I had five pints in all. Okay, so I know that's too much to drive with. But I was all right, you know, not staggering or anything like that. I had been drinking slowly. Anyway, I got into the car and had just moved off when another car rams me from the rear. And when I get out of the car to see what the hell happened, the first thing I see is the check cap and khaki drills. Just my luck. It was a car owned by a cop going off duty. Next thing I knew I was giving a blood test . . . then a quick appearance in court, with no question of pleading not guilty or anything like that, and not all that much later I was in Botany Bay here. I feel as though I have met up with all your ancestors, Brian."

He laughed at that. "Glad to see you haven't lost your sense of humour, mate."

"No joking though . . . it's like that inside. Botany Bay, I mean. There's even guys in leg shackles. The real Chain Gang stuff."

"How about the grub?"

"Genuine cordon spew. Brian, I'll live for years off the tales I can tell about the food and the other things that go on in here. The best story, though, is our mystery prisoners."

"Mystery prisoners?"

"Yeah . . . real mystery. They're five nationals who don't mix, not even with other locals. They don't do any of the field work or anything like that and get regularly taken off to Jilida. That's the name of the long-term wing . . .

you know, same as Fort Jilida? Anyway, they've got us all puzzled and it's the talk of the shop, as it were."

"What are they in for?"

"They're from Razak, up in the Ahmar Mountains and there was some kind of shooting, probably a tribal dispute or something. No one knows for sure."

"You mean the attack on the police station?"

Watson stared in almost disbelief through the glass separating them and sat forward in his chair as he spoke into the phone mouthpiece. "What's that about an attack on the police station and how the hell did you know about it?"

"I was up there about the time it happened. Was doing a section of the book on the mosques of the Jebels. And the place was hotching with military. They had come down from the Jebel Regiment camp at Jiza, high up in the mountains. I know one of the two Brits who are officers in the regiment there, a bloke called Tony Mills. Knew him in Northern Ireland when he was with the Paras. Real nice guy. But different from any other British officer I've ever met . . . different in a sense that's hard to pin down. But different, that's for sure. Anyway, Tony told me the whole story."

"I don't believe it," said Watson excitedly. "Here we are, Yaqoob and myself, racking our brains every night trying to figure out what happened at Razak and all the time you know the story. Right then. Give us all the details."

"Well, it seemed . . ."

Just then a firm hand was placed on his shoulder and when he looked up an unsmiling policeman was signalling to him that the visiting period was over.

"Oh Christ," said Watson when he saw what had happened. "Listen, Brian, before you go. That night I got arrested . . . there was a big party of Press people from London in the Rani. They were here with the Prince and Princess. And some of your old mates were among them."

"Oh . . . I suppose my ears should have been burning. What did they tell you?"

"Everything."

"Tell me more . . ."

A loud buzzing sound came on the line as the policeman put his finger on the cut-off button of Watson's phone and they looked at each other with an expression of forced surrender. As he rose to leave with the policeman, Brian signalled to his friend in sign language, as if he was steering a car and mouthing out the words . . . "w.i.l.l. — p.i.c.k. — y.o.u. — u.p." Watson nodded that he understood and gave him a cheery wave of goodbye in return.

He thought his remaining month at Zamakh would pass quickly. But it didn't. It seemed like an eternity, especially with the arrival of the summer heat when even in the coolest part of the night it was over 100 degrees. In all his years in the Middle East he had never experienced heat such as he was enduring now. Of all the workers in the various countries of the Gulf, it was only those who were in construction and in outside posts in the oil industry, and of course those unfortunate Indian sweepers and tidiers, and the like, who in the 1980s had to really suffer the rigours of the climate. For the majority, who worked in the capitals and other big cities, modern-day life was about moving from air-conditioned flats and villas to air-conditioned cars to air-conditioned shops and offices to air-conditioned customers' premises. They played squash in air-conditioned courts, swam in refrigerated pools, ate in air-conditioned restaurants, drank in air-conditioned bars. The only hazards of a berserk sun were those fleeting moments in between when there was, perhaps, a walk to an unshaded car the steering wheel of which, unless protected by a sheepskin or blanket, would be too hot to touch and the vehicle would be undrivable until the air-conditioning blowers had cooled it. When they did the blast of low temperatures would have a similar effect on the perspiring driver as would a long drink of cool water, making even more sweat gush and saturating clothing from neck to knee. Very soon, though, life would be back to its air-conditioned norm again.

It was only when there was some kind of power failure that you realised how the heat affected everything, sucking every particle of moisture from every fibre, from every molecule, so that in their state of total dessication they gave off a cloying, sickly odour of their own dry death. Even the newly arrived daily newspapers, fresh in their London wrappers, instantly surrendered the moisture from the paper to the searing dry heat, belching off their own nasty stench of moribundity when they were opened. Every inanimate object gave up its personal contribution to the pervading smell of dry rot. Such was the heat and its terrible effect on everyone, everything, you felt it was extracting life out of life itself.

It was at night, when the heat was of an intensity Gordon Watson had believed was impossible, that he had his biggest struggle at Zamakh. There was no sleep when it got to that pitch and lying on the bare concrete arms and legs were constantly on the move, seeking out a piece of floor that was cooler than the piece on which your skin was presently touching. Even the tiniest piece that was slightly cooler was a relief. But within minutes that fresh portion of floor had warmed too and his limbs were on the move again, little by little, looking for a fresh area of concrete that might be just a fraction cooler. Yaqoob could sense his cell friend's agony and as he had done on the first night he had been there would go without sleep himself to bring him cool cloths from the ablutions to help him through the torture of the hours of darkness.

When he left Zamakh after serving the full two months of his sentence, Gordon Watson felt he was leaving an old, dear and trusted friend, which was what Yaqoob the Pakistani had been to him during his 60 days of confinement.

"I'll be back next month . . . as a visitor." he said to Yaqoob as they warmly shook hands the morning he was released. "I can never thank you enough, friend . . . never."

"Look after yourself, Gordon," said the Pakistani in return. "And when you come back in a month I'll have a lot of news for you about our friends the men from Razak and why they keep going to Jilida."

"I can't wait to hear about that."

The Soldiers of God

RELIGION HAS always been a way of life for the Gulf Arabs. It was with them long before Mohammed brought them the unity and discipline of Islam. It was with them back in the days of Sam bin Nuh, the son of Noah. It was with them in the days when they were ruled by the woman they called Saba, and whom the world knew as the Queen of Sheba. And it was with them in the days of the great Marib Dam in Yemen from where the fathers of the Arab nation were spawned. They were to take their creed north across the Arabian Peninsula in great migratory waves.

In families like the Khalfans from Razak, the way of Mohammed not only gave life a reason, He was the reason for their life. He was the purpose for their every thought, their every deed. The Khalfans lived and breathed the word of the Koran; they made no concessions for the holiest of holy books and when their eldest son Said was but 13, he could recite every word of that book.

It was in the name of his God that as a young man Said Khalfan was to become a Soldier of Allah, and it was before him that the group of young men had gathered for their last words of inspiration before going to the attack of the police station at Razak and to their own martyrdom.

"Being a martyr for your God is the quickest route to heaven," he had told them the evening before the day of the battle when they had met together after the Isha prayers. "Remember, that in the last day, the weak shall take their vengeance upon the strong, the unarmed upon the armed, the unhorned cattle upon the horned cattle. For Allah is just and in the end he will make the balance level. Tomorrow you are the chosen ones to take that vengeance. And soon, in the name of Allah and Mohammed, peace be upon Him, I will be the chosen one, insha'allah, for a mission that will let them know in this country that the weak are the weak no more."

Now, as the bearded leader of the five men from Razak being held in Zamakh Prison, he would daily remind the small group of their duties as Soldiers of God and how they must prepare themselves to be martyrs for Him because they were the chosen ones, the ones who would see the smile on Mohammed's face when they went to heaven. They would die in His name.

As children and later as young schoolboys, the five men had grown up together in the old oasis town on the shoulder of the towering Red Mountain. They used to play together round the ancient fort which, it was said, had been there long before the days when the Persians had come across the Gulf and occupied their land. In the long summer days they would splash and frolic in the falaj water channels and when they were chased from doing that, for that was the drinking water, they would scramble barefoot up the mountainside to swim in the pools by the streams that flowed for most of the year, where the wild figs and walnuts grew and there were palms hung heavy with fresh dates so big and juicy that a handful was a meal in itself.

In the evenings in their homes, the same squat adobe and breeze-block houses in which most of the townspeople lived, they would be called to the majlis meeting rooms of their fathers and the friends who would gather with them and, as was the custom of young boys, they would act as the servants to their elders, serving the guests with cool water, then the sweetmeats and fruit and coffee. When everyone had been satisfied, and only then, the boys would be allowed to eat. Then they would sit and listen to the talk of the men.

Said's own father, a respected elder of the town with the title of Sheikh, had years earlier been expelled to Saudi for his deeds in promoting the cause of the Imam, their spiritual leader, whom the Emir had decreed could never live again in Emirate. It had been the history of the Imams in Emirate that they had tried to wrestle much of the power from the Emir. In previous times they had even engaged in war and other acts of violence in order to win that power. Whilst he was the best of Muslims, the Emir would not brook any interference in the running of his country. Hence the Imam and his closest followers, including Said's father, were banished. An uncle had taken the young Said in his care in order that he had the experience of a father-figure in his home and so that he would learn the respect and the ways of their society.

Apart from acting as servants to the men, an exercise principally designed as a lesson in teaching respect, the young boys were not treated as children by the elders. The men of Said's family circle were all Fundamentalists, just as his father had been long before the great resurgence of Fundamentalism in the 'seventies. To them the creation of childhood, adolescence and youth was a Western assumption intended to shut sections of the people out of society. There was only one division in life and that was as the Koran would have it, that being the time when one could distinguish between right and wrong, deemed to be nine years for girls, from which age they were considered old enough to marry, and 16 for boys, the age at which they were assumed to be fully responsible in the eyes of God.

Like his other friends, the young Said would be allowed to sit with the elders as they had their regular evening discussions, which ranged from interpretations of the Koran to the changes that were taking place in the region due to developments in the wake of the discovery of oil. This latter subject came to be discussed by them more and more. Not only were they being deprived of their Imam, they would say, but their society was under threat and the pure Koranic way of life they had known was being eroded by the mass incursion of foreigners, many from the West, to work in the various development programmes designed by the Emir to take the nation into the

20th century. They could see, just as the Ayatollah had seen, how the influence of the Satanic West was ruining their country.

"I was ashamed," said one, "at what I saw in the Capital Area. If you go into those new hotels you can watch them openly drinking their alcohol. And many of them are our own people. People who were once good Muslims."

Another said he had seen them too and not only were there many Muslims to be seen taking alcohol, there were infidel women there too.

The talk of the men burned deeply into the minds of the young ones, particularly the young Said who would often brood about being deprived of his own father merely because he had been an active supporter of their spiritual leader. "How could it be," he would ask his uncle, "that our Emir is always telling us to be good Muslims yet when my father tries to prove he is one of the finest of them he is sent from his own land?"

"Well might you ask," his uncle would reply. "For that is what I and the other elders have been asking for years. And the new generation, like yourself and the other boys, are the ones that we will be looking to in order to change what is happening."

With his friends, now men and prisoners with him in Zamakh, Said would repeat the words of their elders. "We are the lucky ones," he would tell them, "for we are the ones who will be changing the way of what has been. And I am especially lucky for I have been to the land of the Ayatollah and received the inspiration which he transmits to the young."

He had been to Iran all right and in the terms of young revolutionaries he really had been especially lucky for he had spent a year at the great camp in the beautiful park of Manzarieh in the northern suburb of Tehran. There, within sight of the magnificent Mount Towchal, snow-capped even in the warm days of summer, he had learned everything there was to know, for young men in revolt, from Kalashnikov to Koran.

"It was the greatest experience of my life," he would tell them. "We had students from all over the world, even ones who had been studying in the land of the Great Satan and they had first-hand knowledge of what it is like to live in the land of moral filth.

"We would hear too, in discussions with the Mullahs, of the great days of Islam and of the glory of Spain when it was Islamic. And one evening, one very special evening, one Mullah read to us a message from the Khomeini himself in which he told us that to permit the infidels to stay alive was only to allow them to do more corrupting work. He reminded us that the Koran itself declares we must wage war until all corruption and disobedience of our laws is wiped out."

Then he would go over that part of the story of which he was most proud, of the day when he graduated from the great camp of the revolutionaries and had taken the oath and been awarded the crimson headband, the honour which is bestowed on a volunteer for martyrdom. Although they had heard him tell it before, there was still a special look of reverence from them as he would go over the details of this part of his revolutionary graduation.

In Zamakh Yaqoob would watch them in fascination. He would study them every night as they gathered like this, making sure he did so from different parts of the room, mixing with the other prisoners as they played their nightly games of huwayliys, cards and dice. As the nights progressed, there seemed to be an increased intensity in the way their leader would command them in their group sessions, using his hands more frequently as he obviously elaborated points of his message, or whatever it was, to them.

Yaqoob wished his friend Gordon Watson could have been there to see them as they were now. They hadn't been so deep in their discussions before or huddled together for so long like they now were every night. He wondered what Gordon would have said about that. He smiled when he thought about the Scot and how, even though he had suffered terribly with the heat, he had always tried to make light of situations. He had not met anyone from Scotland before but his brother had said in his letters they were a likeable race, much better than the English. "They have many strange and unrefined ways, but nevertheless they are good people," he had written. Maybe he should have gone to Scotland too when his brother had suggested it some years ago. But fate was to bring him to the Gulf instead.

Yaqoob remembered that first occasion back in his hometown of Lahore when he had got the idea that the Gulf would be a good place for him. One evening when he had finished work he had passed one of the little tea stalls in the Dil Mohammed Road, the one next to the big chicken restaurant where the diners picked a live bird from cages they kept at the door. Yaqoob had taken a seat at the tea stall. On benches in front of him was a small audience of about 40 men all watching the pale-blue picture of a small TV screen at the rear of the stall. Admission price was a cup of tea. They were watching a film about the new world of modern Arabia, audibly gasping in astonishment at the scenes of sweeping highways and huge modern palaces they said were airport terminals, hotels and Government offices. It seemed incredible that such fine places existed. Yaqoob had never seen anything like it before.

The man sitting next to him was giving a running commentary about the scenes. He said he had worked in the Gulf and it was even better than the hazy blue picture they were watching. "They even pay the humblest of labourers three times the wages a man can earn here," declared the man. "Not only that, they will give you accommodation and free food," he said, adding that after serving two years there he had been given three weeks' leave and a return air ticket.

Then the picture moved on to show more views of beautiful new buildings, some that even had fountains with high jets of water and splendid gardens. Now, there was affluence. There was nothing like that in the Old City in the centre of Lahore where Yaqoob lived. The only sign of the new world there was the occasional small motor car, small enough to manoeuvre the web of lanes and alleys where little had changed since the Mongol hordes, centuries before, had laid siege at the big gates of their walled Old City.

There were no new ways in Old Lahore with its daily mêlée of people, every one of them a trader or the helper of a trader, like Yaqoob had been when he was as young as five, collecting scraps of wastepaper until he had a filled sack so big he could barely carry it. With the few coins he earned from that he would hire a small charcoal stove and buy raw poppadoms which he would cook and sell at a profit to the strollers in the big parks outside the walled city. On other days, accompanied by his brother, they would hire bigger stoves in which they would roast kernels of sweetcorn, first basting them with spices before offering them to tourists who would come to visit the Lahore Fort.

If you were poor, like Yaqoob's family had been poor, making a living in Lahore was an art form that had to be mastered in order to survive. No opportunity was missed in learning new ways, no chance ever passed up in making a new contact who one day might be able to help in some way.

From cooking titbits in the parks, Yaqoob went on to become apprenticed by day to the roadside motor mechanics of the MacLeod Road and at night operated an almost non-stop pomegranate press to provide the juice they loved to drink with their meals at the karahi pavement restaurants. There he also studied the expertise of the amazing pan chefs who squatted on high stools before their giant girdles and, with long spatulas and ladles and with all the flair of kitchen Toscaninis converted batches of raw vegetables and meats with splashes of ghee and fistfuls of herbs and spices into *cordon bleu* for the proletariat.

A man and his family would have starved in Old Lahore had the breadwinner depended on a living from just one trade. So he mastered the arts of the mechanic and the cook as well as that of the occasional trader, and when it was the season for the sport of wrestling he would work at that too, taking to the ring as King Khan, one of the many used as ring fodder for the full-time professionals on the big countrywide circuit. But even his income from such various sources was little more than sufficient to afford him the most meagre of houses, consisting of two tiny rooms with an outside cooking area and situated off one of the warren of alleys near the Mochi Gate of the Old City. It was there that his wife had borne him six children, two of them dying at birth. And it would be there, if he kept fit and continued to work the hours he did, that he would still be living when he was an old man.

It was the film about Arabia that night in the little tea-stall and the man telling him about the money which could be earned that made up his mind about going to the Gulf. When he told Farida, his lover and mistress, about his plans she said she would give him the money for the agent's fees to get to the Gulf, provided, that is, he vowed to return to her arms one day.

Yaqoob and Farida had been secret lovers for years, long even before he had met his wife. In fact, he was only a lad of 15 when he was first tempted to share her delights. Farida was in her forties then, still an attractive and appealing, if well-rounded, woman and the widow of the owner of one of the big fruit stalls in the Anarkali Bazaar. That particular bazaar was the biggest and best of its kind in Lahore, probably in the nation, to which crowds would throng every day knowing that for the cheapest prices they would get the freshest of produce available. Above one of the hectic fruit stalls, Farida had her apartment, gaudily decorated in vivid blue and startling yellow, but spacious and comfortable, with all the luxuries of life which Yaqoob could never have afforded for his little abode — a television, a colour one at that; a stereo on which she would play Punjabi love songs; and on the floor the best of namda wool mats and Bokhara rugs as well as some rare Isfahans and intricate Kashans with their delicate rose and leaf trade mark.

Yaqoob had been hiring hand-carts then, transporting huge loads of produce from the wholesalers to the stallholders. Such heavy work had laid the foundations of the wide shoulders and barrel chest that was to allow him to graduate into the ring with the wrestlers. He had carried supplies for Farida's stall and although he was merely 15 years of age, Farida too admired his healthy stature. She admired more the fact that, despite his youth, he was more than willing to participate actively in the games of the cushion they were to play. When she took him to her ample body, allowing him to feast his young and wondrous eyes on her huge breasts, she would whisper to him that there were many classrooms in the wonderful university of love. She had studied in all of them. "My husband was one of the great masters," she told the young Yaqoob. "He went to Bombay and brought back the two great books, the *Kama* and the *Kok Shashtra*. In them there is everything there is to know about making love."

Over the years, as he went from boy to youth to man to married man, Yaqoob was to experience the full lexicon of love from Farida until he too was, as she said, one of the great masters himself. Indeed it was the memory of their thousand and one nights of love-making together which Yaqoob had to rely on to cheer the tedious hours of confinement in that crowded and fetid prison cell of Zamakh Prison.

He would contemplate too his life since coming to Arabia. There was the delightful Ahwa, beautiful and young and enraptured with his love-making. Alas, he had only accomplished about half of the many sexual manoeuvres from the *Kok Shashtra* when she had fallen pregnant by him. That was the more pleasant side of getting to know the Gulf Arab.

The men were different. They were a strange lot, he would often think. They had a great pride about them, a superior attitude. You could see it in that assured and upright way they would walk, the casual movement of their shoulders, the confident swing of their arms. Was it this great pride that made them treat the Indians the way they did, or was it because the Indians so often acted the servile way they did? The confident meeting the subservient.

They didn't treat the Pakistanis like that, particularly not the Punjabis like him, invariably big, muscular men with their own pride and to whom servility was anathema. Also the Pakistanis were Muslim brothers and that was in their favour. Despite all that, however, there was still an aloofness about the Gulf Arab which was not to his liking. As for these five, the ones from Razak, with their comings and goings and their nightly cabals, well they were the strangest Arabs of all.

Apart from their nightly meeting together, their pattern of activity during the day continued much as it had done prior to the departure of his cell friend, Gordon Watson. They would be taken from the Hazz Wing nearly every day, leaving the simple one behind, although he was always with them on other occasions when they were in the cell. They still never mixed with any of the other prisoners, not even the other Arabs, and if they ever thought Yaqoob was within hearing distance of them they would revert to speaking in code. He had tried to follow what conversations he had heard when they spoke that way, but they were so fluent in their code he could not follow them. All he could learn about them was that the one with the biggest beard was in fact their leader and was called Said. The simple one was Yousuf and he would only speak with the greatest of reluctance when the others were not there. With a combination of Yaqoob's Old City *nous* and the Razak man's naïveté, Yaqoob made it a point that he was not trying to elicit information from him when they regularly spoke together. He would only ask one question per conversation and would carefully disguise it among other idle minutiae, such as the time of day and the heat and the smell and the foul food. With his persistence and patience, slowly and surely he was able to build up the fragments into the semblance of a picture.

They had many influential friends. That was why they got out of the big cell so often. Sometimes there were nasrani friends, ones from Europe, who would come to see them. That's how important they were. And they had much talking to do. They would not be much longer in Zamakh for their friends were arranging their release, and when they were liberated they would all be going to the Capital Area instead of back to Razak. But what they were going to do there was their real big secret. So secret, said Yousuf on the occasion Yaqoob managed to extract it from him as one of his daily facts, that even he hadn't been told about it.

"And even if I did know what it was," Yousuf had told him when they had once more spoken together, "may the fire, the mother of hospitality, be quenched on my hearth and my father's grave be defiled should I ever tell one word of it."

"And may Allah cut short my life should I ever want to know about it from you, my friend," Yaqoob had reassured him. "Your secrets are safe and will stay with yourself." Then as he turned his back on him to stretch out on the hard floor of the cell, that cruel twist on his face creased into a roguish smile as he thought what subterfuge he would use the next time they had words.

Yaqoob was enjoying his game with Yousuf. Bit by bit by bit the picture was being built up. Eventually he would get to know what their big secret was. But it would take time. At least there was no shortage of that.

About a week after that conversation when the secret had first been mentioned, the two had another chance to speak together. Said and the other three men had returned to the cell at the time, entering by the door at the far end of the room. When Said saw them speaking together he bid the other three to stand where they were in order to observe them. They stood for some minutes before crossing the room, whereupon Yousuf quickly scuttled guiltily away from Yaqoob. There was a corner of the room cleared of other prisoners and Said walked to it, telling the others to bring Yousuf to him. They squatted in a circle, just like they would in the evening, and before he put his back to them to rest on his blanket, Yaqoob could see there were some angry exchanges between their leader and the unfortunate Yousuf.

"What have you been telling the Pakistani one?" Said demanded.

"Nothing, Said. Nothing, I swear."

"This is not the first time we have returned and seen you and him together. What is it you have to tell him?"

"Nothing at all, I swear," he replied, visibly cowering at the ferocity of Said's stare. "May Allah cast me to Jehennan if I tell him your secret."

"Ah, so you were talking about the secret."

"No, Said, No. He knows nothing about the secret. I swear to the Almighty about that."

"May Allah blacken your face if you have even mentioned a word to him. What does the Pakistani know, then? What is it you gossip to him about? About our visits to Jilida? About the attack on the police station?"

"He already knew about that, Said."

"So you have spoken about it! What else, foolish one?"

"It was he who spoke about it. I did not tell him."

"But you acknowledged it. What else has your loose tongue told him? About why we go to Jilida?"

"He knows you go there but he doesn't know why."

"Then only you could have told him that. You have the mind of a donkey, Yousuf."

"What were you talking about when we came in there?"

"Just gossip, Said. About the food and the smell and how terrible it is here in Zamakh. I swear by the Almighty that is all."

"Then he still knows too much. Something will have to be done to stop your gossiping. And soon."

Learning About a Friend

HE LEANED forward, putting his face as close as he could to the blast of cool air coming from the car's air-conditioning vents. Then he opened the top two buttons of his shirt and pulled the collar up so that the air flowed down his chest.

"Oh my God, Brian . . . that is utterly, fantastically indescribably beautiful. Cool air, I've been dreaming about that for the past eight weeks. What a sensation."

"Careful you don't get a chill, Gordon," said his friend Brian Bria, who had come to pick him up the morning he was released from the Zamakh Prison.

"A chill. Brian, I'd love a chill. I've been fantasising about being chilled every minute of every hour of every day. I still can't believe it though. That I was in there. And that I survived it. There was that bad night at the beginning, I told you about that on your visit. And there were some other nights too. Dear old Yaqoob. I don't know how I would have made it without him. He was fantastic, Brian. When he knew I was going through a bad patch he would sit up and go to the toilets and soak rags in water to cool me. I needed him. I really did. One prisoner died, you know? He was an Indian. They brought three of them in one day. They had been accused of a burglary but maintained they were innocent. So they put them in solitary cells. Incredibly small cells they are, with just enough room for one man to lie down. And they just left them there . . . day and night. For Christ sake! In that heat during the day! Anyway, the one who came back to our cell told us he had been in hospital on a drip for a week afterwards. They told him one of his friends had died and he didn't know where the other one went. But somebody said they carted him off insane.

"There was no torture or anything like that. All they need to do is just leave you in some confined space like that in the heat and that's as much torture as anyone can stand. Anyway, that's Zamakh. It will never see me back, except to visit Yaqoob, that is. I promised him I would return in a month to see him. So . . . how're things? How's the gang at the Rani?"

"Great. Nothing's changed much. Big Jock Carlin is back from leave. French has got himself a new bird."

"What's she like?"

"Oh, not bad. A typist at the Ministry. And David Anthony, in his normal fey way, revealed one night he had served with a Scottish regiment. Brummy Marsh retorted, 'What was it, the Gay Gordons?' Poor David. He does ask for it. Little wonder they call him 'Florence of Arabia' behind his back. But he took it well."

"Pity you weren't there that last Thursday night I was there, Brian . . . the night I got lifted. There was this crowd in from the Press who were with the Wales's party."

"Yes, you mentioned that on my visit. You said they had been talking . . . about me?"

"All I said to this bloke, who was a bit snooty at first, was that I had a mate who I thought had done some newspaper work and when I said your name he nearly flipped. Next thing the whole lot of them were talking about you and asking me where you were, how you looked, what you were doing — which made me figure that you obviously didn't want people to know what you were doing. So I didn't tell them too much. I just let them do the talking."

"Oh, I guess it doesn't matter now. If they know I'm here, so be it. I've had a good run. It's taken them nearly a year to find out that I was in the Gulf, and they still didn't get to me. I knew too they would be there that night . . ."

"And that's why you weren't?"

"That's right."

"One of them said you had done a Ross. What was the significance of that?"

Bria laughed. "That would be Tony Shrimpton, one of the few among them that can claim any form of real intellect."

"That's right. His name was Tony. Tall fellow. Dark hair. Thick specs. So what's the Ross bit?"

"When T. E. Lawrence, *the* Lawrence of Arabia, wanted to opt out of the military after he felt the Government had let him down over their dealings with the Arabs, he disappeared from life. He hid himself by joining the R.A.F. as an ordinary aircraftman and used the name of Ross."

"So you were opting out?"

"Well . . . that's one way of putting it."

"So what were you escaping from?"

"Oh, I just had had enough . . . of the job, of the profession, of the people and the ways in it, of Britain. It just all came at once. So I quit. Just like that. No farewells or nothing. The management were very kind to me, gave me an instant pay-off and just let me walk out the back door."

"No regrets?"

"Absolutely none. I did it and that was that. All of a sudden one day I began asking myself the questions I perhaps should have been asking before . . . about the morality of my job. About being the professional butterfly, alighting on other people's troubles, other people's disasters, taking their snapshots then flying off again. Instead of helping them or caring for them or even fighting for them, all I gave them was an f. stop 5.6 at 250th of a second.

Then I'd run off to the next place where there would be more misery to record. In between it would be dizzy dolly birds, absolute empty heads with pouting lips and poke-your-eyes-out knockers or else our TV, quote, stars, unquote. Oh my God, the ego, the vanity of them! No, Gordon, I've got no regrets. None whatsoever."

Whether or not it was because of his arrest later that night, Gordon Watson had remembered every single detail of the evening the Press party had shown up at the Rani Hotel, particularly the part which concerned his good friend Brian Bria. He had been with the usual Thursday night crowd drinking at the bar when they had come in and like other strangers to the bar they were immediately noticed, perhaps more so than the usual salesmen, engineers and architects who frequented the Rani.

"Look like a bunch of theatricals, if you ask me," said one of Watson's crowd.

"Look like a bunch of something else," said another.

"Isn't there a play on at the Sheraton?"

"No . . . it's the Inter-Con."

"That's what they'll be then. Theatricals. Have you been to see my play, darling?"

"Yes, you were divine, darling. Now give me a kiss."

The group laughed loudly together.

"Have you heard them order drinks?" said another who had been near to them while making his own order. "I say, old chap . . . do you have Slimline tonics here? I say old chap . . . do you have Gordon's here?" he repeated in a mocking voice. "Imagine them saying that to our Saby who's got more different gins, whiskies and vodkas on his gantry than half the boozers in London."

"But the English are always like that," said Watson to a chorus of mock derision from his English bar-mates.

"He's off on his Scotch Wha Hae horse again," ribbed one.

"I'll find out who they are," Watson went on, undeterred by the jokes.

Saby, as always, was quick to see his eye. An Indian, Saby was the Rani's head barman. He was handsome and alert with an incisive sense of humour and the reputation of running the most efficient bar in the Gulf. His flashing dark eyes missed little, whether it was a light needed for a customer's cigarette or sensing the precise moment when a customer wanted to order another round of drinks.

"They're journalists," he told Watson. "They're here with the Royal party . . . your Prince and beautiful Princess."

"That's right. I should have known. My boss has got an invitation to the Embassy's Garden Party reception. He's even had to pay his wife's fare over from England so that she can be there. They'd spend their life savings rather than miss out on a chance to meet Diana. God, these English . . . I don't know!"

Saby was tuned in to the regular Scots-English banter he would hear from the Thursday night group and laughed at Watson's comment. Just then one of the Press party came over to the bar. He was a tall, portly man with a ruddy face that looked as though a flash of sun had caught it. There was that slight air of hesitancy which a stranger will signal when he is about to speak and Watson half expected that what he was going to say was some form of criticism of the bar . . . his bar. Which made him all the more surprised when the man turned to him and said, "I must say, old boy, this is a splendid bar you have here in the Capital. Are you one of the locals?"

"That's right, I'm one of the locals, as you call them. But when you get back to London, tell them the splendid bar was in Rani not in the Capital. It's another five miles up the road."

The man exhaled a loud guffaw at that.

What a phoney laugh, Watson thought. "You're with the Royals then?"

"That's right. Mike Langley's the name . . . you know, the one who does the column?" He mentioned a name which Watson didn't quite catch.

He had never heard of the name or the column but shook hands warmly introducing himself. "Maybe you'll know a mate of mine? He's not here tonight unfortunately, but he told me once he did a bit of freelancing with the papers in London. A photographer, like."

"My dear boy, there's about 10,000 freelance snappers in London."

Totally unimpressed, Watson carried on. "His name is Bria. Brian Bria."

A look of amazement came over the man's face as he repeated the name. "Brian Bria! You mean Brian Bria is here? In the Gulf? In this part of the Gulf?"

"Yeah. As I was telling you, he's my mate. And he . . .".

Before he could finish the man had turned round and was calling over to the group he had left. "I say, Tony . . . Jean . . . could you come here a minute?" He introduced them to Watson and told the story about Bria.

"Is it really our Brian?" queried the one called Tony. "Tall, dark with greying sides. Handsome bastard. Pass for a film star, I've always said. A real man's man. But, by jove, he certainly likes the ladies."

"That's my mate Brian."

"God, we'll have to get in touch with him," said the woman, whose eyeshadow had been smudged with sweat, giving her the appearance of having sunken black eyes.

"So you do know my mate?" Gordon asked, staring at the rings which the woman seemed to have on every finger.

"Know him, darling," she exclaimed in a loud voice. "Why everyone knows Brian in London."

"Then he really was a freelance photographer with the papers?"

"The story is," said the big man called Mike, "Brian Bria was the number one photographer in Fleet Street. Not a freelance — a staff man. He was in Vietnam, Cambodia, Laos, all those dreadful wars in Africa, Israel, Lebanon,

South America. All the great war and famine pictures . . . they were Brian
Bria's. Then, one day just over a year ago he disappeared. Nothing suspicious
about it for his bosses revealed he had resigned and that he didn't want any
farewells or the like and that was it. No one ever sighted him again or knew
where he had gone. There were no letters, no phone calls . . . nothing from
him. We never knew why. We thought at first it was some ploy of his
newspaper and that he would turn up after a while with some fantastic
exclusive, but it was not to be."

"My theory was right, then," said the one called Tony. "I always said he
had done a Ross. Brian was different from the pack. He was always going on
about the morals of his job instead of being like the rest of us and just letting
our 40 grand sort out our morals. I fully expected he would be discovered
with his head shaven and reciting mantras, or whatever they do in those
remote monasteries in India."

"I knew him when he came back from one of his Vietnam tours," said the
woman with the rings, now smoking a striped paper cigarette in an enormous
gold holder. "We used to do jobs together and he would tell me things he
wouldn't tell the others, you know? He was involved in a really bad incident
out in Vietnam. I remember the year. It was '68, for I had just changed over
from the other lot and he had just returned. We were out on this story
together and there was a lot of waiting around, you know the kind of thing,
and he told me all about it. They had been right in the thick of the action and
he was in a helicopter that got shot down and lots of boys in it were killed.
Must have been frightful for the poor darling."

"Well, I know the real story about that incident," said Mike Langley. "For
I knew Ian Pringle who was with him. They had been in all sorts of scrapes in
the battlefield, but one particular day they were involved in a pretty hellish
ambush and were surrounded by Viet Cong. They called in a helicopter to be
evacuated and a Marine officer had thrown Brian a gun and said he wouldn't
get flown out unless he took it and used it if necessary. He had no alternative
but to accept the gun. Then the helicopter took off and hit a tree and crash-
landed. There was a real slaughter, apparently. But the thing was, Brian's gun
went off when the 'copter crashed and he killed two or three of the Marines.
That was when the big change came over him."

"Yes, well I told you it was something like that, darling," said the woman
with the rings and the striped cigarette, her sweat-smudged mascara even
worse now, giving her eyes a ghastly cadaverous appearance.

The story all pieced together, Gordon Watson thought to himself, with all
the blanks there seemed to be about his friend Brian's past. Not that he was
over-concerned about the Australian's past for there was a touch of the
Foreign Legion about a few men he had met in the Gulf; some incident, some
event, something from their past which was the *raison d'être* for their being in
the Arab world — not merely, as most of them would say, the money. That
first night they had met, for instance, it seemed to him as if Bria had carefully

rehearsed everything he had said, when it referred to anything they spoke about in the past.

They had met in the Rani — where else? The crowd hadn't been there and Gordon was alone at the bar, nursing the remains of a pint glass. He had had just enough beer to be liberated from his own Scottish inhibitions and he had turned to the tall man who had suddenly appeared next to him at the bar and said, "Just arrived?"

He had replied, "Why, does it show that much?"

"No, but you're still carrying your hotel key and anyone who's living here has just arrived from some place."

Bria had laughed loudly in reply to that and ordered him a fresh pint, introducing himself at the same time.

"Breer . . . unusual name that," said Gordon.

"No, it's Bria . . . B-R-I-A. It's an Italian name. The old grandfather came over with the goldrush, or in the latter part of it. Like most of them he never made his fortune and ended up working in the goldmines."

"Where was that, then?"

"Oh yes, I haven't said. Australia. A place called Bendigo in Victoria."

"You don't sound like an Australian."

"We're not all Ockers. But I guess I don't. I've been away for 25 years and I was nearly 22 when I left. So I guess some of the accent has thinned out a bit."

"So what brings you to the Gulf?"

"A Nikon camera. I'm a photographer. Working on a book for the Ministry of Public Buildings about the mosques here . . . you know, one of these coffee table jobs, big colour pictures and that? Expect it will take me about a year."

"You'll have no shortage of pictures for there's plenty of mosques here. There must be about a thousand of them. They're like pubs in my home town . . . Glasgow."

"Do you know how many there really are? At the last count there were 9,958 of them. And they expect to be over the 10,000 mark fairly soon."

Watson gave a short whistle in amazement. "I'm impressed," he said. "And back to London when you've finished the book?"

"No . . . back to Australia. I've only been back for a couple of brief holidays in all the time I've been away. Now I reckon it's time for me to go back for good. I've kind of fallen in love with the place again, especially after my last trip when I saw it in a new light. D'you know, I've been away so long I stopped calling the Poms Poms! But now I feel like a born-again Australian."

Gordon Watson laughed at that and bought another round of drinks. After that they had become firm friends and he had introduced him to the regular Thursday night crowd who met at the Rani.

Now, by hearing the stories from the people who knew him from London,

Watson felt he knew and understood his friend Brian Bria so much better. He now knew the answers to so many things that had puzzled him in the past, like that day when they had gone together to Qurat Beach and when the Army helicopter had flown low over them, as they often would in mock rescue exercises of young soldiers or police in inflatable dinghies. Bria had buried his head in his hands and repeated over and over, "Christ, I hate those things. I hate those things. I hate those things." And when the thup-thup-thupping had gone he had looked up and said, "Sorry, but I've just got a thing about them."

Then there was the night in the Rani Bar when they had the giant TV screen set up for the European Cup soccer final. As they waited for it to start a film about the famine in Ethiopia had come on — the one where a starved child dies before the cameras against the background music of The Cars singing their hauntingly beautiful *Drive* — "Who's gonna drive you home . . . tonight . . . ?" While they had all been touched, Bria had gasped, "Oh God", and without another word had suddenly rushed from the bar, not returning again that night.

There was another time too, when the Thursday night crowd had been having one of their debates together, this time discussing the plight of the Boat People. One of them quite casually had referred to them as "stupid Gooks". Bria, quite uncharacteristically had reacted violently, grabbing the man by the throat with one hand and telling him, "Never . . . never, use words like that about those people in front of me."

Now Watson knew about those things, and more, about this man Brian Bria sitting beside him as they drove towards the Capital Area of Emirate. "Geez, it's beautiful to see the jebels again," he said as the car glided along the gracious highway, dotted with the ever-present Indian sweepers in their orange overalls, the men who swept and re-swept the motorway every day of the year so that it seemed to take on a sheen in accordance with the fanaticism for the good appearance of the Capital Area. "I love the mountains. They remind me of Scotland . . . without the grass, that is. There's one there that's the image of *Buachaille Etive Mhor* and that one away over to the right, it's the duplicate of *Sron na Creise*."

"Are you talking a foreign language?" asked Bria.

"No. That's Gaelic. Haven't a clue what they mean, except one means the Big Shepherd or something. They're mountains in Glencoe where I used to go a lot when I was young. When I was young! That's the old man coming out in me now. But these mountains . . . they really are just like Glencoe, with a different set of colours."

"And no rain?"

"Oh, geez, aye. You forget that when you're away. The bloody rain."

"Rani for lunch?" Bria asked.

"Are you suggesting there's another place?" Watson smiled in reply.

The Thursday-Night Club

THE THURSDAY-NIGHT CLUB, as their informal gathering had become known, would meet every week in the Tie Bar of the Rani Hotel. The bar got its name from the fact that every company which had come to this part of the Gulf and set up an operations base was asked to contribute a company tie to the bar, provided, that is, that a member of the company had become a patron of the establishment. The tie was then exchanged for another bearing the motif of the hotel — a sheathed khanjar dagger. There were 354 ties neatly affixed to a continuous picture rail around the room of the wide horseshoe bar.

Thursday night was their meeting night because Thursday night in the Arab world was the equivalent of a Friday-cum-Saturday night in Europe. Most of them, like the nationals, worked a six-day week. Friday was the Sabbath and their day off. Therefore Thursday was the last night of the working week and Saturday was the first day of the working week. It was always confusing for the newcomer to get used to the idea that Thursday night and Friday represented their weekend. Even though they got their pay cheques monthly, they would treat Thursday like an old-fashioned pay night. Most of them were there to raise money for their families and a large proportion of that pay cheque was sent home to England and Scotland, to Wales and Ireland and Australia, and to wherever was home for the expat. in the Gulf.

The Thursday-Night Club gathered itself at the far right corner of the bar. There were no formalities about being a member of the club. If you were there and stood with them, you were a member. It was as simple as that. There were those who would turn up once a month, some maybe once every two months, others perhaps twice a month, a few every occasional month, and a core of regulars who to get there would brave the severest of the elements, even the nights of June, the warmest month, when the temperature would only have retreated marginally from the day's peak of 120 degrees and when merely to breathe the dank and steamy night air was painful.

They were a disparate bunch, mates by necessity rather than by choice. Their necessity was the loneliness of the Gulf worker, separated as he was from wife and family. The ones with the better jobs were given married accommodation, but often as not the wives would stay behind, particularly those with children. Unless they too could get work the Gulf could be a trying location for an accompanying wife. Those who did come with their families and stayed were usually wives of men at the top end of the professional scale, managers of banks and companies and the like where the money was good enough, or the company was paternalistic enough, to pay for school fees, with a good company car thrown in and no strain on the salary for the wife to have her own transport.

No one was quite sure just how their Thursday night gatherings had begun, although Jock Carlin, a telecommunications engineer from Kilmarnock in Ayrshire, claimed he had originated the evenings with Bill French, a drug company representative from Preston in Lancashire. Carlin, who was the kind of man who looked ill at ease without a glass in his hand, would explain that he and French had teamed together because both had observed that each drank double vodkas with half pint lager chasers and consumed them at such a rate they had preferred being on their own rather than to have to slow down to suit the pace of the normal drinker. After being drinking partners for nearly a year they had condescended to let others join them. However, they would still stand together on a Thursday night and in between the rounds the others would buy, they would stand each other extra drinks.

By the time Watson had got to know them there was a regular team of about a dozen, at least seven of whom would be guaranteed to be there every Thursday. Among the stalwarts, apart from Carlin and French who were known as the Doubles Champions of the Gulf, and Gordon Watson and Brian Bria, there was Geoff Melmouth, a west countryman and a draughtsman with a Bristol-based company who operated in the Gulf, and Arthur Marsh, a print works manager from Birmingham. Both of these men, it seemed, only came to life after three pints of beer. Steve Powers, from Stepney in London, was a refrigeration engineer with Gulf Beverages. Without the use of "ferk" or "ferkin'" he would be near speechless. Then there was David Anthony, a retired Army major and Arabist who worked for the Ministry of Culture and Heritage and was the supreme example of just how disparate they were.

Such was that disparity, a group like theirs in normal circumstances would have been unthinkable as regular drinking mates, apart from Watson and Bria who had sprung up a genuine friendship and, of course, Carlin and French who shared the same patron. Count Smirnoff.

Melmouth was a Methodist, he would say with a pint in his hand, and would preach tolerance — till he had one too many, that is; Marsh, on the other hand, had all the tolerance of a born-again racist, particularly if those races were Indian, Pakistani or Caribbean and lived in or near his beloved Birmingham. Powers, on the other hand, made it plain he never discriminated; he just disliked everyone who was foreign.

Anthony, though, was the most unlikely member of the Thursday crowd. They referred to him as the Major when he was there and when he wasn't and because of certain mannerisms, the like of which you wouldn't find at a Rugby Club social, he was called Florence of Arabia. As well as being the Arabist, he was a lover of the classics, a patron of the arts, an opera buff, an avid reader and if ever Wilfred Thesiger's name was mentioned he would speak in a tone of reverence, referring to him as The Great Man. These facets of his character gained little appreciation from the others, apart from Watson and Bria.

David Anthony also had the manners of a man whose choice of cuisine would be minceur rather than mince, whose music would be Saint-Saëns never sing-song; he was familiar with Degas but knew nothing about Dallas and when it came to drinking, well, only ORs had pints and all his barmen knew he poured his own tonic in his gin. With that and his various affectations, he was certainly different from the others. As well as calling him Florence, he was a "ferkin' poofter" to Powers and a "bleedin' queer" to Marsh, though neither comment was ever made in a malicious kind of way and certainly never to his face. But to a man they relished his conversation for there was no better storyteller anywhere in the bar than their Major, particularly when the G & Ts were flowing; all his other ways, or sins if they were that, were forgiven because of his likeable manner.

Despite Powers' poofter and Marsh's queer, Anthony was in fact neither. He was a tall, handsome man in his late forties, still with a good head of hair which had once been blond but was now a dark sandy colour and streaked with grey. Once, when they had sufficient drink to ask him about it, he had explained to Watson and Bria that he was aware of his fey ways, the limp hand and the speech littered with "dears" and sometimes "darling", but put it down to having mixed with so many theatricals, art lovers and antique buyers that "perhaps I have taken on some of their ways". He had added, "After all, my dear boy, they're not exactly the type you would meet on a Saturday afternoon at Stamford Bridge or White Hart Lane. And thank God for that."

But there was a certain tolerance among all of them for, as a group, they were a reminder of that norm from which they had come and which so many of them missed. Whatever their particular trade or profession, their work was invariably more trying for them, apart from the demands of the climate, than ever they had known at home. A few, like the Major and Brian Bria may have been there for their love of the Middle East and its strange ways, but the rest of them, like most of those they called the expats, were only there for one reason—the money. Many of them had been victims of the United Kingdom's unemployment explosion and the Gulf had been the last resort for them to keep on working for a few more years to maintain wives and children in standards to which they had become accustomed. For that they were willing to put up with temperature the likes of which they had never known before, to work with people whose ways were not their ways, to get accustomed to attitudes where nothing, it seemed, ever happened today but only tomorrow and only insha'allah. They were Brits abroad and that was their bond. That was why they enjoyed their Thursday nights and each other's company so much despite any misgivings they might have about one another.

The drinks, of course, helped and after two or three rounds they would be as lively and as amiable as any group of real mates in a British pub, particularly if the Scot, Gordon Watson, was in form. With his native Glasgow wit he could convert most situations into a riotous ending, making them overlook the more vicious of his barbs against the English, such as telling them that Hugh McDiarmid, "the greatest Scottish poet ever, was right for describing himself as a hater of all things English". But then none of them had ever heard of McDiarmid and that robbed the jibe of some of its impact.

As he was in the Rani Bar more frequently during the week than the others, big Jock Carlin would often have a supply of the tittle-tattle and various happenings of nights when the Thursday nighters weren't there. Typical of his yarns was the one he recounted about Saby, the head barman and a favourite with them all.

"You should have been in on Monday . . . or was it Tuesday?" he started off, at which point he nearly abandoned the story for the ribbing he got for beginning a tale connected with drink in such a fashion.

"Must have been a good night then, Jock . . . whichever one it was," they joked.

"All right, you wise guys. You've had your laugh. Anyway, Saby was in top form that night. There was this group of newcomers at the bar. They were one of those Chamber of Commerce parties out from England on a tour of the Gulf. From somewhere in the north. Lots of ee-ba-gooms floating round. Pale faces and long-sleeved shirts and that sort of thing. Typical group of Brit. businessmen out for a night to get the flavour of the East and its natives . . . and doing it in the comfort of the Rani. Bet the buggers had never seen anything like it in their Rochdales or Wakefields or wherever they were from. Anyway, I was standing at the bar . . .."

"Not like you, Jock," interrupted someone.

"Aw, give us a break, wee man," Carlin retorted. "As I was saying, I was standing at the bar when they started chatting to Saby. One of them, a bit of a pompous prig with a loud voice, asks Saby his name. Then he says to him, 'And you're from India I suppose?' That was Saby's cue to do one of his mickey-taking exercises. He's brilliant at it — I've heard him before. 'Oh no,' he replies, quick as a flash. 'I'm Italian actually. I'm from Palermo in Sicily. Actually my name is Sabattini. Mario Alessandro Sabattini. I had to leave home as a young boy because of the Mafia. They were after my father—he's also Mario.' And they fell for it hook, line and sinker. Then he goes on to tell them about the way he looked and spoke now. 'You see,' he says, 'I've been working with Indians ever since I left home. So long, in fact, I even speak like one. And this heat and sunshine in the Gulf, it makes us Latins go very dark. Look at me,' he says to them, 'I even look like an Indian now.' And I kid you not, they believed every bloody word of it. God, I'd love to hear them retell it when they get back to their Coach and Horses. I bet it goes . . . 'Eee, lad, when ah was in't Middle East . . .'."

"That's our Saby," said another of the crowd. "Sharpest damn bar manager

I've ever come across."

Other nations' expats and the local natives themselves were often a topic of conversation with them, particularly when Marsh and Powers were there, neither it seemed having a liking for anyone other than the British, and British to them meaning only one thing — English. But while they were vocal about it, there was no shortage of support from the others on the subject, except from Watson or Bria or the Major who would take opposite standpoints to the xenophobia of most of their other drinking companions. A typical such conversation was the night the subject was raised of the continuing riots in the Punjab.

"What I don't get," said Marsh, "is all this carry-on they're having in their country, jumping about with swords and guns and that, and then you look at them here. Have you ever known such a mild and meek lot? Wouldn't say boo to a bleedin' donkey, neither they would. So how come they all behave like football yobbos when they're at home?"

"Maybe it's because they're in a highly civilised country here where people treat each other with respect and one never ever forgets one's manners," was the Major's answer.

"Gawd, come off it, mate," interjected Powers. "Ever been up at the ferkin' Police Motor Registration Branch? Have a ferkin' blink up there and there's three Indians standing in front of you. Sneeze and there's half a ferkin' dozen. Never heard of manners these people."

"The Arabs are the same," added Marsh. "Think they own the bleedin' place, so they do."

"Well, don't they?" asked Watson.

"Yes, maybe that's right," replied Marsh. "But that doesn't give 'em the right to lord it the way they do. Ever seen the way they treat the Indians and Pakis, especially the Indians because they're not Muslim? Have a look at them some day at that big car wash place next to the Hamat House flats . . . you'll know it, Brian, that's where you live, isn't it? Well, they go there with the big Mercs and you have all these Indians to dry and clean out your car after it's come through the wash. The Arab owners get out with their gold-topped canes and go round their cars tapping out with their sticks the bit the 'boy' has missed. That's what they think of them, you know . . . 'boys'. Get a 'boy' to do this and a 'boy' to do that. And if you can't get an Indian 'boy', they'll say, 'Then get a Filipino boy'."

"Hey Marshie, you sounded as though you were almost sticking up for the Indians there," said his friend Powers.

"No, but I mean to say, the Arabs still think of them as slaves and that. You know it was this lot here that started the slavery trade? A quick trip down the east coast of Africa there, round up a few thousand Zulus then bring them back and sell them at a fat profit to the Yanks. That's what they did, you know."

"Arthur, the Zulus are from South Africa," said Jock Carlin.

"Well, you know what I bleedin' mean. They're all the same anyway. Still doesn't get away from the fact this lot here were the big fellas in the slave trade. Did you know the old Emir had them right up to the 1970s. Gawd, he had 'em pulling his car around town. There was wealth in having slaves, see. But you weren't showing your wealth if you let your car engine do the work. That's the kind of mentality they had. And that was only yesterday. Give 'em half a chance and they'd have the Indians here pulling their cars around."

"Yes, and knowing the ferkin' Indians they'd it an' all," said Powers as back-up. "You see," he went on, using his hands to emphasise the point, "the Arab treats anyone as inferior to him who doesn't stand up to him. That's why they'd never treat the likes of you or me that way. But them Indians and others, well they just lay down to them . . . and they get walked all over. Gawd, you should see 'em at our print works. Ferkin' terrified they are. Meet them on the stair and they stand aside to let you past. Go anywhere near a door and two of them'll jump to pull it open for you. And if you need 'em to work late, you just tell 'em and they do it without ever asking for a penny's overtime. Gawd, we must have kicked the stuffin' out of them when we ruled India."

"Don't you believe it," said Marsh. "Ever seen the way the Indian gaffers treat their own lot? Shout right in their faces so they do. Call them all sorts of insulting names. It's their own lot that makes them the way they are. Wasn't us."

The Major joined the topic. "While I'm loathe to agree with dear Arthur . . ."

"Oh God, there he goes again," said Marsh. "Thought for a minute you were going to call me darling there, Major."

". . . as I was saying. There's a nub of truth in what our friend Arthur was saying. The worst of the British in India quickly adopted the ways of the Indian masters themselves. But that's only a portion of the story. The Indians behave the way they do because there's so damn many of them. Goodness, do you know we have them applying for jobs at the Ministry as clerks and they'll have at least one degree, some two, and often as not they've got honours ones into the bargain. And, as well as flawless English, they'll have two or three other languages. After all that education they're quite happy to apply for work as a humble clerk! We pay them absolute peanuts, yet they're over the moon if they get a job for it's about four times the salary they would get as a clerk in India. Now that's the kind of conditions that make people humble. The Arab has never known that kind of life. That's why they can be superior to them. But don't forget the main basis of their superiority. Anyone who has inherited the way of life that they've known for centuries here, having conquered the art of survival in this heat and out there in that desert and their mountains, has got to be something of a superior person. I know the present generation are a bunch of softies just like we are with their air-conditioning and the like, but it was as recent as their own fathers and grandfathers who learned and mastered the way of life out there just as all the generations before them had done for thousands of years. And they did it without ever losing their dignity. I know the pride I'd have if my father and his forefathers had done that for I've been out there."

"Well, if the Voice of Arabia is finished," came in Carlin, "would someone please remind him it's his turn to buy the drink. And Bill and I here are on doubles. With beer chasers."

Just then they had been joined by Majid, a Dhofari Arab whose family had settled in Emirate. He was a big, beefy man with a jolly boyish face, who worked as a civil servant in the Ministry of Information. Majid was one of several nationals who would join the Thursday nighters from time to time. They appreciated each other's company, mainly because, despite the culture chasm, there was only a narrow sense of humour gap between the kind of Southern Gulf Arab who was a regular in such haunts as the Rani Bar, and his British expat. counterparts. It wasn't that the Indians or others who would be there didn't have a sense of humour; it was merely that theirs was a different appreciation of what was funny and what wasn't. Crack a joke with them and it seemed they had immense difficulty differentiating between the fact and the facetious, which made for pained progress in drinking companions' relations. Yet the Arab pub regular was a paradoxical figure of two cultures. His dress would be that of the desert nomad, albeit tailored in the finest quality cotton and updated with such appurtenances as the gold arrow clip of the Parker between the shirt front buttons of the robe. He would more than likely wear designer spectacles and a slimline gold watch, Dunhill and Cartier rather than Rolex or Omega. But with a big pint glass in one hand and invariably a filter tip in the other, he was as much one of the boys as any of the Brits.

"They tell me you're having problems with your maid?" said one of them to Majid.

"No good," he answered. "No good at all. I had to send her back to the Philippines. But look at these," he said pulling a wad of papers from the deep pocket of his dishdasha, each of them with a photograph attached.

"Cor blimey," said Powers. "That's a right lot of brutes you've got there."

"Brutes . . . what do you mean?" asked Majid.

"Ugly, mate. Dead ugly."

Majid bellowed with laughter. "That's right . . . ugly. That's what I'm getting. An ugly maid. The last two were beautiful, but they went out fucking. The ugly ones won't."

Big Carlin shook his head with a look that was somewhere between dismay and disbelief and in that spirit-seasoned voice of his said, "Oh ship me somewhere east of Suez, where the best is like the worst, where there aren't no Ten Commandments, an' a man can raise a thirst."

"That your Robby Burns then?" asked Marsh.

"No, it's your Ruddy Kipling," he answered drolly. "And we're still waiting

on your round of drinks, Mr Anthony."
They were that kind of group.

Lunchtime Questions

WATSON HAD a lot on his mind on the day he was released from Zamakh Prison. He had already impressed his friend Brian Bria about the rigours of the establishment and in particular how he was sure he would have died had it not been for the attentions of the Pakistani Yaqoob. But, apart from that, the confinement had been a jolt to some of his established views on life and although his conversations were generally more surface than substance, he did want to raise them with Bria.

But, more than anything, he wanted to elicit more information from him about the shooting at Razak which he had so briefly mentioned prior to the curt termination of his visit to the prison. With none of their other acquaintances in sight, and the prospect of a good Rani lunch at hand, it was the ideal occasion to get as much as possible discussed. But first and foremost, that shooting.

"You said it was an Army officer you knew who told you about it . . . isn't that right?" he asked Bria while a waiter fetched them drinks.

"Yes. Tony Mills. I met him in Northern Ireland, like I said."

"He's the one you described as not being your usual British officer. You didn't get round to explaining that."

"There's just something different about the guy. Officers have that look about them. Tony doesn't. Got the public school accent and so on, but he's a real rugged individual. And a good bloke."

"So what did he tell you?"

"Everything he knew at the time. There had been this suicide attack on the police station by a group who called themselves a Hussein Martyr Squad. Hussein is not King Hussein or anything like that. This one dates way back in the history of Islam. Anyway, they were Fundamentalists and this was the culmination of a bit of trouble they were trying to create in this part of the Gulf. They don't want them here . . . the Fundamentalists, that is."

"Yes, Yaqoob told me that in Zamakh."

"They don't want any fanaticism here. They won't even let Yasser Arafat visit them. They support the Palestine movement, all right, but from far away. Maybe it's a bit hypocritical, but I can understand it. They just want peace and stability in the country. They've got it and they want to hold on to it. Can't blame them for that."

"So what about the martyr squad?"

"They were wiped out. A few policemen were killed too, but here the cops, who, as you know, are like paramilitaries, are ready for situations like that. Then, after the shooting they rounded up everyone and anyone who might be involved. Apparently there are quite a few of them in the long-term wing at Zamakh."

"That's Jilida."

"Right. And that was about all that Tony could tell me."

"So Yaqoob had it figured correctly. The ones next to us in the cell were Fundamentalists. Yaqoob had ways of telling these things. They would probably have been picked up after the incident, maybe supporters or something, and shoved in Zamakh to cool off."

"But they couldn't have been up to much if they were only in the Hazz Wing."

"That's right. Maybe just way-out supporters or something. But the big mystery still remains. How come they were taken away every day by police for visits to Jilida?"

"Could have been for questioning."

"Every day? And they didn't have to work in the fields with the others. It was like they were on special privileges. They definitely had some connection with the shooting. After your visit, Yaqoob asked the one he had spoken to before if it was the police station attack and he had said it was but was terrified to say any more." Watson had spluttered slightly as he said the word "terrified" and stopped to ask Brian: "Hey! Just how much have I had to drink?"

"That's your first pint you're just finishing."

"Geez, my head is spinning. I feel like I've had about five pints."

"Five pints! You'd better watch that. You know what happened to you the last time you had five pints."

"There's something you've never told me, Brian. How come the Gulf? Why and how did you come here of all places?"

"Have you heard me speak about Billy Bainbridge?"

"Yes, the Colonel bloke who's your boss at the Ministry?"

"That's him. Well, we've known each other for years. Met him first of all in Aden. He was a captain then, serving under Colonel Mitchell in the Argylls. That's one of your lot, isn't it?"

"Aye . . . the Mad Mitch, chasing the Arabs with the bagpipes. I cringe every time I think about that. Sorry . . . go on."

"We kept bumping into each other in a whole variety of places after that. He went to the Parachute Regiment from the Argylls and then the S.A.S. and was on the military attaché's staff in Saigon where he helped me a lot, especially after I didn't file the story about the Gurkhas."

"What were they up to?"

"There was a small detachment of them at the Embassy in Saigon. Merely on protection duties, that's all. Anyway, in '68 when the Tet offensive was on and the VC broke into the American Embassy, which was just down from the British Embassy, Billy caught the Gurkhas with their kukris at the ready and about to break out of the Embassy to go down the road and get a piece of the action. He had to have them arrested at gunpoint and lock them up. Can you imagine the international incident it would have caused had they got out, or the scandal had the story got out? Anyway, it didn't, even though I knew about it.

"We met up in a whole variety of places after that. He did a lot of service in Ireland where he had become something of a counter-terrorist specialist and we used to rendezvous regularly in the Europa, or the Forum as it became. By that time he was a colonel and expected one day to be a brigadier. Then suddenly he quit the Army and put his money with some others from the SAS into one of those protection-security agencies. You know the sort of thing, providing men for all sorts of situations, including other people's wars?

"We met in London one day about a year ago when he was preparing to take up this job here. I assumed he had left his agency, although he didn't say. And it was then that he said if I ever fancied coming here he might be able to arrange it."

"Seems an odd move . . . SAS to a security company to the Ministry of Public Buildings."

"I know. I asked him about that but he said what the Ministry here wanted was an organiser who could get things moving fast. But as you say, it's an odd move. Then again, who thought I would ever be taking snaps of mosques!"

"Or me selling cigs to Arabs!"

"But maybe it's nice for them to have some ex-SAS types around too. He's never said if there are other reasons . . . and I've never asked. Anyway, when I told him I wanted to get away from everything for a while, he got me the job on the mosques book."

"Why didn't you go back to Australia . . . you said you were heading back there?"

"Oh, I am going back . . . for sure. But I wanted a spell in the Arab world first of all. There's a lot of sanity in it, you know."

"What . . . like Beirut, the Palestinians and Mr Gaddafi?"

"That's only a small part of it. Believe me, there *is* a lot of sanity in it. There are a lot of values which they've got right, the attitude to the family and the way they look after each other. You don't get that in Britain . . . or Australia."

"What about the way they treat women?"

"What about it? What about the way we treat them? We prostitute women. The newspapers do it. Flash your tits, love . . . it sells our paper. The advertisers do it. The television does it. And women allow themselves, silly bitches, to be sold for their busts or their bums. Not for their brains, mate."

"You're sounding like one of those feminists."

"Jesus, don't link me with that screwball bunch."

"But what about women here, for instance? Can't go without the veil. How do you never see them if you visit one of their houses? Arranged marriages and all that nonsense?"

"I can't agree with everything that happens to women here. But where else would you see traffic coming to a halt on a highway just because they see some women wanting to cross over? Same in town. A woman only has to step on the road and you'd think she was on an instant zebra crossing the way everything halts. Just little things, I know, but indicative of the deep respect that they have for the female. There are many ways where the respect is shown. Women don't get ogled. They don't get hassled. They don't get raped."

"I've heard of the odd rape."

"Yeah, but it's not a prevalent crime like they have to go about in fear of it. Listen, I'll tell you the respect they have for them. Can you imagine anyone even thinking about using a woman here, and the emphasis is on the using, as a commodity in order to sell their merchandise the way advertisers do in the West? Why wouldn't anyone even think about that here, Gordon? I'll tell you why. Because they've got too much respect for them. And don't think for one minute because you don't see them in their houses that they're some kind of slaves. They rule in their own quiet way."

"Well, you can't marry one, my old son. For they've made a law prohibiting locals from marrying foreigners like you and me. But they can marry other Gulf nationals."

"Yes, I know about that. Does sound a bit xenophobic. Imagine the outcry there'd be in the U.K. if they made a similar law! But again, they maintain it was done in the best interests. They've got the kind of society that they want here and they don't wish it broken down. It was at risk, they say, because so many young students were bringing back foreign wives who could never really understand and appreciate the ways here and who were becoming a force in loosening the fabric of the extended family life. A lot of old local boys were also importing young Muslim girls from India as wives, girls who couldn't speak the language. Because of that the local culture wasn't being passed on to the children. The problem had got so bad they felt society as a whole was being threatened, so they stepped in quick with their no foreign marriages law."

"Funny, I was thinking about some aspects of society here in the East when I was inside. Good God, listen to me talking about 'inside' like I was some old lag. But anyway, it had me thinking. Know what I didn't come across at Zamakh . . . a hard man. I mean, where I come from the hard men, as they call them, they're ten a penny. It's the thing to be . . . to show that you're hard, to act like you're hard. We've got a jail in Glasgow called Barlinnie . . ."

"Know it. Was sent there once to cover an escape. Grim-looking joint."

"You can say that again. Well, I've never been in Barlinnie, but everyone knows all about it and how it's full of hard men. I mean real menacing kind of people, the kind of men who are there for all sorts of vicious assaults, guys whose life is all about being hard; the way they talk, the way they live, the way they behave, and the kind of things they do. Sort of guys you wouldn't say hello to unless you had a smile on your face. A big smile. Even then they would probably say back, 'Hey you . . . who are you fucking laughing at?' That's the kind of people we have in Barlinnie."

"But there's no shortage of them in other parts of Britain these days."

"I know, but in Glasgow we've got an awful lot of them. Yet I didn't come across one like that in Zamakh. I thought there might have been a few convict types, but no. I mean, apart from the fact they don't know how to queue, all these Indians and those from the other Third World countries, they really are a well-behaved and polite bunch. Generally speaking, that is. Yet it's supposed to be us in the West who are better than them . . . more educated, more advanced."

"You're nearly right there, Gordon. More educated, more advanced yes . . . but not better. It's just one of the myths we live with in the West about people from the East. There's a lot more social order and respect among these people than you'll get in Britain. I discovered that a long time ago on my various trips around these parts and the Far East. Although, paradoxically, when they blow up with their racial and religious strife from time to time, they really blow up."

"Yet, they don't do it here in the Gulf, and look at the racial and religious mix they've got with the expatriate workers."

"Must be something to do with the Arab sanity I was talking about. Maybe it's catching. Anyway, these were among the things that made me want to come here. And another reason why Emirate in particular appealed to me . . . there was the bonus of knowing that no one could follow me here looking for a story. If you want to hide from the newspapers, this is the safest place in the world. Every newspaper and television man in the country chased Angela Kay for her story after her affair with the Tory Cabinet Minister. And not one of them got near her. Where did she go? Right here to the Capital. She had a brother who worked at the Embassy and he got her out on a three-month holiday visa. Fleet Street knew she had come here but not one of them could follow."

"The Ministry of Tourism should capitalise on that. You know, 'Come to Emirate; the place where you really are left alone.' They could make a fortune off all those celebrities that the media keep hounding." Watson paused for a while after he had said that. Then, in a loud voice, he turned to Bria, "That's it. Yes . . . that could be it."

"Could be what?"

"Could be why those five from Razak were in Zamakh. Maybe they were put there so that no one could follow them . . . or no one could get at them."

"Feasible . . . but doubtful. But anyway, time you're forgetting all about the

Razak five . . . and Zamakh. Oh, before I forget, Gordon, I didn't tell you I met a new friend when you were inside — God, now you've got me saying it."

"Is he a member of the Thursday-Night Club?"

"Who?"

"Your new friend."

"He's a she, Gordon."

"You old bugger. Got yourself a bird. English? No, bet she's an Aussie sheila?"

"Filipino."

"Oh ho. You know what they say about them?"

"What?"

"If I thought for one minute you didn't know the answer to that I'd tell you. What is she, a nurse?"

"Well I don't fancy the ones in the Kentucky Fried Chicken. The nurses have a bit of education. Do you know, they've all got degrees . . . just to be a nurse?"

"You were almost on the defensive there. Tell me more about her. Where did you meet? Is she a good piece of stuff . . . there are some crackers among them. You see them down Rani High Street a lot."

"She's good looking all right. In fact, she's one of the . . . no, I'll say no more, except she's a beaut."

"Sounds like you've been going steady."

"Yes, when she's not on night duty, we meet once, maybe twice a week."

"How did you meet?"

"I'm ashamed to tell you."

"You picked her up."

"You've got it right again . . . yes, I picked her up. Not really as crude as that, though. I was out for a walk one night. Went along Rani Street, in the direction of the Al Hajjar roundabout and there she was standing at the flower shop just by the arcade. I looked at her and she looked back. And for the first time in a whole year here in the Gulf, Gordon, I got a return look from a girl. I thought at first she was one of those Filipinos who work out at the Al Rawda Hotel so, corny as it may sound, I made that my opening play. And she laughed at the suggestion and said, 'No, no I'm a nurse at Al Nahdha.' Then she said, 'But I don't want you to think bad of me.' I said 'What do you mean, "bad"?' 'You know,' she said. 'Talking to a strange man like this? You will think bad of me.'"

"This sounds good, lover boy. Tell me more. So you asked for her phone number?"

"She's not on the phone. So I scribbled my number down on a card and asked her to call sometime and said that I'd love to take her out to dinner. Gordon, I didn't think for one second that she would. I mean she really is something. And I thought I was way past the stage where a sheila like that would have anything to do with what you call an old bugger."

"So the old bugger got his phone call and the big romance was on. Brian, mate, good luck to you. Just watch the AIDS."

"She's a sheila I said, not a fella. And, anyway, the nurses are all checked out for AIDS before they're signed up in the Philippines."

"Talking of checking out, Brian. Do you think your mate the Colonel could check out the Razak story? I would love to know more about it."

"I told you . . . forget those guys from Razak. You'll become paranoid about them."

"You're right. I can't get them out of my mind, especially since you told me that story about the martyr squad. I mean, if one mob can pop up just like that, how many others might there be? Do you think the colonel might know something?"

"He might. He mixes a lot. I know he's well got at the Ministry of Information. And he goes down to the mess at The Hill a fair bit. That's the Army HQ place. You know what the old military boys are like? I could never really tune into them when there was a bunch of them together. They're such bloody flagrant right wingers. Sometimes I wonder about them. But anyway, maybe he has heard something. Do you want me to find out?"

"Christ, Brian, are you pulling my leg? I'm dying for you to find out something about them. And by the way, make my next drink a tonic water . . . neat. I don't want to get lifted for being drunk and incapable after that one pint I've just had."

"You'll need to go into training, chum."

"Aye, picking up pint glasses. Don't worry. I'll be working on it. By the way, you never mentioned her name."

"Esther."

"That's nice. Esther! Yes . . . I like that."

The Colonel Called Billy

ATER THAT week Bria went to see his friend the colonel at the Ministry of Public Buildings in Al Mushrif, one of the new suburbs of the Capital Area. The building was one of a collection of prestigious new purpose-built office blocks for the various ministries of the Government of Emirate, constructed on a stretch of former saltbush and sandflat country on the eastern flank of the main highway from the Capital to the airport.

The Whitehall of Emirate is an impressive area. The first impression is that here is an array of customised office buildings fitting in their dimension and in the ample two kilometres of land they occupy to represent the infrastructure of a much bigger nation — say an Australia, or Canada, or Belgium or the Netherlands — whereas the population of the country equates with places like Greater Birmingham or Glasgow, or Vienna, Oslo, Stockholm . . . or Minsk. On the other hand, it could also be reasoned that these Ministry buildings are all the more impressive for that.

The offices of the Ministry of Public Buildings were well down the glistening line of solid stone Ministry headquarters, no two of which looked alike, their only similarity being their newness and the fashion in which they were immaculately maintained by the customary army of imported workers doing the kind of jobs with which their ethnic origins had become associated in Gulf manpower terms — Sikh gardeners, Pakistani labourers and, from the base of India, the ubiquitous sweepers and tidiers, those who dusted and polished and ferried tea and water and emptied waste baskets and who would make themselves available for any kind of odd job: the step 'n' fetchits of the 'eighties.

Colonel William (Billy) Bainbridge, MC, ex-Argyll and Sutherland Highlanders, ex-Parachute Regiment, ex-Special Air Service, never took kindly to those he called the "Press Wallahs". Brian Bria was an exception. He treated and thought of Bria as he might one of his senior officers. He was disciplined, trustworthy and his experience on the battlefield was more than any of the new officers in the Army. There was even a touch of envy for the amount of action in which Bria had been involved, particularly his Vietnam experience. The two of them had met there, the Colonel "holed up", as he put it, as a Military Attaché at the British Embassy while Bria had ranged the country from the 17th Parallel right down to the Mekong, with forays into Cambodia and Laos to boot, winning a variety of awards and accolades as the professional photographer. Yes, the colonel would like to have had that kind of experience as a fighting soldier.

He was a small, wiry man who still retained his passion for physical fitness, even to the extent of continuing his daily three-mile run right through the summer months by getting up with the muezzin's hour-before-sunrise call for Fajr prayers. His only concession to his advancing years was that he allowed himself more drink than he had as a younger man in the services.

For reasons he never revealed, he had become disillusioned with Army life in the early 'seventies just after he had returned to England from the war in Dhofar. There had been forgotten wars before and forgotten men who had fought in them, but few had been so overlooked as this bloody and sweaty campaign in remotest Arabia where the consequences of a defeat would have been a Communist-dominated Arabian peninsula and a Middle East with a totally different complexion from that of today.

Billy Bainbridge had been confident that his long experience in the field would have ensured his route to brigadier. But it was not to be. Another more junior colonel had been promoted ahead of him and he had felt more forgotten than ever. It was time to leave the Army. For various reasons other colleagues felt likewise and a small group of them formed one of the new breed of security agencies which were flourishing at the time. They called it Red Alert. The colour was not specifically political but if customers cared to read it that way, so be it.

The company prospered beyond the more abundant of their expectations. Their work covered the full gamut of duties which the new agencies were undertaking. They recruited mercenaries for Africa, the Gulf countries and South America. Their staff, mainly former Parachute Regiment and Special Air Service, played minders to the kind of people to whom fortune meant fear; they made covert deals with shadowy men in Beirut and Belfast, but were clever enough to play them sufficiently low key to avoid the attention others received from the authorities over controversial deals which had brought them criticism in Parliament for such activities as arranging a ransom for a millionaire hostaged in Ulster or being one of the links to Nicaragua in the complex and muddied events of Irangate.

Their senior staff acted as advisers to men in power and, if they considered it appropriate — and the size of the contract could make them most accommodating — they would assist men who wanted power. When the extent of the Gulf contract was made known to them, they were at their most accommodating. Because of his long association with the country and, as chairman of the board of Red Alert, Bainbridge himself took on the challenge of the venture, the culmination of which would be the destiny of an Emir and his country. That was why when Brian Bria made his first inquiries about where and what the colonel was doing, he was told: "He's a security adviser to a Government in the Gulf. But it's hush-hush stuff, old boy."

Bria would report to him every fortnight or so with details of his progress on the mosques project, the pair of them going over his most recent pictures,

selecting ones which would be likely candidates for the book, and planning
out the areas he would cover for new material. When they had finished
discussing the project that day, Bria had mentioned there was another subject
he wanted to discuss.

"By all means, dear boy. What's on your mind?" said the colonel.

"It's about that shooting at Razak . . . you know, where they attacked the
police station and there were a few deaths?"

The colonel went strangely silent and the cheery look that had been on his
face just seconds before suddenly vanished. He had all the looks of a man
who had just heard some bad news. Bria wondered about that. Was Razak
that important? Wasn't he supposed to know? Or wasn't he supposed to talk
about it? He wanted to ask these questions immediately he saw the change
come over the colonel, but thought he would not force the issue and see what
he had to say first of all.

The colonel turned to his telephone and stabbed out three numbers after he
had picked up the receiver. "Norma, I do not want to be disturbed. And that
includes phone calls from anyone, unless of course it's from the Minister.
Understood?"

He turned round again to Bria, looking slightly more relaxed. "Brian, my
friend, when you came here it was on the complete understanding that Fleet
Street was behind you and you would be all three of the wise monkeys . . .
hearing nothing, seeing nothing and saying nothing of what went on here."

Bria cut in sharply at that. "Don't read a wrong situation, Billy. I'm still
playing the ball game I promised I would. The Razak affair has a personal
connection, not a Press connection."

"Do forgive me, Brian, if I assumed otherwise. But it is a very sensitive
subject."

"Obviously."

"How on earth did you hear about it?"

Bria told him the story of his friend Gordon Watson and the Pakistani
cell-mate and how he himself had met an officer friend — he did not mention
his name — who had given details about the police station attack. "So you
obviously heard all about it, Billy?"

"Of course I did. Brian, being an Adviser to the Ministry of Public
Buildings is not my only . . .." He paused slightly at that, obviously wanting to
say the appropriate word. "My only interest here."

"I never thought for one minute it was for a man with your background."

"Without going into any details, let's just say that people such as myself,
and there are others, are necessary here. People who fought in the Gulf, who
know the Gulf and who have the Gulf in our hearts. And will do anything we
can to protect it from the people we consider are its enemies."

"So Razak was that important?"

"It was. Tell me, Brian, how much do you know about the enemies of the
Gulf?"

"Not an awful lot. I've heard about the Fundamentalists and I know they're not too keen on Palestinians, although I don't know if they are enemies or not."

"Let me give you a little history lesson on the subject, Brian. This country has known insurrection for years. They have a history of rebelliousness longer than most everyone, from the time of the people they called the khawarij, the first dissidents, right up to the 1970s. All right, things have been quiet since then. But there are still dissidents of various sorts around. There are the communists who fled from Oman after the Sultan won the war in Dhofar. Many of them came here.

"Then there are those who are supporters of rule by an Imam, that is a church leader. The Emir here, like the Sultan in Oman, dispensed with the rule of Imams. Rule can only be by one leader, not two, they wisely decreed. But there are still those who think otherwise, people with long memories and grudges. And there are some of those people living today up in the Jebel Ahmar mountains of which, as you know, Razak is the capital. At one time, indeed, it was the capital of the whole country. Mysterious place up there. Mysterious people. Same as all mountain people, just like those that live in the Chouf, or in Corsica, or in Afghanistan, they have their own closed societies. They brood like the bloody mountains around them and you never know what they're thinking.

"And the third source of danger to the country — and the most danger-ous one — is the Fundamentalists. They are a very real danger . . . a danger from within and everyone is aware of that fact. For instance, have you ever seen a photograph or painting of the Khomeini here? Of course you haven't. You can go down the Khudra Souk where you can get everything, even carvings and paintings of the Last Supper, but you'll never see a picture of the Ayatollah. That's why the boys over in the Ministry of Islamic Affairs vet all the sermons to be preached by non-nationals in the mosques. They're just making sure that none of the Fundamentalist stuff gets through. But despite all the awareness, you can never be sure about them. They have their 'sleepers', people dotted around the country waiting for the call. People who will wait for years, people who are part of the community and whom you would never suspect of being what they are. Just the same as the Irish plant their own 'sleeper' contacts on the British mainland waiting for the call to action, whatever kind it may be, that will come for them one day.

"The Razak affair is still being investigated, but what we do know is that there was some Fundamentalist activity in the area — pictures of the Khomeini being circulated and that sort of thing. Then this squad from the Hussein Martyr Brigade went into action. And when these boys go at you, there's no stopping of them."

"Hussein! He was from early Islamic history, I believe?"

"Hussein, dear Brian, was a pivotal character in the whole story of Islam as we know it today. He was the Prophet's very own grandson. His father was

Ali who married the Prophet's daughter Fatima. And it's to the man Ali that you can trace the split, which still rocks Islam, between the Sunnis and the Shi'ites. The name Shi'ite comes from Shi'at Ali . . . or followers of Ali. They maintained that the succession of the Prophet should be down the family line, that is through Ali and his family. The Sunnis thought otherwise and that the leadership of Islam should be outside the family.

"But Hussein, the Prophet's grandson, insisted that the succession should be held in the family and in the year 680, together with a small band of followers, challenged those who contradicted their beliefs. They said they would defend their principles with their lives and they jolly well did just that. With less than 100 men and a few women they took on countless odds, proclaiming it was better to die for their beliefs than to live with injustice. Every last man and woman died in that battle which took place near Karbala in Iraq. Because of that, Hussein became the Supreme Martyr. It is not surprising that they venerate him so. As well as his beliefs about the succession of the Prophet, he had wanted to create a totally classless society, a society that had no imperialism, no despotism, no capitalism. I don't suppose we can challenge his ideals."

"Sounds strange coming from you."

He bluffed slightly at that challenge. "Oh, you know what I mean, Brian. However, let me just finish the Hussein story. As the Supreme Martyr, he has followers today who will gladly give their lives for their cause. They are usually known as the Hussein Martyr Brigade, young people who are totally committed to the cause of Islamic Fundamentalism. In war, Brian, as you must know, people's minds can be consumed, and when they are, they are capable of any action for the cause. The dominated mind doesn't have the logic of the battlefield soldier. In fact, the mind goes completely void of all norms. That's why dominated minds can do things like put millions of people into gas chambers, can use aeroplanes with themselves at the controls as human missiles, can put bombs in buildings that blow up hundreds of innocent people without even a trace of remorse. For it's in their cause. It's a dreadful thing the dominated mind. Dreadful and fearful.

"Minds like that were behind a certain event in Beirut in 1983. That was the detonation of the biggest bomb to go off since World War Two . . . bigger than anything that was used in Korea and Vietnam. Six tons of high explosive packed into one big Mercedes truck and driven straight at the headquarters of the US Marines. You'll remember it all right . . . 241 died."

"I do," said Brian.

"And a few seconds later a similar truck smashed into the French base and 58 paratroopers died. At the wheel of both trucks were kids with smiles on their faces . . . the smiles of achievement, of contentment. For, according to their beliefs, to die like that is the quickest route to heaven. That's where these kids believed they were heading. Both of them were from a Hussein suicide squad.

"So to the events at Razak. Yes, there's been some activity in the area. Then out of the blue this suicide squad appears and attacks the police station. After Beirut and knowing what they can do . . . wouldn't you be concerned? And quite a few are. The authorities rounded up as many Fundamentalist supporters as they could. They're in Zamakh where they'll probably be for a long time. As for the ones your friend came across in the short-term wing, well, I don't know about them specifically, but they would probably be only relatives or a group on the absolute outer extremities of whatever following there was. I don't see any significance in them. At the same time, don't ever let the tranquillity of this part of the Gulf delude you. It doesn't fool those in the know. They know there are Communists, Fundamentalists, Imamists and others lurking in the shadows. This is a small country in numbers, but there are few places in the world of more strategic importance, what with the Straits of Hormuz being just out there in nearby Oman and the majority of the West's oil sailing through it."

Then, in that abrupt fashion of his, the conversation suddenly switched. "So where are you off to next with the mosques project?"

"There are a few I want to do in the coastal region."

"Albuquerque was there."

"I beg your pardon?"

"The great Portuguese navigator."

"Oh . . . I thought you meant the place. I was there once. It's in New Mexico. It's the hot air balloon capital of the world."

"Well, it would be named after the Portuguese fellow. He landed at Quriyat, in Oman, burned the place down and had the nose and ears cut off every poor bugger they could catch. Terrible people. But you'll like the coast. The road to it goes through the Hell's Gap. They say it's the warmest spot in the world. How on earth do they measure things like that? Then you go across a wide plain. They used to breed fine horses there. Best in the world, said Marco Polo. Yes, he was in the Gulf too. Didn't go around sacking the place though. And you must make a trip up the Wadi Wahda when you're there. Wahda means a place of solitude. Coming back from the coast it's off the road to the left. Absolutely beautiful spot. Need a Range Rover though."

Then suddenly he stood up, as he always did, military fashion, signalling the end of the conversation or interview, or whatever he was conducting. It was an infuriating habit, but Bria merely put it down to the military man in him, remembering so many staff officers who had done likewise at various briefings he had attended.

"Oh Brian," he said as he made to go out of the door, "eh . . . I wouldn't talk too much about those chappies from Razak. And tell your friend likewise. My contacts tell me they want the whole affair hushed up. You'll do that for me . . . .."

"Yes. Yes, I will, Billy."

News about Yaqoob

GORDON WATSON seemed to be back in his old form that Thursday night at the Rani, the group around him listening intently to some of his tales about Zamakh, interspersed, as was his habit, with some funny aspect of the event.

"See Zamakh," he wisecracked. "One of the best things that ever happened to me. It used to take me six or seven pints to get pissed. Now I can do it on two. It's going to save me a fortune." They enjoyed that.

It was nine o'clock before Bria arrived. They ribbed him about missing the free supper of kingfish goujon which the bar had passed around and about being the oldest lover in town.

As usual they were discussing the highlights of the week and one of them said he had been to the show at the Inter-Continental Hotel. The Gulf showbusiness entrepreneurs would bring a variety of British entertainers out for a series of performances in Gulf cities and towns where such events were either permissible or welcome. Their tours would usually begin up the Gulf at Bahrain, then they would work their way south to such places as Doha, Abu Dhabi, Dubai, Sharjah and Al Ain, culminating at Muscat in Oman. Many of the big names came out, others were the forgotten names, names that were lucky to get the money being offered and the guarantee of expatriate audiences who would treat the shows as an event, as they were often accompanied by pre-show dinner and drinks. What the hell if he/she was a has-been ten years ago? A few gins and the songs were almost good again, the jokes funny — even an offensive ee-by-goom stand-up club comic could get laughs when he dropped his trousers as the highpoint of his act. Well, it was a change from the alternative form of entertainment, a one-dinar rented video film, so crudely pirated in Singapore that the sound track would be inaudible.

"Who all went to see the Scotch comedian?" one of them asked.

Three of them nodded in reply.

"You'd be there, of course?" they said to Gordon.

"I'm saying nothing," he answered in a form of mock disgust.

"What's wrong, Gordon? Couldn't you manage a free ticket?"

"Didn't he tell enough jokes against the English?" another chipped in.

"He offended me," retorted Gordon.

They laughed derisively at that for their favourite drinking companion had never been heard to say anything as bad as that about one of his fellow countrymen.

"I know," cracked one. "He didn't get his autograph."

"No . . . and I'm being serious about this," said Watson, "He really offended me. It was an odd experience, I can tell you, for that same guy has made me laugh till my bones hurt. When he describes us West of Scotland people, it's perfection. He's what we in Glasgow call . . . magic."

"You're making him sound like Des O'Connor," jibed the tall Lancastrian called French.

"Oh, funneee. But listen me out. I went to see him last Monday and I was looking forward to a really memorable night. The place was packed out with expats. On he comes and straight away it was the 'effs' and 'bastards' and 'arses'. Most of them obviously had never heard him before, you know, just out for a night of entertainment, didn't matter who was entertaining? And they get this language. Now, the way he says bad language can be quite funny. When he does it in Glasgow and the like it can be very appropriate. But to come away with it here . . . I mean the purity of this place is catching."

Two of them laughed at that. "Come on, Gordon," said one. "It's not *that* pure."

"All right, maybe not *that* pure, but it's purer than anything we've got in the West nowadays. Sometimes I feel I'm in the Vatican City without the tourists . . . and I'll tell you something, you've got to lock your car if you go there. When did any of you last lock your car here? If you do it's only because of habit. Bill, you've been here, what is it, 12 years? Ever been mugged? Cheated? Burgled? Cursed at?"

Bill indicated he hadn't with a shake of his head.

"What I'm trying to say," said Watson, "is that whether you like it or not there is this air of religiousness and discipline about the place. And when the Scotch comedian came away with the foulmouth stuff, it was just as though he was doing his act in the middle of St Paul's Cathedral, or St Peter's. Know what I mean? This is just not the place for that kind of show."

"Never thought we'd hear that coming from you," said Geoff Melmouth, the west countryman. "I remember you holding court here one night a couple of years back telling us some of his routines."

"Yes, I remember that night. I'm not saying the guy's not funny any more. But I see him in a different light now. I see many things in a different light. Are any of you still reading the London papers? My God, every day it's something terrible. Pensioner mugged. Little girl raped. Couple jailed for torturing their daughter. And the stories of perversion against wee boys . . . Christ, I mean to say, what in hell's happening?"

It wasn't often they heard Watson speak so seriously let alone passionately. The wisecracks stopped and they listened as he went on.

"Okay, so we all have a joke about some of their ways here. Nothing gets done today . . . so, there's always tomorrow, insha'allah. But, for instance, have you ever realised they don't have social workers here? Why not? Because they don't have any social problems with families. The family look after one another. If uncle dies, the brothers, or the cousins, or someone makes sure that auntie and the kids don't starve. That's why there are no children's homes, no orphanages. There's no need for them. For the family takes care of them . . . cousins, uncles, somebody will take the kids in and look after them if the parents die. And old folks homes! Try and explain what they are to a local Arab. They wouldn't know what you're talking about. Putting old grandma or grandad in a home! Must be cruel people that would think of doing something like that, they'd say. Well, we do it. They don't, for they look after the old dears."

"God, Scotch comedian really got at you, Gordon," said Melmouth.

He could see now was the time to change the sombre mood he had brought on the company and in his broadest Glasgow accent with a wide grin he replied, "Christ, I've had a better night at the mother-in-law's."

"Your timing was good there," said Bria as the company laughed and broke into various conversations. "I've something to tell you," he said quietly to Watson. He then related some of the conversation he had earlier that week with the colonel, specifically the information about the men from Razak.

"And he didn't know why they would be going back and forward to Jilida?" queried Gordon.

"Right. But he didn't seem to put any great significance into it."

"He got to know quite quick, eh! You know, him being in Public Buildings and that?"

"Well, as I said, he does keep his ear close to the ground . . . maybe he does have some other cards up his sleeve. I would be surprised if he didn't."

"Oh well, maybe I'll find out some more next week. I'm going back to Zamakh to see Yaqoob."

"Is that a month you've been out already?"

"That's right. And I'm dying to see the guy. He was tremendous. Really. I wouldn't be here if it hadn't been for him."

Seeking permission to visit Zamakh meant a visit to the headquarters of the Emirate Police at Qurat Roundabout. The Police HQ was every bit as prestigious as the Ministry buildings at Al Mushrif and built with the same exhuberance of the young, developing country that wanted to show that it had its feet firmly in the modern, progressive part of the 20th century. There were polished marble floors and tinted glass doors opening to spacious foyers. Outside, Indian gardeners watered and tended trim lawns with colourful displays of oleanders and bougainvillea. And, if you looked closer, there were also built-in tank traps and surveillance cameras on roof corners and other strategic positions to cover every exit, every entrance. The Gulf country that is placid enough to have its police unarmed also displays that it doesn't like taking chances.

Gordon Watson had been to the Police HQ just once before, to have his fingerprints taken, yet another of the new precautions imposed on the expatriate workers. When he eventually found the appropriate counter where the permission chits were issued, he gave a police clerk a note of the one he wanted to see, and was told he had first of all to complete a long form which asked a variety of questions about himself — work permit number, name of sponsor, how long in the country, relationship to prisoner, reasons for wanting to visit, and so on.

It was more than a quarter of an hour before the clerk returned. He was reading the form which Watson had completed earlier with all the details required for the visit. "You say the prisoner's name is Jaffar . . . Yaqoob Jaffar?" he asked.

Watson nodded in response.

"No prisoner in Zamakh of that name."

"But there must be. He had two months to go. I knew him. He's definitely there. Jaffar. J-a-f-f-a-r. Yaqoob Jaffar."

"No prisoner called that."

"But can you check again? There must be a mistake or something."

The police clerk gave him a harsh stare. "No prisoner Jaffar," he repeated sternly, turning dismissively to the next person waiting for attention at the counter.

"Wait a minute. Is there an officer? I want to see a senior officer," Watson interrupted.

The clerk looked at him, with an even angrier stare this time. "You take seat then."

Almost an hour passed before a sergeant came from an office and spoke to the clerk in Arabic. They looked over at Watson and the sergeant beckoned him to come over. "Come this way," he said.

There was a walk down a black marbled corridor, then up a stair and along another similar corridor. Watson thought if only there had been the smell of antiseptic they might be in some newly completed hospital. It had that air about it, the cleanliness, the coming and going of various groups of people, and the silent and ever-present blue-overalled Indian cleaners, dusters in their right hand, bottles of blue Windolene multi-surface spray in their left, rubbing and polishing already rubbed and polished wood and glass and marble.

He was shown into the ante-room of what he presumed was another office. Another police clerk was behind a typewriter and was so intent on the matter he was slowly typing, he didn't look up. The sergeant said something to him in Arabic and a chair was indicated.

There was another wait, but only about ten minutes this time. A buzzer went on the phone beside the typing policeman and he got up, indicating to Watson he was to follow. He knocked at the door of the office, then ushered him in. Watson felt like breaking into a smile when he saw the obviously British face behind the desk. But the face didn't share his feelings. It was that semi-institutionalised face of the regular soldier, its thin red lips highlighting a fair-to-red beard. Was it the beard, he had often wondered, that made the lips of such men look so red? Whatever the answer to that, the lips moved as he approached the man's desk.

"You wanted to see an officer?" he said with Civil Servant formality.

"That's right . . . Mr, eh?" he replied, hesitating where there might have been a name.

"It's Stott. Superintendent Stanley Stott. And what's your trouble?" That last word was pronounced exactly the way Arthur Marsh, one of the Thursday Club, would have said it and he was from Birmingham.

Watson hated when people presumed there was trouble when they were being asked for advice or help. "There's no trouble, actually. I was merely trying to get permission to visit a friend in Zamakh but the clerk at the desk downstairs says there's no one of his name there. But I know he's there."

"And your name . . . ?"

"Watson. Gordon Watson."

"Your sponsor?" That was a favourite question of officialdom in the country, meaning who is your employer?

"International. The tobacco people. I'm a representative."

"And what's a man like you wanting with a visit to a Pakistani labourer-stroke-bus driver in Zamakh?"

His face lit up at that. "So you do know about Yaqoob! You know he's there then . . . I was beginning to wonder when that clerk kept saying there was no one there of that name. Why do I want to see him? Well, he's a friend, of sorts. You see, I was in Zamakh and he helped me a lot. It's not exactly a Holiday Inn . . . is it?"

"So you fell foul of our chaps? What was your problem . . . drink?"

"There's no problem. I was unlucky, that's all."

"We seem to hear that a lot."

"In this case it's true."

"True or not, I would imagine Zamakh has made you think twice about . . . eh . . . being unlucky again?"

Watson was fast taking a disliking to red lips. He seemed to be sneering at him for having been in Zamakh. Zamakh! What the hell are all the questions about anyway . . . he came here to ask about Yaqoob Jaffar. "Excuse me, but Zamakh and myself are a bit academic. I came here to ask you about Mr Jaffar. I want to go and visit him."

"You can't."

"Can't!"

"Yaqoob Jaffar died last week."

Watson was stunned at the pronouncement and sat back in his chair. "God . . . God, that's terrible news. What happened?"

"Jaffar was murdered. He was discovered by the guards in the early hours of last Thursday. It happened when he was asleep. His throat was cut."

Watson gasped in horror. "But . . . but Yaqoob had no enemies. He was one of the most popular men in that cell. Who would . . .? Have they arrested anyone?"

Answering questions didn't come easy to the man in the light khaki drill uniform of the Emirate Police and he hesitated before replying to the point. "No one has been arrested for the offence."

"What about the men from Razak? Are they suspected?"

The man in uniform suddenly came to life. His attitude of clinical formality instantly changed and his hands, which had been toying with a ballpoint pen, lowered on to his teak desk as he leaned forward. "The men from Razak! What do you know about them?"

Watson wondered about the change in the man at the mention of the name of Razak. Should he be told everything or should he pass it off as casually as though they had meant little? How much should he know . . . how much should he be told? Would he implicate himself in some way if he went into detail about them? No, he couldn't . . . could he? There was nothing to be implicated about.

He told him the story as he knew it, of how they had been intrigued by the comings and goings of the five Razak prisoners to the Jilida wing and how they seemed to be apart in some way from the other prisoners, not being called for work duties and the like. The more he told the superintendent, the more the policeman became interested and the more he became amiable towards Watson, trying to make the exchanges between them more like a conversation than an exercise in information gathering.

"But how did you know about the shooting at Razak?"

He thought about Bria and the story his officer friend and the colonel at the Ministry had told him about the shooting, which was how he had got to know.

"Let me see," he said, pausing as if he was trying to recall. "Yes . . . Yaqoob overheard them talking about it one day. He spoke and understood good Arabic. And he had been working in the Razak district, so he knew the local dialect. Yes, I think that's how he got to know. Either that or one of them perhaps mentioned it to him. They were there for two months together before I arrived, you know. And he had travelled with them in the jeep from Razak after they were all arrested. Maybe he even heard in Razak itself."

"I see," said the superintendent, obviously disappointed that he hadn't heard anything more precise, the kind of information that would satisfy the good policeman he considered he was. "Is your family here, Mr Watson?"

That change of tack surprised him. "I've got married quarters and they come out once, sometimes twice, a year."

"Children?"

Now he's really trying, he mused.

"Yes . . . boy and a girl. Pigeon pair. They're at private schools in Scotland. In Glasgow. That's our home town."

Then it was suddenly back to Zamakh again. "How well did you know Yaqoob Jaffar?"

"He was like a blood brother to me. I don't know about you, but I can't go without the air-conditioners when the big heat is here. And in Zamakh, I'm telling you, I nearly died. I don't know what I would have done without the help of Yaqoob. He brought me cool cloths at night . . . did everything to help me pull through. Tell me, does his wife know?"

"The people at Zamakh would attend to all that. Is there nothing more you can think, Mr Watson, about what he might have said about those five men? You know, anything you might tell us could help us in our investigations. We do want to find the culprit who did this, you know."

"So do I. But, really, I've told you everything, although obviously if I think of anything further I'll be in touch."

"How much do your friends at the Rani know about this, Mr Watson?"

"My friends at the Rani?"

The superintendent blustered slightly at the question being repeated. "Well, obviously if a man drinks in a particular place, and I assume you are a Facility Card holder there, then he'll have some drinking companions. And when men drink together they exchange news and gossip and the like. Did you mention the incident to them?"

Without hesitating he replied that he had not. "Of course, I told them about life inside Zamakh and the stinking cells and the rotten food," he said, putting emphasis into the adjectives, "but I didn't get round to telling them about the five men from Razak. It was all a bit tenuous anyway. Perhaps we had just imagined there was something odd about them. What was happening could all have been perfectly routine and nothing out of the usual."

"That's right," the superintendent nodded.

"Do you have a particular friend at the Rani, or at work, who is closer than the others?"

What made him ask that? Did he know that Brian Bria was his closest mate? Did he even know that they had discussed it and that Brian had made inquiries from his friend the colonel? "No . . . not in particular. I get on well with my boss Tommy Torrance."

"So you didn't even whisper it to him . . . or anyone else?"

"No. But why all the concern? I mean, supposing I had?"

"Because I would prefer that you had not . . . and do not. Let's put it this way. There is a murder inquiry going into the death of your friend Mr Yaqoob Jaffar. Now in England when such things happen and when an accused is waiting trial, the matter is what we call *sub judice* . . . before the law. And when something is *sub judice* you are not supposed to talk about it or comment on it. If you do it's contempt of court, a very serious charge I might add."

"So you might be arresting someone?"

"I certainly hope so, but not just yet. However, in the meantime I think it would be a good idea if we considered that this affair is *sub judice* . . . and not for talking about. We would prefer it that way. That no stories get round about any aspects of it, whether it be the murder itself, or the men from Razak or whatever you may have speculated about them as prisoners in Zamakh. I do hope you appreciate that, Mr Watson? It is rather important."

He nodded his head without answering.

The see-saw attitude of the policeman returned to the friendly again when he asked Watson about his hours at work, making it look like he wasn't asking that question in particular but merely having a man-to-man chat. "Keep you busy at International?"

"Yes. The competition is quite fierce. We've got all the big multinationals here in competition and others from India and the like. Yes, we've got to keep on our toes."

"And you're living at . . . ?"

The statement was a question without the answer and Watson waited some seconds before replying on the off chance he might add the answer he was trying to elicit. "Up a dusty road in Al Mushrif in a villa that's built like a fort and costs a fortune to keep cool. And near enough to the local mosque to get blasted out of bed every morning at four o'clock with the muezzin's loudspeaker system. Apart from that, it's a nice house. Where do you live yourself?" He thought that might throw the policeman for he knew he was there to be questioned, not to question.

He blinked before uneasily replying, "Madinat Emir." Then he immediately switched the subject and his mood. "Tell me, Mr Watson, just before you leave, are you planning to go on vacation soon?"

Why was he asking that? And why should he be told that he was in fact, due for leave in two months? "No . . . nothing planned. At the moment, that is. Any particular reason you ask?"

"Oh . . . nothing really. Just in case something came up and we wanted, perhaps, to have a word."

"What about Yaqoob . . . has he been buried?"

"Yes. The following day."

"Here or Pakistan?"

"In an unmarked grave at Zamakh."

He was halfway to the door when the policeman called his name and he turned. "Eh . . . once again, I wouldn't mention this conversation to anyone."

"No. No, I won't."

The door had barely closed when Stott jerked the nearest of three phones on his desk, quickly tapped out a number and snapped two brief instructions into the mouthpiece. "Get me surveillance. And after that get me the colonel."

Downtown in Rani

THERE WERE those who came to the Gulf and saw little that was of Arabia. They played their evening tennis or squash in air-conditioned courts, ate in collar-and-tie restaurants where they could get Western-style food, watched films that were current in London from the video rental shops' pirated tapes for their night's entertainment and habituated the hotels with bars and sports complexes and places like the Emco Shopping Centre which, apart from those customers who wore dishdashas, could have been in Milton Keynes, East Kilbride, Dandenong or any other new town in the West. In the big supermarket next to it they could "ooh" and "ah" at the brown and wholemeal bread just arrived from England; there would be the best Dutch tomatoes — "never heed the price, luv, they are just like we get at home". There was Perrier instead of Emirate mineral water and real tonic water for the gin; Stilton and English cheddar; fish fingers and real cod, albeit frozen; and a magazine rack that had *House and Garden*, the country and car mags and the day before yesterday's *Daily Mail* and *Daily Telegraph*. For high adventure there was what they affectionately named a "wadi bash", a day trip in an air-conditioned Range Rover or Nissan Patrol, on unmade roads or cross-country, to some remote beauty spot.

But there were places in the Capital Area where the old Gulf still lived and there were places too where you could still feel the Gulf as a region, a region that incorporated its age-old trading partners from the subcontinent, places where you really knew you were in that part of Arabia which was the crossroads of Africa and Asia.

On the Thursday evening and Friday, the traditional weekend of the Middle East, Brian Bria would wander endlessly among such places where he felt he was at the furthest end of the world from the West with which he had become so disillusioned and which had shown him too much of its ugly side. It was at such moments that he really felt he was away from it all.

Souk Rani Street was one of the best areas to experience the Emirate of the Renaissance which had been brought about by a remarkable leader and his Government and the sweat and skills of some 300,000 imported workers, the expatriates, most of whom had come from the three principal countries of the subcontinent; the same kind of men who had once come as traders in ships, after a journey that would take them just over a week if the seas were fair and the winds behind them, nearly a month if it was otherwise. Now the Gulf Air and Air India and PIA jets did the journey from Bombay and Karachi in just over two hours, Dhaka and Colombo slightly longer. Although they were scattered throughout the Capital Area, some in rickety camps, most of the imported workers stayed in and around Rani in low- and medium-cost blocks of four- and five-storey flats, the same kind of squat buildings you might find in Rome, Palermo or Athens.

In Bria's Australian terms, Souk Rani Street was no Bourke Street, certainly no Collins Street. It was more like the way Lygon Street in Carlton used to be, or Chapel Street in Prahran, the shopping centres of the districts where he had lodged during the three years he had spent working in Melbourne after leaving his home town of Bendigo and before leaving for London.

The street's one-way traffic was a continuous three-lane flow flanked by the shoppers who would pour there in the evening. There were no pavements for them, just broad strips of wadi dust like grey sand. Some shops had raised concrete "boardwalks" only broad enough for one or two people at a time and there only as a facility to view the display of goods. Shops lined both sides of the long street, off which there were even dustier lanes which led to other souks with smaller shops and maybe better bargains.

The shops were all owned by nationals, for that was the law, but run by partners and their staffs who were mainly Indian. To the newcomer it always seemed so strange that so many of the shops and stores specialised in luggage of all descriptions. There was one entire souk, the one at the Rani Clinic, where almost every shop and stall was a baggage retailer. They sold suitcases of all descriptions. Cases as big as a trunk with a carrying handle, cases that had straps with fancy buckles, cases of tartan, cases that said in big print they were "Made In Shanghai China", and cases with the kind of names that could give status to the humblest of travellers and their baggage, names like Prince and Corona and Highbrow and Diplomat and Goldenman and Long March. Such suitcases, the newcomer soon discovered, were the first thing the immigrant workers bought when they came from India and Pakistan and Bangladesh. With what little money they had left after sending home the remittance that would maintain their wives and children and parents, and often other members of the family and their children too, they would start to fill their cases with presents they would eventually take back. And they would be among the nightly shoppers looking for the bargains they knew would be appreciated in the Punjab and Gujerat and Kerala and Tamil Nadu.

The textile stores were their favourites, particularly when the Ramadan or Eid discount sales were on. They would flock to places like Hotace Readymade Garments, Angara Tailoring, Silky Textiles, the Papoo Stores, Youtex Textiles, Juheima Textiles and the Al Najoom Baby Home. Those with more cash to spend would crowd the gold souks where there were shops like the Arabian Jewellers, the Crown Jewellers and Al Hamra Jewellers, and one, unbelievably, called the Faiq Jewellers which so happened to be directly across the road from the Faiq Money-changers. Neither seemed to suffer from whatever association their names might conjure.

Others would, between shopping forays, pack the little snack restaurants, favourites like the Al Roche, the Sahtain and the Ali Baba Cafeteria, next door to the Ali Baba Bakery, for delicacies like fresh fried wadas, hot and spicy, pakora and samosa, and meat sandwiches of Arab bread accompanied by a glass of freshly pressed orange juice. If they wanted something more substantial, in the Pearl Restaurant they could get a big stainless steel plate, called a thali, of Gujerati vegetarian specialities with rice and as much buttermilk as they wanted to drink for just under £1.

Getting to know who was who in the hustling, bustling Souk Rani Street took the eye of the experienced traveller which Bria had certainly become during his many years globe-trotting in the non-tourist spots of five continents, years when he had used Heathrow Terminal 3 like others would their suburban-line railway station.

The groups that he knew and could recognise would all be there for the night's shopping — Malayalees and Malabaris from Kerala, who seemed to dominate. The Keralites were always quick to tell you if you asked that they were the most literate of all the Indians which was why so many of them were wanted in the Gulf as skilled and semi-skilled workers. There would be the Bori people from Bora, in their loose white shirt suits of cotton and their women dressed Islamic-fashion with black abaya cloaks; Badhkalis from Konkani, almost impossible to tell apart from the Bori, except that they had lighter eyes than other Indians; turban-wearing Kathiawaris from the Ran of Kutch, small, slim men because, it was said, of their vegetarian diet; Sikhs too, big burly men with grandfather faces; Gujeratis and Punjabis; Tamils and Sri Lankans, with their straight, shiny black hair; Pakistanis, in their baggy salwar kameez; the occasional Afghan and Pathan; and, of course, straggles of those anonymous Indian men from various states with their awkward gait and wide, bewildered eyes, dressed in yester-decade's Western fashion of wide flared trousers and spearpoint shirts. The last-mentioned were the labourers who were thought of as coolies and whom no one thanked for their sweat and toil which had done so much to make the Gulf countries the modern states they are today.

Others were there from the Arab world; Egyptians, big, well-fed men with their striped and roomy gallabeyah gowns, accompanied by ample women, in figure-covering fustans and higab headscarfs, who shopped at the Fair Price Supermarket for their gibnah bilfelfel cheese, dotted with chopped chilli, and their bastermah, or beef jerky; Sudanis, even bigger people, their blackness accentuated by their fresh white kaftans, and each looking seven feet tall with their enormous Ali Baba emmah turbans; Jordanians, usually dressed Western-style, the occasional one in thobe and red-checked kaffiyeh; visitors too from the Emirates, Oman, Saudi and the other Gulf countries. Then there would be Filipinos — nurses, hotel staff and communications workers — and Chinese, together with the occasional Britisher, down from their suburban

Madinat Emir to share the experience that was Souk Rani Street.

On one such night spent wandering the street Bria had extended his walk along the adjacent thoroughfare, simply called Rani Street, going past the Mr Softy ice cream shop and the Red Shoe shop. There he met the Filipino girl Esther he had told Watson about. She had been standing by the entrance of the flower shop at the arcade beside the Palace Furniture Store where they sold armchairs as big as thrones. She had returned the look he had given her as he passed and that had struck him. For the first time since he had arrived in the Gulf more than a year ago a woman had looked at him like that. He had walked a few paces past her, then stopped, and when he turned she was looking again and when their eyes met she had continued to look at him. Then, with an aloof turn, she faced another way.

He had to say something to her . . . something . . . anything. What? He fumbled for a moment searching for words that might not be the obvious but when he approached her all he could think of was, "Excuse me . . . but . . . I hope you don't mind. Do you work at the Al Rawda Hotel? In the sea food restaurant? I've seen you there."

He thought at first she wasn't going to reply for she had looked away before turning to look up at him.

"I don't want to talk to you for you will think bad of me."

"Why bad?"

"It is not right that I should talk to a strange man."

"But I know you. You've served me at the Al Rawda."

"No . . . No. It wasn't me. I'm a nurse."

That was it then. Blown it in a couple of sentences. "Hell, this needs practice," he thought to himself. And he was out of it. "Oh, I'm sorry. It's you then who must think bad of me."

"I don't."

"Can I phone you sometime?"

"There is no phone in the flat."

"Oh."

He hesitated for a second. "Maybe you could phone me then? My name's Brian. Here . . . here's a card. Wait a minute. My home number isn't on it. I'll write it. I travel about a lot, but I'll be home most nights for the next month anyway. Will you call me?"

She accepted the card from him, looked at it briefly, then looked up at him again without answering, but he was sure there was the hint of a smile.

"God, she's beautiful," he thought. "Those eyes. That face. Here am I, heading for fifty, and she's half my age if she is that and this whole thing is crazy. Why in hell did I talk to her in the first place?"

She spoke again. "You must not think bad of me."

"But I don't. Believe me, I don't. What's your name?"

"Esther."

He could see she was embarrassed as the street was busy with shoppers and the only thing he could think to say was, "Nice to have met you, Esther. I hope we meet again. Phone me, eh?" And he walked on.

It had been years since he had had the feeling he now experienced when he left her to walk in the direction of the Rani Hotel. It reminded him of his youth back in Bendigo when he used to hang about Angie's Cafe in the Mall. Names like Joyce and Lyn and Val came back to him, girls who had accepted his offer of a date and made him feel so pleased with himself because they had said yes. He smiled to himself, thinking of those days. Then the fond memories suddenly vanished as he contemplated what he had done. "Crazy," he thought to himself. "I'm absolutely crazy. Bonkers. Going troppo. You just don't chat up young sheilas when you're a bloody middle-aged man . . . do you? I mean, you just don't go asking strange girls for their phone number or give them yours. Do you? And here in the Middle East of all places! God, try that next door in Saudi and a bloke could get himself a public flogging. Knew I should have gone straight for a drink with the boys instead of going for that extra walk. Crazy, that's what I've been. But geez. She was nice."

An Evening with China Girl

TO HIS great surprise, about a week later, the girl Esther phoned Bria at his apartment. She would have rung sooner but she had been working late shifts, she said in that distinctive sing-song way of the English-speaking Filipino. Now she was on night duty but would be free in the evenings the following week.

"What would you like to do?" he asked, adding quickly, "No, I'll correct that. What do you usually do when you go out for the evening?"

"Go to the disco."

"You like discos?"

"Of course."

"Esther, you wouldn't like them if I was your partner. But we'll think of something."

They went for a drive instead and then to the Piano Bar at the Holiday Inn, Al Mushrif, the newest of the Capital Area's hotels. There was a Filipino group playing there and she enjoyed that. Later they went upstairs to the hotel restaurant. It was all new and strange to him being with a woman again. After his first and only marriage had broken up there had been the occasional date, mainly with women journalists, whom he didn't particularly like as a breed of female but who were good for talk and gossip about the trade they shared. Occasionally he would escort a well-known model, and he was vain enough to appreciate being seen around some of the places where being seen is a kind of prestige game, even though the conversation tended to be . . . well, in the politest way he could put it, basic. Neither newspaperwomen nor models stimulated him in the way he expected or wanted, even although the latter were more likely to round off the evening in a more sensual fashion than the former.

It was different with Esther from the start. He had imagined there would be that sense of humour gap there always was with someone from a different culture. But surprisingly there wasn't. It was a revelation to him. She could laugh easily and had an infectious chortle when she did so.

He ribbed her about the way she spoke English. "You're like someone doing a bad impersonation of a Frenchwoman who's got poor English."

"That is because in our Tagalog language we speak it like a song, so when we speak another way it is that way already."

"You've got trouble with your already's," he joked. Which she did. Just like she would say, "too much" when she simply meant many, or "that one" when she meant someone or was referring to a particular person whose name she couldn't recall or didn't know.

"You looked lonely that night I saw you, the night you were standing outside the flower shop."

"I was. I am only here four months and I am bored. It is too much already."

"Too much. Already?"

She laughed.

"So why did you come to the Gulf?"

"The money, of course. That is why we all come. Is it not?"

"Mainly I guess," he answered.

"So why are you here? Not for the money? You do not need it?"

"That's three questions. Let's just say, I came for the experience."

"What is this one?"

"Which one?"

"Experience."

"Oh yes. I guess that does need some explaining. But later. So is it worth the money you get to be bored and lonely like you are . . . and just after four months at that?"

"Of course. In my last job as a nurse in the Philippines I was at a hospital in Mindinao. That is in the provinces, down in the south. My pay, if you put it into American dollars was 60 a month. Here I get 600 dollars a month."

"Ten times as much . . . whew! That should make up for some of the loneliness. So how does it feel to be making all that money?"

"Oh, it is not new to me. I was in Jordan for two years before I came here and it was good money there too."

"And what made you leave Jordan?"

Her eyes dropped and the animated look vanished from her face.

"Oh no," he said. "I've asked something I shouldn't."

"No . . . no, it is all right already."

He smiled at the word *already.*

"I was engaged to a Jordan boy. We had been going already for nearly two years together then suddenly one day he disappeared."

"Terrorists?"

"No. His father. He made him leave when he learned we were planning to marry."

"And he went just like that!"

"That's right. He went to Toulon in France. They were in business. Lots of money. They owned stores in Amman. And they had branches in France as well."

"It is difficult, Esther, for the Muslims to accept people from outside their religion," he said sympathising.

"But he wasn't Muslim. He was a Christian like myself. A Catholic. The father just didn't want a Filipina."

"And his son just obeyed him without question!"

"Yes. It was strange. But I understand, too. It would have been difficult for him. His father was a, what you say, a big man. Lots of wasta. You know wasta?"

"Wasta! Yes. Influence . . . power . . . clout. And had he not obeyed him?"

"Well, who knows? They can be like that in Jordan."

"So you left Jordan broken-hearted?"

She looked away at that and didn't reply.

"I'm sorry," he said. "No need to answer that. Tell me, how does the Gulf compare with Jordan for a Filipino girl?" he added quickly to change the subject.

"Maybe we are not so free already."

"What do you mean free?"

"Well, they tell us we must obey their laws, you know their laws about going about with a man who is not your husband . . . and talking to strange men." At this point she looked directly at him and smiled and he interrupted by saying he was glad she had ignored the bit about speaking to strange men in his case.

"Then they put guards at our flats. We must be in by 11 o'clock every night, maybe one night at 11.30 if it is the older one who is on duty at the door. But we are better than the other ones . . . the ones who work in the houses. You know . . . the domestics? They come on a two-year contract . . . two years before they get leave. And do you know some of their employers will not give them a day off in that time."

"How much do they earn?"

"Sixty dinar a month."

"About £100, eh."

"I know some and when they have finished work in their employer's house he takes them to the son's house or the house of another member of the family and they have to clean that one too. And they do worse things. They think because they are Filipina and not brought up in the Arab way that they will give their bodies to them. We have a young one in the hospital just now. She took half a bottle of Dettol."

"Oh, my God. Dettol!"

"Yes, she was desperate. And she has only been here for a fortnight."

"Tell me about her."

"She is just 22 but just a little one . . . you know, a small girl. And when her employer got his family out of the house he made her have the sex with him. It happened more than one time and she got so desperate she took this stuff."

"Will she live?"

"She will be all right."

"So what happens to her now?"

"The police came and told her she must go back to the employer . . . or else she must leave the country."

"Aren't they prosecuting him?"

"What is that?"

"Taking him to court . . . to jail?"

"No. They don't do that. They are just interested if her papers and things like that are all right. It's easy for the employer to cancel a contract and then you are put on the black list and never allowed into the country again. They would not take her word anyway . . . not against an Arab employer. But it is a worse story than that. She is only here two weeks and to get here all her friends in Manila, many, many of them, put together to give her the money for the fare and the agent's fee. The agents in the Philippines charge the domestic girls 500 American dollars to get them a job here and the only way most of them can come is if friends help them. Then they get paid back with the money they earn here."

"So what will she do?"

"What can she do? She has no money so she can not go back. If she doesn't go back to the employer the police will arrest her for absconding and she will go to prison . . .."

"But that's incredible, Esther. Absolutely incredible."

"It will be all right. There are 90 of us, Filipinas, in the Al Nahdha Hospital. We are giving two, some three, dinar each to pay for her fare. We should get her away in a week."

"Couldn't the Embassy help her? I mean, there must be someone to look after you here."

"No, there is no one. The nearest embassy is in Dubai."

"The poor, poor girl. God, that makes my blood boil. Do you have to send money home to keep the family?"

"No. I am one of the lucky ones. My father is working, my mother is working and all the money I send home is invested for me. They have bought a piece of land and when I am finished here it will be all paid."

There were other regular dates after that first night at the Holiday Inn. They went to the shows that would come in the cooler months, to places like the Al Rawda and the Inter-Continental. Even the third-rate knockabout English comedians were funny again when she was in his company. And he showed he could still dance, modern-fashion, that is, when he got up on the busy floor with her during the last two numbers when the rock group Status Quo had come on a farewell tour.

She enjoyed and was obviously well used to the better-class restaurants and together they tried the Capital Area's more exclusive eating houses, such places as the Golden Falcon, a two-restaurant complex, one Chinese, the other Mongolian; the Tokyo Taro Japanese restaurant, where she pointed out that most of the girls dressed as geishas were in fact Filipinas; the Italian and Thai and Greek and French and Oriental nights at places like the Al Rawda, the Palace and Novotel Hotels; and for seafood specialities they would visit the delightful Bait al Shati situated idyllically on the rocks at the far end of Khudra Harbour. During the day the picture windows at the Gulf Hotel's dining-room had by far the best views in the area. But at night that honour went to the Bait al Shati, translation of which meant "House by the Waterside", looking out as it did over the busy harbour, where the storm lamps of so many small fishing boats leaving for their grounds in the Gulf looked like so many bobbing fairylights and where the dhows had real fairylights for festive occasions. Towering in the foreground nearby was the floodlit spectacle of Khudra Fort, crenellated and story-book high, a Disneyworld Arabian Nights fantasy building with a difference — it was for real. The fishermen would deliver the restaurant's supplies straight from their boats as they entered the harbour from the Gulf. On the night he had taken Esther there for the first time they had both chosen the native sharkha, the spiny and spotted lobsters caught further south off one of the big islands and whose ample white meat was robust with the ocean's flavour.

He liked to hear about her life in the Philippines and he would ask her a whole variety of questions about her country.

"What do they call the place where you live in Manila?"

"Pan-DA-cang."

"Spell it. Oh, you mean Pandacan?"

"No, you don't say it that way. You say it this way . . . Pan . . . DA . . . cang. Pan . . . DA . . . cang. It means the place of little people. What do you call them . . . dwarfs?"

"You can be little without being a dwarf . . . but, anyway—now let's get it right. Pan . . . DA . . . cang?"

"Good, that's it."

"Pan . . . DA . . . cang. How far is it from the city centre?"

"Oh, about ten minutes. But sometimes it can be dangerous. You know there are many bad ones these days. Once I was walking and one made me give him a ring I was wearing. Then he ran off. And do you know, two minutes later he came back and grabbed me and was making me take the ring back saying, 'You swallow it . . . swallow it. It's a phoney one.' And he was really making me to swallow it when two other men came to help and he ran off. No, you are better not walking. Better you take a jeepney."

"Jeepney?"

"Yes, like the pick-up trucks here, only they are jeeps and we have thousands and thousands of them."

"And what would you be doing if you were home today . . . Sunday?"

"Oh, Sunday is a good day. Everybody goes out walking and showing their new clothes. We maybe go to the Luneta Park. They have nice restaurants there. And do you know they are run by people who cannot speak? Dumb ones. You call them that?"

"No, not really. Deaf mutes. And they are all like that in these restaurants?"

"Yes. It is the Government who do it. It makes them come into contact with people . . . and help people to know them and their problems. Good, is it not? Or maybe we go to the Rizal Avenue in Santa Cruz. It is the best shopping street. In the morning my father would be up early feeding his cock birds. He does the fighting with them, you know. And my mother is always saying he gives them more vitamins than he takes himself."

"And what does Mum do on a Sunday? Cook the roast lamb?"

"No. We do not have that one. She will probably make kre kre."

"What's that you're saying . . . curry curry?"

"No, it is not the Indian one. It is kre kre. It's our favourite dinner on a Sunday. You do not know it?"

"It's a new one on me."

"Everyone loves it in Manila. We even have kre kre restaurants and that is all they sell for the one dish is a whole meal."

"What is it? Meat or fish?"

"It is everything. I don't know how to cook it. And it takes a long time . . . up to 24 hours. But I know there are lots of things in it . . . there is beef tripe and the inside ones. Intestines, is that it? And then there is pig's trotters and beef head or the nose . . . .."

"Wait a minute. The head and the nose?"

"Only the head if you have a big, big pot. But the nose is special. It gives a good taste."

"Anything else?"

"Oh yes, lots more. There is pork and alamang and banana hearts."

"I know the pork, but what are the other two?"

"Alamang! Little fish, you know? Like tiny, tiny prawns and salted. And banana hearts. You do not have them in your country! They come before the banana grows and we cut them up like a vegetable. Then we put in cabbage and garlic and spices and peanuts and other vegetables."

"All together?"

"Of course. You do not have things like this in Australia."

"Well, they certainly never had it on the menu at Dad 'n Dave's or Favaloro's in Bendigo."

"Then I'll write home for the recipe and cook it for you sometime."

"Can't wait. But your Sundays sound good. Real folksy. Your friends, the other nurses? Do they all have the good family background you have? I mean, you're obviously not struggling at home."

"No. Many of them are quite poor. In fact, most of them are keeping families at home with their pay. Many of their fathers are not working so they depend on their wages. They are not able to buy land like me. Some of them think they are lucky if they can get a new nose when they go on leave."

"A new what?"

She turned profile and pointed to the bridge of her nose. "Many of them don't like this bit," she said. "Like mine. It's flat. They want the nose of the

Western girls. So they save up and get a new one. It costs 500 American dollars, but it only lasts for a year, even less if you let the sun shine on it too much."

"What harm does the sun do to it?"

"It begins to melt and go flat again. It is silicon . . . you know? They inject it from the inside so there are no scars. But it goes down after a year and you have to get the old one out and new silicon in."

"And they do that with their hard-earned savings?"

"Of course. It is what they want . . . what they dream about. And if they've got even more money they get themselves round eyes and bigger busts too and go to the beauty shop and get lighter skin."

"So that's why you never come to the beach with me . . . you don't want to be really dark?"

"I would go black if I went to the beach."

"And no nose job for you when you go home?"

"I will be 25 my next birthday . . . if you can go that long without one . . . well."

"What a funny old world," he said shaking his head. "There are our women in Australia . . . they're never away from the beach. And the English! They spend fortunes getting tans. Do you know they have shops in England with this sun-ray equipment so that people can get a tan. What a crazy world! And there's your lot bleaching their skins to get white and our lot craving for the sun to get them brown. Insane, that's what it is. But then that's the world—insane."

The shaft of light caught his eye and he looked out of the restaurant window. "Oh, my God . . . look at that moon. I know it's the same moon everywhere, but have you ever seen one so big and bright? It's like daylight. Tell you what . . . what time do you have to be in tonight?"

She said it was the "old one" who was on and they could stay till midnight.

"Right. Then seeing you won't come to the beach with me during the day, why don't we go to Bandar Bahar tonight?"

"What is this one?"

"Which one?" he teased and they laughed.

Australians rarely enthuse about beaches in other countries, much like the Swiss find it difficult to appreciate other people's mountains. But Bria did like the beach at Bandar Bahar. Just like Portsea, the handiest ocean beach to Melbourne, was his favourite in Australia, this one was his favourite away from home.

Bandar Bahar was a few miles south of the Capital, along a spectacular new highway which gracefully carved its way into the very heart of the jagged Jebel mountains so that you were as much a part of them as the old mule drivers would have been. From the summit the little fishing village of Qariya sparkled white against the blue-green of the Gulf waters, the road sweeping down in a long curve towards the ocean. About two miles before the village there was a dirt-track road to the right, along which you would meet the occasional bedu family, and after about a mile it ended at the beach of Bandar Bahar, a name which they said was half Arabic, half Persian and meant the town or place by the sea. Although it could be busy on a Friday with enough British and Indian families to warrant two ice-cream vans in attendance, it was usually void of people at other times, which was what he liked about it on his occasional midweek visits there. He had never been at night before and it looked even more spectacular, bathed as it was in the incandescent moonlight, the rocks at either end of the small crescent of the bay highlighting the compactness of its setting.

"Are the beaches as nice as this near Manila?" he asked her as they strolled barefoot and hand in hand over the sand, still hot from the sun it had soaked that day, towards the water's edge.

"Of course . . . and with palm trees too. But they are not without people like this."

"Come on," he said. "Let's walk up over the rocks. There's a footpath I know and an even smaller beach on the other side."

They stood at the top of the rocks for a while, looking out at the many islets in the bay and the light of the occasional fishing boat in the distance.

"But you're right," she said. "This one is beautiful."

It was the time of year just before Ramadan when the stupefying intensity of the summer sun had still to make its presence felt. Nevertheless, it was still over 90 degrees, and would stay that way right through the night. The water was still refreshing though and not as warm as it would be in midsummer when even a swim in the Gulf brought no relief from the oppressive heat.

The neon-brilliance of the moon was such that it was easy to find a way down the steep path to the next beach. Even the sea shells which littered the water's edge reflected the light. She picked up one. "Look. Isn't this one beautiful?" The shells were a feature of some of the beaches, and they could be found in an endless variety of shapes and colours.

"I've made a collection of them from the beach at Qurat. Some others I got down in the south," he told her. "It's a great therapy, you know, just strolling on a beach on your own looking for a new kind of shell."

"You need that? The therapy?"

"No . . . not in the medical or nursing sense. I use the word loosely, therapy meaning something to take your mind off things that worry or nag you. Sometimes when I think about certain events I get a bit down in the dumps and taking a stroll on a beach like this, just doing something simple like trying to find a different shell, well, it's so basic, I guess, and it makes you think about the wonders of nature. Yes, I guess we can all do with some therapy like that from time to time. I'll tell you something about those shells, or the little animals that live in them. Know how they reproduce? They don't even touch each other. They don't even know if the other sex is around when they put their sperm and its eggs into the sea, hoping that some female shell will come along and collect and fertilise some of it. Just imagine . . . wishing for something like that to happen in all that size of an ocean. Yet it happens all right. Or else there wouldn't be so many shells around. Still, I don't think they get much fun out of life, do they?"

"We got told about things like that when we did biology for our degree."

"You've got a degree?"

"Of course. You can't be a nurse in the Philippines without one. Anyway, they told us in biology about the mosquitoes. They have only one hour in a day in which they can mate and the male and female know when this time is and it happens when there are lots of them flying in a swarm and each has to find one to, what you say, make it together and while both of them are still flying."

"Who'd be a mosquito! How about a swim?"

"But I have no . . ."

"Well . . . do you need one on a night like this and a place like here?"

They swam and splashed and cavorted together in the waves and then, with their arms around each other, walked from the water, flopping into a shallow pool to regain their breath.

"Ooh . . . that's marvellous," she said as she sat beside him, the waves breaking into the pool in which they were sitting and frothing over their legs. They lay back and embraced together as more waves came in and they laughed together as one splashed over their heads.

"You know," he said, "this was just the way it was with Burt Lancaster and Deborah Kerr."

"Are they your friends?"

"No, my zany one. They were film stars. Real Hollywood film stars and they played a scene like this once in a movie and if you saw it you would never forget it."

"Don't you mean like David Bowie and the Chinese one in *China Girl*?"

"Same story, Esther. For me it was Lancaster and Kerr. For you it was Bowie and his sheila from China."

Then he held her even tighter to him. As another wave gently caressed their bodies, its coolness contrasted with the warmth that was within them in their long embrace of love.

A Shock at the Fish Market

THERE WAS only a small reception area at the Rani Hotel, but it was big enough to have several armchairs and couches where people could wait to meet friends. As soon as he walked through the automatic glass doors and into the refreshing chill of the hotel's air-conditioning, Bria heard his name being called. It was Gordon Watson, who had been waiting for him in the entry lounge.

"I thought you might come," he said anxiously. "The back bar's full and the crowd are in the main bar. Come on. Let's drive up to the Sheraton. I need to talk to you."

The cavernous Sheraton in the Central Business District suited its location. It was the kind of place which was handy for businessmen and bankers who wanted to impress other businessmen and other bankers with its stately entry avenue, its splendidly uniformed doorman in Fifth Avenue pastel and its abundance of marble, glass and chrome. There were two bars, one in the lower section of the split-level hotel concourse. It was open plan, the drinkers being exposed to the gaze of the hotel traffic. This gave it as much charm and atmosphere as a busy railway station's ice-cream sundae bar. But there was another bar, along American-intimate lines, with buttoned red-leather armchairs and lights so dimmed that it was difficult not only to tell who was who among the customers but also if there were any customers there at all.

"I know it's not your favourite drinking place, Brian, but I had to see you without the others around. So much has happened and I had to let you know all about it. Remember me telling you I was going to see my friend Yaqoob? You know, the Pakistani I met at Zamakh? Well, I went to the Police HQ to get the necessary permission and ended up in the office of a superintendent there. Superintendent Stanley Stott. One of those kind of English bastards us Scots love to hate. You know . . . a right Pom. Cold as a fish. Distant as a horizon. Whatever people say about us Scots, Brian, we're not like that. Anyway, the shock news I got from him was that Yaqoob's dead.

"Brian . . . he was murdered. Had his throat cut as he slept, the poor sod. And that was all he could — or would — tell me. They haven't arrested anyone for it. He didn't even say if they suspected anyone. But do you know what he was more concerned about? That I shouldn't be telling anyone about Yaqoob. Smarmy swine, he was. Do you know he even tried to be matey with me at one stage to find out who my friends were? 'But there must be one person more than the others you're friendly with that you might tell,' he said.

God, I was dying to tell you last Thursday at the Rani. But you didn't turn up. Out with the nurse?"

"That's right."

"We'll need to watch you. How is she anyway?"

"She's a lovely girl. Really."

"Oh God . . . you're away. Aren't you?"

Brian grinned but didn't reply.

"Anyway, you weren't there last Thursday. But even more happened after that. On the Friday I went down to the Fish Souk. Fancied a piece of the old kingfish, fresh off the boats. Brian, you're not going to believe this. But who did I see among the mob there but one of the Razak men? Now don't say it, Brian. Don't tell me I've got a paranoia about these guys from Razak. Don't tell me to get it off my mind. For I can't. And that's it."

"Oh come on, Gordon. I've never known you like this. I mean there are certain things one can get carried away with. Supposing you had taken no interest in any of this at all and had not gone back to the police about getting a visit to Zamakh? You wouldn't know about your friend Yaqoob and you wouldn't be concerned about these mystery guys who were in the clink with you. Sorry about the clink bit."

"Brian, mate. Hear me out. If you think I've got it bad about them then so be it. But I want to tell you it all, just as it happened. As I said, I went to the Fish Souk. It was one of those good days. Big crowd and everything. And the amount and variety of fish! They had everything that morning. Big hammerhead sharks, lobsters . . . never seen so many, and shrimps at three dinar a kilo. I don't know about you, Brian, but I still get mesmerised every time I go down there. I don't know, your mind somehow gets lost in the whole scene. Chinese birds trying to haggle with locals who won't haggle, the Mercedes crowd from the Central Business District buying whole kingfish at the quayside before the stallholders get them, the chicken butchers making a live hen ready for the oven, killed, skinned, gutted, the lot in three minutes flat. You know what it's like. And there I was just dreaming away watching the whole incredible scene and who do I find myself standing beside? One of the guys from Razak. So help me. There he was, right next to me, bending over and showing one of the kingfish sellers how thick he wanted the steaks cut. He was so close he was touching me almost, but he didn't see me. Wait and I'll order a couple more drinks."

Brian was shaking his head in smiling dismay.

"Listen, Brian, I know what you're thinking. But get it out of your head. It's not like that. Just hear me out. So, I turned and walked back a bit so that I could have a good look just to make sure that it really was him. There was no mistaking him though. It was the one we called the simple one. I don't know whether he is or not — simple, that is — but he kept fidgeting a lot. He was the one who told Yaqoob that they were there because of the shooting, but didn't say what shooting, except that it was the 'enemy'.

"So I watched him. He was buying up big. He bought three whole kingfish
— and you know the size of them — and had them all cut into steaks. I
followed him into the fruit and vegetable market where he got himself one of
the wheelbarrow porters. By the time he was finished the barrow was full of
supplies. And off they went. Now . . . I know there's nothing unusual about
that. Plenty of them buy that much and get the porters to cart it back to their
car or pick-up. Some of them buy up for half the village. I know all that. And
that's what he could have been doing. But I couldn't help it . . . so I followed
him and the porter. They crossed the main road — you know, in the direction
of the Muna Hotel? — then they cut up that little side street, the one that's all
sand and dust and that's always jammed with cars. Maybe you know it? It's
signposted Way 177. Well, they went up there towards the old building that
looks like a fort, with the notice that says it's a spice mill, then they turned
right into the maze of narrow alleys that's there."

The Fish Souk at Khudra was one of the places where the flavour of the
old ways survived. The fishermen landed fish there every morning of the week
from their various grounds out in the Gulf to which they would commute
sometimes several times a day depending on their catches, speeding there and
back in their Government-subsidised 20-foot fibre-glass outboard-engine
boats. The quayside souk where they landed their fish was also the main
produce market for the Capital Area and was situated in the harbour known
as Mina Amir, or Emir, depending whether it was being referred to in Arabic
or English.

Across from the souk were a clutch of hotels, the kind which in Britain
might be modestly called "family hotels", and surrounding them was the usual
mixture of shops and traders that you would get in any such small, self-
contained Gulf community. There was Al Khanjary's Barber Shop; the
Mahmeni Restaurant where the menu was confined to whatever cook had in
that big pot you could see back in the kitchen, usually chicken or lamb curry
which they served with scones of nan bread half the size of the table; the Al
Shimaal Sweet Centre; a small grocer's, called as they always were a Food
Stuff Division; and a little mosque. Behind these merchants, and up the
narrow street called Way 177, was a maze of narrow alleyways with little old
houses — concrete shoeboxes with arabesque windows and ornate metal
grilled doors, where splay-foot goats wandered or lingered in the rubbish piles
and hens with broods of chicks would scratch and peck at the nothingness
they seemed to find in the deep grit, and where housewives would sweep the
day's flotsam into the dust sand of the alleyway and would hurriedly bang
their door shut if they sighted you passing.

It was into this little backwater, which might have been any village
community in the Interior, that Watson had followed the man from Razak
and the porter wheeling the impressive pile of supplies bought that morning
from the various stallholders at the souk.

After turning right at the old spice mill they had walked along an alley for about 50 metres until they came to a junction with two other alleyways. Continuing for a few more metres, they had then stopped at the entrance to a house on the left, and had gone inside. He had waited till the porter came out again. This time he was accompanied by another man, a man with a lean Interior face and the old-style untrimmed beard. After the porter left, the man had stood for a few seconds, hawked loudly and spat into the dust. Watson was transfixed in the doorway of the house where, unnoticed, he had been watching the man. He was yet another of the Razak five, the one to whom the privileged prisoners or the guards would always speak when they came to take them to Jilida or wherever it was that they went.

So they must all be there, he thought. That's why they needed so much food . . . the five of them were there. And probably there would be a family living there as well.

He had waited where he was, in the doorway, for a few more minutes in the hope there would be some activity. A powerful BMW with white and red Abu Dhabi numberplates then came slowly along the lane, its black side mirrors like Mickey Mouse ears almost scraping the unpainted concrete rendering of the houses on either side of the lane. He had to stand where he was in the doorway of the house in order to let it go past.

The driver was in Emirates dress of shirt-collared thobe and had his white kaffiyeh folded back over the top of his head. Another man in casual Western dress sat beside him and when the car passed he noticed there were another two in similar attire in the rear seats. He thought they might be Egyptian or Jordanian at first, but the car passed close enough for him to see they had fairer skins than that. He thought it unusual for such a car to be there and stood to see if it could make the tight corner at the junction further along the way. Its bright brake lights came on as it straddled the junction and the front passenger and rear doors opened at the one time. The three men in Western clothing got out, said something to the driver, and the car drove on. Without hesitating, the three men crossed the narrow street and rapped on the door of the house where he had seen the two men from Razak. The door opened and they went quickly inside. He waited for a few more minutes, then walked back down the alleyway to Way 177 and into the Fish Souk again.

"So . . . don't tell me I'm still paranoid after seeing all that lot. I mean, Brian, I'm not seeing or imagining things. What I saw was for real. Not daydreams. Well, what do you make of it?"

"It's certainly intriguing to say the least. But what it all adds up to . . . who knows? I mean, let's face it, all that you've seen doesn't sound sinister in any way. You've seen one bloke doing the shopping for him and his mates and along come three friends from Abu Dhabi or, to be precise, three friends in a car from Abu Dhabi. They could be from anywhere. Then again, let's suppose there is something odd going on. What is it? How will you ever find out about it? Go back and see your Superintendent Stott? Gordon, mate, if these blokes are up to something, you'll never know. And why worry? Take my advice, matey, and forget the whole damn thing."

"Yes, you're right. Maybe I should. But somehow I can't. Ever had a fixation about something? Well, I've got it about this. How about you mentioning it to your colonel friend? You know, maybe it's the kind of thing that means something to him? You can ask him at the same time if he knows anything about Stott the cop."

"Yes . . . I might. Not outright, like. I'll merely mention it casually to him the next time we are talking. He likes the odd bit of gossip. But remember, he wasn't all that interested the last time."

They walked together from the hotel in the direction of the angled spaces where Watson had left his car, neither of them paying any attention to the green Mercedes sitting with its engine quietly running and the louder hum of its air-conditioning operating, its driver looking indifferently in another direction. Brian said he didn't want a lift as he was going for a walk first before going home.

"How about bringing your girl down to meet the Thursday boys?" Watson joked.

"No chance . . . anyway, she doesn't drink."

"I think you're frightened of the competition from the lads."

Brian smiled and waved as he walked away, and Watson got into his car and drove off. As he did so the man in the green Mercedes spoke into a radio telephone and drove off behind him.

Meeting with the Dutchmen

THERE WAS a full turnout of the Thursday Club gathering at the Tie Bar the following week. Bria had said he would be there when Gordon Watson had phoned to say there had been a "development". He had also added that it was "most definitely" not his imagination this time. So they had agreed to meet in the smaller Snooker Bar before joining their other friends.

"Don't tell me," said Bria. "You've been back to the Fish Souk and you saw all five of these Razak blokes together and they saw and threw you into the harbour. Right?"

"Very wrong. And it's no joke what's been happening. I've had my house done over . . . and I've been followed."

"Oh, sorry, mate. That's really bad news. Getting your house done, eh? That's rare. Did they take much? And being followed! Tell me more."

"Well . . . the house first. They didn't take anything. But they went through the place with a fine tooth comb. No mess, or anything. Well, no real mess, that is. But you can tell when someone has been in your place. Drawers all mucked up and that. I'm Mr Tidy about the house, you know, so it makes it easier to tell."

"But nothing taken?"

"Not a baisa. I even had a bank envelope with a 100 dinar in fives and tens lying on top of a cabinet and it wasn't touched. Nor was the telly or the stereo or video. Mrs Percy, the next-door neighbour, saw them. She's an old nosey and doesn't miss a trick. Says they walked straight into the house as though they owned it. Had a key and everything. And they came in a green Mercedes."

"And what about the being followed bit?"

"Well, after Mrs Percy told me about the green Merc I remembered seeing one in my rear mirror a couple of times and thought it a bit odd. I didn't think any more about it at the time. I mean to say, you don't think about cops and robbers and that kind of thing here. But don't the police use green Mercs?"

"Well, it's always a green one they use at the radar speed trap between the Wadi Duka roundabout and the slip road for Mina Fatima. But I don't know if that's conclusive. When did you say all this happened?"

"Last Saturday. After I saw you on the Thursday I went back to the Fish Souk on the Friday . . .."

"That was on the cards," cut in Brian.

"Well, I had to, didn't I? But I saw nothing. I hung about that little alleyway and Way 177 where I had seen them go and kept my eye on the house for a while, but not a thing."

"That's what I call progress," Brian smiled.

"Well, I could have been lucky. Anyway, whoever it was that came to my house did so the following day when I was at work. I phoned the agent's and asked if they had given anyone the spare key but they said they hadn't. Indians, you know? They're all shit-scared of the cops and would tell you anything to save their skins. But the green Merc. I definitely saw one a couple of times behind me. Seriously, Brian . . . what do you make of it all? Do you reckon it could have been the police?"

Brian looked thoughtful and his reply was matter-of-fact. "Yes . . . sounds like it was. They're checking you out, I would reckon. You went and saw the superintendent bloke, told him all you had learned about the Razak men in Zamakh, and, being the good cop, he was doing a double take on you just in case you are involved in something."

"Like what?"

"Well, I don't know. But they've obviously been checking up anyway. How about the tail? Have you seen it since? Tonight, for instance?"

"Christ, Brian, I can hardly drive the car without looking in the mirror. But the answer's no. And tonight I came by taxi. Remember . . . it's Thursday. Big drinkies night and that. I don't want another couple of months in Alcatraz."

"Right. It is Thursday. Fun night. Remember! Good chat with the boys. Come on, forget everything and let's go through to the main bar but, just before we do, tell me something, mate. In your wildest of wild dreams, what did you imagine was going on between the Razak guys and the others? Some kind of revolution or something? An armed takeover? Gordon, this is the most secure country in the Gulf. They've got the best-trained army . . . well, they were trained by your lot."

"The Scots?"

"You know what I bloody mean. The Brits. Then there's the Palace Guard who can sort out any internal problems and, clever people, they've got a paramilitary police force that's been deliberately spoiled rotten with money and conditions so that they can be relied on to be yet another back-up if any of the other forces were to do some kind of about-turn. So, if your most fanciful dreams were thinking along these kind of lines, forget it. This place is too secure."

"Yes . . . I suppose that's what the Shah thought too when the Ayatollah was holding his press conferences in that villa outside Paris telling everyone he was going back to Iran to take over. What a joker this guy must be, everyone thought. Didn't they?"

"But there are no bloody Ayatollahs saying that about here. Are there? Come on, mate. You need some company to take a few things off your mind."

The pop duo Comfort, a lively and very engaging couple from Ulster, were the resident entertainers and with the aid of some Japanese electronics had the same effect on the lounge as a full blown band. Some of the more enthusiastic Arab males were up dancing with each other.

"If you can't tell the difference between an African Arab and an Arab Arab, just watch them when they start really swinging it," said Watson. "It's the African blood. They just can't help themselves. Look at the movement they've got. God, wish I could move like that. What rhythm!"

By the time Comfort had finished their little show, they had given the Tie Bar customers their version of the pop hits being performed by the current stars. Everything from Jennifer Rush to Laura Brannigan to Donna Summer, Bruce Springsteen to Elton John to Stevie Wonder to Neil Diamond. Their final number *Susannah* was met with wild applause and shouts of "Encore, encore," particularly from the locals and especially from the African ones whose tables were littered with the big litre cans of Fosters they favoured so much.

"And we're supposed to be in Arabia," joked Bria as conversation resumed with the end of Comfort's performance.

"Wish my local in Stepney was as good as this," said Steve Powers, the Londoner. "They've really taken to this group. I was in the other night and some of the Arabs had Indian fellahs up dancing with them. Nothing queer or gay, like. They were just using them like substitute birds. Talk about laugh."

"Were you in the night the one they call The Dancer did his act?" asked another of the group. "God, you should have seen him. He's a local like. Of African descent. Well, he gets up on his own when they're doing the *Susannah* number. Blimey, he was like that Michael Jackson bloke in a dishdasha. See if they put him on the telly at home, he'd be a star. I'm telling you."

Geoff Melmouth, the West Countryman, said he didn't see why they didn't have nationals on the local TV doing Western pop. "Ever seen their kids in the tape shops? Mum and Dad are looking for all the ethnic stuff and all the kids want are these crazy pop groups from England."

"Yes, but that's as far as it goes," said David Anthony, the major and the Arabist. "You see, places like this and letting the kids have their noisy tapes are just types of safety valves for them. There's no way they're going to let our new Western culture come here and affect them. Pardon me for using the word 'culture', for what we have now in the West is anything but culture. Now the ruling family here, they really like Western culture and I'm using the word in the best sense. Go into any of their houses and you'll hear delightful Beethoven and Bach and Mozart being played. That kind of culture, my dears, is welcome any time here. Do you read what these people do on the stage nowadays in England? They spit and throw cans of beer at their audiences and they put safety pins through their noses. Will someone please explain to me what's going on," he said shaking his head in obvious disgust.

"We're going to the devil, mate," said Powers. "That's what's happening. Right . . . whose turn for a round then?"

The major continued to shake his head.

Bria turned to speak to his friend Watson but he had gone. A few seconds later, however, he saw him in deep conversation with Saby, the head barman.

"So what was that all about?" Bria asked when he came over.

Watson was smiling. "I hesitate to tell you."

"Oh no . . . ."

"All right . . . all right. Don't imagine the worst. But see these big blokes at the other side of the bar?"

"Yes, I spotted them when I came in. Haven't seen them before. What are they, oilmen or something?"

"They're Dutch. Saby has just been telling me about them. They're fish buyers. Over here trying to do some big deal involving Gulf fish for the European markets."

"Sounds a great idea. Enough fish here."

"Yes, but that's not the important bit."

"Go on, then."

"Brian, three of them are the guys I saw go into the house with the Razak men. So that probably explains everything about them being down there at the Mina Emir port."

Brian shook his head smiling.

"Now listen, mate," said Watson. "Don't you start taking the mickey out of me. Okay, so I know you told me there would be a logical explanation for everything. I know you told me there was nothing sinister going on."

"Agreed. I'll say no more. Not a word."

"Tell you what," said Watson. "Let's go and have a chat with them. I might find out a bit more about the Razak guys . . . I mean, what their part in the fish operation is."

There were five of them and they were all, as Watson had said, big blokes. Two of them had the classical Dutch looks, the fair hair, lean faces. All of them were superbly fit-looking men and could have passed off as team members in some top sport. They were an easy group to mix with, but then most were in the Rani's Tie Bar. It was that kind of place where, if you didn't wear a dishdasha, you had come to the Gulf from some distant part and that in itself provided a form of fellowship.

Watson had been joking with them about the hooliganism that had now spread among the Dutch soccer fans. "It was Den Haag, wasn't it?" he asked. "They were the ones who had the trouble last year?"

There were some "Ja, Jas," in agreement, one of them saying that it was terrible and not like Dutchmen to behave like that. Johann Cruyff's name was mentioned and one of them, after saying he had been the world's best player, added that he didn't care about Den Haag or the other teams because he was an Ajax Rotterdam supporter and that was the best team in Europe. "They will be European champions next season," he said. And there was a chorus of "Ja, Jas" from the others.

"So you're Ajax Rotterdam men?" Bria asked and they all nodded. "Well, maybe you can tell me this. There's no argument that Cruyff was your best-ever player. But who would you say was the best after that . . . Joop Zoetemelk or Henni Kuiper?"

Watson looked at him puzzled.

One of the two fair-headed men replied. "Kuiper was good, but I would say the other one, what's his name?"

"Zoetemelk."

"Yah, yah, Zoetemelk. He was the best after Cruyff."

"Do you all think that?"

One of them shrugged his shoulders and another looked round at the bar but the other two said they agreed with their friend about the one called Zoetemelk.

Watson then changed the conversation to ask the men about their fishing business, adding that he had seen them in the vicinity of the harbour at Mina Emir. They replied they were making a study of the market here as reports had told them of the vast and virtually untapped source of fish that was available from Gulf waters.

"But they will need bigger ships," said one of them. And they laughed together at the size of the little outboard craft which the Arab fishermen used to hunt for hammerheads and kingfish and the big yellowfin tuna and other fish which were in abundance in the Gulf of Oman waters of the Arabian Sea. "They are all right for feeding the locals who go to the fish souks, but what they need are the big trawlers if enough fish are to be caught for the world market," the Dutchman added.

Bria asked them if they would like some more Heineken but without waiting for a consensus, one of them announced that they had had enough and that they would have to leave. He was the one who had shrugged his shoulders and turned his back when Bria had been asking the questions about the Dutch footballers. He made it patently obvious he was the group's senior man, or boss. No one dissented from his comment that they would have no more drink and they quickly emptied their glasses and left.

"Well, that was a bit of a revelation from you," said Watson.

"Revelation?"

"Yes . . . knowing about Dutch football like that. Never heard you talk soccer before."

"I'm not just a pretty face, mate."

"Nice blokes, though," said Watson. "Don't meet all that many Dutch here in the Rani or the other hotels. You know why that is? They're mainly from Shell and when they come here they work for the P.D.E. oil people. Some outfit that. Got the best of everything. Best club in the country, best pub, best beach, private and all. They even import their own entertainment, groups and the like, from England. And the wages they get . . . making a small fortune some of them."

Bria was musing into his drink and didn't reply to his comments about the Dutchmen and the good conditions at Petroleum Development Emirate.

"Bet you were thinking the same as me, Brian?"

"What was that?"

"That you were right all along about everything . . . particularly with me thinking all sorts of odd things about these guys who turn out to be nothing more that a bunch of fish buyers. My mind was in one big whirl about them and the ones from Razak. You know, I didn't say to you at the time, but I was thinking when I saw them that first day down at the harbour that they were some kind of infiltrators and were linking up with the Razak men for something sensational. See watching these one-dinar pirated James Bond videos! Plays havoc with your imagination, so it does. Geez, Brian, I'm glad it was only you I told. Can you imagine the laughing-stock I would have been had I told that Thursday crowd! God, I would never have heard the end of it. Especially Melmouth and Marsh . . . they would have done a double-act on me for the rest of my days here."

Bria was still looking into his drink, a faint smile on his face, but not replying to his friend's comments.

"Come on, Brian. You must have something to say. Not like you to go all quiet like this. What are your views?"

"My views? Well, Gordon, I'm glad your mind is settled and you're thinking the way you are."

"And what about your mind?"

There was no reply.

Watson was about to ask the question again when he was interrupted by the unmistakable voice of David Anthony, the major and frequent Thursday companion.

"I say, old chaps, what lovely boys you were talking to there. And just my luck not to meet them. I saw them from the other side of the bar and when I turned round to come over they had gone. Weren't they handsome! Did you say something rude to them?"

"They were Dutchmen," said Watson. "They're in the fish business."

"How terribly fascinating," said Anthony. "Now speaking of fish reminds me," he added, turning to Bria. "Are you still coming over for dinner one evening?"

"What's this?" asked Watson.

"Mosques," replied Bria. "David here, as you know, is one of the best Arabists we've got and the Ministry have asked him to do a foreword for the book."

"So what night then, Brian?"

"Well, Ramadan is due to start tomorrow . . . if they sight the moon that is."

"Oh no," said Watson. "That's the bars all closed for a month."

"Shall we make it one night next week?"

"Lovely, my dear boy. I'll have cook prepare something nice. Meat or fish, Brian? Or should I say lamb or fish? We don't touch that terrible meat they bring here from goodness knows where. Fish you say? Splendid. I'll shop for it myself."

The "Sleeper" is Aroused

P. CARL SABAMONTES was surprised when he was told that day at work there was a telephone call for him. Normally he only received a regular weekly call, on a Sunday evening, from his wife in Bombay. This was a Friday morning. The voice was deep and masculine and well modulated and he presumed it was that of an Englishman by the way he asked, "Are you Mr P. Carl Sabamontes?"

"That's correct," he replied. "May I know who is calling?"

"You don't know me, Mr Sabamontes. My name is Van Est. Arie Van Est. I am here with four colleagues. We have just driven from Abu Dhabi and we stopped at the airport to make this call to you. We are here on a business trip connected with the fishing industry in Holland and a mutual friend said you would be an excellent contact to offer us what help you could."

"Are you sure you have the right person?" said a puzzled Sabamontes before the man could continue any further.

"Oh, yes, I am sure you are the person. Our mutual friend said that there was no one better than Boris One to help."

There was a gap of several seconds before Sabamontes spoke again. "Oh! Oh, yes. Yes indeed. I can help. I will be only too willing to help you. Where are you?"

"As I said, at the airport."

"I'm sorry, I forgot. I've been expecting this call for a long time now. It's been nearly two years. I was beginning to think . . ."

"Mr Sabamontes," the voice cut in. "We can perhaps speak at length later. We have had a long car journey and would like to get good accommodation as soon as possible. Now our requirements are two adjoining rooms in a three- or four-star hotel with a good restaurant, a swimming pool, gymnasium and centrally situated. Where do you recommend?"

Without hesitation he replied that the Rani Hotel had all of these essentials.

"How far is it from the airport?"

"About 30 kilometres and easy to find. Just follow the signs for the Capital Area, then after a while you will see ones for Rani and the hotel is right in the centre of town. Everyone knows it."

"Will there be vacancies?"

"Of course. All the hotels have vacancies. There's been a recession since the oil prices dropped. But Mr . . . ," he fumbled for a name but continued speaking although none came. "I mean to say, goodness, it is so wonderful to hear from you at long last. I have been so anxious to do something to help and . . ."

"Fine, Mr Sabamontes," the voice cut in again. "I would like to see you this evening. Come to my room at about 8 o'clock. And the name again is Van Est. Arie Van Est. And we are from Holland."

The man who answered the door of Room 25 at the Rani Hotel that evening reminded Carl Sabamontes of the big Texans who would frequently come to the Capital Area from their oil camps in the Interior. They always stood out from the crowd because of their size and their slow and casual gait. This man in front of him who seemed to fill the entire door frame was exactly like that, except for the hollow cheeks and the pinched waist. His English was also much better than the strange form the Texan men spoke.

"You will be Mr Sabamontes," he said rather stiffly and with only the faintest trace of a smile as they shook hands. "I'm Van Est. Please call me Arie."

There were four other men in the room deeply engrossed in a game of cards and only one of them, a young fair-haired man, looked up. Like Van Est and the others he was that bronzed way white men would go when they had had long exposure to the sun.

Although none of the others obviously shared his pleasure, Sabamontes couldn't contain his feelings at the occasion and was still beaming widely when Van Est showed him a seat at a coffee table piled with dirty dishes and about a dozen empty beer cans.

"It's as good a way as any of replacing the body fluids," said Van Est when he saw Sabamontes looking at the cans, most of which had been crumpled into grotesque shapes. "Would you care for something?"

"No," he replied, still smiling. "You know, Arie, this is indeed a great day for me. And I will be only too pleased to do anything I can to help."

"Right," said Van Est, obviously uninterested in what gratification the Indian was experiencing from the occasion. "There are some things I would like to know. We have good maps of the area round about the Capital but a street guide would be a help. You know, one of those tourist type things? There were none in the hotel shop."

"I will get you one, no problem," Sabamontes promptly answered.

"After we booked into the hotel this morning, three of us went for a short tour in one of the cars which brought us here from Abu Dhabi. We had some difficulty before finding a particular location in the vicinity of the Fish Souk. The street guide would have helped, for the streets and alleyways there are a bit chaotic. And while I'm on about the Fish Souk, can you get me a list of the various kinds of fish they land there. If we are supposed to be in the fish business, we had better have some details. Now I assume you know the Capital Area fairly well. How near do the public roads go to the restricted areas at the Jebel Azraq TV mast and to the Ordnance Depot at the Army base?"

Sabamontes was delighted he had instant answers to these questions. He explained that the restrictions at the TV mast were only by signs on the public road but at the Army base there were gates and armed sentries were always on duty.

"What about the oil terminal at Mina Fatima?"

"That's like the Army base. There's a gate which is always manned by sentries."

"We will be travelling a lot by taxi. Do you have to make an arrangement with the drivers before you hire them?"

"No . . . no, not at all. They are remarkably honest, although many of them don't know where certain places are and you have to show them. Hardly any of them have English, but most have Hindi as well as Arabic."

"That's not a problem to us."

"What are the drinking regulations? Is it free like Bahrain or is it like the other places?"

"All the big hotels have bars where the residents or members of their Facility Clubs can drink. You will only be allowed to drink here in the Rani as it takes months to get a club membership. However, the bars are all closing next week for the Ramadan fast, but you will be allowed to get drink in your rooms."

"What's police activity like . . . I mean plainclothes people, special branch and the like?"

"They have them in the bars. Some are there to watch the nationals and their drinking habits, others watch the foreigners. But it is not all that bad."

"Are telephones tapped?"

"Some people say they are. I don't really know."

"Night life . . . does it exist?"

That question prompted some reaction from the card players, one of them looking up and saying something in a language Sabamontes didn't understand. Whatever it was must have been funny for the others laughed and even Van Est managed a smile.

"No, you will not find night life. The town begins dying at 9.30 when the shops start closing. By 11 o'clock only the cats are on the streets. A couple of the hotels have discos but only couples are admitted and they are all expat. workers."

"Are there many Dutch people around? Will we meet any in the bar here?"

"Yes, there are quite a few Dutch people in the country. But they are mainly working with the P.D.E."

"What is that?"

"Petroleum Development Emirate, the Government's oil company. They are in collaboration with Shell which is why you have the Dutchmen. But you don't find them so much in the bars for they stick to their own clubs at the P.D.E.

which are better and cheaper than the hotel bars."

"What about if we go out running in the morning? Will that draw attention to us?"

"No, I don't think so. I see quite a lot out running. I think they are mainly Englishmen and no one takes any notice of them."

"What about wearing shorts?"

"That's all right for your running or for any sport. But you can't wear them at any other time. But do you go running at this time of year? It's over 100 degrees every day now."

"Heat, my friend, is only a state of mind. There is no heat that nature supplies which the fit body cannot endure. And in our regiment we spend a lot of time maintaining fitness."

"You are soldiers?" exclaimed Sabamontes, surprised that he was hearing something about them.

"That is right. We are from the force known as Troops of Special Designation. I am the platoon commander. You will want to know now what our mission is here. But I can tell you no more, even although I know you are a friend and are trusted by our intelligence people."

"No, I don't need to know any more. But it has all been so confusing for me. You know, first of all you saying you were from Holland. I didn't expect that."

"That is our flag of convenience, my friend. We can hardly go about this part of the world saying we are from the U.S.S.R. . . . now, can we?"

"Of course not. No. Of course not," agreed Sabamontes promptly and emphatically.

"So, for the period we are here, we are all Dutchmen making a survey of the fishing industry in this part of the Gulf with a view to importing some of it to the Netherlands."

"It is still all a great surprise to me. It's just not what I expected all the time I've waited here for the call . . . you know, for someone to say the words Boris One?"

"And what did you expect?"

"Well, I did have things explained to me by Mr Burenkov . . . .."

"Burenkov," cut in Van Est sharply in almost Pavlovian reaction to hearing the Russian name. "Who is he?"

"Mr Burenkov was one of the two gentlemen who came to see me in Bombay and recruited me to work for them . . . your people, that is."

The Russian nodded and let Sabamontes proceed with his story.

"He said that I was to come here to Emirate and that one day, but he had no idea when, someone may call on me and I was to give them whatever help I could. Somehow I always imagined it would be just one man."

The big Russian laughed loudly at that, breaking the stiff formality he had displayed so far. "You mean, Carl, that you expected someone to whisper in your ear one day that he knew your code name or else you would get a phone call saying you were to retrieve the newspaper you saw the man with the white shoes and dark glasses put in the litter bin beneath the big clock at the airport at precisely 13.08 hours and when you did that and turned to page five there would be a message for you. In code, of course." He laughed again before continuing. "No, it is not all like the American films. Nothing is ever like it is in the American films. So, no master spies, Mr Sabamontes. Just five soldiers of the Spetsnaz on a secret mission for their country. Sorry to disappoint you."

"Please, please, Arie, believe me. I am not disappointed. Just surprised. And delighted that the day has at last come."

"Delighted, Carl. Why delighted?"

"Because at last I am of some use to the Soviet Union. That is the only reason I am doing what I am. I have never stopped being a Communist, even although I had to end my work for the Party in Bombay because of the police. I was beginning to give up hope that my services would ever be required here and that was a great disappointment to me."

"But you would have been paid anyway, whether you were used or not. Is that not the case?"

Sabamontes's conciliatory attitude changed dramatically at that. "Please, my friend, do not think I am doing what I am for the money. It is nearly two years now since I have seen my wife. My son was only weeks old when I left home and I have not seen him grow. I have endured that and the strange environment of this country and all the many hours of loneliness for just one purpose . . . that what little I am doing for the Soviet Union will bring that great day just a little closer when the country I love most, my India, will have Socialism and its people will be rid of the terrible poverty. That is the great passion of my life, Mr Van Est. So please, I ask you, do not associate me and what I am doing with any money I get paid."

The Russian stared at him, unsmiling, for a few seconds after he had finished speaking, but made no comment. And Sabamontes was no longer smiling.

"You were given a short course on radio communications and weapons, I believe?" said the Russian, changing the subject.

"That's right," Sabamontes replied. "My instructor said I would be quite a good marksman. But will I be required to shoot?"

"On a mission such as this, comrade, one can never predict what may eventuate. But it is good to know your capabilities. And, of course, your patriotism."

The Magic of the Souk

THEY WOULD gather early every morning by the green fawn canopied stall of Haji bin Beeri atl Hadjali, the tea and cake seller. Some would buy his tea with a slab of his thick yellow cake while others would sit on the furthest chairs from the stall waiting on the coffee vendor. They would hear him before they would see him as he tinkled his little cups, six of which he would carry in the same hand that held the small bucket for washing them. In his other hand was the big enamel coffee kettle beneath which was slung a neat charcoal brazier packed with hot coals to keep his brew warm. Hadjali couldn't really complain about them using some of his seats for, as his notice-board said, he was the tea and cake man and who would offend a man if all he wanted was one of his chairs to enjoy the drink of the coffee vendor?

They were the merchants of the souk, men who, you could tell by their ways, their mannerisms, their language and their appearance were from the world of trade. Even in their simple dishdashas and ornately embroidered kooma hats they had that air of well-being about them; men who had done well, lived well. In London or New York they would be the men of the best coffee houses, the more selective of hotel lounge bars, the men who would gather in the places where city gents met. In Emirate they met at Al Hadjali's tea and cake stall.

Every community in the Arab world has its souk. They range from the Grand Bazaars of the vast cities to the humble rag-tags of itinerants' stalls by some outback oasis or wadi course which would be set up before the Dhur midday prayers and be gone by the evening Isha prayer to appear somewhere else another day. There were no Grand Bazaars in Emirate, but there was the souk, the Khudra Souk, the principal trading centre, wholesale and retail, of the country.

The wealth of Emirate like its neighbouring Arab countries, came from its oil. But the commerce of the nation was founded by the merchants of the Khudra Souk. For centuries they had traded in the essentials of life of the country, the fish and the pomegranates and the limes and dates that went out, and in the spices and pulses, the rice and wheat and tea and flour that came in. They had their souk by the harbour so that they would be there to meet the slope-sailed ghanjah and dhow boats which came to them from up the Gulf, from Africa and from Bombay or Karachi, and from the ports of Persia. In the Renaissance of Emirate which followed the bloodless coup of 1970, the traders of the souk went forth and became the agents and importers and the partners of a whole new breed of names that were to appear in the country for the first time, the names that were the symbols of the new way of life which the open door had suddenly given them, names like Mitsubishi and Mercedes, Nissan and British Leyland, Wimpey and Cementation, Safeway and Sony. They still dealt with their spices and pulses, but now they dealt too with things like cars and pick-ups, trucks and tractors, radios and televisions, refrigerators, air-conditioners, washing-machines and the full range of requisite commodities for the acceptable part of the Western way of life. And they prospered like they had never prospered before.

From their traders' houses adjacent to the souk, in the ghetto they called that of the Liwatiyas or the Khojas, the Shia sect whose origins were either in India or Persia, many moved out to residences that some called villas in Qurat but might more appropriately be called mansions, even palaces, handsome and modern and spacious, with uninterrupted views over the azure waters of the Gulf across which had sailed the ships that had brought their forebears and the merchandise from which they had made their wealth.

Unlike the Arabs of the regions away from the coast or the coastal villagers themselves, the men of the souk were worldly men, men who could converse in Persian and Hindi, Baluchi and Gujerati, and Urdu as well as Arabic, for if they couldn't, neither could they have traded.

The ones who had moved their homes away from the souk to their stucco palaces by the sea still kept some kind of connection with the old market place, some through members of their family who still traded there, others continuing to run their new empires from the old office above the stall where they had started their business life. And some, just as successful and wealthy, preferred to retain their homes in the old Liwatiya ghetto with its warren of alleys and lanes which lay behind the big gates next to the Shia mosque on the Corniche seafront, a mere 100 metres from the souk itself.

Haider Barjani was one of the men of the souk. He was in his sixties and remembered well the timelock life of the country and of Khudra before 1970 when in the evening the roll of drums would be heard coming from the vicinity of the gates and then after the booms of three cannon shots men of a trusted Interior tribe would ritually pull shut the two massive doors of the gates of Khudra, enclosing the town for the night.

For those who did wander forth within the town walls there had to be the accompaniment of a lighted oil lantern to demonstrate that they were not a footpad or villain, which those without were deemed to be. They would be arrested on the spot and incarcerated in Fort Jilida.

Haider was and looked the typical Khoja: tall and portly, clean-shaven and light-skinned. He wore the shirt-collared dishdasha instead of the traditional one of the national. Legend has it that the Khojas were originally from the south of the Gulf and centuries ago had wandered as traders and silversmiths across the Arabian Sea or the Persian Gulf to Sind and Kutch-Gujerat in the subcontinent of India and to Persia itself. Then later they had returned, in the same fashion as they had left, as traders and silversmiths, to be the founding fathers of the great trading community of the Khudra Souk.

In his time Haider had exported dates and limes and salted fish and had imported sandalwood and ivory. As well as his import-export business he had run one of the biggest and most successful stalls in the area of the market known as the Cloth Souk. In 1970 when the country opened its door to the world, Haider had been one of many men from the souk who had become agents for the Japanese companies which came flooding into the country. With the money he had made from that enterprise alone he could have well afforded to have had a Qurat mansion by the sea, but life for Haider was about the souk and he continued to live on in his centuries-old merchant's house in the Khoja ghetto.

Brian Bria had got to know Haider well during his first few months in Emirate. He had been referred to him as an elder of the Shia community and one likely to give him the assistance he might require for photographing some of the Shia mosques. Haider had been more than helpful and had told him all about their community and the Shia sect and how they had lived in harmony with the majority sect of the Sunni and how they would even visit each other's mosques on their Friday Sabbath day. And from time to time Bria would return to the souk which ran from the water's edge up the slopes of Jebel Dawhah and sip the coffee vendor's brew with him in his favourite seat by Al Hadjali's tea and cake stall.

Haider had once told Brian that nothing, "but nothing my friend", happened in the souk community without it coming to his attention. No one could come, no one could go without him knowing. "I never tire," he would say, "of the faces you see here. Look at them . . . there's a representation from almost every part of two continents there, as well as those from throughout the Arab world. I know of no other place where you can get a mix like that, not even in the Grand Bazaar in Cairo would you get so many different faces." And he had rhymed off to him the 14 languages that were spoken every day when he had been a young man in the souk: Arabian of at least a dozen dialects, Persian, Baluchi, English, French, Swahili, Somali, Hindustani, Sindhi, Gujerati, Goan Portuguese, Pushtu, Armenian and Turkish. And there was the occasional Russian too. Nowadays you don't hear so much of some of them every day, but there are a whole lot of new ones to replace them from the new workers and others who have come in recent years: Dutch, German, Italian, Finnish, Norwegian, Chinese, Japanese, and the Philippine one, Tagalog, and so on.

As Haider spoke, he would pass between his thumb and forefinger, one of the polished marble beads he always carried, the beads the English usually called "worry" beads or "prayer" beads but which were neither. They were the Muslim's sebhah beads and were used for the triple repetition of three litanies with each of the 33 beads — that everything was of the glory of God, to the praise to God, and that God was great — together with the reminder that for each bead there were three words of glorification for God and every good Muslim could tell you what those 99 names were. If you ever asked what was the hundredth the reply would be: "Only the camel knows that."

It was after his last meeting with Watson and the group of men who said they were from Holland that Bria had gone to the souk early one morning. As he had expected, Haider was sitting there in his usual place at Hadjalis, the end seat of the bench at the junction of the alley that was called Lane 839, narrow and dark as a tunnel and leading to the Spice Souk. He had sat with him for a half an hour or so, exchanging the ritual inquiries about health and family and friends, asking about each individually rather than collectively and exclaiming the *al hamdu lillah,* praise be to God, after the news that each was well.

"You haven't been here since the flood," said Haider. "My God, it was terrible. Look . . . look over there at those cloth stalls. You can still see the high point of the water. My goodness, it's more than four metres high. This is an old wadi bed, you know, and you cannot change the ways of nature. When the flood came it swept down from the jebel up there and right through the main alley of the souk. All the traders at this low part lost everything. And look how all their shutters are broken and smashed. That was done by cars that floated past with the flood. Everything went . . . straight into the sea. And the next day not a drop of water to be seen, just the devastation that it left. But it was the will of Allah.

"So what brings you back to our souk, Mr Brian? Are you still taking your photographs of all our beautiful mosques?"

Bria said he was and joked that he reckoned he had seen the inside of more mosques in the country than the Grand Mufti himself. "Tell me, Haider, what do you know about the community who live by the Fish Souk?"

"The Fish Souk!" he exclaimed with a chuckle, fingering two more of his sebhah beads. "Some say that in certain parts of that area you will find all the bad things that ever happen in Emirate."

"Why would some men from Razak be living in a house there?"

"Which house?"

He described its location.

"Yes, I know the one. There were some illegal arms dealers operated there once. But that was many years ago . . . during the time of the Imam revolt. There would be a Razak connection then . . . maybe there still is for some reason."

Bria let the conversation drift for a while after that, not wanting one inquiry to be linked with another. Eventually the discussion turned to the subject of the Government and he said, "I believe Mustafa Abdullah came from the souk?"

"His Excellency Mustafa Ali Abdullah, the Minister for Public Buildings? Do you know him?"

"Well, I've met him twice. He's my big boss in a way. It's his department I'm doing the book for and I heard it said he had come from the souk. What kind of man is he?"

"In one word . . . ambitious. But then the family were all like that. They were traders here, but not like us Khojas. We have trading in our blood. But they were there to snatch every opportunity they could. They wanted to be rich by the quickest way they could. And it seemed it didn't matter which way. We could not be like that. Mustafa's old father was one of the most ambitious men I've known. He was one of the first to become really rich through all the new trade we got after 1970 when the world was allowed to come here. And they quickly forgot his connections with the men from Razak and the Jebel Ahmar."

"Razak . . . Jebel Ahmar! What was that all about?"

"It was 30 years ago when the man who was the last Imam challenged the Emir. He and his followers wanted to declare their independence up there in the mountains and there was a war. The Imam was a man called Khamis. Khamis bin Ali. He had a brother called Hamed and together with a Sheikh Khalfan, who deemed himself the King of Jebel Ahmar, and their followers they declared themselves an independent state. And Razak, in the shade of the Jebel Ahmar itself, was their capital.

"Old Ali Abdullah's connection with them was that he came from a village along the coast in the vicinity of the airport and he was arranging arms for them, smuggled in on boats from Saudi Arabia. For a time it looked quite bad for the old Emir and Ali Abdullah saw an opportunity, if the Imam's men won, to be there in some high post in their new Government. It's very hard to fight men up in these mountains and after more than a year or so the Emir had to get your people in to help."

"My people?"

"Yes, the Englishmen . . ."

Bria smiled to himself but didn't interrupt.

". . . and they fought away up there and they had to bring in aeroplanes to bomb the villages before it was all over."

"So what happened to the men from Razak?"

"Oh, they all fled to Dammam in Saudi and to Cairo for they had Nasser backing as well."

"And old Abdullah?"

"Oh, he just lay low for a while. He was lucky not to end up in Jilida. I think he paid some money and kissed the right hands and vowed his allegiance to the Emir. And now he is the respectable old merchant with the son who is a millionaire many times over and is His Excellency the Minister."

"What about the others from Razak . . . the ones who didn't get away to Saudi and Egypt?"

"Oh, they are still up there in the mountains. They'll be older men now and many of them will have passed away but the stories linger."

"Could the same ever happen again, Haider? I mean an attempt like that to take over from the ruler?"

"It could never happen that way again, by challenging the Emir and his forces. They are too strong, too loyal."

"But it could happen by other means?"

"Of course. You never know what goes on in men's minds. Once they have achieved great riches there is only power to be gained after that. Ambition can be an evil quality. It can be such that it can make man reach out for the heavens, and if he were ever to find them, he would still not be satisfied."

"And Mustafa, the son, did he make his money with the father?"

"No. Like so many, he left the country in the days of the old Emir and made his fortune up the Gulf. Then, when the young Emir took power he came back with the others, loudly proclaiming loyalty to the new monarch. But we who know think their loyalty was elsewhere. In their purses, my son."

The coffee vendor was by them again and he took their proffered cups to refill. It was sheer artistry the way he could pour the dark, unsweetened liquid, holding the big pot at arm's length from each of the thimble cups, then letting the required amount pour in a long stream so that it bubbled and frothed and gave off all the delightful aromas of the kawah and cardamom.

They sipped it together as they looked in silence and appreciation at that glorious tapestry which was the passing scene of the souk at Khudra.

Dinner with the Major

MAJOR DAVID ANTHONY was a tall, strikingly handsome man and despite his effeminate postures, the way he would pucker his lips, womanlike, from time to time, and his speech littered with "dears" and "darlings", he was accepted by the Thursday gang as "one of the boys", whatever the accuracy of that description might have been.

He had been a professional soldier and had seen action in the Gulf, hence the occasional reference, "Well, I did fight for His Highness", meaning the Emir and the service he had experienced in the Jebel Ahmar insurrection. He had fought too for the Sultan of Oman in the Dhofar war in the south of the country. It was also known that he had served in Kuwait and in Aden and had retired from the Army during the cutbacks of the 1970s with sufficient pension and legacy from his mother to pursue a life of "Arabic studies". Now he was back in the Gulf on an archaeological project under the auspices of the Ministry of Culture and Heritage and it was through his old military contacts, he explained, that he had got himself a grace-and-favour house at the Bait al Bonni, the military camp which surrounded the fort of that name in the heart of the Capital Area. The fort had once been the headquarters for the combined services of Emirate and there was a small estate of old colonial-styled bungalows there which had served, and still did, as married quarters for senior officers.

While the other great forts around the Capital, like Jilida and Khudra, had an aura of fairy-tale fantasy, the fort of Bait al Bonni was pure P.C. Wren. It had tall towers with battlements and crenellations encrusting the ramparts and with the merest of blinks you could hear bugles and barked commands and rifle shots and the screams of death coming from this strategic stronghold which stood sentinel on the gravel plain that was the advance on the Capital. In fact, scenes such as that had been enacted around the fort in very recent Gulf history. In the early part of the century thousands of dissident tribesmen, again under the influence of a wayward Imam, began a revolt against the grandfather of the Emir because he had imposed a restriction on the importation of arms. After they had captured many of the Interior forts, 3,000 of them on horse and camel besieged the crucial Fort Bait al Bonni and the vital hillocks it commanded on the flat sweep of the wide gravel plain. The history of the country would never have been the same had that force won the fort and access to the Capital. But with the combined efforts and courage of tribesmen loyal to the Emir, backed by his friends, the British, with the King Edward's Own Grenadiers and Russell's Infantry, quickly brought in from India, the fort held in an epic battle of charging men with flowing robes on daring steeds. They were death and glory days and the glory, as providence would have it, was for the ruling family of Emirate.

These were changed days at Bait al Bonni. When it became too cramped and antiquated as a services headquarters for the sophisticated forces which now defended the country, the building was given a major renovation and, like so many old military establishments of its kind, turned into a museum. Plantations of trees and shrubs quickly flourished and it now had the appearance of a suitably scaled Central or Hyde Park, a haven of peace and solitude amidst the bustling traffic that continually moved around the three towns of the Capital Area.

The major was there at the security gate when Bria called to keep his dinner engagement that evening and they walked together through the avenue of tall gums past the gleaming white fort and then up one of the broad paths to some of the bungalows which had been built on the hillock. There most of the blood had been shed during that epic battle.

"What a delightful place," said Bria. "God . . . that smell from the gums. Now there's a reminder for me."

"Why, of course, my dear boy, you're from Australia. I never did manage to get there."

"How lucky you are, David, to live in such a lovely spot."

"I never stop appreciating that, particularly as I remember the old fort I served in when I first came here. It wasn't the crisp white way it is now. It was an old brown building then. That's what Bait al Bonni means . . . the Brown House. There were no trees either. No electricity. No air-conditioning. It was fans and old punka wallahs yet it wasn't all that long ago. Just shows you how dramatic the change has been here. I mean, it's just 73 years since a great and historic battle took place right on this very spot. It was as important to them as Waterloo was to us, maybe more appropriately as Gettysburg was to the Union forces. And they fought it in the same fashion men had been fighting battles for thousands of years."

He stopped to point out the crest of the hillock where the Grenadiers and those loyal to the Emir had stood firm and to explain the details of the conflict. "Can you imagine that sight . . . those charging tribesmen? What courage they had to do that. And those stout defenders, the Grenadiers and others out there in the open with musket and sword. Think of their courage too. You know Brian, I would have given an arm, and I really mean that, to have been here in that battle. God, it must have been wonderful. Sounds abysmal, doesn't it, to talk about death and injury as being wonderful. But what was wonderful about it was the manhood . . . the bravery . . . the devotion of those men. Every damn one of them. That was the kind of war that men were really about. One man against the other, each fighting and ready to die for his own cause. Each directly facing up to his counterpart, never flinching. Each out to show the other who was the stronger, the more daring. God, they were splendid people. And I'm talking about those on either side.

"But, sadly, everything in life seems to have degenerated, war perhaps the most. Now it's all secondary combatants they take on. They blow up people in airports or on aeroplanes or sitting in restaurants and pubs and try to tell us the innocents they've just killed were the victims of their struggle. They take hostages and say we must blame the hostages' government for what they have done, but not to blame them. They sneak up behind policemen and shoot them in the head. They mail parcels that blow up in some unsuspecting face. Or they press a tit on a piece of electronics and, whoosh, a bloody rocket thing flies off and blows up a ship 40 miles away. And their leaders and the people who motivate the ones who do all these things speak of them as heroes. Heroes! Bunkum, dear boy. There are no heroes now. But there were when they attacked this fort in 1915. And the poor major here didn't arrive till 1957 . . . 42 years too late, alas."

His house was near the summit of the hill on which part of the battle had been fought and was screened by thick bush-tree, just like the way the tea-tree screened many houses on the Mornington Peninsula, which had been one of Bria's favourite haunts near Melbourne.

"So you were here as far back as the 'fifties, David? You must have known Billy Bainbridge?"

"Oh yes, I know Billy Bainbridge all right. I was a young second lieutenant when I first came here and he was a full lieutenant. We were in the same regiment actually."

"I didn't know you were with the Parachute boys."

"Well, one can hardly go around swinging the lantern, can one?"

"So you are old mates?"

He didn't answer that point.

"Do I take the silence as significant?"

"Yes, I suppose one can say significant. We met up in the Paras, both of us having come from different Scottish regiments. Billy was an Argyll, although his Scottish connections are somewhat tenuous. Being lobbed out of planes together does foster a special kind of comradeship and one does get to know people rather well. Being part of a regiment is like being part of a rather large family and although the Paras was not our parent regiment, it nevertheless had that close camaraderie. Alas, like the best of families, situations can arise and if I sound a bit vague about it all it's because of my reluctance to speak about events of the past. So, enough tittle-tattle about two old soldiers.

"Now tell me, Brian, do you like malt with your Mozart? I've got some Glenfiddich and some delightful Glenmorangie. Do you know it took me seven years of drinking whisky before my senses were educated enough to appreciate a good malt. But then that's like all the good things in life, one must teach the senses to appreciate them. And I can think of few more provoking or lingering taste sensations than beautiful Glenmorangie, except of course Glenfarclas which you just can't get here in the Gulf."

"You said that with all the affection of a Scot for his, what is it they call it again? Yes . . . Their dram."

"Oh, the Scottish blood is there all right. Dear mother. A Douglas from an old Covenanting family in the Lowlands. That's why I started off in the Cameronians before going to the Parachute Regiment. It was her dearest wish that her one and only son should serve in the regiment which had defended the Scottish Presbyterians."

"You in the kilt, David!"

"It would have been quite fetching actually. No, dear boy. The Cameronians didn't have the kilt. We wore tartan breeks, or trews as they called them. We were part of the Rifle Brigade, just like the Gurkhas. There were many similarities between the two actually. Both were little men, one lot with yellow faces, the other lot with the pale faces of the boys from those dreary, wet little towns and villages of Lanarkshire. But, my God, what fighters. The Gurkhas had this obsessional thing about their kukri. But the Jocks didn't care what they used . . . knives, razors, bottles, stones, boots, fists. What tigers! We had a battalion of them out here when the Jebel Ahmar thing was on. I was in the Paras by then but a lot of my old fellow officers were with them. Even one of the old ORs, a rifleman by the name of Scally, was still with them. He was the one I remember after this enormous pub brawl in which they were involved when we were in Germany and in which they had caused incredible damage — God, you would have thought a bomb had hit the place, When I was reprimanding him for his role in it, he replied to me: 'But, surr . . . you should see us at hame.' They were great days. Brian. Great days. But you've been around yourself, dear boy. All those horrible wars in Africa, and several tours of Vietnam."

"Who told you that?"

"You should know Emirate is a very small village. There are not many secrets here. Was it as dirty as they say?"

"Dirtier."

"But there's that kind of element in every war. I mean, they haven't all been like the battle for jolly old Fort Bait al Bonni. But when you say dirty, just how dirty?"

"So dirty that it was like a disease that instantly corrupted everyone who had anything to do with it. Vietnam was where dishonour became an art form. And the state of the art was total immorality. Men behaved like they had some form of mental AIDS. Maybe they should have called it AIMS — Acquired Immunity to Morality Syndrome. Minds became totally immune to all forms of carnal, venal and martial immorality. The accepted morality *was* immorality. It bastardised us all in some kind of way."

"You too, Brian?"

"Me too. No one was immune. Some just got it worse than others, like the ones who did what they did at My Lai. They just happened to get the publicity. My Lai wasn't just a village. My Lai was an attitude."

"And how did it affect you, Brian?"

"It affected me so that I didn't cry out when I should have when I saw and heard the things that I did. It made me laugh at the brothel queues. One after another they would wait to dip into some poor wretch who would be feeding her family and her parent's family and probably her brother's family and maybe a sister's family too with what money that was left after the pimps who leeched on her took their cut. I laughed at that, David, instead of feeling for that poor bitch lying there with her legs up in the air taking one after another into her. And I'm not like that. But it did that to me. It demeaned and it debauched and I'll carry the mental scars of it for the rest of my life. I don't know why I'm telling you this, for I never speak about it."

"Perhaps the Glenmorangie helps."

"Yes. Perhaps it does."

They spoke for a long while after that about the mosques of the country, the reason for their dinner that evening, the major having an extensive knowledge of mosques not only in Arabia but throughout Northern Africa, India, Pakistan and Turkey. He had visited hundreds of them. Bria was amazed at how, without reference, he could recall their names and their architectural highlights, even the ones in remote places like Timbuktu, where he had been, as well as on the lonely islands of Socotra before the Communists had taken over.

"Take the basic minaret, for instance," he said. "Did you know we have still not proved to this very day whether the purpose of it really was for the calling of prayers or if they had meant it for some other use. Some were initially used as lookouts for observing the coming of the caravan trains. Others, particularly along the Red Sea, were utilised as lighthouses. So what came first, their utilitarian use or their spiritual use? It's chicken and egg, isn't it?"

It was obviously a well-learned monologue of the major's and Brian let it run its course as it went from minarets to mihrabs, the spot where an Imam stands indicating the direction of prayer, to minbars, the mosque pulpit, while at the same time he watched the little gecko lizards cavorting for insects in the exposed laths between the open beams of the house. When he thought he had explored the subject sufficiently without it seeming obvious that he wanted a change in topic, Brian asked him, "What do you know about Razak, David?"

"You mean the mosques there?"

"No . . . just Razak. The town. What kind of place is it? What kind of people live there?"

"What, are you thinking of going on a wadi bash or something up there?"

"In other words you haven't heard anything?"

"About what?"

"About Razak."

"We seem to be talking in riddles, dear Brian. What is there to hear about Razak?"

"You know Gordon, our Thursday-Night Club Scottish friend? Well, he got involved in this situation arising out of his time in Zamakh. Remember, he was booked for a drink-driving offence and jailed? Anyway, it has become a bit of a saga."

He related all the aspects of the story to the major, about their strange cell-mates in the prison, about the Pakistani Yaqoob who was murdered and the subsequent sighting of the men together with some Europeans in the houses behind the Fish Souk.

"I have an old friend, he's called Haider, one of the Khojas at the souk, and he gave me some of the background about the Imam Revolt and the Jebel Ahmar affair and its three protagonists. Who were they again? Sheikh . . .."

The major cut in. "Sheikh Khalfan and the Imam Khamis bin Ali and his brother Hamed, or as we referred to them, The Three."

"So you remember them!"

"My dear Brian . . . that was my reason for being in the Jebel Ahmars in 1958 and '59. They were tough and cunning beggars up there in those awesome mountains and they took some rooting out."

"Yes . . . I've been reading what there is to read about it. But there's not much, is there?"

"No, I'm afraid they don't like too much literature about their recent history. It's hardly the thing the children will be taught about at school, although they should for the Emir at the time had a lot of courage in standing up to them. It could so easily have gone the other way. But getting back to Razak which was the centre of so much that was happening at that time and where so many of the men came from who fought on the Imam's side. Well, it's a most colourful and very ancient town. Its fort, which is immense and absolutely gorgeous, dates back to before Mohammed, back to the time when the Persians were in these parts. Razak has been popping up in this country's history for centuries. When the nation was divided and ruled by a variety of sheiks, Razak was often the capital of the area in the mountains. And before the present ruling dynasty there was a previous dynasty who made it their capital while they ruled.

"The war of '57 to '59 was the culmination of considerable trouble in the area with lots of comings and goings between here and Saudi and Egypt by the three men I mentioned. They formed what they called a Bureau of Free Emirate and enlisted lots of expatriates working in countries up the Gulf. At one stage they even persuaded the Council of the Arab League to put the subject of the country on the agenda of the United Nations General Assembly, accusing the old Emir of imperialism and blocking the self-determination of his countrymen.

"Mind you, the country under the old Emir certainly wasn't exactly a bastion of freedom and liberty. Well, you know the stories about curfews and lanterns at night and all that business? They were all true, you know. But the old chap meant well. He just wanted things to stay as they were and be damned to the rest of the world. Which, when you see the way of things in some of our developed West . . . my God, maybe the old boy had it right. But it was at terrible cost. The disease and the poverty! And the mentally disturbed . . . they had them going about in chains, poor souls. Anyway, you say your friend Gordon thinks he may have stumbled on something that smells of evil and has a connection with Razak. Brian, if you would take my advice for what it's worth, tell him to leave well alone. The security forces here are remarkably efficient, you know. They have their I.S.S. . . . have you heard about them? The Internal Security Service. A bit like our Special Branch boys. You know, one must always be on guard in nations like this for the coup that can always be just around the corner. Look at the little problem they had last year in Sharjah. And that was between brothers! Tell your friend Gordon that nothing's likely to happen without the I.S.S. boys getting to know about it."

"So you think that all the events which he experienced and the meeting with the European men he saw at the house near the harbour and who we later met in the Rani and who told us they were Dutchmen . . . you think it all perfectly innocent?"

"Well, I certainly don't read anything sinister into it if that's what you mean. Through various contacts, some of them old military chums, I know a fair bit about the security service and what they're up to here, Brian. You can believe me, they've got everything fairly well sewn up. By the way, when you spoke there about those men, the ones you met in the Rani, it sounded to me that you didn't think they were Dutch."

"Because I put it that it was they who said they were Dutch?"

"That's right."

"Perhaps I just put it badly then."

"Do you like the hamour? I think it a wonderful replacement for our cod, don't you? And cook has excelled himself with the sauce. It's made from coconut milk. Suits the fish so well, I think."

In the Garden of Eden

RAMADAN, despite the heat, was a good time to get away from town. The hotel bars were shuttered for the month and every restaurant, cafeteria and snack bar closed during the hours of daylight. The non-Muslim could not help but be impressed by the discipline and fortitude of the believer who, for a month, would forego any form of food or liquid, even the slightest sip of water on a day when the sun was at its most intense. Muslims would do so without the merest of murmurs about it being a burden of any kind. On the contrary there was a great reward in it for them, the reward of achievement. They would tell you that it fostered a discipline of all the senses and their minds would be refreshed, so that not only would they do without sustenance and water but neither would they think of any kind of vice "and the tongue would not indulge in the telling of lies". Well, that was the case with the good Muslims.

The Christians and others, the nasrani and kaffir, tried to show their respect by not mentioning food or drink during the day or by smoking in the presence of those on the fast. Even the Hindu and Sikh roadmen, their clothes habitually stained with sweat, would look about them making sure no Muslim was in sight before taking a swig from the insulated water barrels that kept them refreshed.

Brian and Esther had spoken about going away for a weekend, not to a hotel for that was illegal and could have merited an instant visa cancellation for her and some kind of trouble for him were it discovered that as unmarrieds they had shared a room. So they planned a trip by four-wheel drive vehicle to some Interior beauty spots and intended to carry the equipment to camp for a night or two.

She had telephoned him, as planned, the night before they were due to leave but her news was that she couldn't make it.

"What? Have they switched your shifts again?" he had asked.

"No . . . it's not that. A Filipina has turned up at our flat and we will have to help her. Remember the one I told you about with the Dettol? Well, it's a story like that. Only this one did not take anything. She has just run away and a friend brought her to our flat and we will have to do something to help."

"Then bring her with you for the weekend. If she's got problems like that then it will do her good to get away from it all with us. I've got a spare camp bed. That's if we need it. Maybe you'll want to share mine?"

She laughed at that. "Brian . . . it is that time already."

"What time?"

"You know, that time of the month already. So maybe we better put it off."

"Come on, you don't think I go with you just for that. I enjoy your company, love."

"That is nice. You don't mind then if I bring this one along?"

"You bring *this one*. No problems. What's her name anyway?"

"Amar."

They were to meet at the usual place, by the flower shop in Rani Street next door to the Palace Furniture Showroom beside which was the building where the nurses had their flats. There would often be Filipino girls waiting there, some in their white cotton trouser-suit nurses' uniforms, smart and fresh and waiting for the bus that would take them to the Al Nahdha Hospital, others off duty waiting on friends. The Oriental girls stood apart from Arab counterparts, each at either end of the ethnic and cultural scale, the Filipinas with their round Oriental faces and polished black hair, the slender Arab girls with their high cheekbones and aloof profiles, one lot from the furthest East but with attitudes that were of the West, the other of an East that would forever be East; one so casual and informal, the other so disciplined and formal.

They were both waiting when he arrived with the big balloon-tyred Nissan Patrol he had hired for their weekend trip. They had been obscured at first by a group of young Arab youths who were passing at the time. Although no one called them such, they were the local equivalent of the English mods, the label referring more to dress than behaviour. They wore the conventional dishdasha, but there are things that can be done to make even them modish. They would have them tailored so that the more adventurous they were the wider they got. They liked colourful ones too and while modern city gents were experimenting with soft pastel shades for theirs, the mods boldly went for the crimsons and violets and dramatic blues and even the occasional black, the spaciousness of the garments making them billow in the breeze like Victorian nightshirts. Their hair was part of the fashion, long and bushy, and to show it they would most daringly have their heads uncovered, either carrying their cashmere head-dress or draping it round their necks. But very rarely were they indisciplined or would they break the strict Arab code of manners and as they passed there were no comments or gestures, not even a sideways glance at the two pretty girls waiting on the broad pavement.

The girls were both in the usual gear favoured by the Filipinos, light, brightly coloured trousers and gay blouses. Esther was wearing sunglasses and he wondered, as he had done before, why Orientals behind dark glasses always looked so mysterious, almost sinister; but then he invariably concluded that would be just one of the old prejudices surfacing. Nevertheless, they did.

Because of Esther's large dark glasses, his first eye contact with them had been with the girl accompanying her. She was smaller and slimmer than

Esther and she was darker too. He stared, captivated, into her eyes, just as he had done with Esther that first time. She had that classical face of the Filipina beauty, the one that represented the loveliness of more than one culture: maybe it was Malay and Chinese; maybe Malay and ethnic Filipino, whatever; but the eyes were Spanish, that was for sure — wide and round and, God, he thought, as he stared at her before getting out of the vehicle, how do you stop yourself looking into eyes like that?

"You from Manila too, Amar?" he had asked.

Esther laughed. "No, she's not. We are not all from that one."

"I'm from Baguio," she said. "That's up in the mountains. The Cordilleras. It's a real nice place. They come to us from Manila when the weather gets too warm."

"Hey! You say you're from Baguio? That accent is more like Chicago. Where on earth did you get the American voice?"

She smiled for the first time, revealing the same toothpaste-advertisement teeth as Esther. He momentarily reflected it must have something to do with diet.

"From my teacher, I guess. That is the way with us. So many of us have teachers trained by Americans or who have been in America. But I don't think I am speaking American."

"But the pair of you . . . you're so different: the way you speak, the way you look."

"But that's the way of it in the Philippines. Did you know we have more than 7,000 islands in our country? We've got eight different major languages."

"So you've had a rough time, Amar?"

"Worse than I ever imagined. All right, I was prepared not to have a day off. Other Filipinos I had met who had been here told me that it sometimes happens. So I put up with that for more than a year."

"Not one day off in a whole year?"

"No . . . not one. I had to go to my employer's sons' houses. There were two of them. And their wives left all the work for me. But I accepted all that for I was getting much more than I could ever earn in Baguio."

"How much was that?"

"Eighty dinar a month."

"That's about 30 quid a week . . . quids . . . that's English money. I can value things better when I translate it to English currency. God, Amar, seven days a week for that kind of money . . . that's bloody bondage."

"But I didn't mind. It was enough for me to send home 150 U.S. dollars a month and save money too so that I could buy presents when I go home for my first leave next year. But it was when one of the sons . . ." Her voice tailed off at that point.

"Esther told me, Amar. You're safe now. No need to worry about that any more."

She sat silent for some minutes before speaking again.

"And he said he would tell the police I had been stealing from all of their houses if I told what he did to me. And that would mean I would go to the woman's prison for a long time. They would never believe my word against a national."

"Yes . . . I know. They've got so much going for them that's right. Then they go and spoil it with things like that."

Esther spoke up at that point. "They think because we are Filipinas that we are all bad women and know nothing. But we are educated and have been to University . . . Amar has a degree in the arts. They only treat us this way because they know we make so little at home."

"So you packed your bags and left them. How did you find Esther's place?"

"The girl who shares Esther's room is from Baguio. We were at school together and she used to come and visit me at the house in Al Mushrif where I worked. I don't know what I would have done without her for when I was not working for them I could only stay in my room. I could only go out at night when all the work was finished and if they didn't need me to look after the children. But where can you go in Al Mushrif? My friend told me that if I ever got in any kind of trouble I could come to the nurses' flats and they would look after me. We have a sense of honour to each other like that."

"They are terrible people these Arabs to do that," Esther interrupted.

"But they're not all like that, Esther. Lots of other girls are here and are not treated badly."

"What about the one who took the Dettol? And I know others."

"I bet you have those who behave like that in the Philippines too. Look at the wages they pay you there for a start."

She nodded in agreement at that, although she didn't say any more.

The girls were soon laughing then screaming, the way women would, as their station wagon bumped and bounced alarmingly. They had left the main coast road to take the dirt-track road that was signposted for Hail al Ghaf, then from that on to a smaller and bumpier dirt road for Al Misfa. When that took them into the mountains they turned off at a sign for Jizarre to begin a precipitous and undulating cross-country trek, following where they could the wheel tracks of previous traffic. It was a roller-coaster ride. One minute all they could see was the dazzling blue of the sky as the powerful Nissan snailed up tight slopes in lower ratio first. Held in that gear, the engine screamed as it plunged down the opposing incline. Then, when the road seemed no more, Bria swung the vehicle into the crystal water which was flowing in the wadi and drove upstream for another few kilometres. They stopped in the shade of some steep rocks by a wide pool. Dotted around them were the embers of previous campers' fires.

"So this is Wadi Wahda! Wow, it really is something," said Bria when they got out of the vehicle to view the scenery around them. It was nothing less than dramatic. Ahead of them was a huge escarpment of limestone rock rising sheer from the head of the wadi to about 4,000 or 5,000 feet, a sensational beige-yellow amphitheatre.

The girls said they were amazed that water should still be flowing after at least eight months without rain.

"It's like the Cordilleras . . . only there are no trees," said Amar.

"But look at the colours . . . the wildflowers, the bushes, those rocks and that sky. Those ones are oleander . . . have you ever seen such a variety of colours? And those other bushes, whatever they are, look at the colours in them. Wish I knew my flora . . . oleander is the only one I can put a name to and that's because someone pointed them out to me just last week. Anyway . . . how about a swim?"

The girls said they would stay in the shade of the rocks where it was cooler. "I know," said Brian. "You're scared you get a suntan."

After they lunched, they drove on to the sea then turned south on another unmade track, the one that followed the coast past a series of communities not marked on his map, little fishing villages by freshwater wadis around which there were date palms and banana plantations and even papaya trees.

It was already nightfall when they decided to stop near a deserted wadi where there was a dam of fresh water which trickled into the languid sea. Although there was no moon it was light from the brilliance of the stars and they parked the Nissan by the wadi dam and just above the high-tide mark on the beach.

"Well, you two. How about a swim now? You won't catch any suntan this time."

"You and Amar go," Esther replied. "It is not my time for swimming. I'll listen to the radio."

"It's near midnight . . . try for Voice of America. Willis Conover should be on. Plays the best modern jazz of anyone."

Amar appeared from behind the vehicle, dressed only in the briefest of briefs and as she approached, Brian, in surprise, could only stand and stare at her. She was smiling and relaxed and so different from the shy and nervous girl they had picked up that morning. Her body was that of a shapely teenager, her pinched waist emphasising her shapely bust and her abundant and erect nipples.

"Well . . . are you coming?" she said, her smile now an ample grin. "I'm not going swimming on my own."

They splashed and laughed together as they played in the gentle surf and she held his hand affectionately when they came out of the water, shrieking at the phosphorescent dots that covered their bodies. "Cripes . . . it's like something out of Disney," yelled Brian as they wiped the tiny lights from their skin. "Must be some kind of luminous plankton." He turned and ran into the water again to emerge once more with his body dotted in the peculiar little lights and the pair of them screamed and laughed as he wiped them away once more. "That stuff made me look like the Incredible Hulk — without the body," he said taking her hand as they walked back towards their campsite.

She seemed to hold his hand extra tight just before she released it . . . or did he just imagine she did? There were so many things that women did that could play on the imagination and had so often played on his: little touches, maybe just a finger even; the way they could smile and their language of movement which could mean so much; little subtleties which no man could initiate and only man could appreciate. It was as though in the space of that swim and from the way she had stood so unashamedly near-naked before him and the way she had touched him when they were in the water and held his hand after that something had passed between them. Yet not a word had been exchanged.

"God, there I go again," he thought to himself. "Bloody imagination. Bloody women. They set traps, wait and see if you jump and then if you do they're liable to walk away laughing. That's what they like . . . the ensnaring bit. It's their only chance to show their superiority. What a old bloody fool I must be to be even thinking like that. And there's me already ensnared by one . . . and thinking about another. I must have flipped. The heat must have got to me. Or is it just age? Yes, that's it. Age. My bloody oath it is. You're 30 one day and before you bloody know it you're almost touching 50. Then some doll squeezes your hand and you think you're 30 again."

"It sounded like that was fun," Esther said when they got back to where they were camped.

Amar, still topless, lay down on one of the camp beds and Esther stripped likewise, saying how warm it was.

"Did you hear the forecast this afternoon on Radio Emirate? You know, the one read by the woman with the terrible American voice? D'you know she can't even say George Shultz's name. She makes it rhyme with dull. Like Shull-tz. Anyway, she said the minimum temperature tonight would be 36 Celsius or 97 Fahrenheit. I reckon it's warmer. It was close on 120 today."

Esther had found the Voice of America station and, for a change, it was coming over with a strong and uninterrupted signal. The midnight news was just finishing and, as always, it would be followed by Bria's favourite jazz programme, the one with the DJ Conover he had mentioned. The prospect of it put him in an even happier mood and with the sharp crack of the ring pull on a can of lager, he announced to the girls. "Here he comes . . . ten past midnight every night of the week except Sunday when it's orchestral hour, the world's best DJ — Willis Conover. Wait till you hear how laid back this guy is. If he spoke at 50 words to the minute he'd be in a hurry."

He mimicked the American when he came on air with the same announcement that had made him something of a radio legend to VOA listeners around the world for the past 30 years. The introduction was always the same. First the bass drum beat then the trombones and the opening bars of Ellington playing Ellington and *Take the 'A' Train*. Then on would come Conover and that deep, urbane, and so unhurried speech of his.

"Time . . . for . . . jaaaazzz.

"W-i-l-l-i-s C-o-n-o-v-e-r in . . .

"Washington

"D.C. with

"The Voice of

"America

"Jazz

"Hour."

"How did you know he would say that and the way he did it?" they asked him.

"Because I've had a mis-spent adulthood. I was weaned from every other kind of music by that very same Willis Conover. Do you know, I think I've heard him on that Voice of America programme in at least 30 different countries? Funny thing is, about the only place you can't seem to pick him up is in the States. I owe some of the happiest moments of my life to that guy . . . he introduced me to Stan Kenton, Gerry Mulligan, Stan Getz, Lee Konitz, Kai Winding . . .."

"Who are these ones?" Esther asked.

"Do you know any of them, Amar?"

She shook her head.

"What a couple of squares you are. Okay, so I like Madonna and Springsteen too . . . but I'd still rather have the musicians Willis Conover plays."

The drinks were still cool in the big double-skinned Esky boxes in which they had brought their supplies for the weekend. Conover was playing a programme of Modern Jazz Quartet music and the girls said they liked it, though admitting they had never heard of them before. There was a slight breeze and it was eddying to and fro from the sea and then back behind them off the jebels, varying the temperature startlingly, the jebels having soaked the stupendous heat of the day's sun then released it with the breeze like some gigantic storage heater, making their bodies glisten even more with sweat. Then it would switch towards the sea again and the relief seemed all the more as the sweat beads cooled, then chilled slightly. It was a delightful sensation.

"You know," said Bria, flipping back the tab of another can of beer, "this whole scenario, as the Americans would say, is for unreal. Unbelievable really. Here I am by the edge of the Arabian Sea . . . this glorious heat where you can lie out all night under the stars with not a stitch on . . . that water gently lapping down there . . . a can of cool Fozzies in my hand . . . that lovely music from the MJQ . . . and two most gorgeous girls right by me. You know, it's stories like this they don't believe in pubs in London or Melbourne.

"Did you see some of those Arabs further up the coast today beside those little communities with their freshwater wadis and all that food just hanging off the trees and the sea out there literally boiling with sardines and kingfish?

And there they were up on the hillsides. You could see them, lying asleep in the cool shade of cavemouths and other places. They say the Garden of Eden was up the Gulf. I reckon they got it wrong. These ones up that coast there . . . that's a real paradise kind of life."

Reporting to Billy

THE FIRST THING he had wanted to ask Billy Bainbridge when he reported to him later that week for one of their regular meetings on the progress with the book was if there had been any developments in the story of the men from Razak. But he didn't want to place any undue importance on the subject and so, as usual, they spoke first of all about the work.

"The more photographs I take the more difficult I'm finding it," he told the colonel. "What I don't want to do is miss out any of the gems. In order that that doesn't happen I think I'll have to visit every one, well every one in the Capital Area at least. Do you know how many there were at the last count? Five hundred and eleven, and that's just in this one area. And every time you turn your back, there's another new one."

"But the Minister wants the very best of them, Brian. He places a lot of importance in this work. I mean, being the politician he is, there can be, what shall we say . . . advantages, prestige-wise, that is, in being seen to be the inspiration behind a project like this. I know they are all good Muslims but showing the religious authorities that you are that bit better . . . well, it can't do any harm, can it?"

"Is that why some of them have spent fortunes to build mosques of their own, like that one they've just finished with the dome of leaf gold? God, the dome itself must have cost a mint.   Anyway, work is progressing, but painfully slowly at times. Some days I'm lucky to get two done in the same day. You know what it can be like. They'll read my letter of clearance from the Ministry first of all then they'll want to make a phone call to check that I am who I say I am and that the letter is really geniune. And after that they'll either say 'tomorrow insha'allah' or else it's prayer time and I've got to wait. But what I do most of the time now is wander around like some innocent tourist taking shots for the family album. It's an old Fleet Street dodge. And it works. I did five last Tuesday and wasn't asked a question once. Part of the trick too is getting your timing right to avoid the prayers. I reckon I must be the *Observer*'s most faithful reader of the daily guide column which gives the five prayer times. Bit like studying a railway timetable."

It was the colonel who changed the subject and Brian could scarcely conceal his delight that the question was about Gordon Watson. "By the way, Brian, how's your friend, what's his name, the Scottish chappie who was in Zamakh?"

"Oh yes," he replied, as though he hadn't been giving the subject any thought. "Gordon Watson you mean? Yes . . . yes, he's fine. Still getting over that terrible time he had in Zamakh. It must have been really grim. And he got a real shock when he learned from the police later that the Pakistani acquaintance he met there was murdered."

"Murdered, my goodness. What happened?"

"The police say they don't know. They found him dead in his cell with his throat cut. Anyway, I did tell Watson like you said that he wasn't to speak about the Razak affair and he accepted that. But then the other day when he was down at the Fish Souk he spotted a couple of the men from Razak who were in the same cell block as him."

"Should there be something unusual in that?"

"Well, what with them being sort of mysterious-like inside the prison and him being kind of fascinated with their various activities there, he decided to follow them. They went up a few alleys and lanes at the back of the market and there they met up with some Europeans who came in a car with Abu Dhabi numberplates. I know you like to keep your ear close to the ground on things like that. What do you read into it?"

"Where did he follow them to, did you say?"

"Oh, I didn't pay all that much attention to him. But it was to some particular house in the vicinity."

"On that evidence, Brian, my view is that the chaps from Razak are running a brothel and had found themselves some sailor boys as customers. Nevertheless, though, I'll make a few inquiries. You never know about these things."

At that he stood up in that same abrupt fashion he always did when announcing that the interview was over.

"Bloody hell," Bria thought to himself. "I'll beat the bastard to it one of those days."

The buzzer went on the secretary's phone as Brian Bria closed the door behind him. "Norma . . . make an appointment for me with the Minister. But first of all get me Superintendent Stott on the line. That's right . . . Superintendent Stanley Stott at Police Headquarters in Qurat."

The voice was more cheerful than normal when he was told who was on the line to him. "Good morning, colonel. Are you surviving Ramadan well?"

"Oh, we'll get there all right. Though I do miss popping in to read the *Telegraph* with a gin at the English Pub in the Inter-Continental. But never mind, it will all be over soon, thankfully. Oh, seeing as you've mentioned it brings me to just why I'm calling you. There's a chap that's been reported to me who's got a bit of a reputation for driving under the influence. I'm told he's been in Zamakh once already for it but he doesn't seem to have learned from that experience. He drinks mainly at the Rani. Has a Thursday night smash there, so my informants say. Then he's damn lucky not to have another smash on his way home, silly fool. And not even Ramadan has kept him sober. Drinks around a few friends' houses and still drives around."

"You've got his name?"

"Yes. It's Watson. Scottish fellow. Gordon Watson. Well known about the place, I'm told."

"Leave it with me, sir. We'll take care of him."

"Good show, Stanley. How's the family?"

"Fine. My eldest daughter was married at home last week."

"Goodness . . . that age already! Right. I'll keep in touch."

"Spoil Me"

THE LIGHTS were burning in his sixth-floor flat as he drove into the courtyard of the magnificent 11-storey block they called Hamat House. Brian Bria smiled to himself. He had given Esther the spare key and she said she would be there in the late afternoon to prepare a meal for them.

Hamat House was rated one of the finest blocks of flats in the entire Gulf. The builders had subcontracted to a German company and all of the interior fittings had been shipped out from Germany: the double glazing; the heavy, natural-finish wooden doors with special keys, the numbers of which every tenant had to have noted, for if they were lost replacements would only be made by the company which supplied them in Germany; kitchens by Bosch and Alno; and each flat with a main door that had a real novelty for the Gulf . . . a spy-hole. They didn't need or use such devices in the Gulf but that was the way the Germans supplied their sturdy outside doors and, so be it, the first spy-hole doors had arrived. Such were the standards that one of the Germans who lived at the flats had confided to Brian one day: "Do you know the nationals here are not ready for these houses? I mean, they are of our best German standard. They are not ready for that. Already one of them has had a wedding party . . . in the underground car park! And we found another family keeping their Indian boy down there too. I'm telling you, they are not ready for these houses yet."

Esther answered the door, wearing the briefest of shorts and a blouse which had an extra button undone.

"Now, I hope you used that spy-hole before answering the door," he said, holding her close in a warm embrace. "God, if that had been someone in a dishdasha and you opened the door to him like that, the poor bloke would have fainted. Or else raped you on the spot. Hey, what's cooking? That's a great smell. What have you been making?"

"Kre kre. I wrote to my mother for the recipe. We made the first part at the flats and I've brought some here to put in the other parts. I've never cooked it before. I hope you like it."

"Kre kre! That's the Filipino dish you told me about. The one with the beef nose, tripe, trotters, peanuts, garlic, salted shrimps, cabbage and everything else. Don't see it taking over from steak, egg and chips. I'm only joking. Smells super. It really does."

"You shouldn't have come already. It will be more than an hour yet."

"Good. Let's crack a bottle of Australian champagne."

"They make it in Australia? That one, the champagne?"

"Esther, love, they make everything in Australia. When it comes to making things for drinking, well, they're past masters. Make the best beer. The finest wines. And this is not a bad little number in the old champers line. I know you don't drink, but you will join me? I'm trying your Filipino dish with the name that sounds like committing suicide, so you might as well try a little drink of Aussie bubbly. It's harmless stuff. A bit like lemonade with a grape flavour."

"Mmmmmm," she smiled after taking a sip from the glass he had poured for her. "It's so bubbly. But it's not too bad. Won't it make me do strange things?"

"Just watch me object if it does, love. Gosh, you've no idea how glad I am that you're here tonight, Esther. I've had a bloody horrible day worrying about Gordon."

"You said on the phone he had disappeared. Why is that?"

"I wish I knew. No one has heard a thing from him for five days now. I've checked all his mates, his office. And I'm no further on. But I'm going to have to do something to try and find him. Then, maybe I'm worrying too much. He'll probably turn up wondering why we were so concerned. God, that champagne is going down a treat. Here, have another glass."

"I'm sorry about your friend, Brian. It is not nice what has happened, eh?"

"No. No, it's certainly not nice."

"And Brian, I have news. We got word this week, some of the other nurses and myself. We have to go to Jordan for our examinations, you know the C.G.F.N.S. one?"

"Yes, what does it stand for again?"

"The Commission of Graduates of the Foreign Nursing School. If I pass I can apply for a job as a nurse in America."

"I thought you were coming to Australia with me?"

"Do you still want that? Men, you know, say things and make many promises, and then sometimes without even telling you they can change their minds. It is no good, eh?"

"No, it's certainly no good. But I still want you to come to Australia. You can work there with your C.G.F. . . . whatever it is. When do you go to Jordan anyway?"

"Tomorrow. We will be there for one week, returning on the Gulf Air night flight on the 19th. The exam is in two parts and is very difficult. Only a few of the last lot of Filipinas who went there passed it."

"You'll be there for a week, you say? That means you will miss the big Eid al Fitr festival, you know the one that marks the end of Ramadan? It's due next Tuesday. That's May the 17th I think. Yes, that's right. Today's Thursday the 12th. And you don't come back till the 19th. A pity. Some of the nationals at the Ministry were telling me all about Eid the other day. They were saying it was one of the best times of the year to be here."

"But they have the Eid celebrations in Jordan too."

"Yes, but it would have been nice had you been here. We could have gone out together and joined the crowds. It's a bit like Christmas, they say, with everyone all dressed up in their best togs, carrying presents for visiting. It's quite an occasion apparently."

"Yes, I remember it once in Jordan. It was so different for they don't have many celebrations, these Arab ones. Not like we do in the Philippines."

"Will you be seeing him when you go to Jordan?"

"Who?"

"You know. Your old boyfriend."

"What would you say if I said I was?"

"I wouldn't say anything. I might think a lot, though. Well, you haven't answered. Will you see him?"

She laughed and took his hand. "You are a crazy one, Brian. Of course I'm not. I never want to see him again. What about you? Will you be seeing Amar when I'm away?"

"Now there's a strange thing to ask. Why did you think I might?"

"Because she likes you."

"How do you know?"

"Women can tell these things much better then men. And you did not say yes or no."

He laughed at that. "Now who's the crazy one? Esther, darling, Amar is the furthest thing from my mind at this moment."

"So what is on your mind?"

"You. You and the way you looked when you stood there at the door tonight. And that blouse . . . it does something for you." He slowly unbuttoned it. "And it does even more for you . . . off."

She was wearing only a loose nylon slip top beneath. Her ample nipples stood erect through the transparent material. Then she stood up slowly after he had taken off her blouse and, with a sensuous smile, lazily crossed her arms to her waist and pulled the slip over her head. Then she slowly unzipped her shorts, stepped out of her skimpy briefs and stood in the dim light of the room, before laying down on the couch beside him, helping him to undress.

"God, you spoil me, girl. You really do," he whispered into her ear as they embraced and she folded into him. "You spoil me . . . spoil me . . . spoil me . . ."

A Red Alert Meeting

LONDON, 1987. The two men had met in the Dorchester Hotel in London. The choice of meeting place was, like most things in Mustafa Ali Abdullah's life, meticulously pre-planned. If he were to go down in history as a man who made his mark in the story of the Gulf, then the part he played would be told with great flourish and detail. As part of that detail it had been a fact that one episode in the history of his area of the world had ended in the Dorchester. For it had been in this very hotel that the exiled former Emir had spent the remaining years of his life till his death in 1978. Mustafa planned that if one chapter of his country's history had ended there then another should begin in the same place.

The arrangement was that Mustafa and Colonel Billy Bainbridge should rendezvous in the Promenade Lounge of the hotel for a pre-lunch drink. Mustafa and the colonel had first met in Kuwait and had got to know each other through regular British Embassy meetings and functions. Bainbridge had been a captain at the time and had been posted to Kuwait following the ending of the Jebel Ahmar War in 1959. He was to remain in Kuwait until 1961, when the British left in the hasty withdrawal from colonies and possessions and areas euphemistically deemed Protectorates that lay East of Suez.

Abdullah had been as fastidious about his contacts as he was about his pre-planning. A note was made of everyone he met . . . everyone, that is, he thought might be of some use to him at some time in the future, no matter how distant that point in the future might be. Every person had a worth to him — they might be able to provide for him or he might be able to make use of them, whether by favour or by other means. Time and time again such contacts had paid off in a variety of ways, not least being the means of an introduction to someone else who could help in a business negotiation. They had spoken highly of Bainbridge at the Embassy, saying that he was a man likely to go places in the Army. That alone was worthy of an entry in the voluminous notes he kept about such contacts.

After he left Kuwait, Bainbridge was posted to the Parachute Regiment Depot at Aldershot but was to return twice to the Gulf on detachment to the Trucial Oman Scouts, where he again met up with Mustafa during business trips to Abu Dhabi and Dubai. Later, after Mustafa had returned to live in Emirate, they were to meet many times when Bainbridge, by this time a major, was serving with the SAS in Dhofar and would spend many of his leaves in Emirate. There were few facilities in the country in those days, but there was always comfortable room for him with good food and drinks at the Abdullah family home, an old verandahed building filled with the stench of dry rot situated just back from the jewel of a harbour on to which faced the British Embassy and the Emir's Palace.

More than 15 years after that period the name Bainbridge was to come to the attention of Mustafa Ali Abdullah once again. He had sent his eldest son to London in order to make an assessment of the new generation of security/protection firms which were springing up there. They were mainly staffed by former Special Air Service, Parachute Regiment and Special Boat Squadron men — people whose lives had been dedicated to the art of war, the skills of survival, the business of death. The pattern for many of these *nouveaux* agencies was to litter their board rooms with names of utter respectability. British firms had been doing that for years, of course, but some of these security companies thought there was a greater need than usual to be seen as respectable. Particularly favoured for their boards were former chief constables, senior Army commanders and the like, especially those men who had made a notable mark in public life and who in their time had become well-known faces in TV interviews and in the Press. One such firm had just signed a Commissioner of the London Metropolitan Police to join their staff which already included a previous Commissioner, as well as a former Commander of the Army in Northern Ireland. There was work galore for these new private armies and they were well able to afford the huge sums that were needed to recruit such men as former London Police Commissioners, the last one having left a job that had paid him more than £62,000 a year. The new firm was able to improve on that sum. Considerably.

Some of the firms relied on their achievements in certain areas of security work, others on their knowledge and expertise in particular locations of the world. Some restricted their activities to the conventional, others built a reputation for the questionable. The Beirut bomb that was meant for Ayatollah Fadhl-Allah, spiritual leader of the Lebanese Party of Allah, was arranged through one of the latter. The bomb, incidentally, missed the man for whom it was meant and 80 innocents were killed in one of the city's worst bombings. In the same category were the companies mentioned in the Irangate hearings who were hired to carry out operations in Nicaragua.

Mustafa had rejected the use of such companies. The firm he wanted had to have no "form" or anyone asking what they might be up to next because of a Gulf connection. Neither did he want the biggest of the agencies, particularly those with board-room men who had previously been such prominent figures. He had suspected that their directorial boards would be too reputable and of such esteem that they would still be the kind of people who had the ear of men in the Cabinet rooms of more than one country. What Mustafa had in mind was for the ear of no one else.

Red Alert's brochure appealed to him. It was on the short list recommended by his son after his visit to London for that purpose. Under the heading "Special Forces Skills", the company detailed some of its activities:

Counter Terrorist Teams;

Quick Reaction Forces;

Counter Insurgency Expertise;

Arabian Gulf Specialists.

But the most appealing item in the publicity matter was the name which headed the roll of directors — Colonel B. Bainbridge, M.C. A few telephone calls quickly established that it was, in fact, the same Bainbridge who had been the captain he had known in Kuwait, the major he had entertained so frequently in Emirate. He would be the perfect man for the job. So Red Alert it would be.

The meeting was set for midday and Bainbridge, the punctilious military man, was there ahead of time. He paced the long Promenade Lounge, admiring the gold-topped salmon marble pillars and the five magnificent brass lantern lamps which dominated the spacious and imposing lounge. He stopped to gaze at the delightful Dorchester Charity Polo trophy of two prancing horses in bronze, then turned to cast a disapproving eye on the exposed threads of the patterned carpets, thinking that if he were in charge they would have been replaced. The sight of the tailed waiters cheered him, however; they seemed smart and efficient and there wasn't enough of that in the Britain of 1987 where so many standards had fallen off. There were two girl waiters too, formally dressed in jackets and skirts, but just as smart and cheerfully efficient as the men.

"It will be because of this 'We're an equal opportunity employer' thing," he thought. "Oh well, it's all right if they're as damned smart as these girls."

One of them approached, smiling, and proffered a drinks list card. He said he would wait for his friend but studied the card when she had left, raising his eyebrows at the £82 price charge for a bottle of Taittinger Blanc de Blankes Brut '79, and raising them even further at the £86 for the Cuvée Dom Perignon. "Bloody disgraceful," he mumbled.

Dead on 12 o'clock Mustafa appeared. Bainbridge was sitting where he could see the entrance lobby and those who came into the hotel and was caught unawares by Mustafa who had recognised him first. It had been the first time he had seen him out of his national dress and without his head covered by the usual Gulf Arab head-dress or the casual kooma cap. The Gulf élite could look quite splendid in their national dress, particularly in their full costume when they topped their dishdasha with the gold-fringed black bisht robe and wore their magnificient khanjar daggers of gold, ivory and silver. Savile Row had no such splendour. Mustafa's full head of dark, wavy hair helped display a much more youthful man than Bainbridge imagined he would be after such a time. He hadn't realised it before, but seeing him as he was in his expensive Western dress, the tailored shirt, the silk tie with its large diamond tie stud and other diamonds glistening on his gold watch, doubtlessly an Ebel, he thought him the image of that famous Egyptian film star, the one whose name, like all film stars it seemed, he could never recall but who had played his supporting role so well in *Lawrence of Arabia.*

They greeted each other in Arabic, going through the customary ritual of inquiries about wives and children and friends and health and how each other was keeping, Mustafa then switching to English to comment that it was the first time he could recall meeting Bainbridge out of Army uniform and how his civilian clothes made him look much younger than he imagined he would.

"Now there's a coincidence," replied Bainbridge, "for I was having similar thoughts about yourself, seeing you dressed as you are. Life is obviously doing you well."

"I have no complaints."

They had drinks first and a brief navigational sort of discussion before adjourning to the Grill Restaurant, which Mustafa said was one of his favourite eating places in the city. The sommelier made it obvious that he was known to him, calling him Mr Abdullah and inquiring, "Will the usual be all right, sir?"

"I assume you don't mind a little champagne, Billy?" he inquired. "I find it most refreshing at this time of day." A bottle of the Cuvée Dom Perignon was quickly cradled beside them. Billy did not lift his eyebrows.

"Champagne and fine food," smiled Bainbridge. "Didn't Ramadan begin last week?"

"You're thinking that I have a troubled conscience about such things. Aren't you? Well, I don't. I'm a good Muslim in my country. But I feel no guilt in breaking our religious code when I am here. Mind you, I would be ashamed if it were known that I was breaking the fast. But it will not be known, therefore there is no shame. There is such a gap, you see, between the ethics of our life in the Gulf and the degeneracies of the West. So our reaction to such things as having drink and good food during Ramadan is a bit like one of your businessmen going to the naughty places of Paris or Amsterdam. One tends to partake in such delights when released from the strictures of home . . . does one not?"

Without saying so, Bainbridge equated the analogy with some of his own experiences in much less salubrious places than London and smiled and nodded in agreement.

"I know you understand . . . Colonel. Congratulations, by the way, on reaching that rank before you left the Army. Tell me — and I hope you don't mind my asking — but was it a very great blow to you when they passed you over for promotion to brigadier?"

He studied him closely for his reaction knowing the impact of the question. A waiter serving their meal gave him the blessing of an interruption and a better opportunity to assess his response. "The salmon for you, Mr Abdullah, and the rib of beef for you, sir," he had said.

Mustafa let him linger with his thoughts as he praised the salmon. "You know, I simply adore the fish here. So full of flavour. I think our warm waters in the Gulf do something to our fish. Doesn't have that same, what's the word for it . . . piquancy?"

"So you know I was passed over? Word does get around, I know. Nevertheless, my compliments to your sources. But how did I feel, you ask? Yes . . . I was aggrieved. It was unjustified. And it made me turn my back on the thing I loved in life most of all . . . the Army."

"You know, I was reading about these people of yours who have turned traitor and had all these books written about them, you know, these spy people. Well, it has been noted that most of them had one thing in common and that is they were passed over at one time or other in their work. And it played on their minds so much that they devoted the rest of their lives working against their employer, which, of course, meant them working against their own country. It was their kind of way of getting their own back on the boss, as it were."

"Yes, I know such things can have a devastating effect on a man, particularly when the man is so dedicated to his job, so dedicated that it becomes a greater love to him even than his family. Then one day, for no apparent reason, his master betrays that love by appointing someone ahead of him. It is perfectly understandable that they become traitors. Nevertheless, I still abhor treason and those who are party to it."

It was Mustafa who changed the line of conversation. "Your company, Billy . . . Red Alert. It interests me greatly. In fact, and I hope you don't mind, but I've been making inquiries about your organisation and its activities."

"Yes, your son went to considerable trouble in his investigations."

"You knew he was here?" said Mustafa, concealing as best he could his great surprise that his son's visit to London had been known about.

"Oh yes," said Bainbridge, matter of fact. "He started with two other companies first of all — Pegasus then Special Activity Services, who as you can imagine called themselves that for the connotation of their initials — before he started his dossier on us."

"Purely out of curiosity . . . just how did you know? I mean, did he make it all that obvious?"

"Not at all. Your son behaved with every discretion . . . every discretion, that is, of the untrained information gatherer. He even went to the length of checking out the private detective agency he hired to help him. And his conclusions were right too. They were a reputable company . . . yes, very respectable lads they were."

"But that doesn't tell me how you found out."

"Well, I take it your son mentioned that our staff isn't entirely made up of those hairy but rather handsome and very active ex-SAS soldiers. We also have some very pukka gentlemen who left good positions with MI5 and MI6 to be with us. There's not much they miss, particularly when anyone is asking questions about us. In fact, people who make inquiries about us are the very first people we, in turn, start making inquiries about. You never know why some people want to know about you. And that includes our own Scotland Yard who spend countless hours assessing us. It is rather imperative that we keep an eye on those checking on us. I mean to say, how would it be, for instance, if a Minister of some foreign government were to come and ask our company to perform a very hush-hush job in his country . . . and then word of his actions got back to his leader?"

It was the colonel's turn now to study reaction and there were no hovering waiters to give the man sitting opposite him a respite to manufacture his reaction. There was no concealing his surprise this time and it was all he could do to prevent himself from visibly gasping.

"I think it's time for a fresh bottle of Dom Perignon. And for you, Billy?"

"I'll share."

Ordering the champagne bought him the time it needed to get over the shock of wondering just how much Bainbridge knew. "So after you discovered my son was collecting his information, you and your men started making inquiries about me and my country?"

"Naturally. I wouldn't have liked coming here today unprepared and without some knowledge of why you wanted to see me. That would have been most unprofessional."

"And what did you find out?"

"Enough to compile our own small dossier, which is now very obviously highly classified. But in your case, Mustafa . . . an old friend, and a potential customer, I think I can tell you. The conclusion of the dossier is that you resent being your country's Minister for Public Buildings and you would very much like to be something more . . . prestigious, shall we say? Your resentment is quite natural for you are an able and talented man, much more so than many of the Ministers who are senior to you. In fact, as you mentioned yourself, you are exactly in the category of our men, you know, the spy people who turn traitor. You love your country but you feel you've been passed over. I share your feelings. But we weren't quite sure, however, just where Red Alert would fit in. Several theses were made, but I wasn't all that happy with their conclusions. And that's about all I can tell you."

"I'm most impressed. Well, at least you have justified the work and the recommendations of my son. He will get a special thanks for that when I return home. Now I take it that you haven't been back to the Gulf since you left after Dhofar?"

"That's right. But I've been keeping abreast of developments. I read every report I can. I meet as many visitors as possible here in London, which has increasingly become the Arab's second home. And many of my old Army buddies are still out there."

"Might that not be a handicap should it be that you were to return one day?"

"That surely would depend on the job that would be involved in any return."

"Supposing that job meant doing something of which your old friends there would disapprove?"

"I don't ask old chums to approve or disapprove of any of my actions. If I did, there wouldn't be a company called Red Alert."

"But you couldn't keep it from your old friends . . . the fact that you were back in the Gulf again."

"No, that is true. The word would get around very fast. But none of them would ever dream I would be involved in anything that you might have in mind, such as a coup or the like."

"Colonel Bainbridge . . . your mind moves very fast."

"Slow minds tend to get left behind, particularly in the kind of business I'm in now."

"You mentioned the word 'coup' there. Was that mentioned in any of the theses your men thought out and which you rejected?"

"No. None of them came up with that. Coup was my thesis."

"I see. And it didn't put you off coming here today and discussing that very subject?"

"No . . . discussions don't put me off."

"But you are interested enough to want to find out more?"

"That's right."

"Tell me, Billy, do major tasks not concern or daunt a company like Red Alert? I mean, really major tasks?"

"Daunt . . . no. Concern . . . yes. The concern being for the customer and whether he is able to cope with anything we might achieve for him and his associates."

"What would be your thesis, then, on the ability of this particular customer to cope with anything which you might achieve for him and his partners in his country?"

"I did think about that. My conclusion was that you were as competent as anyone at governmental level in your region of the world to handle whatever may come your way."

"Your confidence in me is appreciated."

"Right, Mustafa. Isn't it time we called off our little war game . . . and played at actual war itself? What do you have in mind for me and Red Alert?"

"Quite briefly, to create the sort of conditions whereby I could form a new Government and take over the leadership of my country."

"A tall order. A very tall order. I must know more. Why, apart from your own ambition, should you want such a dramatic change of events there? I mean, everything seems fine in your land. You're one of the most stable areas in the Middle East. Oh, I know the volatility is not far below the surface . . . there was the Sharjah affair earlier this year and that was between two brothers. That showed up the rivalry between Abu Dhabi and Dubai, each backing the other. There's Saudi ready to stir up trouble with its Communist neighbours in the two Yemens and Bahrain and Kuwait have had their bombings and assassination attempts by the Fundamentalists."

"It's time we had change. The Family have been in power too long. New blood is needed. We have become too complacent, too reliant on the Americans. We need to stand on our own feet more and not be a mouse that runs when the big cats around us bare their teeth. There is still much to be done. We have had a proposal now for years to build a new oil pipeline which could bring all the oil from our side of the Gulf through our country to our ocean terminal. Do you realise what that would mean? No ships would ever have to pass through the dreaded Straits of Hormuz or go up the Gulf again, for they could collect the West's oil at our terminal which is outside the Gulf. But instead of going ahead and building it ourselves we are waiting on others. It would only cost one to two billion dollars at the most and be ready in two years. The money could be raised . . . easily. We have become too conservative in our thinking. And I mean conservative with a small 'c', not your lady leader's kind of conservatism."

"And what kind of scenario do you imagine could bring about the kind of conditions which would be appropriate in your country for what you have in mind?"

"Something on the scale of the events of 20 November 1979 and 6 October 1981 . . .."

The colonel cut in at that. "The attack on the Grand Mosque in Mecca by Mahdi and his followers and the frontal assassination of Muhammad Anwar Sadat of Egypt with his generals?"

"Your contemporary Arabic history is quite sound, Billy. But then I didn't expect it would be otherwise."

"These were events of considerable magnitude. Enormous magnitude."

"But you said your main concern at Red Alert was whether your clients could handle the results of what you achieved for them, not the actual achieving itself."

"Yes, quite so. But that was in relation to the scale of what firms, such as my own, and including the biggest of them have done in this sort of work so far. But this . . . well, this is a considerable escalation of security agency work as we know it."

"Moving into another gear, as the Americans would put it."

"Precisely."

"Well, are you going to be the first who moves into overdrive?"

"The stakes are, to say the least, quite fantastic, Mustafa. I mean, playing with the future of an entire country."

"Not playing, Billy. Changing."

"Are the rewards commensurate with the scale of the operation?"

"I would think so. One million pounds deposited in your company's account the day after you take on the commitment and another million when the mission is accomplished."

"The money . . . the two million . . . is it all your own money?"

"The amount would be of no problem to me. But the answer is that we are a consortium. The wealth from our oil made many people rich and it made some people very, very rich."

"Getting back to the scenario once again. The attack in Mecca and the assassination of Sadat were, as you know, carried out by Fundamentalists. What is their presence at the moment in your part of the Gulf?"

"Well, if you ask any of the mullahs or the civil servants at the Ministry of Religious Affairs they will proclaim to you that there are none or if one does confess that there are some, he will assure you that they are of such a tiny number that they do not constitute any form of problem. But they know and I know that we have them. We have Fundamentalists of varying degrees. We have many Shi'ites who have been living and working in our country from India and Pakistan. They have been coming to us for the past three decades or so and there is strong support from many sections of them for the Fundamentalists.

"There is also Khomeinist activity directed against our country by way of the recruitment of militants and infiltrators who encourage as many as they can to listen to Tehran Radio's Arabic programme. We are not without their attention. Four years ago the Iranians were speaking about seizing one of our islands. Revolutionary Guards even had a rehearsal of how they would take the island. But then their war with Iraq diverted their attention from that. Yes, we have the Fundamentalists all right and when they have finished their war with Iraq we will be getting a lot more attention from the Iranians."

"But your proposed coup wouldn't change any of that."

"No . . . but then perhaps there is a Fundamentalist streak in the consortium who are promoting the coup."

"Oh . . . so that's the way of it. That being the case, then, why are you not masterminding the takeover yourselves?"

"My friend . . . that would have involved us dealing with our fellow countrymen. Despite what may be happening to you English in recent times, the behaviour of your sporting followers and the way your standards, your morals are, shall we say, not the same as they used to be, despite all that, I still attribute one great quality in you . . . trust. I would not so easily trust any of my countrymen to do what I am asking of you. There would be perfidy. Also, most of the wars in which you were engaged were against the insurrectionist. You know how they work. You know their minds. You know how to manipulate them. My faith is in you and whatever specialists you require to bring with you to achieve what we wish."

"Are you anticipating lots of bloodshed?"

"Not lots. Only the appropriate. Wars are where you have bloodshed and suffering. I would not wish that on my country. Only those who are vital must be put out of the way."

"But getting back to my point that our concern at Red Alert is whether or not clients can handle the results of what we achieve for them, how do you expect you and your new Government will handle the Fundamentalists if it is seen by the population that they were the force behind the coup?"

"My game of chess has many moves. The only media in the country is that owned and controlled by the Government. Together with the news of the event it will be made clear that the new rule is not of those who perpetrated the terrible deed but that we are only in power because of that deed. Therefore our new Government will be immediately accepted by the people and the revenge will be for the followers of those who carried it out. The Fundamentalists will be contained . . . the natural course of events will see to that."

"But what about the Fundamentalist streak in your consortium?"

"There are Fundamentalists of many shades. They are not of the shade of the Ayatollah's men."

"So, in short, you wish Red Alert to bring about the conditions that will inspire the removal of your leaders. And the timescale for all this?"

"Well, this is Ramadan, 1987. I would want everything concluded by the end of Ramadan, 1988."

"And your proposals for getting me and whoever I want to accompany me to your country . . . it's not the easiest land in the world to get into."

"Everything has been taken care of. You are coming as my public relations adviser at the Ministry of Public Buildings. And one of your first assignments — overt assignments, that is — is to mastermind a book for the Ministry on all our beautiful mosques. One of these very prestigious things, so hire the best photographer you know. Working on that and some other things for the Ministry will give you all the freedom you desire to move around and make the — what is it you call it? — the field study that will be necessary for the main mission. The book, by the way, is no pretext. I really do want one published."

"And supposing I need to bring out some of my . . . specialists?"

"There's no problem there. We can arrange business visas for them which will enable them to do whatever they may have to do."

"Of course, one of the main problems will be maintaining the secrecy of the operation. I mean, there are many ears apart from your Internal Security Service."

"Such as?"

"The Russians, of course. They have Spetsnaz units operating in the area ready to move at instant notice to any part of the region where they think they can be of use."

"I'm sorry, but I'm not aware of these people . . . Spets . . . ?"

"Spetsnaz. They are the most élite of all the Russian specialist forces and, dare I say it, even more élite than our SAS men. And that's a fact I know but never breathe."

"And you say they are ready to go where they think they can be of use?"

"Yes. Just like in Sharjah earlier in the year. They were preparing to go there and stir up trouble. But they were called off at the last minute when it was seen that the affair would quickly blow over. Stirring up trouble is their speciality. They infiltrate. They create havoc in a situation where trouble and chaos is the required remedy in the hope of toppling a government, then they move quietly out again before anyone even knows they have been there."

"Spetsnaz . . . have I got it right?"

"Correct. Spetsnaz."

"And they specialise in havoc and disorder and making the conditions ripe for a change of government?"

"That's precisely what they're about."

"And you say there are some of them in our region?"

"There is a force of them in the People's Democratic Republic of Yemen. They're probably based at the Soviet submarine base on the Socotra Islands. They get that in return for the $1,400 million in economic aid that they're giving to the PDRY plus of course building them a power station in Aden, reconstruction assistance and the establishment and funding of oil exploration units, although the joke is they're not having much success at finding oil for the Yemenis."

"And they use submarines for travel?"

"Well, they're not exactly the kind of people who arrive in your country with forged passports and visas. Yes, submarine landings by night is their usual method. They could land anywhere in that entire Gulf without being detected . . . and move off just the same."

"And when they do the work they have to do they simply move out again just as they came in?"

"Yes . . . and I'm not that slow, Mustafa. You see them as a help rather than a hindrance to your plans."

"Why not? I presume you would have it in your power to make some form of contact with them?"

"They're not in my telephone contacts lists, but I know what you mean. Yes, I'm sure they would jump at the appropriate bait. Take, for instance, supporters of the People's Front for the Liberation of the Arabian Gulf? You and some of your neighbours still have them around. If they were to get wind of what was happening, it would soon go to the people to whom they report in Aden."

"And from there to the Spetsnaz?"

"Undoubtedly. But that's just one example. There will be various other ways we can get the bait to them."

"Well, I must say, Colonel Bainbridge, this is a much better meeting than I anticipated."

"Even though I haven't said whether or not Red Alert will take on the commission?"

"One can assume, can't one? However, I'll be more direct. Can Red Alert handle the project?"

"Yes . . . we can handle the project all right. I'm just mulling over the morals of it all."

"The morals! Morality, I thought, was the prerogative of the politician, not the soldier, especially the mercenary."

"Mercenary is a rather harsh word for us, Mustafa."

"Nevertheless, appropriate. Organisations like yours have men of great honour serving with them . . . honour, that is, for Queen and country one day, and the very next day their allegiance is to the company and the money it pays them. I know what they've been doing in Ireland and Beirut and the Iran connection. Mercenaries are a fact of life, as you well know. I'm not condemning them. Indeed, I couldn't be thinking about what my project might achieve without them . . . could I? Red Alert can do the project, you say. But will they?"

"Yes."

"I'm so pleased that's the answer. Of course, the venture is not without danger, as you no doubt appreciate. And while you are under my care as my public relations adviser at the Ministry, the rest of your work — your *real* work, that is — will mean your being on your own. If anything comes to light about what you are doing, I will completely disown you. You must realise that. There must be no hitches of any kind in your mission. If there are . . . then you cannot look to me for help. You and whoever comes with you are on your own until all the necessary arrangements are made and finalised. And when that is done you will be on the next plane to London — with the final instalment of your fee."

Revolutionaries, Dissidents and Others

MANY PARTS of Arabia are littered with the supporters of various factions who have been in wars that they have lost or else are the scattered remnants of other causes whose wars are still going on. They are one reason for the high state of tension and the intense security in so many of the Gulf countries, causing them to be among the most exclusive nations in the world in which to gain entry.

Those with a dissident past can trace their revolutionary heritage to a variety of causes and the lands which fostered them around the world. There are those who fought in the war in Dhofar against the forces of the Sultanate of Oman. When that war ended most of them accepted the amnesty offered to them by the Sultan, becoming loyal supporters and stout defenders of his realm. Others, however, went to live in the People's Democratic Republic of Yemen to enjoy the Communist society for which they fought in Dhofar. Some wandered to the new societies of the north where there was work and the chance to save some money and wait for the day when they might be needed again. Among them were men highly skilled in the art of guerrilla warfare, for under the auspices of the Popular Front for the Liberation of Oman and the Arabian Gulf they had been to some of the finest schools in the world to learn that art. Some went to Palestine, others to East Germany, and many to the Chinese who, being fellow Asians, had taken the Arabian revolutionaries under their wing.

Scores of them travelled in the late 'sixties and early 'seventies on charter flights via Bahrain and Bulgaria to China. They were sent to various training centres there, some to the Peking Military School, where they participated in an eight-month intensive course on the theory of guerrilla warfare, followed by several months on an even more intensified term at the school's field operations centre north of Peking, beyond the Great Wall of China where on the horizon they could see mountains higher than any they had ever seen before and the distant land of Tibet. Others were selected to go to Mokanshan in the Province of Chekiang for training at the famous Chinese Intelligence School. There they were joined by students from all over the world, in particular many from the United States, young student anarchists, together with black power negroes, as well as those from the Philippines, Latin America, Thailand and India.

The dissident heritage of others is that of Dr George Habash's Popular Front for the Liberation of Palestine which has proclaimed on many occasions that their work is not confined to Palestine and that their overall strategy is to relieve other countries in the region of their "imperialist puppet régimes". When they list such countries, Emirate is among the forefront of them.

And as the Muslim sects become even more polarised, there are those of the Shi'ite faction who have been participants in the events that have taken place in two neighbouring countries of the Gulf, Kuwait and Bahrain. After Iraq, Kuwait and Bahrain were rated the number two and number three enemies of the new Islamic régime in Iran and with their support there have been several attempts made to overthrow the leaders of both countries. In January 1982 Kuwait suffered a series of attacks on cinemas, restaurants, schools and libraries. Cars belonging to pro-Iraqi businessmen were set on fire and some women wearing un-Islamic clothes, which could mean simply that they were not veiled, were viciously attacked in the street. A year later, with the Party of Allah firmly established in Kuwait, there was a further series of attacks, this time with bombs. Among the targets were American and French embassies and several big business firms. In May 1985 an assassination attempt was made on the Emir himself, Sheikh Jaber al-Ahmed al-Sabah. Several people were killed but the Emir escaped uninjured. Undeterred, the revolutionaries struck again later that year when there was a wave of terror on popular restaurants in the city, places that had committed another Fundamentalist sin. They had allowed men and women to eat together at the same table. At least a dozen people died and more than 100 were injured. The Emir ordered a crackdown by the police on the Fundamentalists and other dissidents and scores of them fled south to Bahrain, others to the scatter of countries on the southern shores of the Gulf.

Bahrain had already experienced its own problems with those in revolt. There had been a coup plot in 1981 by a group who labelled themselves the Islamic Front for the Liberation of Bahrain, whose origins could be traced to the bedsitters of mid-'seventies London. The Bahrain plot was followed by yet another series of expulsions, which cast hundreds out to seek their revolution elsewhere.

Then there are those who consider themselves the élite of the revolutionaries, for to study the subject they have been to the highest universities of their kind, where the masked face and the AK-47 waved over the head were merely the basic elements. In the background of the terrorist game are the learned ones, the manipulators and the plotters, those who enlist and encourage, who conceive and achieve. They were schooled in the land of the great Islamic revolution — Iran. Through contacts mainly in Kuwait and Bahrain, young people from the Gulf joined other students recruited in London, Amsterdam and Paris for the journey to the home of Fundamentalism. There they were graded and sent to the various camps to which they were best suited.

Those considered to be the top grade went to Manzarieh, in the northern suburb of Niavaran in Tehran. It was there that the Shah had his palace and in the splendid suburbs around it were the finest of villas where the wealthy of the capital lived and where the only blight on their beautiful homes was the daily clatter of the comings and goings of the Shah's many helicopters. Apart from its lovely homes and the Shah's palace, Niavaran is known for its fine orchards and open spaces and the huge national park of Manzarieh with its uninterrupted views north to the snow-covered slopes of Mount Towchal in the beautiful Elburz Mountains. In 1977 the park had been the site of that year's Boy Scout Jamboree. It was jamborees of another sort that were to take place there in the 'eighties.

The camp at Manzarieh is the biggest of its kind in Iran, probably the biggest of its like in the world. It's Harvard-Oxbridge of the student revolutionary. A degree from there gives a man status in the eyes of those whose will it is to change the world to their ways. Students from more than 30 different countries regularly attend the lengthy courses which have a curriculum designed only for the dedicated. The day begins with pre-dawn prayers and half an hour of recitation from the Koran followed by an hour and a half of strenuous physical training. Then it's time for ablutions . . . and all that before the 7 a.m. call to breakfast. The pre-dawn activities set the pattern for the rest of the alumni day in which the volunteers are subjected to a régime which approximates that of novice monk, college student and infantry soldier. Graduation for the Iranians among them means a posting to only the finest of regiments, perhaps a unit of the Revolutionary Guard. For the others it means a posting to the action taking place in their own country or else, should their country be at peace, they are told to preach and promote the way of Fundamentalism or else to wait there as "sleepers" until the call comes for whatever kind of revolution may take place there.

There are various other similar institutions in Iran, each with its own speciality, just as any other country would have in its university infrastructure. These include Bojnurd, 370 miles east of Tehran, run by the Revolutionary Guard; Tariq al Qods, north-west of Tehran, for the young men of the Iraqi ad-Da'awah (People of the Call) Party; Ghayour Asli Base, near Ahvaz, in Khuzestan, in the south-west of the country, also used for training Iraqi as well as other Arab guerrillas, all instructions at the camp being in Arabic; Abad, near the holy city of Qom, like Manzarieh, a huge camp where one wing specialises in terrorism; Eram Park, in the outer suburbs of Qom, formerly a hotel and now concentrating on the training of activists from the Middle East, India and Pakistan; Parandak, in the vicinity of Tehran, once used by the National Railways of Iran to train mechanics and drivers, now the home of more than 500 young cadets training for war; Beheshtieh, about 13 miles north-west of Tehran, for women whose call is terrorism and with students from the Arab world as well as America and Ireland.

Then there are the schools where the students can specialise in the refinements of their trade, places like the one at Kharg, a branch of the Beheshtieh school, where hundreds of women are in training as Volunteers for Martyrdom; Mashhad, near the Soviet border in Eastern Iran, for the study of popular models of Boeing passenger aircraft by potential hi-jackers; and Shahid Chamran, in the Bushehr Peninsula, for the grooming of suicide attackers, like the ones who drove the trucks into the American and French camps in Beirut and including pilots ready to take on the American Fleet in the Gulf.

The Shi'ite communities of the Gulf are other areas of likely dissidence. Once they were passive and small in number but with the huge influx of workers from Pakistan and India during the past three decades they have grown considerably. After the events in Iran, many of them turned their eyes — and ears — in that direction. They have become eager audiences for the daily radio programmes in Arabic and Urdu specially broadcast to them from Tehran. Others, in certain locations and with an appropriate TV antennae, can pick up the programmes from across the Gulf which begin in the early evening with the 5.30 news in English read by chador-clad young women with UCLA accents, strange babushka figures with new world voices and old world minds. The newscasts are often followed by lengthy reports from the warfront, where they are living World War One all over again. Often too there will be documentaries on aspects of guerrilla warfare and what better for the medium than to show viewers such enlightening tips as how to dissect and maintain your Kalashnikov AK-47?

The countries of the Gulf have their portion of the revolutionary of one kind or another. Dissident, reactionary, Fundamentalist, agitator, Communist, Imamist, factionalist . . . they are there in a variety of shades. And Emirate has its share of them too.

The Ambitions of a Minister

MUSTAFA ALI ABDULLAH, the Minister of Public Buildings, came from a family which had initially made its fortune from the souk. In the medieval days prior to 1970 there was little need for men of enlightenment in Emirate. Skill and enterprise and knowledge of the tools of progress were anathema to the régime. When those with money sent their sons off to the fine schools and colleges of India and Egypt and England there was little scope for them to put that education into use in their homeland, unless they wanted to be doctors working without the aid of modern drugs or equipment, or to confine themselves to a career with the mosque. The most primitive country in all Arabia didn't want its sons as lawyers or teachers or engineers or architects, for all of these things smacked of advancement and of the ways of the West. They would have none of that in the land on the eastern extremity of the Arab world.

So there was a great migration of people with knowledge and foresight, of those who saw that the better ways of the West were an improvement in life and of those too who thought that the ways of the Muslim and the ways of the modern world could go hand in hand. Thus Emirate had its own diaspora. Some went to East Africa; others to the Gulf countries which were using their new oil wealth for the material benefit of the country and its people and where there was an enormous demand for the educated or entrepreneurial Arab.

Mustafa Ali Abdullah had first of all considered joining the family firm which operated out of the Khudra Souk after his education in Bahrain, the most English of all the Gulf states, where there has been free education since 1919. From Bahrain he went on to Cairo University where he studied law. After the enlightenment of Bahrain and Cairo, the ways of his homeland seemed all the more primitive. Besides, there was much more scope for a man of his ambitions in other lands and, like so many others, he joined the exodus, choosing Kuwait at the head of the Gulf as his particular destination.

With his perfect English, good Hindi and Urdu, as well as his native Arabic, Mustafa Ali Abdullah had little problem in finding himself work away from the family import-export business. His ambition was to become much more than an importer-exporter. They were commonplace in the Gulf but were not the kind of men who scaled the real heights of money and power, where Mustafa Ali Abdullah was convinced his destiny lay.

His first job was as a translator for the Americans, who had just elevated their Consulate to Embassy status. After some months he changed to the British Embassy doing the same work. The pay was less but the job was with the commercial section which he knew had great potential for him as he would get to know the people who negotiated the contracts for some of the huge development projects going on. Realising his aptitude for this work, his employers quickly promoted him to assistant in the department and he in turn showed his great flair in establishing contacts and linking up companies with the appropriate kind of work they were trying to secure.

As an employee of the Embassy he was forbidden to have any commercial dealings of his own. His view was that such rules should never be bucked. One had to show enterprise, instead, to find a way round them. He did. A cousin was enlisted to front a company whose objective was to secure and negotiate contracts for the major overseas builders and contractors who were flooding into the Gulf. By re-routing contracts which came through the Embassy to this front company Mustafa Ali Abdullah prospered beyond even his most fanciful of dreams. He secured so much work for one particular Greek-Cypriot contractor that he was taken on as a secret partner. The company was to flourish spectacularly due to his inside knowledge. Eventually, after they had won contracts in other Gulf countries, the dimensions of the Greek-Cypriot company were such they required Mustafa's full-time supervision as one of the senior men on the board and he left the staff of the British Embassy. When that time came the Ambassador himself thanked him on behalf of Her Majesty's Government for all the valuable work he had done on the part of so many British companies.

Apart from a great longing to return to their beautiful country, and particularly when that beauty was viewed against some of the featureless areas of the other Gulf countries, the expatriates from Emirate thought little else about their homeland. There was nothing for them there, apart from turning the clock back to the Middle Ages. Even if they wanted to return they couldn't for that was forbidden. Freedom was so restricted that just to travel out of one's own district meant having to get approval from the old Emir himself. And he lived secluded and remote in his Palace guarded by retinues of black slaves. There were no telephones, there was no electricity. Everyone was a virtual prisoner.

In the mid-'sixties when the development boom was gaining more and more momentum in the Gulf, there seemed little prospect of the expatriates returning for many years. The Emir was in his mid-fifties and reported to be in good health and likely to be the monarch of his ancient country for another 20 years. He had a son who had been educated in England and went to Sandhurst. But on his return to Emirate it was quickly demonstrated to the young prince that he had as much freedom as the ordinary subjects of his country and he was kept a virtual prisoner in a villa near the Palace.

When they heard the news about their prince being held under house-arrest conditions, many of the expatriates working in countries throughout the Gulf gave up hope of ever returning to their homeland. The fact that they had heard of events was remarkable enough, for getting any real news from their country was a rarity. Letters were exchanged but all they ever contained was word about immediate family. As for news of the country itself, there was invariably none. There were no newspapers, no radio, no means of knowing what precisely was going on at the Palace, no one to tell them if there would ever be doctors, or hospitals, or schools, or even roads; no one to explain to them what was happening to the money from the oil that was now gushing from more than one well; no one to ask as the 1970s approached why they still slammed shut the gates of walled towns when night fell throughout the land; why men with long muskets in countless hilltop watchtowers still had to stand guard against raiders who might descend on them from the vast and lonely interior of gravel plains and deserts they called sand seas; why they should have to suffer the horrors of yaws and leprosy, tuberculosis and syphilis and have an infant mortality rate which could be as high as 75 per cent; why they should have to remain the most backward country in the Arab world, with life going on just as it had when they were born and when their parents had been born and their parents before them. The timelock was cast and set. Emirate was to be the forever yesterday land.

The news of the events of that day in early 1970 spread in an instant from community to community among the exiles in the Gulf. They rejoiced in Doha and Abu Dhabi, in Bahrain and Kuwait, in Basra and Baghdad, and in Amman and Cairo. The old Emir had been overthrown. The young prince had taken over. Their country was about to be reborn.

For Mustafa Ali Abdullah it was the chance to achieve many ambitions, not the least of them to move in on the prospect of the biggest new market in the Gulf. Whereas other areas had been mainly progressive developments, what would happen in his native country would be immediate and universal. The basic requirement was quite simple. They needed a new country. Roads would have to be built; an airport that could take the new jets; offices; highways; hotels; hospitals; schools; mosques. And all the infrastructure that went with them. His ancient and neglected nation would be crying out . . . build me! Mustafa Ali Abdullah was going to make sure he would play a big part in that building.

Before returning, however, there was business to be done. Within days of hearing the news about the opening up of the country, he was on a plane to London where he would invite tenders to build a new cement-producing plant in Emirate. They would need cement by the shipload and if he could produce it in-country he could undercut all the other suppliers and corner the market. While he was doing that he had his eldest son move quickly to the Capital from the offices in Kuwait to get companies registered and to secure land for the building of a new headquarters. By the time he returned to his homeland to swear his allegiance to the new monarch he had laid the foundations for a new phase in a business career which had already seen him amass one fortune.

The new Emir was quick to show that he could get things moving and development came even quicker that many of them had anticipated. But Mustafa had made good plans and with his cement works producing and his companies acting as the local partners for a major British construction company as well as the Greek-Cypriot company with whom they had been partners in Kuwait, he entered a new golden age of immense wealth and prosperity.

There were other nationals like him with parallel careers, parallel family histories. All of them had dreamed of the day when they could return, but never imagined it would happen so quickly. Their country was there for the having and they were going to make sure they had it. The new Government was quick to agree with them that the foreign speculators should be kept out. They could come if they wished with their manpower and plant and expertise, but they would be forbidden to own any land, to own any house or property, or to solely own any company that operated in the country.

The signboards proclaiming the Ali Abdullah companies with their English and other partners could be seen everywhere, or so it seemed. They were there too on the five-acre site on the coast, on top of one of the best sweetwater wells in the district, where they were building a beautiful new palace of white stucco and golden domes. Around it there was one of the greatest displays of wealth in the Gulf — grass lawns. Only the wealthy could afford to have grass and the water it required. At the new home of Mustafa Ali Abdullah there were two acres of it with automatic sprinklers as well as fountains and shrubs and trees and a gazebo as big as a Madinat Emir villa.

With his wife, a Lebanese beauty, and his three sons and two daughters, who had all been schooled in either Cairo or London and had finished on the playgrounds of the Côte d'Azur and Switzerland, Mustafa had everything a man could wish for . . . and more. His riches were far in excess of anything he had ever imagined they might be. As well as the new palace by the sea there was a small country estate in Surrey and a flat in Kensington where they could escape from the rigours of Gulf summers as well as live and enjoy the less disciplined Western way of life. There was just one thing missing from his life. Power.

He had made it known that he wished to help the Government and with his experience as the thrusting businessman and his reputation for being a ruthless achiever, he was quickly made an Under-Secretary, a government rank which gave him the title of His Excellency. It was to be nearly four years before he was to become a full Minister and the reason it took so long, as the stories would have it, was because he had spent so many years out of the country. They, meaning the Ali Abdullahs and those like him, should have been with us here during the hard days, said some of the ones with the power, those who had endured running the country in its dark age under the old ruler.

Another point he resented was that his Ministry was one of the junior ones, and that particularly rankled when he looked around at some of those in much higher posts than his. He considered himself superior to them — in many ways he was — and knew that he had done a lot more for the country than many of them. But then they were close to The Family, either by blood or some point in history.

He knew about the whisperers, those who said he had only returned, like so many others, to make another fortune, and he knew too about the closed ranks of the Establishment. But Mustafa Ali Abdullah knew he was a better man than any of them. He had gained everything in life by his own hands. He didn't have to follow his father into the family business to make his money. He had wanted to do it his way and he had. Now he had amassed a fortune greater than any other member of his wealthy family. He had a wife of fabled elegance, a splendid family. If only he could have power too he would be the completely fulfilled man.

He was a handsome, courteous man and performed the greeting ritual of the well-mannered Gulf Arab with the same grace and charm, no matter the visitor — rising from his chair to warmly shake them by the hand, asking how they were, asking how the family was, asking how their friends were and replying to them himself with a courteous "Praise be to God" in a fashion that was less perfunctory than the normal. He had the distinguished air about him of those described as Mercedes Arabs and not even the uniform collarless dishdasha, albeit that his were made of the finest cotton, each individually tailored, could detract from his elegant appearance. He was clean-shaven, apart from the moustache which was more Rhett Butler than Zapata and his skin was the light olive of the coastal Gulf Arab.

He rose to greet Colonel Billy Bainbridge when he was ushered into his office, quickly adjusting the volume of the choral music coming from the two picture-frame stereo speakers on facing walls. They exchanged the customary greetings litany in Arabic before the Minister asked in English, "Well, Colonel, what have you to report? Everything going to plan, as they say?"

"Yes, everything is working out. Most of my problems have been sorted out."

"Excellent. I'd like you to go over all the details with me once they are near finalisation. Are you in a position at this stage to name a likely date? I've been getting inquiries from some of the others of our consortium."

"You gave me a year. The research work has been long and painstaking. That's ten months now. All the in-country arrangements have been made and, as the Americans used to say, I can see the light now at the end of the tunnel."

"Wasn't that in Vietnam they first said that?"

"A clever observation, Mr Minister. Yes, perhaps it was but the light I am seeing is most illuminating. I have no worries. As for a date, well, I think you'll find the light shining brilliantly about the end of Ramadan."

"You have heard then about the ones we hoped may come and create the required chaos?"

"No, not yet. I'm about to embark on that any day now. Everything has been a question of timing. With everything else in place I will now concentrate on them. Have no fears, Your Excellency, everything has been planned with precision and everything will eventuate in that fashion."

"I am so glad to hear that, Billy. So glad."

Casting the Bait

THE AGREEMENT between Mustafa Abdullah, the Minister for Public Buildings, and Colonel M. Billy Bainbridge was that the mission for which he had been engaged should be finalised in the period of one year. With that in mind, the colonel knew there would be little time to spare if it was to be done in the fashion which they had conceived, with no accusing fingers pointing anywhere in their direction once it had been carried out.

In late May 1987, the colonel and his party left London Heathrow on a chilly and wet evening on the night flight for the Gulf. They arrived the following morning at the ultra-modern Renaissance Airport, to the north of the capital city of Emirate, stepping out from their plane into sunshine so brilliant it smarted the eyes and into a gasping heat that was already over 105 degrees.

Together with him were three other men from Red Alert whose work visas listed them as "specialist-mechanics". One of them, a gaunt-faced fitness fanatic in his mid-forties called Bob Thomas, had served with the colonel as his driver bodyguard in his two campaigns in Arabia and had gone with him when he had started the Red Alert Company. The other two were younger men, Gerry McDaid and Francis McQuade, inseparable mates from the Parachute Regiment and before that diehard schoolchums from Liverpool. Although they had been with Red Alert for more than a year, the exploits of McDaid and McQuade were still the talk of the 2nd Battalion of the Regiment. Each of the three had known the front end of the soldier's game and the colonel felt little fear with their like around him.

If anything went wrong, Mustafa had warned him, he would be on his own. He didn't take the warning lightly for he knew that should the situation ever arise, the Minister would be the first to turn on him. That possibility was easier to live with when he had his three helpers on call. All flanks were covered when they were around.

As soon as he had settled into the spacious new villa which had been arranged for him in that area of the upmarket suburb of Madinat Emir reserved for high-ranking Ministry officials, the colonel set to work. His first task was to make a close study of all the dissident factions in the country who might be incorporated by him into his plan of action. Accompanied by at least one of his men, he spent weeks travelling through the districts they called the wilayats, exchanging gossip and news with those he met in the souks and the coffee meeting places, always willing to listen, to note.

He made a study of the regular radio broadcasts in Arabic from Tehran and with his house situated high on the hill at Madinat Emir and fitted with a tall antenna, he had little problem picking up Iran TV, except on the nights when the atmospheric conditions were bad enough to "snow" it off. And he spent countless days pouring through all the dissident literature which he could obtain. Most of the publications from Iran were dedicated to long communiqués about the war or else lengthy diatribes against the Great Satan of America and the other Satans of the West. But he persevered, working assiduously through every one which his sources brought to him, not knowing specifically what he was looking for, but hoping that there would be something to provide the spark he required.

In his sixth month of this tedious, non-stop research he came across the very item in one of these pieces of literature for which he had been searching. It was in a magazine called *SAFF* . . . the Line of Combat, published in Qom, the holy city of Iran. *SAFF* was the organ of the Committee for Exporting the Islamic Revolution and specialised in reports, as it would describe them, of "acts of selfless heroism by the Soldiers of Allah" throughout the world Hussein Martyr groups were always featured in the magazine which would describe with great flourish the groups' "selfless devotion" and how they were "the valiant of the valiant and had to be looked upon as an inspiration to all the young of Allah".

The report which had caught his avid attention gave details about the work of such a group in Emirate and how they and their supporters had attacked an Army patrol in the Interior near the Old Capital, meaning Razak, inflicting heavy casualties on the soldiers before they themselves had been wiped out. "The spirit of revolution lives on in Asima Qadima (the Old Capital)," read the headline. The story went on: "Many centuries ago, long before there was the family of the Amir, the young men of this part of Arabia had demonstrated the best principles of Islam by rebelling against those who were not in the name of Allah. In the words of our great Ayatollah Khomeini, monarchies by their very nature are Anti-Islamic. And so too are the Amirs who act as little monarchs. To have a true Islamic country, the monarchs will have to be vanquished. And so too should the Amirs. And just as they did centuries ago, the new men of Asima Qadima are rising again. Already they have fought a valiant battle with the forces of the Anti-Islamic Amir. In the months to come there will be other battles. When the story of these battles is known throughout the land, there will be a great uprising of the people. After Iraq then Kuwait and Bahrain are freed of their despotic leaders and their tyrant Governments, the beleaguered peoples of the other Gulf countries will have their day of liberty at hand. So have patience, dear brethren, and be inspired by the Martyrs in your midst. Every deed of theirs is a day nearer your great day of liberation."

Next day, together with Thomas, McDaid and McQuade, the colonel left for the area. Anticipating such a journey, his men had prepared an Army trailer which their Range Rover would tow. In it they had stowed a complete camp consisting of a three-roomed tent, rugs, fly netting, cooking facilities and a powerful Yamaha generator for their electrical equipment which included a freezer and fridge, television and lighting.

The fish were running, the colonel reckoned. It was time for the fisherman to come off the bank and prepare to cast the fly.

They camped outside the town in the vast gravel plain which preceded the desert. "Just like the old days, eh boss?" said Thomas. "No wonder the buggers keep raving on about the beauty of the place. It really is fantastic, you know. Especially at night. Never seen stars as bright or moons so brilliant. And the way they light up the mountains and the peace and quiet of the place . . . especially when you don't have to worry about the adoo (enemy)."

"You almost sounded like a romantic there, Thomas," said the colonel.

"I reckon the sun's got to him, boss," quipped McDaid, adopting the SAS nomenclature. He and his mate McQuade were having their first experience in the Gulf.

They cleared the gravel for a site then set up their big Arabian-styled tent with its wide door and majlis meeting-room. Scattered around the wall-to-wall rugs were cushions where their visitors could lounge as they sipped their coffee and enjoyed the halwa and other sweetmeats they would prepare for them.

Acting as couriers, Thomas and McDaid had made contact with the senior elders of the district and, one by one, they came to the camp to pay their respects to the man they had been told had been one of the great soldiers who had helped them when the Jebel war had passed their way. They came dressed in the full costume of elders, wearing their ceremonial khanjar daggers — the more senior the elder the more elaborate and ornate the curved dagger. Wearing such daggers in magnificent silver-tooled sheaths strapped to their belts and carrying their carved walking sticks, the elders were splendorous old-world figures, even though their mode of transport was by the latest model Toyota Pajero or Nissan Patrol.

The first essential of the Gulf Arab was his manners. Many of the expat. workers found it difficult to comprehend that the workmate or associate with whom perhaps they had a vicious argument the day before would the following day greet them with a peace-be-upon-you and then inquire about their health and the health of their family with a polite shake of the hands. It was difficult to live with a grudge when confronted with such daily gestures. Despite the pressures and the advances of modern-day living and conditions, the manners remained and not even big city life, as is its wont, or the experience so many of them had gained on their world travels, or the presence of the multinationals, detracted from their code of conduct. Workers would still shake hands even more than the French. Managers in city offices would still stand to greet the visitor and offer him what hospitality they could.

But it was in the country where manners were at their most lavish and

most formal and where they were displayed with the same flourish as had
been the way for centuries. It was unthinkable of them to communicate with
one another unless a set pattern of manner-ritual was performed. Then, and
only then, when every little nuance of the ceremony had been accomplished,
would men relax together for conversation. And when the village elders began
making their calls to the camp of Colonel Billy Bainbridge, they did so in the
time-honoured fashion and were received likewise by the man who not only
was experienced in their ways but an advocate of them.

They would begin their meetings, as always, with the full ritual that the old
friend or traveller would receive on calling at someone's camp, talking as if
they were long-lost friends. The colonel was well practised in their ways and
could go through the litany with the expertise of a priest at prayers. Peace-be-
with-you . . .. Let's shake . . .. How is your family? . . . Praise be to God in
good health . . .. How are your companions? . . . Praise be to God in good
health . . .. How is your group? . . . Praise be to God in good health . . .. How is
your family group? . . . Well, no one complains . . .. How is your health? . . .
Praise be to God in good health. . .. How are your friends? . . . Well; praise
God . . .. How are your close friends? . . . How are your neighbours? . . . How
are your children? . . . How are your sheikhs? . . . How are the old ones? . . .
How are the little ones? . . . All answered with the muttering of the "Al
hamdu lillah" — Praise be to God — over and over again.

The first formality over, it was then the procedure to ask what news there
was. But this too had to be performed in the prescribed fashion. It was the
custom that the honour of asking the question should go to the eldest or the
most senior of the group and when the subject was raised there would ensue a
friendly argument on who should be the one to ask the question, just in the
manner of two friends in the West bantering over who should buy the first
round of drinks. When they had settled who it should be, he would then quite
formally inquire, "Is there any news?" Just as formally, the reply would be
that there was no news. Then, when the second or third man asked the same
question of the others, followed by the inquiry whether there had been any
incidents, again the reply would be that there had been none and that, praise
be to God, everything was quiet. The colonel understood the routine well
enough to know that when they did ask each other such questions, it was the
custom to reply that there had been no news or incidents irrespective of
whether there had been or not. At that point they would be invited into the
majlis of the tent and offered hospitality.

These various set pieces of age-old custom were based mainly on respect
and the desire never to show greed. The eldest or the most important among
them was always the one who was given the most respect. If there was ever
any dispute about who should go first, whether it be in being served or who
should lead the way through a door, the honour would always go to the eldest
even though he might have to be reminded, "After you, you are the most
senior."

The desire never to show greed was derived from the Bedu. It was one of the sacred principles of their way of life. Despite their incredible hardships in the desert or on the cruel and barren gravel plains where they may have gone for long periods without nourishment, they would always insist when they did dine that the other person should eat first or eat the most. They would even argue and grumble among themselves when dividing their meat that they had been given too much and that the other should take more. Often to save such arguments they would draw lots to save having to complain they had been given more than someone else. It was anathema to them to complain that they had not been given enough for that indicated greed and greed was to be despised.

The colonel's three men had set out the majlis room of the tent in the appropriate fashion or, as McQuade had quipped, "Like something out of your bleedin' Arabian nights." And it was. There were cartwheel brass plates piled with various fruits, mainly melon, banana, oranges and the finest Khalas and Khanaiza dates, big and fat and juicy and sweeter than anything that the foreigner associated with the humble and abundant Arabian fruit. There was also a variety of halwa, their favourite sweetmeat which they would sell in little containers not unlike egg boxes from the specialist halwa shops. They said that the halwa in this part of the Peninsula was the best in all Arabia. It was the Arabian version of Turkish Delight and nothing like as mundane as the halwa of Greece and the Levant. It was made of flour, sugar, ghee, rose water, cardamom and saffron and flavoured with grated almonds, all mixed together in the fashion of men treading grapes. Or so it was said. It was then cooked for four hours and thereafter left for a day to set.

Also laid out on the rugs of the floor of the majlis were brass vacuum flasks, shaped, as was the popular fashion for them, like old Arabian coffee pots. The guests were served iced water from them while they ate the fruit and the halwa. When they said they had had enough, they were brought finger bowls and paper towels to dry their hands, for, whether it was a main meal of lamb or goat stew or a light snack of sticky fruit and halwa, it would be eaten with the hand, the right hand.

Then the coffee was served. Thomas had made it from a mixture of light mocha and a darker roast bean, grinding the beans himself with a traditional pestle and mortar and flavouring them with cardamom seeds which he also ground. He had brought it to the boil three times before allowing it a long time to settle. Then he served it with great flair, holding the pot in the proper fashion with his left hand and pouring it in long and glistening streams into the little cups he held in his right hand. The brew would spring forth with the pungent aroma of its strength which was much appreciated by the men who were about to receive it. At this point the ritual would come into play again and they would hold up their hands in refusal when offered the coffee, saying that the host should be served first and he in turn would refuse until they would settle, the honour of the first cup going to the oldest of the company or else the one they considered to be the most important. And it was only then, having sipped the thick and unsweetened coffee and shaken their cup from side to side in the direction of the pourer to indicate without words that they wished no more, that they would impart what news there was, despite the fact that only minutes earlier they had been saying in their greetings that there was no news.

A variety of them had visited the little camp, some too young to remember the war they had in their jebels, others who did and who remembered the deeds of the colonel. Or so they said, anyway.

It was on their fourth day in camp outside Razak that he came. The colonel knew he would be there one day. It was just a matter of time. It was at that time of day when people begin moving again after the long afternoon siesta. A heavy duty cross-country pick-up, the kind Toyota called a 4WD Runaround, high-sprung and robust, came driving from the direction of the mountains where there were many villages and small communities who lived and ate well off the abundance of fruit, nuts and vegetables they could grow in the narrow strip terraces with their plentiful water supply. The driver of the blue-coloured Runaround, and they all seemed to be blue, had an ammunition bandolier round his shoulders. He got out of the vehicle quickly to help his passenger dismount. The passenger was a thin, elderly man with a straggle of white beard. He wore a magnificent khanjar dagger and carried a rosewood walking stick, carved in the fashion of a coiled snake with a head of gold.

Bainbridge walked to greet him and they held each other by the arms as they salaam alaykum-ed and went through the greetings exchange, smiling with pleasure as first one, then the other, replied to the questioning.

Fresh dates and halwa and melon which Thomas had bought that morning at the souk market were offered with the coffee as the man with his driver, who carried a Belgian self-loading rifle, sat down with the colonel in the majlis, meeting-room, of the tent.

"And how long is it since your return to the country, Issa?" the colonel eventually got round to asking after they disposed of the remainder of the greetings and inquiry formalities.

Issa replied that it had been nearly seven years and that it had been with the knowledge of His Highness. "He said two of The Three could also return, but not the Imam and because of that the others are still in Saudi."

Issa and The Three, as they had been known, were central figures in the war of the Imam in which the colonel had served on the side of the Emir. Issa, the Arabic name for Jesus, had been the cleverest of the commanders of the jebel men and the colonel's troops had nicknamed him Rommel because of his daring military tactics which had outsmarted them on so many occasions with a skill and polish which some of the officers said would have won him honours at Warminster. The colonel, then a captain, had finally outsmarted him and taken him prisoner after one of the bloodiest battles of the campaign. Issa had expected to be put to death by the enemy and, in fact, would have been had he been captured by national troops. They had even sent a firing squad to report to the soldier called Captain Billy who they expected would arrange Issa's execution. But the captain refused and said he would be treated as a prisoner-of-war and be given the due protection and care demanded by the Geneva Convention.

Having fought against each other for so long, the two soldiers felt they had known one another for years. A strong bond grew between them during Issa's first few days of captivity. But near the end of his first week in their custody Issa, together with three of his warriors, had escaped by cleverly duping a Baluchi guard. He had left a letter for the captain thanking him for being an "English gentleman" and expressing the hope that one day, insha'allah, they would meet again.

"So you are a servant of His Highness?" said Issa.

"Actually I prefer to think of myself as one who serves His Excellency rather than His Highness."

"Your loyalties are with the Minister then?"

"That is right."

"And what is the word of your Minister?"

"The word of my Minister, my friend, is that he knows and understands his people better than anyone. Better than anyone even in The Family and that he knows there are many who would wish for more understanding."

"Indeed, your Minister thinks wisely for there are many in these parts who have similar thoughts."

"Including the new Fundamentalists?"

"You know about them?"

"Yes. I have spoken to some of them and read about them. I am aware of what is going on."

"There is a new thinking among many people today. They do not like many of the things that are happening in our country. And they are inspired by what is occurring across the waters of the Gulf. It is not like the days when we fought as soldiers. Today many of the young ones see themselves as soldiers of Allah and the quicker they go to their death the sooner they will meet Him. But that is the way of life, that people constantly change. One must be prepared to adapt oneself to them. If your Minister has the understanding which you say he has, does he have a message for me and my people?"

"Yes, the message is that perhaps that understanding might be even greater if The Family were replaced by others."

"That has already been spoken of by the people here. We have some among us who have been to Iran for training and already we have several martyr squads awaiting their instructions. These people are fearless and already they have shown the Army near here their determination in a battle which they had recently. Soon there will be another attack which will focus the news of the country on the Old Capital. And one day, insha'allah, they will do the same in the New Capital."

"Supposing the word of the Minister was that through myself we could make it easier for that great day to dawn for you? Supposing it was to be that there was ammunition and the best of direction to help your men . . ."

"Captain Bainbridge, I did not say they were my men."

The colonel didn't flinch at being called captain again, in fact it brought back some of the nostalgia he had for the days when he had soldiered in these parts.

"But they are men that you know of and to whom you can pass the word. Again, let us suppose that you were to get that word to them with the details which I have given you. What would be the reaction of these men?"

"I think the word back from them would be that if Issa, their most respected elder, were to say it was wise, then wise it would be. And so be it. It would be done."

The fly had been cast . . . and taken.

About three months later, after the attack on the police station at Razak, the colonel returned to visit Issa.

"I heard the news in the Capital about the attack," he had told him. "It caused quite a bit of concern among the Ministers, I'm told. When I heard I knew it was the event which you spoke of when I was here last."

"Yes, indeed, it was. We did it to demonstrate to the Emir that his beloved police are not unassailable. Have you seen what they did to the police station and the barracks? They are half destroyed. Men of a Hussein Martyr Squad carried out the operation. Four of them only and they caused scores of casualties among the police before they were wiped out. Now we have the Army and extra police everywhere. They have reacted viciously because we have the whole country talking. The soldiers and policemen are everywhere and are being very cruel to families they suspect of having anything to do with the Fundamentalists. They have put scores in jail, including the five men who were the volunteers for the next Hussein Martyr Squad and who were preparing for you and the work that has to be done in the New Capital."

"That is very bad news, Issa. Extremely bad news. I was relying on them to carry out the operation. Are there others?"

"Yes, but these were the ones who dedicated themselves to the mission that they know will make them live forever."

"Have they been sentenced?"

"No. They did not find them with arms or anything. They merely suspected them and took them together with many others. Perhaps they will release them soon for I hear they are in the Hazz section of the prison and they only keep the ones there who will not be with them for a long time."

"That perhaps will make it easier for us, then," said Bainbridge. "For we must have them soon for training. They have to get acquainted with the weapons we have for them. I am sure with the Minister's wasta we should be able to arrange something."

But the Minister's influence, the wasta which the colonel had spoken about to Issa, wasn't all that easy to exercise. There was great sensitivity about the men from Razak in prison. The best he was able to do for them at first was get them preferential treatment. It was arranged that they would be taken daily to visit with the prisoners in the Jilida long-term wing, the work being much easier there on the principle that hard labour should be reserved for the short-term inmates. The food was also better there, being made intentionally rough and spartan at Hazz. The preferential treatment for the Razak men also catered for them to have visitors without the customary restrictions which enabled them to meet and plan together within the walls of Jilida. The visitors were Issa, their elder, and Colonel Bainbridge, and between them they ordained the destiny of a leader and his country.

Ultimately, however, the Minister's wasta was to pay off and the five men were released from Zamakh. Waiting for them were Bainbridge's men, Thomas, McDaid and McQuade, in two vehicles, their Range Rover and a Hilux Pickup. From Zamakh they were taken, as they had expected, to the New Capital and the house of an old Razak family who were friends of Issa, their elder . . . the house along the narrow lane off Way 177 at the Fish Souk.

The plan was taking shape. Only the element of turmoil and chaos which the Minister perceived would facilitate the emergence of the new grouping of leaders which he would be heading had to be arranged.

Bainbridge wasn't unduly worried about the fact that there were only weeks left of the year he had been given to complete the job. When word was passed to those who would organise the men he was positive would come, they would move fast. They wouldn't come, as they would say, in mawa'eed Arab . . . in Arab time, words which even the Arabs themselves used to describe their own relaxed attitude to timekeeping. No. They would come in mawa'eed ingiliizi, English time. And that was always punctual. What had been more of a concern to him wasn't their actual coming, but how the right word could be got to those who were their masters. He had worked hard on that, however, and he was sure he had the right answer.

To Turmoil and Confusion

BECAUSE THERE was no Soviet Embassy in the country, Colonel Billy Bainbridge had to make do with the recently established Soviet Trade Mission in the Capital as his first contact with the men from Moscow. Their offices were located in one of the older blocks in Rani Main Street and there was the usual haris (watchman) at the door, as there were at many offices, a haris being an acceptable job for a national. Although they were paid the lowest of wages, there was much more dignity in being a haris than a labourer, which the national would never be. A Gulf national wouldn't labour for another man. Why should he? Indians were for labouring and there were always plenty of them. Gulf nationals only did work which they considered had dignity. There was dignity in being the manager of other men. There was no dignity in being managed. There was dignity in making decisions. There was none in doing the work required by decisions. They could get good money if they wanted to work in restaurants or hotels. Attending to other people's needs? There was absolutely no dignity in that. Much better being a driver or a guard or a watchman for they were people who made decisions all the time; they were people of authority. There was dignity in that.

The office was on the second floor and an Indian girl came to the inquiry window. "Mr Chanov, please," Bainbridge said. "I telephoned him earlier today. My name is Brown. Mr William Brown."

After some minutes she returned and ushered him into a starkly furnished office with no air-conditioning and with three ceiling fans on maximum power creating so much air turbulence that even the numerous paperweights on the desk were struggling to retain their various charges. The room stank with the heavy smell of dryness you would get when there were no air-conditioners and was accentuated by the whirling fans.

The man was having an exasperated conversation with someone on the telephone, explaining the intricacies of import-export licences, having to elaborate each point, repeating some of them two or three times before the caller apparently grasped the meaning. He indicated to the colonel to be seated, then impatiently told the caller he had no more time and that if he required further assistance he should make a personal call. That meant another explanation about where to locate the office and again he had to repeat this information twice, shaking his head as he did so.

He was a big, overweight man with an untrimmed walrus moustache and gave another exasperated shake of his head after he hung up the phone, taking a large, soggy handkerchief from a drawer and mopping his perspiring forehead as he did so. "That's the third time this week the air-conditioning has broken down. And when do they come to fix it? Tomorrow, insha'allah. It's always tomorrow. And always insha'allah." His accent was Eastern-bloc caricature. "You are the gentleman who phoned this morning about an appointment to meet one of our officials at our Embassy in Oman. Can't I help you with whatever you want?"

"Thank you all the same, but I would prefer to visit your Embassy in Muscat."

"We have an Embassy also in Abu Dhabi."

"I know. But I haven't been to Oman for some time and I would like to see the place again. As well as speak to one of your people there, that is."

"But I can easily pass information on to them from here."

"I would prefer to pass it myself."

"Can I have the nature of your information, Mr Brown?"

"Let's just say it is about a situation which will be of vital interest to them."

"We are in close contact, you know. I can have it relayed quickly from here. And confidentially."

"I mean no disrespect, Mr Chanov. But I came here for you to open the door, as it were, to your Embassy in Oman. Either I give the information I have to them, or I don't give it at all."

Chanov scribbled a number on a pad and handed it to Bainbridge. "That is my home telephone number. Call me this evening after nine o'clock. Hopefully I will have some news for you."

True to his word, there was news for him when he called that evening at his home.

"Ah yes . . . Mr Brown. I have spoken to our people in Muscat. They say you should be there the day after tomorrow. The telephone number is 56437. Ask for Mr Bessonov. Mr Pavel Bessonov. He will be expecting your call. I believe Gulf Air fly down that morning."

"That's right. I was planning to go on a morning flight."

He had been to Oman many times before, but not since the early 'seventies when he had been stationed at the Bait al Falaj camp, which had served as the HQ for both the armed forces of the Sultan and the British troops helping him in their war in Dhofar in the south of the country. He found it hard to believe the sights that greeted him after his arrival at the Seeb International Airport, about 20 miles north of Muscat, the capital, on the Batinah coast road. They had told him the changes would be dramatic. But the transformation he was to see on his way from the airport to the hotel amazed him. It was difficult to conceive that a country could leap the centuries as it had done.

He remembered the old road from Muscat north to Seeb. It was a bumpy Land Rover-only track with wadi crossings that regularly washed away what semblance of a route there was. Now in its place was a six-lane highway with bougainvilleas in the central reservation, roundabouts that looked like botanical gardens, and a modern Arc de Triomphe they called the Renaissance Gate which heralded the start of the handsome highway south to the Capital Area.

There were flyovers and cloverleaf junctions, mosques with golden domes, dazzling white mansions, the occasional palace in suburbs overlooking the sea and the ubiquitous Indian roadsweepers, even more of them than there were in Emirate, sweeping little piles of dust from what must be one of the most well-tended roadways anywhere in the world. Only the jebel backdrop was unchanged, barren red mountains that were something of a cross between those of Arizona and the Moon. There had been smaller jebels too which blocked the route to the south and these had been altered, the occasional one having been removed to allow a graceful double-lane highway to gently rise and curve to its destination somewhere. Others had been merely manicured so that instead of the mountain rising in its natural line from the roadway, it did so in a series of giant gravel terraces.

The highway signs had many names he recognised, places like Qurum, where he remembered there had been a good beach and where regiments of big crabs used to scramble sideways to the sea in the late afternoon at low tide, and Ruwi, which had been little more than an adobe village where the Indians used to have many shops, and Muttrah, which began on one side of the jebels and descended to the sea, forming a twin town to Muscat, two to three miles along the rocky shore, one the centre of business, the other the seat of power. The taxi went via Muttrah, the market town by the sea.

It was still recognisable as the Muttrah of old, the latticed balconies of the old merchants' houses which looked out on the half moon bay to the harbour and the ships from India, Africa and Persia which brought them their lifeblood. They were all still there, even some of the old-style dhows and booms, bobbing in the harbour just like the old days, but in the background now at what was obviously a container terminal, there was the perpendicular outline of container vessels which looked as much like a ship as a floating dry dock.

The facelift the once-scruffy Muttrah had been given was quite astonishing. In place of the rubbish-strewn shoreline where the waves lapped an evil-smelling donkey track which also served as the sewage disposal area there was now a splendid double-lane highway proudly signposted "The Corniche" and a walled promenade with seats where people could relax and look out on one of the most beautiful harbours in the world. The backdrop was much the same, the sawblade jebel mountains, more ragged even than he had remembered. At the far end of the bay was the huge Muttrah Fort, an Arabian Edinburgh Castle, now with its very own Princes Street and with the added bonus of the rich blue of the gentle waters of the Gulf of Oman.

After Muttrah the highway continued, becoming a boulevard with a central plantation of thick-trunked palms tended by Indian gardeners, then a park with grassy slopes. If you had told the people of Muttrah 20 years previously that within walking distance of their houses they would be able to see and enjoy, as they could now, the luxury that green grass is in Arabia, they would have run for the police to report a madman in their midst. There too, across from the park, on the waterfront was a seafood restaurant which resembled a small fort. Nearby, also on the water's edge, there was a huge rock, maybe 100 feet high, which had been converted into a natural fountain with water cascading down it on the side which faced on to the roadway.

He travelled on past the tiny village of Kalbuh, with its little mosque and watchtowers on the highest jebels, then into Muscat which, at first, looked as it always had, charming and relaxed. But then capitals often were by comparison to their nation's business centres. They went past the Sultan's sparkling new Al Alam Palace, Arabian-flashy with flaring columns of gold and blue that looked like giant upturned trombones, and surrounded by fountains and pools and the most beautiful gardens he had seen in Arabia.

The Minister had been right about the Al Bustan Palace Hotel being the finest in the world. About three miles south of Muscat it nestled in a setting of mountain and sea so beautiful it was overwhelming. The hotel itself looked even more imposing than the Sultan's Palace, in fact even to call it a hotel was to detract from its magnificence, with its grand entry promenade adorned with gushing waterways, pools and fountains and gardened car bays. Once inside there was still little that resembled a hotel. Its foyer was a cathedral of sculpted white stucco as ornate and delicate as Spanish lace and so vast that not even the hustle and bustle of reception could break the delightful tranquillity where the only background sound, it seemed, was the soft tinkle of the central fountain and some soft Mozart muzak.

Using a lobby telephone, he called Bessonov at the number he had been given. He didn't have to explain who he was. Bessonov said he had been expecting the call.

"Would you care to come to the Embassy, Mr Brown, and we can discuss what you have to tell us?"

"I would rather not, thanks."

"What about the Sheraton Hotel then? It's a nice place and we can have a drink."

"Don't think I'm being difficult, Mr Bessonov. But I would prefer no hotels, if you don't mind. I know the kind of people they have watching in them."

"Then nearby the Sheraton there's an Indian restaurant called Copper Chimney. It has none of the problems which concern you."

He was a much younger man than Bainbridge imagined he would be. Not much more that 30, he thought, as he studied the handsome and smart young man who had walked alone into the restaurant. The lightweight suit was sharply tailored and there was a confident and casual New World openness about his demeanour. One of the new *glasnost* brigade, he mused. Under one arm he carried a copy of the *Financial Times* as he had promised on the telephone, and Bainbridge rose from his seat to greet him. The accent was more Massachusetts than Moscow and Bainbridge found it difficult to realise he was speaking to a Russian, albeit a second consul at the Soviet Embassy, and albeit in all probability a member of one of their intelligence agencies.

He was in no hurry to ask Bainbridge about his business and spoke about how much he liked Indian food, how he considered the restaurant one of the best he knew and how beer was transformed into a refined drink when served in golden goblets as it was in the Copper Chimney. They were offered menu cards, but the Russian waved the waiter away with a casual dismissal of the hand, saying they would prefer to have some drink first of all.

"Your good health," he said politely raising his goblet of chilled beer to Bainbridge. "And do tell me, what makes you honour us with this visit . . . Colonel Bainbridge?"

"I would have been more surprised had you not found out who I was," replied Bainbridge coolly. "Your Mr Chanov, or someone, obviously did a little homework."

Bessonov smiled, but didn't reply to the remark which was an implied question.

Bainbridge resumed the conversation. "Yes, what I have to tell you is important enough for me to have come here. And it's important enough for you to be in contact with your Government to let them know that there will be changes soon in Emirate which could greatly improve your country's representation in Arabia. That, I imagine, would be most welcome news to the Kremlin bearing in mind their desire to win the hearts and minds of the people of the Gulf and hopefully one day those of Saudi Arabia itself."

The Russian snapped off another piece of poppadum from the silver rack in which they were placed on the table. He was obviously in a listening mood, and was studying the colonel attentively without reply or comment.

"So, do I assume you wish to hear more?" Bainbridge asked in order to prompt a response.

"Please, Colonel Bainbridge. My silence is because of my interest."

"Word has come to us — that is, a certain faction of the Government — that there will be an event occurring on or about Tuesday, 17 May, that being the first day of the Eid celebrations which mark the end of Ramadan. As a result of this event, and if the country is reduced to sufficient chaos because of it, a new grouping is ready to step in and take control away from whatever members of The Family are, how shall I put it, not affected by the circumstances of this occasion."

"Can the change in those who rule only come about as a result of this chaos?" asked Bessonov.

"The change can only come about effectively if it is seen that the new grouping did not instigate the removal of the main members of The Family and that they are there to save the country from further chaos. You see, even though the principal members of The Family are disposed of, and forgive me for stating it so basically, there are many others of the same clan who will try to win control. That's been the trouble with the country for so long, its neglect for centuries of the elective principle. Heredity is acceptable in a ruling family provided that rule is only titular and not authoritative, and I say that as a devoted and most loyal subject of Her Majesty Queen Elizabeth of England."

"And will chaos follow the anticipated demise of the ruling family?"

"Those who aspire to become the new leaders certainly hope there will be, for that is the only means they see of effectively winning control . . . and the backing of the populace."

"Then presumably they are taking steps to induce this chaos?"

"Not really. Their knowledge is that the event is going to occur. They did not conceive it. They are only witnesses to it. Witnesses who are letting events take their predestined course. If they were seen to be participants in any way then they would have very little chance of gaining power."

"And if they take no steps to encourage the chaos they see as their route to power, how do they expect it to come about?"

"That is the chance they are taking. It may well be that following the forthcoming occurrence there will be no great panic and alarm and that the country will continue to be ruled and governed by people with the same name as for the past two and a half centuries."

"Then why is it you want my people to know all this?"

"Because, being the forward-looking people they are, the people who think they will be the new leaders are anxious to let future friends know of their intentions."

"And is your mission to pass the word to other future friends?"

"No. Some future friends may take steps to prevent what is to happen on the day in question."

"Then your people, Colonel . . . are they seeking assistance from those they consider will be their new friends?"

"Assistance? No. They cannot be seen to be assisted, particularly by people who are to be new friends."

"Even if there were ways?"

"I think at this stage they would prefer not to know of any ways. Except one, perhaps."

"Do tell me, Colonel."

"The volunteers who are about to change the course of history in the country I am serving, have the most basic of arms. Their leader has been trained in Iran but their armaments leave a lot to be desired. This has concerned my Minister. For there to be the real confusion that's desired, their supporters and others are in need of supplies. The Ministers, despite their power and wealth and influence, daren't be connected with any form of armaments, even in the most remote sense. For that is an area under total surveillance by Internal Security. Any movement of weaponry from within the country would be immediately traceable as there are many eyes and ears willing to sell themselves to the authorities."

"Likewise, Colonel Bainbridge, there would be difficulties for new friends in supplying them. But, nevertheless, if it was to be considered and approved by the people to whom I report then it will be done. Presumably you will be leaving me some future contact point. And you say what is likely to happen takes place on or about 17 May? That is not long!"

"That is correct. For a contact point, can you take a note?" He pinpointed the location of the house by the junction of the narrow lane off Way 177 at the Capital's Fish Souk. "All that is required after that is to ask for 'the men from Razak' and they will be accepted."

"You will appreciate, of course, that I only relay information and that there is little likelihood of any form of reply except, that is, when and if it may be decided to contact your men from Razak to further the cause, shall we say, of a new friend." Then he repeated the words, smiling as he said them. "A new friend . . . in need of turmoil and confusion."

The colonel smiled widely in return. "Yes, you put it well, Mr Bessonov. I'll raise my golden goblet to that. Turmoil and confusion."

Their goblets met with a metallic clink. "Turmoil and confusion," the Russian replied.

The colonel's plan was working, and much better than he had expected. Bessonov and his superiors would have been wary had they been openly asked for a Soviet force to come to their aid. That was why he had stressed that all the assistance they required was weaponry. Of course they could have got the arms to the men from Razak themselves, but Bessonov had obviously believed the story about that being a problem. When the Russian's commanders knew there was a country ready and waiting to offer them Embassy facilities, and perhaps other favours, there would be very little chance of them passing up the opportunity of lending the required help, especially when all that was required was a detachment of their specialist forces.

Yes, indeed, the Spetsnaz would be despatched. Nothing was more certain. He was convinced of that.

"Your mentioning of the Fish Souk, Colonel, has implanted the thought of food. They do wonderful giant prawns here. They're from the beautifully clear waters around Masira Island, you know the place where your B.B.C. has its main relay station to the East? Well, the chef here cooks them in the most glorious of light curry sauces and with the accompaniment of some kingfish kebabs from the tandoor we will have a truly wonderful meal."

"Then I'll let you order, Mr Bessonov."

Mustafa Abdullah grinned appreciatively as the colonel went over the story with him.

"It's the very chance they've been looking for here. Mr Gorbachev can have all the openness he wants but he's still got the same problem with his KGB as Reagan and his successors have with the CIA That's what happens when you create a power faction which has the mandate to take the action they deem necessary. They can become more powerful than the Government itself. The events of Irangate and the characters it threw up proved that all right. And when the Soviet intelligence gets Mr Bessonov's details, there'll be weapons *and* Spetsnaz here within days. If I was a betting man I'd put my money on that."

"You already have, Colonel Bainbridge," said Mustafa Abdullah smiling. "A million pounds. Remember?"

The Spetsnaz

THE RUSSIANS know them as the "Spetsialnoye Nasnachenie", which translated literally means Troops of Special Designation. Others, particularly Western Army Commanders, knew them simply as the Spetsnaz. While the Soviet leader has his openness and his declared desire to reduce the world's nuclear tension, there is never any mention of reducing the numbers of Spetsnaz forces. If anything, they are on the increase. Military commanders in opposing countries fear them as much as they do nuclear weapons. You can have all the nuclear treaties you want, but there will never be a Spetsnaz treaty, they argue, and while they are around, there is always a threat. They know and have studied the Spetsnaz. That is why they feared them so. They know how effectively they can neutralise a country. That is their speciality. They can live among foreign populations for they are as academically brilliant as they are physically perfect. They are already established with bases in many countries of the world; watching, assessing, reporting back to HQ units in the motherland. They are the ultimate military machine . . . the soldier-spies.

Units of them are already operating in Britain. Defence chiefs have known about their operations for some time but it wasn't till 1984 in a Government Defence White Paper that a slight, almost passing reference was made to them as a threat . . . "not of large-scale invasion but by small squads of specially trained troops".

The Spetsnaz men have their main British targets prepared. They know their vulnerable points and they know how and where to cause the maximum damage. Among the 100 targets they have listed is the dump for submarine missile nuclear warheads at Faslane in Scotland and the others near the English air bases at Brize Norton, Bentwaters, Upper Heyford, Woodbridge, Weathersfield and Greenham Common. The key US signals centres sited in Scotland, which are the contact points for their underwater fleets, are also on their list. So too are the 14th U.S. Submarine Squadron base at Holy Loch, again in Scotland, and its nearby British counterpart on the Gareloch; the submarine repair yard at Rosyth; RAF High Wycombe, the RAF and NATO HQ; and Northwood, the Royal Navy and NATO Eastern Atlantic HQ and many others. The Spetsnaz know and have studied them all.

The Spetsnaz training camps in the Soviet Union are located inside a triangle formed by the towns of Rovno, Lutsk and Lvov. These are situated in the Carpathian mountains in the south-west corner of the region and near the

Hungarian and Czech borders in the military district of Ural and Volgo.

When a Briton thinks of the supreme soldier he thinks instantly of his own Special Air Service men. They are indeed the most select and most highly trained men in the country. Their story is as fabulous as it is fabled, much of the latter deriving from the often-publicised fact that no SAS man may have his photograph shown, unless he is killed in action that is, and from the hooded warrior image of the dramatic and televised ending of the Iranian Embassy siege in London.

But there's a big difference between the SAS men and the Spetsnaz. The SAS — and their equivalents in a variety of other countries — are first of all ordinary soldiers who volunteer from other regiments to undergo the stiffer training that is required of the parachute soldier. If they are among the very best of that regiment they can go on to the even higher military "university" of the Special Air Services, where they undergo the most gruelling of courses, out of which only a small percentage qualify to become members of the "Who Dares Wins" regiment. The Spetsnaz, on the other hand, are no mere soldiers before being selected to serve. They are chosen as youngsters, much in the fashion of the British football player selection system whereby talent scouts study school and junior teams looking for potential stars. The football scout is an anonymous man who watches endless youth soccer games hoping that his eye for talent catches some potential star. As a bonus for his efforts, perhaps there will be a share in a signing-on fee. But there's little anonymity about the Spetsnaz scouts. They are highly paid senior officials from the two main units which control the Soviet Special Forces . . . the KGB and the GRU The KGB is the State Security Police, the GRU the Chief Directorate of Intelligence of the General Staff. Each controls its own Spetsnaz units, the KGB for use in conjunction with the security interests of the Soviet state at home and abroad by protecting diplomats, guarding embassies and the like; the GRU units are solely for action in foreign countries.

Schools, academies and sports clubs are visited by the talent spotters from the two organisations searching for the appropriate potential they require, youngsters of unswerving loyalty to the party, who have both academic promise, particularly in languages, and athletic prowess. If they get top marks in all categories, the scouts will recommend them as potential Special Forces' recruits.

Between college and their actual call-up for service, they will be sent for three years part-time training in the paramilitary DOSAAF youth organisation. When they have finished that course they will be qualified parachutists, experienced underwater frogmen, skilled as sharpshooters, competent users of various radio equipment, and practised first-aid men. At the same time, desk studies will have taken them to university degree level. And all that before they go into the Army to begin their training as Spetsnaz men.

As would be imagined, the men who train them come into the near supermen category. Many of them are among the champions of Soviet sports teams as well as being outstanding soldiers. Those who train the young KGB Spetsnaz recruits are invariably from the Dynamo Club, which is not merely the football team known to British soccer supporters. The Dynamo Club is a nationwide sports organisation which fosters sports teams at the highest level in the USSR. Training the youngsters going into the overseas GRU units are the finest coaches of the ZSKA, the Armed Forces Sports Union.

The cream of Soviet youth is transformed by these champions into the cream of Soviet soldiers. Or, in the eyes of the men in the Moscow citadel, la Kremlin de la Kremlin. Included in their training, apart from the customary fitness régime which is something akin to that of an Olympic champion, there are regular trips to the countries in which they will specialise as Spetsnaz units. Already proficient in that country's language, the purpose of these visits is to accustom and acclimatise them to the ways of the land in which they will ultimately operate.

The first of these trips are undertaken quite openly, usually as members of sporting or cultural delegations, being fully qualified to participate in either or both if the need be. Later they may travel in a less open fashion. Some will arrive as deck hands or cabin crews on ships and planes from the Eastern bloc. Some will go as tourists. Others as lorry drivers. And all in the quest of gaining more experience of the country to which one day they'll be destined as one of the Spetsialnoye Nasnachenie.

At their schools high in the beautiful forests of the Carpathian Mountains they will learn the other arts of the Spetsnaz trooper, such refinements as espionage and sabotage, assassination and subversion, and how to maximise confusion and disruption in a country when it is experiencing a period of turmoil.

They were there in readiness in Britain during the year-long miners' strike. Their women members were there too among the females of Greenham Common. British security pinpointed some of the "safe houses" they had established in the area of the marathon feminine protest. They were there in 1968 when Czechoslovakia was occupied, representing perhaps one of their outstanding achievements for such was their groundwork that the regular Soviet forces were able to take over the entire country in just 24 hours. They were there in Afghanistan in their capacity as the most versatile of frontline forces. The Mujahideen feared them more than any others they had ever fought, particularly because of their adaptability in the mountains. Most of the successful battles in the war were those where the Spetsnaz were in action.

The Arab world knows them too. They have been in action in Lebanon, specifically in Beirut for a rescue mission of Soviet hostages. And they participated in the brief but bloody civil war in South Yemen . . . the People's Democratic Republic of Yemen. Most of the 5,000 Soviet advisers stationed there were withdrawn during the uprising, but the men of the Spetsnaz stayed on to direct operations, suffering several casualties among them in the bitter fighting. More of them returned together with the bulk of the Soviet aid teams when the war was over. They wear the same uniform as the other Soviet military personnel who are there, plain khaki slacks and shirts with no emblems or badges of rank. Most days you can see them dressed like that and shopping for souvenirs in the Crater district of the capital, Aden. If you want to pick out the Spetsnaz men from the others, merely look for the fittest and most erect of the casual strollers, or listen to the ones who speak fluent Arabic with the shopkeepers. They are the Spetsnaz men. They are from the small detachment chosen from the three units whose speciality is the Arab world. It was from this small force in South Yemen that they used men for the quick operation in Beirut.

The war in South Yemen was something of an embarrassment to the Soviets and they had done their best to get it over as quickly as possible. The Soviet intention in that part of the Arabian Peninsula is to show what a good and stabilising influence they are. They need to demonstrate this in order to woo other countries on their side. Of course, while they are there, they have the added bonus that they are in the ideal position to monitor any likelihood of their need should a neighbouring country undergoing some kind of turmoil require the extra impetus which will reduce it to a state of chaos. Nowhere in the world do they await that call more eagerly, for it gives them the chance to expand their influence and be one step nearer their ultimate target in the region . . . Saudi Arabia.

It was their Intelligence Unit stationed at the Little Aden base in the PDRY which first picked up the word of the impending trouble in the Emirate. It came to them through local agents who had gone to live there after fighting on the opposing side during the war in the Southern Peninsula in the late 'sixties and early 'seventies. Several such agents had taken up residence in a variety of Gulf countries and regularly checked with the base at Little Aden about developments in their locations. The information was sketchy, however. More precise information was passed on by Bessonov via Moscow.

On receiving the information the Duty Intelligence Officer in Aden requested a computer check on the country concerned and within seconds he had before him a print-out with the relevant and most up-to-date information, such as areas of vulnerability, the locations of armed forces with emphasis on the country's own specialist units which it listed as National Security, Internal Security Service and Task Force. Members of the Special Designation Force had already been there and knew the local dialect, what modes of travel were immediately available and other relevant matters. It also listed a contact agent who was stationed there and who was available for help. He was named P. Carl Sabamontes, Indian, code name Boris One. The print-out also gave the names of a five-man unit serving in one of their South Yemen bases. They were named as the Volgo Platoon and had served together for nearly a year. Two of them had already been in action in Beirut in a clandestine operation.

As well as their Arabic, they were also fluent in Dutch and English, the latter being as vital a language as Arabic for anyone serving in the Gulf.

The Chief Directorate of Intelligence of the General Staff in the Soviet Union was informed about developments and ordered a top priority on all information on the subject. A command alert order was simultaneously despatched to the Socotra Islands where the men of the Volgo Platoon were on exercise in the Martian mountains of one of the world's loneliest island groups, situated in that part of the Arabian Sea pointed to by the Horn of Africa. Ocean travellers used to welcome sight of the islands as they marked the end of the longest stretch of the voyage west across the Indian Ocean from Australia and meant that they would soon be in the sheltered waters of the Gulf of Aden.

A radio message was flashed to the base at Tamrida on Socotra and from there to the Volgo Platoon who were high on the incredible pinnacles of the islands unclimbed mountains. They were to rendezvous at a map reference point where they would be picked up and returned to base in order to prepare for a possible mission. The following day a coded message was received at Little Aden from the Chief Directorate of Intelligence and was then relayed to Socotra. The message when decoded read: "Despatch Unit Volgo immediately on T. and C. operation." T. and C. needed no further translation. It was the primary objective of the Spetsnaz. Turmoil and Confusion.

That night the five men of Volgo Platoon, having been lifted by helicopter from the mountains, were driven from their barracks to the naval yard on Socotra, one of the Soviet's most vital sea bases which serves the fleets that patrol the vast Indian Ocean, the Red Sea and the Persian Gulf. They were taken to the far end of the harbour, past various warships, two Berezina replenishment ships, and submarines of varying sizes, from the huge nuclear power Delta and Hotel Class down to a more conventional India Class rescue sub with its two Deep Submergence Recovery Vessels affixed on its after casing. Their vehicle stopped at the end of a long quay where there was a jetty leading to a waiting submarine. But first they were taken into a quayside office and introduced to another man. Within an hour of their arrival at the harbour, the diesel-electric engines of a Kilo Class patrol submarine were quietly humming and its six new passengers were resting in the officers' wardroom as the vessel cast off. It sailed past the harbour entrance lights and out into the blackness of the Arabian Sea where it set a course for due north.

Destination . . . the Persian Gulf.

Reported Missing

THE WAIT in order to see Superintendent Stanley Stott was the same as Watson had experienced. He was exactly as Watson had described, the red lips accentuated by the reddish-fair beard, the unsmiling semi-institutionalised face, the clipped formality of his Midlands accent. There was no greeting or introduction when Bria was shown into Stott's office, only a perfunctory, "Well, what's the trouble?"

"It's about my friend, a Mr Gordon Watson. He works for International, the tobacco people. He's gone missing."

"Missing! That's strange. Very strange indeed. People don't go missing just like that in this part of the world, at least not the expats."

"Well, Gordon Watson is missing. We haven't seen him now for nearly a week and we're really concerned about him. I've done all the checks . . . with his mates, his office, I've even phoned his home in Scotland, although I never let on to his wife that we didn't know where he was. I just said he had asked me to call as he had to leave for the Interior on an important business trip. So I'm here in case maybe you . . ."

"We've got no missing persons on our books Mr . . . ?"

"Bria . . . that's B-R-I-A."

"I think I remember your friend, Mr Bria. He had a bit of a drink problem, didn't he?"

"Drink problem! You must be joking, Superintendent. Gordon is no drinker."

"He was inside for it though."

"Listen, I'm telling you . . . my friend Gordon Watson is no booze artist. Okay, he was unlucky one night when someone pranged his car and he had a pint too much for your breath test or whatever you do. But the guy is no lush. He has a couple of nights at the Rani every week . . . four or five pints with the boys. Like the rest of us, he'll keep a few cans at home. That's it. He's most certainly no drinker."

"Well, whatever. We've got no missing persons on the books, not British expats anyway. There are always the usual Indians and Filipinos absconding from their employers, but no Brits. And we've got no bodies in the morgue waiting identification. Maybe your friend has gone to Dubai? Lots of good bars there."

Bria flashed angrily at that remark. "You can forget that line."

"Merely a thought, Mr . . . ?"

"Bria . . . ."

His mood was slightly more subdued this time. "But people do take off. Once you have the visa it's fairly easy to move around this part of the world. He may have gone up to Bahrain or taken one of the tours they have started running to Oman."

"No. That's not him. Like most of the guys here, he sends most of his pay cheque home to the wife and kids every month and there's just enough left for a few nights with the boys . . . and at £2.40 a pint I really mean a few nights. He's just not the type to up and off somewhere for a fling. Superintendent . . . did he tell you the story about the men from Razak?"

There was a slight delay before he answered and his words seemed more calculated than they had been. "Yes, he mentioned something but it didn't seem all that relevant to me at the time and I didn't take the details. Why, what was there about Razak that was of any importance?"

Brian wondered for a moment whether or not the policeman should be told everything. He decided that there could be no harm in telling him about Gordon and the mystery men from Razak. He told the full story as he knew it.

"Finally, it became an obsession with him. He was sure there was something clandestine about these guys from Razak and he was only put off when he met the Dutchmen at the Rani Bar. At least, that's what he told me. But I'm certain that even after that night he was still sure something was going on. That was the last time I saw him. After that there were several phone calls between us and we had our usual chats, mainly gossipy sort of stuff . . . about who was going on leave, and so on. He seemed perfectly normal and cheerful. His last words were that he would be arranging a night at his place for some of the boys to have a drink and he would let me know. Now let's get the dates right. Our last night at the Rani, when the Dutchmen were there, was just before the start of Ramadan. The last time he phoned me was on Saturday, the 7th of this month, for I remember he mentioned the date and it was only ten days till Ramadan finished. Tommy Torrance who runs the International Tobacco Office in Rani says he came into work on the Sunday morning — that would be the 8th. Then he went out on a call to a customer and never returned. That was the last they saw of him.

"I've been round all the group, you know the gang of us who meet at the Rani, and I've been to see his neighbour, but with no luck. Mrs Percy, that's the neighbour, knew he was away, she said, for his lights hadn't been on since the Saturday night. She had heard him leave for work on the Sunday and when he didn't come home that night she just assumed he was off on one of his usual rounds of customers up country."

"What about his car?"

"There's no sign of it."

"Well, that could mean something, Mr Bria. He's off and his car is away too. I mean, it does sound like he's just taken off somewhere."

"Superintendent . . . he hasn't. That is most definitely not him."

"Well, I'll have him recorded as missing. But you realise we can't muster the entire Emirate Police Force in order to look for one missing man. We'll make the usual checks. And just for the record books, I'd like some details of yourself, Mr Bria. English, I take it?"

"No . . . Australian."

"Oh," he said, looking up from his pad with what Bria suspected was a look of slight disdain. "You don't sound it. And your sponsor?"

"The Ministry of Public Buildings."

"You may know Colonel Bainbridge, then. He's the Public Relations Adviser to His Excellency the Minister."

"I do indeed. In fact, I work for him. We're doing a project together on the mosques of the country. I'm a photographer, you see."

"Have you mentioned any of this to the colonel?"

"No . . . not as yet. Should I have?"

"Oh, that's entirely up to you. And you say you informed Watson's wife in England?"

"In Scotland . . . yes. But she doesn't suspect anything and seemed to understand quite readily when I told her he had been called away on business."

At that Bria leaned forward in his seat, thinking an appeal of sorts to the cold-eyed policeman sitting in front of him might elicit some form of response. "What do you think, Superintendent? Do you think there was anything in these five men that intrigued Gordon so much? Could it be that there was something and that they are in some way the reason for his disappearance?"

The policeman pondered before looking up at Bria. "That I don't know. Your friend touched on the subject when he came to see me about the Pakistani chap who was murdered in prison. I did say to him then that if he thought there was anything suspicious to report it to the proper authorities and they would make the appropriate inquiries. That is what the police are for, you know. However, it was merely mentioned by him at the time and no report was made of the incident. You say he had been following the men to try and find out something? Just what did he expect to find out?"

"I don't quite know. I think he had let his imagination run away with him. He was thinking up all sorts of things . . . that they might be spies or involved in some big smuggling operation . . . that the Europeans might even have been from the Mafia. He was thinking everything. That was the way it had become with him."

"I don't suppose you developed any such thoughts yourself, Mr Bria?"

"Not until he disappeared I didn't."

"And since he disappeared?"

"I don't know. Now I'm ready to be suspicious about anything after the way he vanished like he did."

"Not to the extent, I trust, of you too trying to play detective with these men from the Fish Souk?"

"Well, I certainly feel like doing something."

"Mr Bria . . . take my advice and leave the investigations to the people who are experienced in such matters. If there's anything to Watson's story, we will find out. In the meantime, I will institute inquiries about your friend."

The phone was in the superintendent's hand the second Brian Bria left his office and he was speaking to his secretary-assistant. "Get me the colonel on the line. And quickly."

Bria had gone straight from the Police Headquarters to the Ministries Area and the offices of the Ministry of Public Buildings. He always loathed going to the Ministry offices for he could never get into one of the shaded car ports they had there and that meant an instant sauna as soon as he returned and sat behind the wheel of his Toyota Cressida.

Colonel Bainbridge was in his office and was free to see him as soon as he arrived. "You look concerned, Brian, dear boy. What's on your mind?"

He told him the story of the disappearance of his friend Watson and how he had just been to see the superintendent at Police HQ. "Remember you said you would make some inquiries, Billy, when I told you about the five men Gordon had spotted? Did you find anything?"

"Yes, well, I did make inquiries like I said I would and my contacts promised they would put out feelers to see if there was anything funny going on. But so far none of them have come back to me, which makes me assume that any reply will be in the negative. I must say, though, it is a bit strange your friend going off the way he did. Not like him I take it?"

"Not in the slightest. He hasn't gone off anywhere, though. I can assure you of that. Something has happened to him. Something drastic. I know that . . . I just know it somehow. There's too much of a coincidence about those guys from Razak and the ones they met . . . the Europeans."

"Those are the ones you said were Dutch?"

"That's right."

"Well, are they the Dutchmen you said that they were?"

"I don't know."

"But why don't you know? What else could they be?"

"I don't know, Billy. I'm really puzzled. Why would Dutchmen be buying fish from guys who aren't fishermen?"

"What makes you think the others weren't fishermen?"

"Well, for a start they were from Razak, up in the mountains and about 100 miles from the sea. There are about as many fishermen up there as you'd get living in the middle of Coventry."

"Yes, but they're here by the sea now and living at the harbour. They could be in the fishing business now. Perhaps that's why they came to live here. One never knows."

"I suppose you could be right. On the other hand . . . Billy, I'll need to make inquiries myself before I'm really satisfied."

The colonel's face flushed slightly at that and he landed a clenched fist firmly on the table as he spoke. "Brian, for God's sake you be careful. Have nothing to do with this. You've told the police, let them get on with it. And supposing there is something, whatever that something might be. Do you think a tobacco company rep or a photographer, with all due respect that is, is going to find out?"

"Logically I have no case. I know. But I still have a friend who's missing and I've got to do something, even to satisfy myself that I just didn't let him disappear without making any effort to find him. It's the very least I can do. Besides, as the superintendent said, there's not much they can do. And your inquiries with your contacts didn't turn up anything. So, at the moment we know nothing about these guys who were in the jail with Gordon, and worse still we know nothing about Gordon himself. Billy, I want a week off from the project. And you can't quibble about that. Haven't taken any time off since coming here. And that's nearly 11 months now. I need a break and I want to do something about finding Gordon Watson."

"Well, as no words of warning are going to deter you, what can I say? Take the week then. What are you doing about your car?"

"Oh yes . . . I got that Ministry memo about handing your car in if you get leave. Bloody regulations. Do we need to tell them I won't be at work for a week?"

"I suppose in your case not. What is it you've got anyway?"

"A Cressida. Toyota Cressida."

"Oh, yes I know. That vivid red thing."

"No, it's silver grey actually, with the Ministry emblem on the passenger door."

"That's right, so it is."

"Unlike Gordon who went walking down all those little streets behind the Fish Souk, I'm just going to sit in the car and observe everything that's going on. I did it last night actually, but couldn't stay for long as I was expecting someone at the flat. But I'll be back again tonight and I'm going to sit there till I see something."

"Well, I'm going to say nothing more on the subject. You know my views about what you are up to. Just be careful, especially down in that harbour area. I don't want you disappearing too."

"Don't worry, Billy. She'll be apples."

"I beg your pardon?"

"Oh, sorry about that. Everything will be all right."

In Gordon's Footsteps

HE SWITCHED off his headlights as he turned his car from the main harbour road into Way 177, the broad but short, dusty street which led up to the spice mill. This was the point Watson had told him he had turned right down a narrow alley to the house where he had seen the men from Razak and the others. As he approached the spice mill with only his side lights on, he slowed the car then stopped to look at the scene.

To the left there was a stretch of vacant ground about 100 metres square. He remembered having parked the car there on occasions when he had been at the Fish Souk. At the far end, to the left of the vacant ground, there were some other houses and narrow lanes which led out to a main road adjacent to the harbour road. To the right he could see the long lane Watson had described. About 50 metres along it he could see a junction. He remembered Watson had said that the house was on the left at the far end of the junction.

Just as he had described it, the lane was only wide enough to take his car, with only a few inches to spare on either side of the protruding wing mirrors. He drove slowly down in first gear and when he came to the junction he could see lights on in the house which faced up the street. A window in the house had only half a curtain and he could see figures moving about inside. One man appeared to be in Western casual clothing, but Bria couldn't be sure as he also had to keep his eyes on the close proximity of the houses between which he was driving.

At the junction he turned the car sharply to the right, down another narrow lane, and eventually came out on the main harbour road again. There he turned right and a minute later was back at Way 177 from where he had started. This time he only drove as far as the spice mill where he stopped the car and switched off the engine, leaving his side lights on. He got out of the car and studied the mill.

It was two storeys high and the tallest building in the vicinity, all the others being squat adobe houses typical of the kind that could be found in any of the villages of the Interior and in which people had been living for hundreds of years, each marking the arrival of the new world with a three-metre TV antenna. At the side of the building there was an outside flight of stairs which led to a landing on which there was a door. Beside the landing there was a short iron ladder, fixed to the rough stone wall of the side of the building and leading up to the crenellated roof of the mill. This had obviously been the little community's fort at one time as it was on the highest ground in the area and commanded a view of the entire suburb.

Tony Mills, his Army friend, who had been promoted to major and posted from Jiza in the mountains to the Emir's Armed Forces Training Regiment near the capital, had loaned him a rifle night-sight which he was assured would enable him to see clearly up to 250 metres, even in the dimmest of light. Checking to see that no one was around, he climbed up the stairs and then the ladder of the mill building and lay down on the roof, using the night-sight like a telescope between the short crenellations.

"Ouch," he grimaced as his bare elbows touched the metal of the corrugated roof, still burning hot from the sun it had soaked that day. "Bloody hell . . . I'll get roasted alive if I lie here any longer." He squatted instead, having made a pastime out of practising it Arab-style, crouch-sitting as they would in groups for hours on end with their feet flat on the ground and looking as comfortable as perched birds. Then he focused the sight on the little house down the narrow street.

He was amazed at the clarity of the picture through the blue tinted glass. It was as though someone had floodlit the whole scene as it brought into view the little house and the window with the half curtain. It was only a flimsy net curtain and the sight was so powerful it could see through that as well. There was some movement in the room into which he was looking, then a man came into view. He could only see the lower half of the body, but that was enough to determine he was in Western casual dress just as Bria had thought when he had caught a glimpse as he passed earlier in the car.

Then, as suddenly he had come into view, the picture blurred and he could see nothing. His perch on the roof of the building was a giant hotplate and the sweat was pouring from him. Some of it had trickled into the sight's eyeglass. He slipped off his light cotton shirt, dried his face and cleaned the moisture from the sight, moving to squat in an even better position at the corner of the building immediately over the street. As he thought he might be seen from the street below, he took a careful look around to ensure he hadn't been observed. It appeared there was no one around. The little narrow streets were motionless and only the sounds of radios with their incessant Arabic music, one louder than the others playing one of those Egyptian orchestras the Arabs seemed to love so much with their strange musical cacophony, so perfectly discordant it seemed almost harmonious. There were televisions too with their own noises and their staccato blue flashes eerily lighting the darkened street. Then a loud clatter from a nearby corner made him look up sharply. It turned out to be from a flock of goats grubbing in a rubbish heap, one of them knocking over a big can.

He could hear a car engine in the distance; then its headlights came into view and it stopped at the far end of the big piece of waste ground, about 80 to 90 metres away. Without using the sight he could see three men in European dress stepping from the car, then he turned away presuming they would be going into one of the houses nearby. There was stillness again and he was sure that no one was around. He focused the night-sight once more on the little window of the house. This time he could see a man sitting on a wooden chair. Then, slowly, he turned the prism of the sight, bringing the man even sharper into focus. "God, it *is*   him. The bloody big Ja Ja Dutchman who had them all saying they were Ajax supporters." He smiled wryly to himself at that, as he wiped his face once more and dried the sight again.

He took extra care this time in refocusing the sight and was more amazed each time he looked through it how it transformed the dark night scene into one of almost daytime brilliance. He remembered the story about the night-sights when he was in Ireland and he thought, "No wonder all the squaddies had wanted them." The Ministry had said then that they couldn't afford the £2,000 price for each one.

He could see the big man still sitting there in the chair. He was using his hands as though he was demonstrating something to people around him. Others were there in the room for he could see shadows and movement to the right of the window. Then someone in a dishdasha stood with his back to the window and obliterated the Dutchman. Bria cursed at not being able to see him properly.

The roof of the building seemed to be getting hotter, although he thought that would be impossible, and he wiped the sweat once more as well as the eyepiece of the sight.

The man had moved away from the window by this time and the Dutchman came into view once more. He had something across his lap and was again using his hands, in an even livelier fashion than before. Then he grabbed hold of the long black object that had been lying across his thighs and held it towards his chest.

"Christ . . . a bloody gun. A bloody Kalashnikov."

The man with the gun disappeared from view once again as another man, in national dress and with a full beard, crossed the room and stopped in front of the window.

It was the blast from the explosion that hit him first. A puff of furnace air flashed on the right side of his face, followed by a great whoosh sound and the most enormous of bangs, then the cracks and the tinkling of glass shattering and the clattering on tin roofs of debris. It seemed to continue for ages but in fact lasted only a few brief seconds. Then for a short time there was a strange silence, eerily accentuated by the roar it had followed. The first sound after that was of a car starting up and driving off. And suddenly the little community startled into life. Doors opened and men were shouting and women and children were screaming and the once dark piece of vacant ground lit up with the bonfire brilliance of the twisted and shattered ruins of what had once been his car.

Too frightened to move, even to wipe the streams of sweat running down his body, he had stayed on the roof for over an hour after the explosion. The fire brigade had come and extinguished the blaze. So too had several police cars which waited, for an eternity it had seemed, before slowly prowling the area and finally leaving. He had found another ladder which went down from the roof at the rear of the mill building and from there he got to the Muna Hotel on the harbour road, from where he was able to phone the Training Regiment to speak to Tony Mills.

An hour later they were sitting in the coffee shop in the ground floor of the cavernous Inter-Continental hotel, the bar being closed for Ramadan.

"There you are, Brian," said Mills, surreptitiously pouring a large measure of Cognac from a hip flask into his friend's coffee. "I brought that along, for you sounded as though you obviously needed it. Right, now let's get it . . . right from the very beginning."

He went over the story mentioning every detail he could.

"So you saw this guy sitting there with the Kalashnikov. How do you know a Kalashnikov anyway?"

"That curved magazine, it's so unmistakable. Hey, are you forgetting where I've been?"

"Sorry about that. But go on . . . there was a guy with a beard."

"Yes. It was one of these full ones. You know, the ones that seem to stick out from their chin . . . like all the Fundamentalists have. It was when he stood in front of the Dutchman that it all happened."

"Did the whoosh come before the bang or the bang first?"

"It all seemed to happen together, except for the debris falling. That made a helluva din, rattling on all the roofs like it did and the windows of the houses shattering. It was quite a commotion."

"But getting back to the whoosh and the bang again. Which do you think came first?"

"The very first I knew was this puff of hot wind hitting me on my right cheek and then all the noises. When I think about it, though, I'm sure the whoosh came first. And then . . . yes . . . and then when it was all over, I could hear a car start up and drive off. That's right, it would be the car that had driven up to the waste ground just minutes before. I remember it now for I wondered if they could see me. Three guys had got out of the car and I got the impression they were Brits which I thought unusual down there for you never get a Brit up these back alleys."

"What made you think they were Brits?"

"I only glanced at them, thinking they would be going into one of the houses and I was sure they had fair skins. Of course they could have been anything. I just got that impression somehow about them being Brits. I was too interested in what I could see with the night-sight and only gave them a glance just to make sure they hadn't seen me."

"And the whoosh and the bang once more . . . you think it was the whoosh that came first?"

"Tony . . . so much happened all at once. But I think that's the way it went.

The hot air, the whoosh, the bang, the clatter, the silence, the screams, the shouts, the brilliance of the fire . . . geez a car can really burn, can't it! What do you make of it all, Tony?"

"That you're one lucky guy. That rocket was meant for you."

"Rocket! . . . Rocket! . . . What do you mean?"

"Your car was hit by a rocket. I didn't say at the time, but when we drove past what was left of it you could see the impact hole."

"For Christ sake, Tony, the car was all holes with the fire and gas tank going up."

"Yes, but the hole I was talking about was on the driver's door which had got blown off and was lying propped up beside the wreck. It was a projectile of some kind which did that. Looks like they used an anti-tank rocket of sorts. And the whoosh before the bang. That was it coming at you. Whatever it was and whoever fired it . . . they didn't want any walking wounded."

"I just assumed that somehow it had gone up of its own accord . . . you know, an electrical fault or something? It happened to a friend of mine only last week with a new Range Rover he had bought. He had stopped, got out of the car and up it went and so quickly, he said, he couldn't believe it. Are you sure, Tony?"

"From what you tell me of the events and from that hole in the door I'd stake my reputation on it. And what about the car that drove away! Why would a car drive away after an explosion like that? Surely just out of curiosity even they would have stayed to have a look? Your Brits or whoever they were don't seem to like you, old chum."

"They warned me, you know. And they repeated it over and over that I shouldn't go and that I should leave it to them and that I shouldn't be interfering."

"Who was that?"

"Stott, the cop, and Bainbridge."

"Who knew you'd be there tonight?"

"The colonel did. And Stott would suspect I'd be nosing around. You know I did a check on Stott?"

"What kind of check?"

"Got an old workmate from the paper I used to work on in Fleet Street, or what used to be Fleet Street that is, to do a cuttings check from our library. Sure enough, Stott gets a couple of mentions. One was the report of a trial in Ulster where he was a sergeant in the Paras and was accused of shooting an unarmed IRA suspect, but was cleared. The other was when he was in the Prison Service. He was commended for bravery after a big jail riot in the North of England. But the interesting part was in the first clip, which was back in the early 'seventies. An officer at the trial spoke of his exemplary service in the Paras both at home and abroad. And the officer . . . Colonel Billy Bainbridge. I didn't mention it to Billy and he's never let on to me that he and Stott have an old connection. He should have . . . shouldn't he? I mean, I did tell him I had seen him about Gordon but he said nothing, which puzzled me. Stott I don't fancy. He seems a real cold fish. Gordon thought the same too."

"And he suspected you would be here tonight?"

"Not specifically tonight, but he would know that I would be looking around sometime."

"But Bainbridge knew you would be there?"

"Yes . . . for I asked him for leave because I said I had to do something in order to try and find Gordon. I even asked him about keeping the car . . . ." He stopped suddenly as he said that and grasped his friend's wrist tightly. "Tony. The car. That's it. The car. He asked me what I was driving and what colour it was. That's it. The car. He knew where I'd be and what I was driving. Even the bloody colour . . . and with the Ministry logo on the door. Christ, I even told him I would be sitting inside it tonight — at the Fish Souk, watching everything that was going on. He knew."

"Hold it, mate. Who knew?"

"Billy. Colonel Billy Bainbridge, the bastard. He knew. What in hell is going on, Tony? Why would Billy want me out of the way? I kept wondering why he had asked me about the car. He doesn't talk that kind of trivia. What kind of car do you drive and what colour is it? That's not him."

"So the colonel and Stott must be in some kind of collusion?"

"Looks like it. But why? And why me, Tony? There's no reason to get rid of me."

"Of course there is."

"What, for Christ sake?"

"You were making the same inquiries as your friend Watson. He obviously discovered something and now he's vanished. You discovered something too, even though it was just a big Dutchman sitting with a gun on his lap. But it's the one thing you have in common. You were making inquiries that they didn't want you to make and had warned you off making. Your friend Watson suspected there was something sinister. Well, it looks as though the poor bloke was right. Whatever it is it must be something big with the likes of Bainbridge and the superintendent being involved. I mean, this is not smuggling cigarettes or even coke. This is something big-big, Brian. And you're right up to your neck in it."

"And do you know, Tony? Somebody else warned me off. It's just come back to me. David Anthony. He's a drinking friend at the Rani bar. And he's an old Army chum of Bainbridge's. He told me about that himself."

"So he could be in whatever it is with them?"

"I don't know, Tony. Anything's possible now. Although David! No. That's really stretching the imagination. I can't conceive him wanting to . . ."

"Bump you off? Did you suspect Billy would either?"

"Not in my wildest dreams. And I still can't realise it. Surely not, Tony? He's an old friend. We've known each other for years. He brought me out here for this big prestige project with the book. He needs me. Why should he want to get rid of me?"

"Back to what I said. Whatever you've stumbled on has got something to do with him, the cop and perhaps this David Anthony. Then there are the guys who came in the car tonight. They were somebody's henchmen obviously. Could they have been some of the Dutchmen?"

"No. They weren't the Dutchmen. These guys weren't that big. The Dutchmen are all giants, not one under the six-foot-plus mark. And another thing. Although I keep calling them Dutchmen. They're not. That's something I know for a fact."

"What are they then?"

"Haven't a clue. They're the five guys who speak good English, presumably good Dutch, fittest looking guys you've seen, but there's no way they're from Holland."

"You know that for sure?"

"For sure. And they've got something to do with Gordon's disappearance and my rocket. How about your Intelligence guys at the base? Any chance they've heard about anything funny going on? Maybe there's a whisper that something's in the air. You know this part of the world. Anything's liable to happen. Maybe there's a revolution or something afoot and maybe these guys are arms dealers . . . or even advisers of sorts, you know like the Americans and the Russians have in various countries?"

"Like Spetsnaz even."

"What are they again . . . Spetsnaz?"

"Like Russian commando groups. We've had several lectures on them. They've got units of them down in the PDRY but they only move them into countries that are having problems, although they do lots of recces to get to know various areas. But everything's quiet enough here."

"Except for what happened to Gordon and myself. Tony, you should know better about the Middle East. Everything's quiet till it happens. Remember King Faisal . . . a crazed cousin shoots him dead at point blank range. And Sadat at the big parade. And look at the cousins, brothers and uncles and sons even that have done in the old man over the years in this place."

"I'll see what I can find out. Where are you going to stay tonight?"

"Thanks for reminding me. I was just going home to the flats. But I can't now. Can I!"

"You better come with me then. We've got plenty of spare rooms in our block at the barracks and with this being Ramadan, nobody is much caring. You know, if ever you wanted to take over this country, Ramadan's the time to do it. Mostly everyone's gone home on leave and those who are around just sleep most of the day as they stay up half the night eating and playing their card games and the like."

"Could that be it, then? Is someone planning something while the nation is half-asleep? Doing a Yom Kippur on them?"

"Hardly a Yom Kippur, Brian."

"You know what I mean. Taking them by surprise when they're all at the mosques or else switched off."

"But who? The neighbours are friendly and the days of the Saudis marching in with thousands of horsemen ended when they tried to take on the Omanis at Buraimi."

"I know, Tony. The neighbours are friendly all right. It's the people in your own house you've got to watch in these parts. They say the guv'nor fears some of his own senior ministers more that he does anybody. While he was busy building up the country, they were busy building up the company. Do you know one of them is listed in the world's richest men ratings? And there are two lots of brothers who between them, it's reckoned could buy out the Sultan of Brunei. It could be any of them that's up to something. You never know, Tony. More likely, though, it's someone connected with Billy Bainbridge. Of course, that's it. Mustafa Abdullah, the Minister! He's the one I've been told that's the most ambitious man in the country. His very own father was involved in a takeover bid at one time. What's more, it was with people from Razak. It runs in the family. And there's no way that Billy Bainbridge is here purely as a Public Relations man for the Ministry of Public Buildings and organising a book on mosques. What date is it anyway?"

"That's easily answered. It's the 13th. Friday, 13 May 1988."

"Might have known it was a Friday the 13th."

"I don't know, Brian. After what you missed tonight, this has been your lucky day."

"That gives them three more days then."

"Three days for what? And who are them?"

"The Eid al Fitr is next Tuesday, 17 May. That's the first day after Ramadan ends so that means they've got only three more days of Ramadan left."

"And then?"

"Bainbridge . . . Stott . . . The Dutchmen . . . The Minister . . . David Anthony even. Who knows? But something is going on. Something is going to happen. I'm convinced of that. And I plan to find out. But I need your help, Tony."

"Count me in. I'm bored out of my mind at the Regiment. At least out in the desert we got the odd pot-shot at smugglers. I could do with a bit of action. So what's the plan, Brian?"

The Plan Revealed

BRIA AND his Army friend Tony Mills discussed their plan of action.

"It's up to me to do something now, isn't it? I mean, I've been thrust right into this. But that's the way of life. I've got a boss with three goons on the loose looking for me with rockets and God knows what else. There's a cop who I'm sure is one of them. And I can't hide anywhere — well, for long that is."

"Well, we'll need to get moving, Brian. The Dutchmen are the key to it. If we can find out more about them it should help us figure out the five guys at the Fish Souk."

"Okay, we'll do that. I was trying to pump some information about them out of Saby. You know, the head barman at the Rani where they're staying? He didn't have much to say about them except to confide that he thinks they're in Holland's marathon team for the Seoul Olympics. He says they still go out every morning at 4.30 — 4.30 for God's sake! — running their heads off. They don't come back till about six then they go straight into the gym for about an hour and on to the swimming pool. And that's before breakfast. He says the other diners have been complaining about the way they come in and empty all the buffet trays. So why don't we go and check out their rooms when they're out training tomorrow morning?"

"I doubt if you'll find badges saying 'I'm a Spetsnaz'."

"I know, I know. But there's got to be something . . . just something that takes us a bit further. Saby's brother-in-law Vijay is the Head Housekeeper at the hotel. Maybe he'll fix it up for us. But first of all I'll need some things from the flat. Don't like your shaving gear for a start. And where did you get that after-shave . . . the QM's store? Real cheapo it is. And I need my Nikon."

"Think they'll pose for pictures?"

They drove into the car park at the rear of the Hamat House flats. Mills parked the car near the main entrance. "I'll run up myself," said Bria. "Won't be more than five minutes."

It was always nice to step through the big glass doors that opened into the marbled entry foyer of the flats; the coolness of the air-conditioning provided a relieving and contrasting chill to the muggy and sweltering conditions outside the building. As he waited for the lift he stood beneath one of the big air-conditioning outlets in the corridor relishing its gentle and refreshing breeze.

Everything seemed normal at his sixth-floor flat, but then no one could get through those stout German doors unless they had special keys. He quickly packed an overnight bag, thinking it was just like being back in London when the office had called telling him to come to work ready as there was an overseas assignment. Before closing the bag he had a final look at the contents — shirts, slacks, socks, underpants, toothbrush, shaving kit, camera, spare film. That would do. "Oh, and some money." He was on his way to the kitchen for a drink of cool water from the fridge when the doorbell rang. It was one of those cheerful three-chime bells which went down the scale slowly, but loudly . . . doh, soh, ray. He presumed it was Mills.

"Maybe he doesn't think I'm hurrying enough," he thought and just as he was about to turn the double mortice lock in the door, he checked through Germany's contribution to the house construction of the country, the spy-hole, Funny, he had never thought of using it before. There never had been any need. Strangely enough, somebody had blacked it out. He took another look as the doorbell went one more time and for a few fleeting seconds he could see who was standing there before a hand was raised to block out the view again.

"Jesus," he gasped as he stood back from the door, shocked at what he had seen. Two of the colonel's "mechanics", the ones called McDaid and McQuade, stood there, each with an automatic rifle in their arms.

The bell went again and the doh, soh, ray wasn't cheerful any more. He retreated back through the vestibule from the big main door. The hefty main door of the flat opened into the house, but the second door, which went from the vestibule into the hall, opened back into the vestibule itself. When locked it couldn't be forced as it had to be pulled. It was just as robust as the outside door and it too had a double mortice lock. He quickly locked it, turning the key twice. Then he ran through the house to one of the verandahs to try to attract the attention of Mills.

He couldn't see him. The bell went once more, an idiotic menacing ring about it this time. Then he could hear hammering at the door and shouting. It was just then that the gun — or was it two guns? — went off, sounding like there was someone out in the corridor at work with a pneumatic drill. The guns stopped and the men were shouting again. "We know you're in there, Bria." Then there was the sound from the other nearby flats of terrified women and children screaming.

He ran quickly through the house again to the bedroom balcony to have another look for Mills but there was still no sign of him. He checked the distance to the balconies of the flats below on the fifth floor. Yes, he would make it all right with two sheets tied. No problem. Only about ten feet from the bottom of his balcony's teak balustrade to the top of the moghul arch of the balcony below, then he could swing through the high point of the arch and jump.

The guns started again. It sounded as if they were through the front door.

But the second door would hold. It had to. The guns went off yet again. Inside the first door they seemed louder this time. Bullets were coming through the vestibule door into the flat and hitting the wall of the long hall, knocking huge lumps off the plaster and stone. The door still held and the guns stopped for a brief second before starting again. As soon as they did there was a heavy thump as though something had fallen against the door. The guns stopped. Then a man's voice shouted "Bastard" and a single shot rang out. There was another muffled noise like someone falling and the loud clatter of something metallic hitting the terrazzo floor. Then silence.

"Are you all right, Brian? Brian, are you there?"

It was Tony Mills.

The side of the vestibule door facing towards him looked like it had been attacked with a hundred axes, the inch-and-a-half veneered board holed and splayed with bullets. Yet the double mortice had held and the key turned normally with two clicks. Something was obviously lying against the door which wouldn't open.

"Hold it a minute, Brian," said Mills.

The pungent smell of burnt cordite hit him as soon as the door was free to open. The vestibule was sprayed with blood and the bodies of two men were on the floor. One had a piece missing from the back of his head, out of which blood was still pumping.

"Not a pretty sight, are they?" said Mills, standing over them with a pistol in his right hand. "McDaid and McQuade. Who would ever have thought it would have ended like this."

"You know them then? They were working for Bainbridge. They're two of his men."

"It figures. I was their platoon commander in the Paras and they left to be mercenaries. Last I heard they were in Sri Lanka. But then they would be booted out when the Indians went in. I didn't know they were with Red Alert."

"And you shot both of them?"

"No. Only one. McQuade. McDaid must have been an own goal," Tony replied coolly, almost casually, like a man who seemed used to killing. "They were still firing away, bullets flying everywhere when I ran along the corridor and, just as I got there, one of them fell. The other one stopped firing and when he looked up I was standing with my gun pointed at his head. For the tiniest fraction of a second he knew it was me and I knew it was him. He shouted out and I shot him. I knew then that the other one would be McDaid. They were always together. Couple of right rascals. Bloody good soldiers, though. But that was always the way of it, whether it's the British Army or . . . or any other army. Right, Brian," he then said with some urgency. "We better make ourselves scarce very fast. We're both right in it now. Here, you take McQuade's gun. I'll get the other."

"But . . . ."

"But nothing. If this is what the colonel thinks of you, you're going to need some kind of protection."

Tony Mills went on his own to the Rani Hotel to speak with Saby, the Indian who managed the Tie Bar. He sat at a table alone away from the crowd around the bar and waited. Saby, he knew, regularly patrolled the bar making sure customers never had to wait for a drink.

"Regimental bugger," he thought as he watched him asking customers what they would like at the precise moment they had downed the last of their drink.

Saby shook his head when Tony asked if his brother-in-law Vijay would let them into one of the bedrooms. "No . . . no, he wouldn't dream of allowing that," he answered. "It's against all the rules."

"But Saby. You know Brian. He's in a real spot. I can assure you this is a matter of life and death. And I really mean that. These Dutchmen are not the businessmen you might think they are."

"Oh! Then what are they?"

"Well, we think they're involved in something. And it's all linked up with the disappearance of Brian's friend. You know, the Scottish chap, Gordon Watson?"

"Have you not heard from him yet?"

"No. But there's a connection with these guys. Saby, we must get into their rooms. Don't worry, we'll be in and out quickly before they come back from their morning training run."

"Why don't you tell the police if it is that bad?" the Indian answered with a concerned look on his face.

"Because there's something going on that involves lots of influential people and it's not the time for the police to be interfering. We think there's one of the police mixed up in it anyway."

Saby looked around the room at that. "You know, there's about six of them in here tonight. Never had as many cops as that before. Don't look over, but in the table in the corner behind me there are two plainclothes men from the Rani Police Station. At the other end of the room there are two from Internal Security. One of the barmen tells me there are another two from one of the other intelligence organisations. Is this to do with your friend Brian?"

"More than likely. If he can just find out about these Dutchmen everything will be cleared up, I'm sure. Don't worry, Saby, you or your brother-in-law won't be involved. I promise you that."

He hesitated before replying. "You'd better speak to him yourself. He comes to work about 4 a.m. to supervise early breakfasts and calls. Tell me, Mr Tony. These Dutchmen. What do you think they are? Gangsters or something?"

"Yes, Saby. That's a good way of putting it. They're gangsters all right. International gangsters at that."

At precisely 4.32 a.m. next morning, Sunday, 15 May, Bria and Mills watched from their car in the high terrace park above the hotel entrance as the five men emerged wearing shorts and running shoes. Two of them had small packs on their backs. With some obvious gusto they ran up the steep slope from the big doorway of the hotel to the main road and, in single file, headed along Emir Street in the direction that led away from town.

"God, look at them!" exclaimed Mills. "That's not a jog they're off for. That's real running."

With great reluctance Vijay said he would take them to their rooms. "Mr Gordon, your friend, lived in the hotel when he first came to Rani. Very nice man. I'm doing this because of him. We better go round the back of the building. I don't want you going through reception. The less you are seen the better," he said earnestly.

He took them through a door at the rear which led to a stairway and they climbed to the second floor. "They've got adjoining rooms," he said. "Numbers 23 and 25."

"Neat buggers, aren't they?" said Mills as they walked into the first of the rooms.

"Their rooms are always like this," Vijay said. "They even make their beds sometimes. Wish we had more guests like them. Only thing is they never leave the room unattended when we are cleaning them out. There's always two of them here. It's as though they don't trust us."

It didn't take them long to search the drawers, being careful not to disturb anything. In the open compartment of one of the bedside cupboards, Mills found some newspapers. "Look at these, Brian. *De Volkskrant, Het Vaderland* and *De Rotterdammer*. Dutch aren't they?"

"Yes, and here are their five passports, all with the Royal Netherlands stamp. But I expected that. You can't go around saying you're Dutch and not have a Dutch passport. But they're still not Dutch. No way."

"Checked the tabs on their shirts and vests?" asked Mills.

"Yes, most of them have none. The ones that do are either Taiwan or Portugal."

They looked over the toilet gear in the bathroom. There was an electric shaver, a Remington; a half-empty pack of disposable razors, Wilkinsons; a big economy can of Gillette shaving foam; and a tube of Signal toothpaste.

"Well, they were wise enough to do their shopping locally," remarked Bria.

"You didn't expect Mockba wall posters or GUM department store carrier bags, did you?"

"Well, not the GUM carrier bags. I've been there. They don't give them."

"What about this big cupboard in the hallway," Mills asked Vijay as he pulled at its doors.

"It's locked, but I've got a key," he replied. He opened the wide doors of the big walk-in cupboard, at the bottom of which was a neat row of canvas-topped boots with rugged, mountain climbers' soles and three suitcases sitting on top of a heavy-duty tin trunk, the kind which they sold in the local souks and which the expats from the subcontinent would pack with goods and presents to take home when their contracts were over. It was padlocked.

"Got a key to fit that?" Brian asked Vijay.

"Perhaps. I keep a ring of keys which can open any suitcase or padlock. People are always having trouble with luggage and losing their keys."

The two men continued to search the room when Vijay had left to get the extra keys. "Not many hiding places in a hotel room, are there?" said Bria. "You can't even hide anything underneath the carpets the way they glue them down."

"What about beneath the bottom drawers of the cupboards? Let's take them out and see if there's anything there."

There wasn't in one room nor was there anything in the first three they pulled out in the second room. Then they came to a small cupboard beside a bed. Mills got down to put his hands into the space beneath the vacated drawer.

"Bingo Brian . . . look what Uncle Tony has found." He pulled out a handgun. "Hold it. There's more." He produced another two. "And wait, there's something else," he said as he pulled out a thin satchel made of cheap plastic material. He held up two of the guns to Bria. "Well now, what do we have here. This one in my right hand looks like the small Jerry Walther, but it's neater and slimmer . . . and Russian. It's a 5.45 PSM, which is Ruskie for Pistol, Self-Loading, Small. And this bigger one is a 9mm Makarov . . . look, it's even got the five-pointed star on the grip. Lost count of the lectures I've had on them. The little one's used a lot by their police and our you-know-what friends."

"Five guys but just three guns?" Bria queried.

"But weren't two of them running with small haversacks on their backs! No way would these guys go out unless they were armed in some way. Bet your boots they've a couple of Makarovs with them."

Brian picked up the thin satchel which he anxiously unzipped, taking from it a sheaf of about a dozen foolscap papers which had writing on them.

"So you really were right about them not being Dutchmen," said Mills as they studied the neat Cyrillic script of the papers.

"And you were right about your suggestion of them being Russian."

"And if they're Russian, then they're Spetsnaz. Nothing's surer."

They studied each of the papers carefully to see if, perhaps, there would be something they could decipher. There wasn't. The contents of each of the folio sheets was of a different length. Some were a mere half-dozen lines. A few were about a dozen lines. Three of them were more than 20 lines. They were all neatly hand-printed in what looked like the same hand. Each sheet was a photocopy of an original and it appeared that they were copies of messages of some kind. The last sheet was of a map of an urban area and again was a photocopy. They didn't recognise it for a minute until they realised it was upside down. It was of the Capital Area and its environs and marked with several five-pointed stars. Each star was numbered and it was obvious they were reference point markings.

"Look, there's the Emir's Palace with a star and the small mosque across the road from the Palace, you know the one they call the, what is it again . . . ?"

"It's the Saghir Mosque. It means the Little Mosque. I spent about a week trying to get permission from its Imam to photograph it."

"And look, there's another star at the houses at the Fish Souk and we know who lives there, don't we? And another one, now where is that? It's along the shoreline, north from the container terminal. Of course, it's Mina Fatima, where the oil tankers load. And Jesus, look there's one at The Hill, our barracks where you're sleeping tonight. Wait a minute, it's a little way to the south of it. Right . . . it's spot on. The Ordnance Depot. And there's one more. It's on the main jebel ridge to the west of the capital. Now what the hell is up there? Of course, the big TV mast at Jebel Azraq which serves the whole bloody country. Boy, have they got the place sewn up. If these are their objectives and they knock them out then you've got a no-function country. Total chaos. A classic Spetsnaz operation."

"But how about the Palace and the mosque? What does that indicate? Are they going to take them out too? Don't tell me they're going to assassinate the old man?"

"Doubt it. That's not their scene. Get caught at that game and the backlash would be enormous. Would topple *Glasnost* himself. Maybe it's referring to something else."

"Like what?"

"Don't know. But it means something. Could be that it's to do with the nationals in the house. Your friend Watson told you that the guys in the house were the ones from Razak who were in jail with him. The attack on the police station at Razak was by a Hussein Martyr Squad. And you said Watson also told you there was a connection between the five guys in jail and the police station attack. If one lot was a Hussein Martyr Squad, then so too could be their friends at the Fish Souk. As for the Dutchmen, well, if they are Spetsnaz like we now think, most of these star markers are on locations which are typical targets for them, facilities the lack of which can instantly reduce a country to chaos. The Palace and Saghir Mosque could be the targets for the Razak men. Now, we know the Emir stays in the Palace when he's not at one of his other palaces or the villa at Nice or the estate in Buckinghamshire. But what gives with the little mosque?"

"They pray in it every Friday, of course. And . . . and . . . yes, that's it. It's the Eid mosque. I remember now its Imam telling me how proud they were that the Emir often came to the mosque which he had restored and refurnished for them so that it's like a little jewel. And the only day of the year that his congregation couldn't all get in was on the first day of the Eid al

Fitr when the Emir together with all of the family and the most senior members of Government walked together from the Palace, out through the big courtyard and across the street to the mosque. The crowds all know about it for it had become a custom over the years and apparently the previous Emir had done the same. And the Eid al Fitr day is the . . . God! It's the day after tomorrow."

"So we've got one day."

"But wait. Let's see what's in the trunk first. It might just be simple things."

"Like Easter eggs or something?"

When Vijay returned he was carrying a thick bundle of small keys of varying shapes clustered round a large ring. "There's a key here," he said smiling, "for every known suitcase or padlock."

They pulled the big trunk out from the cupboard, struggling as they did so because of its weight. Vijay told them it had taken two of his men to bring it up to the room when it was delivered the day after the men arrived. "They told my boys it was special fishing tackle which they were going to introduce to the country," he said.

Mills took the keys and tried to select the appropriate ones which might fit the heavy brass padlock on the trunk.

"Maybe it's a Ruskie job," said Bria.

"No . . . no worries. It's a standard brass Viro which you can get locally, just like the box itself."

Vijay left the room again in order to photocopy the papers they had given him from the satchel. He urged them to hurry before leaving, telling them that they had already been there for more than half an hour and there was always the possibility that the men might return earlier than usual.

Mills busily worked his way through the big ring of keys. "I was sure the third one was going to do it. This is the 13th now. Here goes. Oh damn. Not a budge. Number 14 now . . . God, that was nearly it. You could feel it slipping into position. It'll be one just like it that will do it." The lock sprung apart with a loud clunk. "That's it . . . got it," he exclaimed excitedly, removing the lock and lifting the heavy latch which kept the trunk closed fast.

He raised the lid slowly then looked round at Bria, shaking his head as the pair of them stared at the contents of the big box. Packed down one side of it, at the rear and in a neat polystyrene mould, was a rack of five Kalashnikov AK-47 assault rifles, each cocooned in a plastic filmspray. At the front of the box was a double layer of the curved magazines used by the rifle. In between the weapons and their magazines and occupying the entire central section of the trunk was an assortment of hand grenades and explosive pouches, layered in thick yellow fibreglass packing, like the type used by householders to insulate their lofts. Neatly wedged between the two piles, keeping them in place, was a single rifle, much longer than any of the AK-47s and with a peculiar hollowed butt.

"They mean business with this lot, Brian. That's for sure. Some of this explosive stuff put in the right place would soon knock out the Jebel Azraq mast and the Ordnance Depot and I'd hate to think what it would do at Mina Fatima oil terminal."

"And a Kalashnikov each to play with. What about that single rifle?"

"Well, it's only there for one purpose. It's a Dragunov SVD . . . a sniper's rifle. Look, built-in sight, flash eliminator . . . a very lethal weapon. Can take somebody out at up to 1300 metres. Wonder who? As for the AK-47s, well they're for bang-bangs. Move around with them at night to all these points on the map and let off a few rounds every now and then and you would have the place in absolute turmoil. Just imagine it. Five unseen guys going from place to place knowing precisely what they're doing, one minute up in the jebels, next minute down on the waterfront and every now and then a big bang takes out some installation and you keep hearing the firing of their automatics in between. You would think the bloody Russian Army had arrived. Or somebody's army. And the next day, not a trace of them. Off in the night to a sub lying offshore somewhere, leaving behind them a country that was in a shambles wondering what in hell had hit them, with no TV or radio, their main oil terminal ablaze and an army without a spare bullet. That's Spetsnaz tactics. And that's what these boys are here for. Nothing's surer."

"Right," said Bria. "Get the trunk shut quickly before Vijay returns. We'll tell him we found nothing, except the papers he's copying. The less people know the better."

At nearly 5.30 they left the hotel. The sun had risen but still wasn't high enough to come over the smaller jebels which separated Rani from the sea and the main mountains were full of the same long purple shadows with which they were creased in the evening just before sunset.

"I've never seen them at this time before," said Bria, looking around at the spectacle of the changing colour of the hills. "Bloody beautiful, aren't they! When you think of how red and gaunt they become during the day, almost like they were molten, and then you see them now, so soft and gentle with all these colours and shadows in the folds. Really something, isn't it?"

"Crickey, Brian, you certainly pick the time to go all poetic. We've got a lot to do today. And a lot of decisions to make. First of all, what are we going to do with all these notes in Russian? Can't very well bowl up to their Trade Mission offices and ask if they've got a translator."

"Haider will know someone who can do it for us. He's a friend down at the souk."

"Should you be wandering around down there?"

"Probably not."

Haider told Tony Mills that he should speak to the one they called Mohsin and that if he asked anyone in the vicinity of the Shia mosque they would point him out. He explained that Mohsin's mother was from Turkey and his father, a Khoja, had lived there for many years.

"It was in Eastern Turkey, on the Black Sea, not all that far from the border with the USSR, where the ships from Odessa, Sevastopol and the other Russian ports would call. Trabzon, yes, that was it. Trabzon. I should know, for Mohsin is always speaking about the place. His father built up his business by trading with the Russians who regularly went there, supplying their ships and the like. Only the ones who knew the language well got the trade. Mohsin was born there and Russian had become a second language to him. Clever man is Mohsin," said Haider. "He has English, Turkish, Hindi as well as Russian, Urdu and Arabic all at his command and he was one of the best traders here in the souk."

He was an old man, maybe in his mid-seventies, with the light skin of the Khojas. He now spent much of his time, as many of the old ones did, sitting on the steps outside the Shia mosque on the waterfront, his marble sebhah beads in one hand, a walking stick in the other. It was as good a place as any to watch the day go by and there was nowhere better to meet everyone you knew and exchange gossip. With great flourish he read each of the documents out loudly, first in Russian then in English, Tony Mills nervously wondering whether any of them might contain something sensationally revealing as he scribbled down their translation.

When Mills returned to the barracks, the two men went over the notes in English of each of the papers.

"They're dynamite, Brian," Mills said excitedly. "Could hardly get back here quick enough to let you see them. Just as we suspected, they are copies of messages they've been sending back, either through a courier or else by straight telex or fax to somewhere. And thank God they're couched in such terms that they didn't mean anything to old Mohsin. If that had been the case then the whole town would have known I'm sure."

Then he read from the pad on which he had written the Khoja's translations. "This is the first one. Reads a bit like a holidaymaker's postcard. It says: 'Arrived safely and staying at the Rani Hotel.' Then after that it gives telephone, telex and fax numbers of the hotel. The second one goes on about the supplies having arrived and having been checked and declares everything in working order and the trip going according to plan. Now wait till you hear this next one. 'Have met the fishermen and have gone over details of their fishing grounds with them, where the good catches can be found and how much we are likely to harvest. The Netherlands will be pleased with their product.' Wonder what The Hague would have to say about that, eh? The one after that asks for details of when the fishing tackle samples will be arriving from Rotterdam and says, 'We will arrange transport and deliver it to the fishermen.' Now listen to this one: 'Fishermen have now received their supplies. They say the Dutch equipment far superior to any they've used before. They plan to take it with them for use on their big fishing trip, details as follows. They leave for fishing grounds at about ten o'clock on the morning of Tuesday, 17 May, and plan to begin fishing at number one star map point at 11.30 a.m. local time. Our own equipment tests will begin that night. Have checked out the fishing grounds and see no problem in using the equipment at all of them on the same night in order to complete everything before sunrise. Will advise of our departure details.'"

"Well, Tony, that certainly makes the picture a lot clearer. Funny, I'm not as surprised as I thought I might be at all these details. It fits the kind of scenario we had figured out. The Razak five are an assassination squad; a suicide martyr squad, for they know that anyone who takes on this job will be cut down within seconds by the Palace Guard. And with all the crowds who will be there it will be bloody mayhem. A bit like trying to shoot down a group of guys at a football match."

Mills took over the rest of the outline of the plot as he saw it. "And then that night the Spetsnaz will go into action when the nation is reeling from the shock of what happened in the morning. They'll create their own havoc then slip out the back door sometime early in the morning. And your Colonel Bainbridge's man, the Minister, will make his big bid for the country. That's got to be how the story goes."

"Christ, Tony, and all we have is just that one day . . . tomorrow. Well, whatever we're going to do we will have to do it in double fast time."

"Yes we will, won't we?"

"Tony . . . you've been a real sport getting yourself involved like you have in this. Every time I've said we've got to do this or we've got to do that you have gone right along with it. You've laid yourself right on the line for Gordon and myself. I do hope you don't feel I've dragged you into all this mess. Everything just seems to have snowballed crazily. Had you told me any of this a couple of months back I would have laughed in your face."

"No question of me being dragged, Brian. I was a very willing partner when you told me about what was going on. I couldn't have lived with myself had I not shown some kind of response. There are too many people go around with a blind eye to things. My philosophy is if you see a wrong then you've got to do something about it. It might sound a bit prissy, but that's one of the reasons I chose a career as a soldier. I just thought it was a right and proper thing to do. Funny old life, isn't it? Once one was upright and respectable if you did the right and proper thing in life. Now people, especially in UK, laugh at you for it. Anyway, apart from all my feelings about things, I just don't fancy the idea of these Fundamentalist guys bumping off the old man. And who would pass up the chance of being the first British officer to take on the Spetsnaz?"

"And beat them!"

"Of course. And beat them."

The Day of the Eid

MAY 17. That was the day scheduled for the Eid al Fitr, the first day of the month of Shawal which followed the month of Ramadan and marked the day when the Muslim holy fast was over and a time of celebrations would begin. The Islamic Lunar Calendar is counted from the year of the Hijra, the departure of the Prophet Mohammed from Mecca to Medina, an event as important to the Muslim as the birth of Christ, from which dates the Western calendar. To the Christian and those who lived by their calendar it was the year 1988. To the Muslim it was the year 1408.

The first day of the Eid al Fitr celebration is a great occasion for the Muslim. He anticipates it with the same spiritual feeling and relish as the Christian does Christmas Day. There is a great sense of deliverance; of liberation from the rigours of the fast and the deprivation endured during the month when any form of sustenance, even a sip of water, is forbidden during the hours of daylight; in temperatures which are well over 100 degrees such self-denial takes considerable fortitude. Yet it is done and it is seen to be done. No one flagrantly breaks the fast rules: in the devout countries of the Arabian Peninsula remarkably few infringe them even surreptitiously.

So the day of the Eid begins with great relief; relief that no longer does one have the daily ordeal of waiting till that time of evening when the light dims enough that it is no longer possible to distinguish between a white and a black thread and it is therefore deemed to be night and permissible to drink and eat for the first time. At the midday prayer services throughout the Islamic world there are bigger than usual crowds rejoicing together in prayers of thanksgiving for the spiritual uplift which they have experienced in the time of Ramadan and in appreciation that, once again, they can eat and drink as they do normally for the rest of the year, thankful that they have survived their great test of discipline. The mood everywhere is one of festivity and enjoyment. They dress in their best clothes and flock into the streets carrying presents for their visits to friends' houses. Children too get presents for their Eid; and for the poor, some of whom will gather at the mosques, there's the Zakat Fitr, the extra alms that they receive on the day of the Eid.

It was the only day of the year when the Emir was known to be in a particular place at a particular time. For it had been the custom, as it had been that of his father before him, to meet that morning with all the members of The Family at the Palace in the Capital. Precisely at 11.40 they would all leave together, walking across the garden-fringed courtyard to the massive brass-spiked gates which, for that occasion, would be opened wide. Huge crowds would be waiting for them but they would respectfully clear the way as The Family approached through the gates and continued to walk together across the public highway to the blue-domed building with the marble-fluted minaret called the Saghir Mosque. And there, after speaking to members of the congregation and wishing them Eid Mubarak, said in the kindred fashion to Happy Christmas, they would take their places in the front of the prayer crowd, kneeling on the layers of Bokhara and Persian rugs on the floor of the mosque.

The Grand Mufti of the country, the leader of the nation's Muslims, would be there and to him would go the honour of leading the prayers being attended by the most important family in the land. When the prayers were over, His Highness and the others would retrace their steps to the street again. This time their procession would occasion great cheering and dancing of the traditional ardha and waving of swords over their heads. It was always a great day for the people of Emirate for not only could they celebrate their Eid, they also got the opportunity to see, and show their appreciation to, their Emir.

There was no other day in the year when they would know where and when he or any member of The Family would be, for advance details of their movements were never released. Even on the day he went to the Saghir Mosque there was never any prior publicity. It was just known that he would be there and people would go to greet him. Otherwise they never knew where and when he would be until they would read it later in the newspapers or see him on television. A tour of his country along the lines of a pre-publicised British royal visit was unheard of. A royal walkabout unthinkable.

And so it would be, they had planned, that on the first day of the Muslim month of Shawal in their year of 1408, at about 17 or 18 minutes before the hour of 12 midday, as the long rank of The Family walked out of the gates of the Palace, the men from Razak would throw off their bishts, the outer robes they would be wearing, and open fire with their Kalashnikov AK-47s. Not many seconds later they knew, they too would be as dead as the men they had come to kill. They would die the happiest of assassins for they had been taught that this was to be their particular way of meeting their Allah. Just like the ones who committed the massacres by driving their Mercedes trucks into the American and French camps in Beirut, they would have smiles on their faces at the knowledge of what they were about to achieve for their cause and for themselves. That was the meaning of life for those who were members of a Hussein Martyr Squad.

Cats on a Hot Tin Roof

WELL AFTER midnight on that morning of Monday, 16 May, Brian Bria and Tony Mills had gone to their beds in the adjoining room of the officers' quarters at The Hill, headquarters of the Emir's Defence Forces' Training Regiment. It was so late, in fact, that the Voice of America early morning jazz programme featuring Willis Conover had come and gone as they had sat discussing what action to take on what they had figured would be the last day before the Hussein Martyr Squad and the Spetsnaz would go into operation.

They considered all the options. The first was that it was now time to report everything they knew to the police. But Stott, the Superintendent, would be some kind of stumbling block there. Bria, in particular, would probably be arrested on the spot. The deaths of McQuade and McDaid at his flat were reason enough for that. Getting the Army involved would be as unlikely, Tony had considered. His own colonel, another Briton, was on leave and the few other senior officers still around the camp were all nationals who would want reports in writing to pass on to more senior officers. With Ramadan and the Eid celebrations coming up that would take days.

"There are a couple of national officers, very switched-on guys, and they would listen but like half the camp they're away on leave."

"Then it really is up to us," said Bria. "There are just no options on that score."

"You're right. No options."

Stage by stage, detail by detail, figuring out their timings, they worked out their plan for the day ahead, stopping from time to time as Bria debated the morality of what they would be doing.

"Okay, so I realise we have no options. But, God, this really is taking the law into our own hands. I've been condemning people for that all my life."

"What about me?" Mills came back. "I'm Old Morality itself when it comes to that point of view. But, let's face it, others made that decision for us. The law, or the rule, has been thrust right into our hands. We're not taking it. We've been given it. And if you don't think that argument right, then conjure the consequences if we don't take action. There's going to be the most horrific bloodshed at that mosque and more than likely the Emir is going to get bumped off and goodness knows how many others with him. I mean, we still don't know precisely what they're going to do. Maybe they're going to bomb the mosque like they did the Marines in Beirut. Think of the results of that. We can only really guess about what they're up to. It could be ten times worse than anything we've speculated on."

"Everything you say is right. I know. It's just that the doubts still linger about the principle. But I'll have to live with that. As you say, there's no way out. Is there? We've inherited this thing. We'd better see it through. Let's get some sleep."

That was easier said than done for Bria, who lay awake for what seemed like hours thinking about the events of the last two weeks when the whole world, as he knew it, had gone completely topsy-turvy. He had been enjoying life to its fullest. He was satisfied and fulfilled at his job in taking what he had considered the best quality photographs of his career; not the rash and rushed get-it-on-record work of the normal news photographer, but fine and studied architectural compositions, executed with what he had considered near technical perfection. In his free time he was enjoying to the limit the company of his many friends at the Rani and elsewhere, together with a highly satisfying and rewarding love affair with the beautiful Esther.

There was the pleasure too of just being in the Gulf; he was captivated by the fascination of its people and their way of life, so deeply disciplined so vastly different from that of the West with which he had become disenchanted; and the daily appreciation of the beauty of this part of the East, whether that be in the charm of the Old Capital, or in the changing colours of those amazing jebel mountains as they went through their daily kaleidoscope of colour shades, principally red, from Venetian to ochre to vermilion to red lead to scarlet, before softening into the various pigments of brown and then purple, and finally merging black with the night.

But now it had all changed. His best friend had disappeared. He was no longer free to see his other friends, even to walk the streets, for fear of the police or whatever men Bainbridge still had at his disposal. How would he have been, he thought, without the acquaintance of Tony Mills? Funny how people could reveal themselves in as many different shades as those jebels. He reflected on the number of times he had been badly let down by those he had trusted, when a bond had been broken, a relationship shattered; and how that had always hurt. But here it was in reverse. He had never figured the young officer Mills as a friend. Acquaintance, yes. But a true and loyal friend! No. He had never considered that. Maybe it was because he had put people in what he had thought were appropriate boxes. It was wrong, he knew, but he had. Mills had been in his Army officers' box. They were all right chaps in that box. Up to a point, that is. Good to mix with now and then. Helpful enough, usually, to work with. The odd one could even let his hair down, like Tony Mills had done on the two or three occasions when he had met him in London and taken him along to mix with the Fleet Street crowd. But people in the Army officers' box could never be real friends. Could they? There was always that allegiance to something else with them. Like a sort of priesthood. You could go so far with people like that, but if there was ever a test it became clear that their allegiance would always be to Queen and country and the regiment. At least, that's what he had always thought. He would never have imagined Mills as he considered him now. The ones in his officers' box didn't do things like this; they would have preferred to do it by the book, old boy. Wouldn't they? He had always thought there was something different about Tony Mills. He didn't know what. Just different. Despite that, he still wouldn't have thought of him as he did now. Funny how you could be so wrong about people. Indeed, sleep wasn't easy that morning.

Mills came into his room about nine o'clock with a big cup of coffee. "Sorry it's only that instant muck," he smiled as Bria sat up in bed. "But it's hot and it's sweet."

"Nine o'clock, you say? I feel as though I went to sleep at five to nine."

Mills was in uniform. Shirt sleeve order in olive green, light desert boots and matching beret, with the red and purple striped belt of the Training Regiment.

"You're a trim bastard in that uniform, mate."

"Oh thank you, darling," Mills joked.

"No, seriously. You wear it like you were made for uniform. Not too many officers like that. Clothes and the Englishman are not the best of mix. I know the Paras officers always look better tailored than the others. Perhaps that's because they're more vain. And if you don't mind me saying so, and I've always thought this, you even stood out from the normal Para officer. Maybe it's your face. You don't have an officer's face."

"Officer's face!"

"That's right . . . an officer's face. They've got them, you know. Come on, you know that. There's an officer's face just like there's a squaddie's one, just like there's a sergeant's one and you bloody well know there's a sarn't major's one."

"So whose face have I got? Don't tell me a corporal's."

"I don't know. It's difficult. But you've got a face that tells something. Just like a boozer's face always tells a story. If I didn't know you like I do, I'd be tempted to say you almost had a burnt look . . . please don't be offended, old mate."

"Burnt look! What do you mean?"

"Burnt! You know, done time. And I did say don't be offended."

"That coffee's doing you no good," Mills replied before shaking his head and breaking into a wide grin. "Are you having me on, Brian?"

"No, not really. There's an edge about you, a hardness if you like, that's contrary to the public schoolboy accent and the regiment and all that jazz."

"Has someone told you something about me?"

"No. What is there to tell? You mean I'm getting warm?"

"Sort of."

"Ah, so there is something there. You couldn't have done time or else you wouldn't be in the Army and here. Reformed alcoholics keep a 'look' about them, but it's not that either. You're too fit for that."

"You bugger, Bria. Reformed alcoholic indeed."

"Well, it's not the first time I've thought about it, you know. I mean, about you looking different, not the alcoholic bit. I thought it even back in Ulster when I first met you and then again recently when we met that day up at Razak and you were in combat gear. You stood out from the other officers in it. Combat gear and your appearance go very much together. The ones with the normal wah-wah accents look so out of place, in that gear. Like they were wearing old clothes to go out and do the garden. You wear it like you were somehow meant for it. That and the cocky angle of your beret. Come on . . . what is it? There is something, isn't there?"

Mills was grinning even more widely this time and, laughingly, he said, "You're an astute old bastard, Bria. I guess what you're trying to say is that I appear institutionalised and an officer and a gentleman never looks that way. Well . . . I know I've got that look. I can see it for myself. As for a reason . . .." He looked down, shaking his head once more, his grin becoming a quiet chuckle before he started speaking again. "Brian. This is my third army. I'm a soldier of the Emir and before that it was for Her Majesty and before that it was for the President."

"The President!"

"Yes . . . The President of France. I was in the Legion Étrangère."

"Bloody hell . . . a Foreign Legionnaire!"

"That's right. I did a full engagement of five years beginning when I was 17. I cheated a little. And I was with them till I was 23 when I got an honourable discharge. A very honourable discharge."

"What in God's name possessed you to join the French Foreign Legion?"

"Beau Geste had only a very little to do with it. It attracts all types and for all types of reasons, and not necessarily running away from something, although perhaps I was in a way. Running away from myself. Running away from young Antony Mills whose whole life had been pre-ordained by two very lovable and doting parents. A youngster couldn't have wished for a better start to life than I had. Born into a very comfortable home in Highgate. Went to the best of schools . . . Westminster, actually. Was all set for Oxford and then it was to be Sandhurst. And after Sandhurst it was to be into Dad's old regiment. He was with the Fusiliers during the war. Even got himself an MC in the D-Day landings. He wasn't a career soldier but had loved the Army wartime life and young Tony here was to fulfil his dreams of being a professional soldier. Well, I fulfilled them all right. But on my terms. A bit like changing the order of batting, one might say. That's why I went knocking on the door of the old Fort de Nogent in Paris and, incredibly, I was accepted as a Legionnaire."

"Incredibly?"

"Oh yes, they don't take any old riff-raff these days, you know. There were about 40 of us turned up that weekend. What a bunch! They ranged from tramps to cowboys to out-and-out thugs. And me in my grey flannels, my blazer and Westminster school tie. Out of that 40, only two of us were accepted. Myself and one of the out-and-out thugs. But he was a bright guy. Came from Dijon and we ended up good mates, even though we started off by having a scrap on the train going to the camp at Aubagne, down near Marseilles in Southern Provence."

"Well, that's quite a beginning to your story. But how in hell did an English kid of 17 take the transition to that kind of life?"

"With difficulty. Great difficulty. I had two advantages . . . a good education which included A-Level French, and I had been good at athletics. But I was no man at 17, Brian. For nights I cried. And I mean cried. Tears . . . sobbing . . . the lot. Homesickness. It was terrible. God, I missed Mum and home and everything being done for me. But there must have been some streak of obstinacy that just wouldn't make me give up, not even in the toughest of the ordeals they put you through in training, like running tanks over you. And don't associate that trick with the way you see it done in the American movies. They do it two ways in the Legion. One is that you have to stand in front of the tank as it charges up to you and you've got to keep standing there till it hits you before you fall back with it and let it roll over you. That's the easy one. The other way is that you have to let the actual tracks rumble over you. They give you a trenching tool and as the tanks advance you have to dig yourself a four foot bottle-shaped hole with a narrow neck—the narrower the better. When you're in the hole you are completely unseen by the tank crew but you are in a position that's in line with its tracks. Then you get into your little hole and hope for the best, praying like hell that the earth around you doesn't collapse under those tracks. One guy's did. He was in a terrible mess. His head was crushed so badly it was fused together with his helmet.

"Once you are into that sort of training, you stop crying for Mum. At least I did. You are too busy thinking about self-preservation or else too exhausted. Anyway, I seemed to do well at Aubagne. I was posted to Camp Raffalli, near Calvi in Corsica, for training with the 2nd Foreign Parachute Regiment. Now this lot are a breed apart. And if you think there's a little bit of the swagger about me with my uniform, well I got it from these guys for I was to be with them for the next four and a half years. So there you are."

"Well, for God's sake don't just stop there. What happened after Corsica?"

"Are you sure you want to hear more?"

"Of course I do. Every single detail."

"Well, after Camp Raffalli things really moved fast. We had just finished our parachute training when we were dropped into action in Zaire. Remember Kolwesi?"

"Only too well. I was to go there for the paper, but we couldn't get visas in time. One of the agency men was already there and he had got all the action photos. So you fought against the Katangan rebels?"

"We weren't really there to fight against them. But after the Zairean troops had run like hell leaving the civilians, many of them Europeans, to the mercy of the Katangan Tigers, as they called themselves, we had to go in and stop the bloodshed. That's where I killed my first man. Four of them actually, all with one pull of the trigger. They were in an armoured car at a crossroads and had been indiscriminately shelling civilian houses. I hit them with one shot from an 89mm Anti-Tank Launcher . . . something similar to the one they used on your car. And it had the same effect. I had just turned 18 and wasn't a year out of Westminster, but killing those four guys in that vehicle seemed to justify all the doubt I had about becoming a soldier. OK, I had killed, but I had saved a lot more lives than I had taken. Innocent lives, people who had nothing to do with their rebellion. And to me that's more the role of the modern-day soldier than the ones of old. There's no going about the world knocking off another country as a conquest. Those days are over. Anyway, after Zaire it was Chad, then Djibouti, my first experience in the Arab world, and finally Beirut and Lebanon. We did a lot, lived a lot and learned a lot in all of them. So . . . hence the face. The Legion does leave its mark, you know."

"Hey, Mr Mills. That's quite a tale."

"I can assure you, Brian, it rarely comes out. I mean, one can hardly pop it into the conversation . . . 'Well, when I was in the French Foreign Legion'."

"I know precisely what you mean. So you left the Legion after five years?"

"That's right. I was a chief corporal by then, *un caporal-chef*, a rank that's between corporal and sergeant. OK, I'm a major now, but that is absolutely nothing compared to having been a *caporal-chef* at the age of 23 in the Deuxième Bataillon Étranger de Parachutistes — pardon the French and pardon the boast, but that really was something. I think I was the youngest who ever who made it. I had promised my parents I would leave after my five years were up, but I was sorely tempted to stay. The Legion had become like my family. There were some remarkable people I served with . . . officers who had been in the last stand at Dien Bien Phu, then there was the lot that had served at Sidi-bel-Abbes, or just Bel-Abbes as the old hands called it — you know, the legendary old fort in Algeria that was their HQ in North Africa? Amazing characters, some of them."

"They wanted me to train as an officer, which would have been a year at Strasbourg followed by another year at St Cyr. Now that was a great temptation, even though it meant having to become a French citizen. However, I kept my promise and went home. Not very long afterwards I was at Sandhurst and the Royal Fusiliers and all that. And that's the story."

"Some story, mate. What did your folks think about it all?"

"I suppose that's the sad part. I think it broke their hearts when I told them I was off to France to join the Legion, particularly Dad. Poor Dad. His greatest ambition in life was to be there with Mum to watch me in the Sovereign's Parade at Sandhurst. He died the month before. Mum took it like a brick. She's a lovely dear. When I went off to the Legion she told me she didn't want me to go, but said she understood what I was doing. Wasn't that sweet of her . . . to tell a 17-year-old that she shared and comprehended his feelings? She was there that day at Sandhurst, all done up in her finest. Can still turn a few eyes, old Mum, for she's a good-looking woman. Keeps teasing me about being in the Emir's Army. 'But you're a not *real* Major are you?' she keeps saying. Anything but the British Army and you're not the real thing, she thinks. She's a dear. You must come and visit us, Brian. Avenue Road, Highgate. Kingsmead House. Lovely old place. Lots of ground with trees and little squirrels running about the garden."

"Yes, I will. That's a promise. I'd love to come and meet Mum. By the way, what I didn't ask was why are you in uniform today?"

"Have you forgotten already? We spoke about it last night."

"Must have forgotten."

"I'm on duty today but that will give me the chance to get what I need from the stores. Then I'll go out with a driver and do that recce of the Fish Souk area and check at the hotel about the Spetsnaz . . . don't worry, I won't say that's what we think they are."

"It's all right, I remember everything else. I had just forgotten the bit about you being on duty. God, last night seems like it was only half an hour ago."

"Oh, I've also got an errand I want to do at the hospital. So I'll be back here to pick you up as we planned at 3.30. You can use my Corolla if you want to do anything. It's got Army number plates so you'll be safe with it. It will also help you get out and back into the camp again. No more second thoughts on what we decided last night then?"

"Second thoughts! Yes, tons of them. Third, fourth and fifth thoughts as well. But, no worries, Tony. None of them affect the plan. We'll go through with it."

"Whew! Thought you were going to say something else there. So what are you going to do till this afternoon? You can stay in bed if you wish. No one will disturb you here."

"No. I may go down and see how that girl Amar is getting on, you know the Filipino I told you about who was interfered with by her employers' sons and had to run away? She may have heard something from Esther. But won't go to the Rani, Inter-con, the Al Rawda or my flat. Promise. See you at 3.30 back here."

An old *haris* (watchman) was sitting by the stairs which led up to the nurses' flats from the shopping arcade in Rani Street. Bria assumed he was the one Esther had said was more lax than the others — when he offered a dinar note he accepted it without even looking up to see who had given it to him.

Amar's face lit up in a wide smile when she opened the door and saw who was there. "I thought it was one of the girls returning our iron. Come in."

"Sorry, love. No iron. But I was thinking about you and wondering whether you had got away or not. That's why I'm here."

"No. And now it is more complicated. Another one has come. A Filipina.

She is more unlucky than me. She is pregnant. It was her employer who did it. When they found out they threw her out of the house. It's so easy for them. They just tell the police that you have absconded, which is against the law, or else you have been stealing and you end up with the others in the women's wing at the prison, what is they call it . . . Zamakh? Is that right?"

"So how does this other girl affect you?"

"Well, they want to get her home quickly because of her condition. So I will have to wait. And Esther is in charge of getting the money raised for me so that has delayed things too. But I don't mind if it will help the other one. At least I am not in her condition. I think I would commit suicide if I was."

"If I'd known for certain you were still here we could have gone out for a meal. I would have come sooner but I've got a big project on at the moment and it's kind of occupying my time."

"Is she nice?"

"Is who nice?"

"The big project that's occupying your time," she laughed.

He smiled as he replied, "No Amar, dear. Nothing like that. Anyway, how could I look at another girl when I've got Esther and you."

"And me?"

"Yes . . . and you. That night when we went swimming down the coast. I thought there was . . .. You know . . . ?"

"What? You mean the way I looked at you when we first met and the way we held hands when we went swimming and when I held your hand that tight way. Yes . . . there was something between us then. I felt I had someone to protect me. It was so comforting to be in the company of a man who just liked being with me and not for my body. Esther is a very lucky girl to have you as a friend."

"But I take it you think of me as a friend too?"

"Yes, I do. But not the way that Esther does."

She took his arm as they walked to the door and said how pleased she was he had called. Even though she was with other Filipinas she kept thinking, she said, that the next knock at the door would be the police or someone from the family for whom she had worked.

He reassured her she would be safe where she was. "And I'll make regular checks to see that everything is fine till Esther gets back."

"Esther gave me your card. Can I call you?"

"No. Not till after tomorrow, that is. The project I'm on should be all cleared up by then. Insha'allah."

"Insha'allah," she smiled in reply. "Brian, I want you to know how safe I feel having a friend like you." She made to kiss him as they stood inside the doorway of the flat and he put his arms round her and held her closely in a warm embrace.

"There are times Amar, dear, when one needs friends. And God, don't I know it." He kissed her once again. It was the second embrace that did it. He knew and she certainly knew it was more than an embrace of friendship. It was long, warm and lingering. When they stopped it was only for a second and they kissed again and held each other so tightly they could sense all the arousals which their embrace meant.

"Oh, Brian," she whispered to him. "I want you so. So much. But it is wrong. Ever since that first day I saw you I wanted you. Tell me it's wrong, Brian. Tell me you must go away. Tell me. Tell me."

They lay naked in each other's arms on the bed of her little room.

"What is it that's happening to us, Brian?"

"Do you need explanations, Amar? I know I can't explain the way I felt that night at the beach when we went swimming and you held my hand the way you did. Let's put it down to confusion. I'm confused. You're confused. But does that mean we pass up a golden opportunity which we'll remember for the rest of our lives . . . at least I'll certainly remember it for the rest of my days. You said earlier that it was nice to be in the company of a man who liked being with you for your self and not for your body. Has what happened changed your view?"

"No, Brian. I still believe that. You didn't want me for that alone."

Then she ran her hand slowly down him and he turned and held her to him again. They began kissing passionately once more.

Mills was in his billet when they met back at the barracks at 3.30 as planned. He was on the floor of his room sorting out the contents of two big rucksacks he had brought from somewhere.

"How did you get on," he asked. "See the girl okay?"

"Yeah . . . saw her. Everything's fine. And how did you go?"

"Great," he said enthusiastically. "Got everything done. Did my recce of the Fish Souk. The police are watching the house. In a green Merc, you might have guessed. And they're sitting in the one spot, near where your car was blown up. But it won't affect us from using the roof of the spice mill building. We can still get access from the rear and I've found a good place to park the car where we won't be seen by them. I've also been to the Rani. Our friends have informed the hotel they're returning to Holland tomorrow. Like the good citizens they are, they've asked for their bills to be made up and they also inquired about what the usual percentage was to leave staff for tips. But the good news is that they also told reception they would be going out for their usual jog and their daily call for 4.15 a.m. has been booked. So, remarkably, no hitches so far."

"And what's this lot here? By the looks of it you would think it is us that's taking on the nation . . . ropes, guns, grenades, and what the hell is that?" Bria asked, pointing to a large bulbous object which stood about a foot and a half high.

"That's dear Twiggy. But let me go over everything in detail. First of all, two 25-metre lengths of nylon climbing rope. Part of every good commando's kit. Two high-powered torches, both checked and in good working order. A box of first-aid gear just in case old Brian scratches his knees. Three bottles of Masafi mineral water, straight from the Emirate of Ras al Khaimah and according to the label full of calcium, magnesium, sodium, potassium, iron and bicarbonate and just what us two cats will need on that hot tin roof tonight. Some glucose tablets to keep up the energy during the stake-out.

"And then there's the hardware. First of all let me introduce Twiggy. Twiggy is a night-sight. But a special one. Remember that one I got you before? Well, that was a toy by comparison. Feel the weight. There's nine kilograms in that. And, despite the shape, that's the official name listed by Rank Pullin's, the manufacturers . . . the SS69 Twiggy Night-sight. When we get this set up on that spice mill roof you'll see them so clearly you'll be able to tell what they had for breakfast. Do you know, they even use it for aerial reconnaissance? We used to use them on the roof of the Divis Flats in Belfast. In the blackest of nights, and you know how black they can get there, we could spot the Paddy getting up to all sorts of tricks. They could never figure it out how we spotted them. And the things the boys used to spot looking through house windows! Won't put you off your supper, old chap. So that's Twiggy.

"I hid the guns we took from McDaid and his mate. I'd rather use these ones here. Much more familiar with them. They're Steyr rifles, or 5.56 Army Universal Guns to give them their proper name. Austrian. Great little weapons. Can be used as a rifle or a submachine-gun with a 350mm barrel. You can convert them to a carbine, an assault rifle, or a light machine-gun. That barrel there is the 620mm one to make it a light machine-gun. I'll fit one up with that and the other with a 350mm barrel. Look how easy they are to change. See. There are these eight lugs around the chamber end of the barrel — one half turn and she's off. Just like that. In automatic they can fire 10.8 rounds a second and you can do a 15-second burst without them overheating."

"And they're made in Austria, you say?"

"That's right. By the Steyr-Daimler-Puch company. They're our standard weapons in the Army here. They're a good enough little gun, but the main reason they were chosen is because one of the Minister of Defence's companies happens to be the agents for them."

"Well, that figures. That's why all the Ministers are millionaires. Every Government contract of any size goes to one of their companies. They don't call that corruption. It's all done openly and everyone knows — unlike in the U.K. or Australia where it would be illegal but they do it just the same in some underhand fashion. What else has Santa brought?"

"Well, we had to have a couple of revolvers. Brownings they are. Very good weapon. Heavy, but effective. Each takes 13 rounds which can be very handy. Might as well show you how they work now. For the pistol, you just hold it in your right hand, like this, and with your other hand grasp the top of the assembly here and pull back. That's the safety catch there, pull it back for on. Push it forward and the gun's ready for firing. The rifle's just as simple. Again, hold it in your right hand with the pistol grip and trigger assembly, then with your left hand you simply pull the cocking handle here straight back and release it. The safety catch is just forward of the pistol grip, just here, look. Push it from one side of the body to the other. When you see the red dot that means the gun is live and dangerous, the white dot and it's safe. It will be on automatic fire so just give it short, sharp bursts when you're shooting. Right, Brian, that's the weapon training lessons over."

"What about this lot here?"

"The grenades you mean? They're for my exclusive use. I thought they would be the best thing for the Fish Souk job. Get it all over with quickly and without too much fuss. They're HG 78 fragmentation grenades. Each has got 5,500 pieces of frag in them and if you use them in a confined space, no one survives. All very beastly I know. But these are the tools of our trade in the Army."

"It's at this point that I feel like walking away from it all," said Bria shaking his head. "Just seeing all that stuff lying there. Knowing what it can do. And knowing that someone is going to be at the receiving end of it in a few hours time. They're not my tools of trade, Tony. And I'm not frightened to admit I'm dead scared of even touching them. The last time I held a gun . . . No, it's too long a story."

"But Brian, we went over all this last night."

"I'm sorry, Tony. I know we did. And we'll still go through with it. Just understand my feelings at seeing all this collection."

"Don't worry. Remember, as we discussed, your role is covering me. I know what this gear is all about and I'll be the one that's using it. I know precisely what needs to be done . . . where, when, and how to do it. Everything I have learned in the Army has been to this end. Now I'm about to put some of that training to use. I'm even going to keep my uniform on tonight just to remind me of that and anyway, if I'm fighting for the old man, I might as well do it in his uniform."

As they couldn't predict the precise movements of the men from Razak, their plan was to take up a position on the roof of the old spice mill and observe them through the night with the aid of the Twiggy night-sight.

"Maybe they and the Spetsnaz will get together for a big farewell," Bria had joked.

"Wouldn't that be super? Then we could take them all out together. Four HG 78s through that little window and there'd be nothing but the sound of silence when the din had died down."

There were to be no get-togethers or farewells. Only the men from Razak were there. They all left the house together when the muezzins' cries went up from the four mosques which surrounded the area for the evening Isha prayers, timed that night for 8.10, the point of the day when it became completely dark.

"Allaa . . . aaahu."

"Akbar," sang the muezzins, the first words "God is the . . ." stretched out in a long singing note. Then followed quickly and abruptly with "Akbar", meaning Greatest.

The cries and the proclamations followed. Not only was Allah the Greatest, there was no other God but Him. The streets were filled, as they usually were at that hour, with men walking to their various places of worship.

"Good God, this Twiggy is incredible," said Bria as he studied the men in the house and could even continue to see them after they had put the lights out and emerge into the dark lane to walk in the direction of the mosque. "Gordon kept talking about a simple one," he went on, still observing them. "That's got to be him, walking on his own at the rear. He keeps jerking his head. He's got an odd sort of walk too. It must be him. There's nothing unusual about the others. Yes, that's the team all right. They've all got the shorter dishdasha and the Fundamentalist beards. And the one at the front; he's the one I kept seeing through the window last Friday. He's got one of those fuzzy, step beards — classic biblical."

"Hardly biblical," quipped Mills.

"Yeah, you're right. Automatic, isn't it, for us to think of everything in our terms. Tell somebody he had a Koranic beard and they'd wonder what you were talking about. But biblical, that's okay. They've turned into another alley now. I know, that's the one that goes straight down to the Shia mosque by the waterfront."

"What are the police doing?" asked Mills.

Bria turned the big night-sight round to focus on the green Mercedes in the waste ground, its nose pointing in the direction of the principal alley that led to the junction and the house where the Razak men had been living. "One of them is speaking into his radio."

"Bet he's saying 'Can I come in for supper, sarge?'" joked Mills in a broad Lancashire voice.

"You could be right, mate. They're moving off."

Still looking through the sight, Bria followed the car as it turned and drove over part of the waste ground, then turned left down Way 177 to the Harbour Road, where it turned right and then sped off in the direction of the Capital.

"They'll be back, though. Probably think they don't need watching when they've gone to the mosque."

Nearly an hour later they could see the streets filling again with men coming from the mosque. Bria focused the night-sight once more on the alley the Razak men had gone down towards the waterfront. "There are two of them coming back. The one with the big beard and another one."

"Right, that's it," said Mills. "You take the night-sight and head back towards the car. There's an opportunity here. So let's grab it."

"Opportunity . . . what . . . ?"

"No time for details, Brian. I'll go first. See you back at the car."

It was nearly half an hour before Bria saw them, Mills and the Arab walking casually along the narrow alley towards the intersection where there had been room for them to park their car behind a big jujube tree. He was obviously talking to the man and when he approached Bria who was standing by the car, he said "I've been telling this gentleman how we got terribly lost and he's very kindly offered to show us the way."

It was one of the Razak men, the one with the head that twitched and the strange walk, the one Watson had said was the simple one.

They exchanged *salaam alaykums* and then the Arab started pointing in one direction with one hand, then in another with his other hand. Mills said something to him, which Bria didn't understand, then opened one of the car's rear doors saying, "And he's very kindly offered to come with us to the main road. How splendid."

Mills got in behind the wheel and drove the car off. "Right, Brian. That's one down. Four to go. When he starts to panic, turn round and show him the ugly end of that Browning that's in the glove box." He explained the rest as he drove. "It was too good a chance to miss getting one of them as a prisoner, particularly this one. We'll take him back to the barracks and make him talk."

"What if he doesn't?"

"He will. There are ways."

"That sounds ominous."

"Don't worry. I don't mean by tying his balls to an electric circuit like my former confrères did in Algeria or even any of the tricks we used against the Paddy."

As the car unwound itself from the maze of lanes in the direction of the main thoroughfare, the man told them his name was Yousuf and that he came from Razak and lived with four other friends who also came from there. Then, when he realised they weren't stopping the car at the main road, he became suddenly agitated and began shouting and trying to open the car door.

"Ajlis fi makanik, wa kun hadi!" said the Arab despairingly.

"Sit still and be quiet," Mills shouted gruffly, Bria at the same time pointing the Browning at him.

"Aina nahnn thahiboun?" said the Arab despairingly.

"There you are," said Mills. "Scared already. He'll talk all right."

They took him to Mills' quarters where they made him sit on the floor, tying his hands together in front of him. "Now tell us about the men from Razak — *al an haddithna an ulaika al rijal min Razak.*"

The man shook his head.

Mills then threatened he would take him to the Baluchi soldiers. "They will make you talk within five minutes. You know that."

Again the man shook his head.

"I know your house in Razak," said Mills. "It's near the big fort."

The man looked frightened when he had said that.

"Yes, I know it all right. Near the big fort and just by the souk where the trees hang heavy with dates."

The look of fear intensified at that and Bria looked on in amazement as Mills walked round and round the man speaking in Arabic, which he didn't understand. He knew by the man's reactions that the words meant something threatening or fearful.

"Your children go splashing the cool water of the big *falaj* that runs past the fish stall." Mills went on, still pacing round and round the man.

The nervous movements of his head became more accentuated. Nevertheless, despite his pathetic and terrified appearance, he still wouldn't talk. Then Mills stopped the questions for a minute and went over to one of the haversacks which he had left earlier in the day. From it he took a parcel which was wrapped in what appeared to be a plastic carrier bag. He threw it at the man and it landed in his lap. The man stared at it wondering what might be inside. Then Mills leaned over him and emptied out the bags contents.

His screams were those of someone suddenly possessed and he began jabbering incoherently as he rolled wildly away from what had fallen from the bag into his lap and was now lying on the floor.

"Jesus Christ," gasped Bria as he caught sight of the foot.

"Ugly thing a human foot," said Mills blithely. "Especially when it hasn't got a body attached to it."

It was ugly all right, its scarred and wizened sole an ash-grey, contrasting with the darker skin of the ankle and the bottom piece of the leg.

Mills picked it up and threw it in the man's lap again and he let out another horrific yell. Mills spoke to him, even more coarsely this time. "*Yousuf, hathda yantami li zawjatikum sa uhdir al akhar ghadan lau iltazamta al samt. . . .* It belongs to your wife, Yousuf. I will get the other one tomorrow if you don't talk."

The man went silent and just stared at the foot . . . muttering incomprehensibly.

"Talk," shouted Mills. "Tell us about the men from Razak."

The words came fast and non-stop. He was not one of them, he said. He had only been their manservant. They were his townspeople and he had always been a helper to them. He had been with them when the police and the Army had come after the shooting at the police barracks. That was why he had ended up in Zamakh. He had only come with them to the Capital to help them in their house, get them food and see that they were looked after. But he was not part of their group in the other way. He had not been with them in the lands they had gone to across the Gulf for the training that had made them experts in the use of guns and other things. He was not part of that. Nor was he a part of what they would be doing just before midday prayers at the Saghir Mosque.

"What, Yousuf? What are they doing at the Saghir Mosque?" Mills shouted at him.

"I love the Emir," he said. "But if it is the will of Allah that he must go, then so be it."

"How are they going to do it?"

"With the guns. The guns the other men brought, the strange men. The white ones." Then his eye caught sight of the foot again and he lapsed once more into an uncontrollable muttering, none of which Mills could understand.

"So it's just as we figured. They are Hussein Martyrs and they're going to do a Sadat on the Emir. Right, Brian, we better get back to our sweat box on top of the spice mill. We'll take Yousuf here, I know a track that goes to town via the jebels. We'll dump him up there. It'll take him a day at least to find his way back."

The quick turn of events had left Bria speechless and he carried out orders without question, untying the Arab's hands, then retying them behind his back, escorting him to the back seat of the car then pushing him out of the vehicle when they had reached the spot high in the hills.

It wasn't till after they had left Yousuf and were driving towards the harbour that he was composed enough to start asking questions. "How in hell did all that come about? How did you know where he lived? And that foot! Good God, Tony. What's been going on?"

"I'm not that clever, Brian. Most of it was bluff. I know Razak very well. Spent a long time up there — you know at Jiza? — and we were always in and out of Razak. Everyone lives near the fort and with it being an oasis, everyone lives near a palm tree with dates. Most of the kids splash in that particular *falaj* water channel. He just assumed with me saying all these things that I knew his particular house. That was the bluff part. The rest was chance. I figured he would be married. Well, they all are, aren't they! As for the foot," he laughed. "Now that was real opportunism. I reckoned there would be a one in a hundred chance of that working. I figured, you see, that we might be able to take one of them as prisoner, like we did Yousuf. And if we did, how could we make him talk? Then I remembered this trick."

"But where did you get the foot? I mean, was it a real one?"

"Oh, it was real all right. Angelo, the Filipino who arranges the catering for the officers' mess here has a brother who is in charge of the mortuary at the Central Hospital. I went there today on my way from the Fish Souk to the Rani Hotel and there was a female body all shrouded and ready for burial. He quickly arranged one of her feet for me. A bit unethical perhaps, but she'll be buried now and the family will never know she was minus a foot."

"You say you remembered the trick. From where?"

"Oh, it was used in Beirut when I was there with the Legion. But not a foot from a dead body like the one I used. They hacked the real foot from the real wife. It was a technique used to persuade kidnappers to release hostages. They told them they would be back with the other foot the next day and the day after that they would come with the hands. They meant it too."

"Who were they . . . your Legionnaires?"

"Oh, we might have done that okay. But it wasn't us. It was Spetsnaz. A couple of Russians had been taken hostage so the Soviets sent in a small detachment of 'the boys'. Result . . . they got their hostages back in one piece. And no more Russians have ever been taken. They know the Spetsnaz don't fool around. Nor did the story ever reach any of your papers."

Brian was nonplussed and shook his head. "Tony Mills, you young bugger. I never realised you were such a bag of tricks."

It was 2 a.m. when they returned to their lookout post on the roof of the little spice mill. Surprisingly, the police car hadn't returned and they settled down for their long vigil which they knew would end just before dawn. To stay awake and alert, they had spoken to each other, mainly about events in their past lives. For Mills, ever the opportunist, it was the ideal moment to find out about a subject which had intrigued him.

"That story about you and the gun, Brian. Whatever happened?"

"Am I what you call a captive audience?"

"There's no way out from here, chum. Anyway, it will make you forget this damned heat. Tell me about it. Was it in Vietnam?"

"Did you know?"

"No. But I thought it probably might be."

"Vietnam was a long time and another world ago. Another world I hope never comes back."

"Was it a friend you lost or something?"

"No. Not a friend. Just a couple of youngsters, kids not all that long out of High School. It happened up in the north. We were flying out of Da Nang on Medevacs, you know evacuating the dead and wounded from battlefields? We were flying in twin-engined Sea Princess helicopters, a version of the big Chinooks. Horrible things. No windows. No doors, And the noise and the way they shake! You wonder how they can fly. Anyway, we were diverted on one return trip to pick up a group coming back from a long jungle patrol. As we were making our descent they radioed that they were involved in a firefight with some VC. The pilot went down just the same. As usual I grabbed the camera to take some shots and this very belligerent officer shoved a rifle in my hands and said, 'This ain't Pan Am, bud. You fly with us, you work for us.' I was stuck with this gun. There was no chance of debating the issue with all the action that was going on. So we got the wounded and the Grunts from the patrol on board, then took off. We had put down in a tight landing spot and when the big chopper took off one of its rear rotor blades hit

a tree and folded up. It dropped like a shot bird. There was a helluva smash
and a lot of guys got badly injured. It was then that it went off. That bloody
gun I had been given. I don't know how. Could have been my finger on the
trigger or the jolt of the crash. I'll never know. And two of the boys we had
picked up, a couple of fresh-faced kids that's all they were, well, they got hit.
Killed outright. They had been out there in that hellish jungle for days and
there they were, one minute thinking they had made it, the next minute lying
dead. That's my gun story, Tony. And it's been my life's nightmare ever
since."

"I'm sorry, Brian. I didn't think it would be quite like that. But these things
happen. It was not of your making. We had some bad incidents like that in
the Legion, like the tank crew who ran over and killed that guy in training I
told you about. They took it bad."

"Oh, I know these things happen. I just wish I could convince my
conscience of that."

"I hope you don't think I'm being personal, Brian. But were you married
when you were going off doing those various wars?"

"Yes . . . for a while. She was a lovely girl. She was called Rose. A genuine
beautiful English rose, in every sense of the word. We set up home in
Guildford, which was her home town. And all she ever got from me was an
evening phone-call saying things like, 'Sorry, love. Can't make it home
tonight. Been kept late on a job.' Or else, 'Sorry about the holidays, dear. I've
to leave for the Far East tomorrow. Don't know when I'll be back.' It was
cruel. So we did the right thing before we had any kids. She remarried and
has a family. And I stayed married to a camera."

"But now you seem pretty serious with your girlfriend. Esther, isn't it? I've
still to meet her, you know."

"You will. She's a beauty. You know, I've been so lucky here in the Gulf
meeting a girl like her. I mean, unattached females aren't hanging on every
tree. Are they? And we've really hit it off. Can't wait till she comes back from
her exam in Amman on Thursday night."

"Will you marry her?"

"Now there's a question. And the funny thing is we've never discussed
marriage. It's understood she's coming with me when I leave here. The
original plan was that I'd be going back to Australia, but that could change.
Whatever way, we'll be coming to visit you and Mum in Highgate. That
reminds me. I've still to check what time Esther's due on Thursday night. It's
flight GF 046 she said."

"I'll take you to the airport if you like."

"You're on, mate. And you can meet her at the same time."

At about a quarter to four in the morning the lights went on in the house by
the junction of the alleys which the two men were observing from their roof
perch. The police had been back twice during the night but had only stayed

for about ten minutes on each occasion.

The men from Razak hadn't checked whether or not Yousuf, the simple one, was back in the house. If they had and had seen that he wasn't there it would not have made any difference to them. He had done his duties on their behalf. What they had to do now was not for him. Their remaining hours as soldiers of Allah would be spent in devotion and in preparation for their big day ahead.

There was a washing area in the small yard at the rear of the house and one by one they went there to go through the Muslim ritual of cleansing in preparation for the Fajr dawn prayers. Bria watched them in fascination. It was the Prophet Mohammed himself who had decreed that every person should wash before praying and that as well as the water which removed any pollution from the body, there should also be a symbolical cleansing of the mind. With what lay ahead of them for the day, there was some extra zest put into the washing ritual as they readied for this very special Fajr prayer on the morning of Tuesday, 17 May. It would be their last prayer on earth.

When the muezzins next called, for the Dhur prayer, when the sun would be at its zenith at nine minutes past 12 o'clock that day, they would have done what they had been trained to do and what they had come to the Capital to do. And they would be united with their Allah.

They first washed their hands and then rinsed their mouths and their noses, casting away every scrap of dirt and phlegm before finally washing their faces. Their arms were next, first the right one, then the left, each being thoroughly washed in the prescribed fashion from the elbow down to the wrist. Then they rinsed their hands once again and stroked their hair with some water. Next they washed their feet, again as the Koranic law dictated it, the right foot first and then the left. Such routines were important for it was a basic premise of their religion that everyone, everywhere, should do things in a similar fashion so that in their adoration of their God there would be a oneness in all of their actions. They would prepare together likewise and they would pray together at the same time of day in relation to the position of the sun in whatever land they lived. When they gathered for those prayers they would turn in the direction of Mecca in Arabia where the message of Allah had been revealed to Mohammed. Every mosque in every country of the world where Islam is practised had its special mark, the mihrab, which indicated that direction. The mihrab was a revered place in the mosque, usually a niche adorned with columns and the point where the Imam would stand during the prayer services. There were mihrab indicators too in most houses for the benefit of the stranger who did not know the direction of Mecca from that spot. Even in the little house in that lane off Way 177, there was a mihrab mark, a simple blue paint mark on the wall of the majlis room, facing the direction of south-west.

After the washing ceremony, they gathered together in the majlis to declare the Shahada, the daily proclamation whereby they bore witness to the fact that there was no God apart from Allah and that Mohammed was the messenger of Allah. Standing in a neat row they prayed together, again in the ritual fashion. First they stood in reverential silence and concentration, composing themselves to pray and asking for the help of the Almighty to pray correctly. Then they raised their hands to their ears, repeating together those same first words of the muezzin, *"Allahu akbar"*, Allah is the Greatest. There followed the other rites of bowing, then prostrating in glorification, again by the uniform method of the toes of both feet, the knees, the hands and the forehead, all touching the ground at the one time. They would perform this twice, thereafter standing erect and finally sitting, the four positions which a man can assume to show reverence. As they had started, they finished the routine together, saying "Peace be on you and the mercy of Allah".

It was a simple and touching act of devotion. The universal conformity of it was its uniqueness, perhaps its strength; and there was a solemnity about it to match that which the great cathedrals were supposed to instil in men's hearts.

"Should we get them in the middle of prayer?" Mills had suggested as they had watched them go from the wash place to the majlis room to begin the first of their solemnities.

"How could you even dream of that?" replied Bria.

"Quite easy," said Mills. "In this game you shoot sitting ducks. Let them fly off and they're liable to turn round and shoot you."

"No. No, I couldn't," Brian maintained. "Give them a minute."

Mills knew the prayer routine and when he saw them at the sitting stage he knew it would be over within minutes. "Right, Brian. That's it now. Let's get the night-sight and the other gear back in the car and then go for them. How are you feeling anyway?"

"A bit like they must have felt before going over the top."

"Don't worry, mate. You'll feel okay once there's some action."

As the police car hadn't returned since its last brief visit, they approached the house down the main lane from the wasteground. As planned, Bria stopped about 15 yards from the house and stood in a doorway in order to give cover to Mills who went on alone.

It would be as simple as Mills had said it appeared. Some grenades through the window with the half net curtain followed with a few rounds from his Steyr just to make sure.

The bullets riddled across the narrow alleyway right in front of Mills, sending up tall spouts of dust. Then another burst slammed into the wall of the house behind him. At the same time the door of the house which was their target opened and a man with a protruding beard appeared with a gun.

The two guns fired almost simultaneously; Bria's, from the doorway where he stood, firing off a short volley at the man on the roof who had been shooting at his friend, and Mills with another burst hitting the bearded man the moment he had opened the door of the house. He caught the full impact of the two-second burst which Mills had fired and it hurled him back into the house. The man who had been on the roof fell into the lane with a loud thud. At the same time Mills was by the doorway of the house. With his back to the wall he began lobbing in his grenades. There were some loud shrieks from the men inside and then the muffled explosions of the grenades going off in the confined space. Mills ran through the cloud of dust belching from the doorway. There was some more gunfire and within seconds he was out again.

Just as he emerged, the headlights of an approaching car speeding down the lane caught the pair of them, blinding them for a moment in the full glare of high beam.

"Give it to them," shouted Tony, "right between the headlights."

The crack of their automatics' fire was followed by a series of loud screeches and grinding noises from the car, which suddenly came to a halt with its lights out and a cascade of bright blue and pink sparks coming from beneath its engine. Mills fired a rapid round in the direction of the sparks and there was an instant fireball of flame. They could see two men scrambling from the vehicle and running back up the lane in the direction they had come.

"Right, Brian," Mills snapped. "Follow me."

They ran back towards the house where he paused for a moment to look inside. "Yes, there are four of them all right. The one on the roof must have been an *askar* (sentry) they hired for the night. Funny we didn't spot him with the Twiggy. Keep going, though. It's five lanes in this direction, then left, then another left after the sixth lane. That's where the car is."

"I'm glad of that two hours I spent walking around there today," said Mills as they drove along the main road towards the Rani Hotel. "A job like that is always ten times easier if you do a good recce."

"I can't believe my luck in hitting the one on the roof," said Bria. "I just aimed the gun at him and let fly and down he went. If I'd missed he could have got the pair of us."

"And how about the one at the door! That was your biblical beard. He would never have known. He just opened the door and got them right in the chest. They hit him so hard they blew him right back into the house."

"I keep thinking some film director is going to step out from somewhere with his clipboard and say 'Cut'. It really is like playing in some movie. And how about those two policemen turning up! Wasn't that a stroke of bad luck?"

"Yes. For them," smiled Mills. "Now, just how are they going to explain that to Stott? Oh, nearly forgot. Time-check. Four-forty, eh. Not bad. They'll be ten minutes into their run, so that gives us plenty of time to get set up for them on their way back. There should be a lot less problems with this lot. At least there'll be no one up on a roof taking pot shots at us."

The Sixth Man

THEY COVERED the same distance, traced the same route every morning for their one-and-a-half-hour training run. They had discussed it often with the gym instructor at the hotel. The route they chose, they had said, was one that they considered the most pleasant, for that made their training all the more bearable, and one that also gave them the challenge they required to remain in peak condition. "You see, we have to be this fit," they had told the instructor, "because we are all speed skaters and go in for all the big canal races back in Holland."

They certainly couldn't have chosen a better route for delighting their emotions, satisfying their brawn. After leaving the hotel, it took them along the six-lane highway they called Emir Street, alongside which there was an old track where they could run free of the traffic. That went past a straggle of Indian shops, to a roundabout off which there was the road leading to the imposing Hamat House luxury flats, where Bria lived. The flats were a solitary unit and there were no other buildings within a quarter of a mile. Behind them was the wide course of the Wadi Duka, bordered on either side by a range of small jebels about 1,000 feet high. The area was criss-crossed by a variety of tracks, many of them made by the power grid men when they were installing the big red-and-white electricity pylons which strode up and over the jebels to communities on the other side. They made ideal running roads, lonely and free of traffic, and were tailor-made for the kind of work which the Spetsnaz men wanted for their early morning work-outs. After leaving the main road at the roundabout, they would run the full length of the Wadi Duka. At its far end they would climb into the jebels and run back again towards the Hamat House flats along the summit ridge of the steep hills, then descend down a shoulder which brought them back to the point in the wadi where they had started. From there it was just over a mile back to the hotel. It was an arduous seven- or eight-mile run and one which would have tested the fittest of athletes. And they ran that course every morning.

It was just going on five o'clock when Tony Mills nosed his car off the road behind Hamat House and took it down the wadi track. They stopped and got out.

"Couldn't be better, eh Brian! Not a living soul around."

Apart from the big block of flats about a quarter of a mile to their rear, there was nothing. The night sky had been broken, with the first light of the day displaying a dramatic contrast of blue and black. The jebels were the deep purple-black of early dawn, their innumerable rifts and folds still waiting for the sun to burst them into their daily rhapsody of the many variations of red.

"Jesus. Look up there," said Mills excitedly. "That's them right up on the summit ridge. Look at them."

They were easy to spot because of the movement of their silhouettes, small as they were, black against the blue of the new day that was getting brighter by the minute.

"That's them okay," said Bria. "They've gone up the pylon track which goes to the summit and they'll run right along till they come to the end of ridge then down the far shoulder by the other track that's there. It descends to a point near the bridge at the beginning of the wadi. I haven't been on them, but I feel I know every inch of these tracks for I can see them from the windows of my flat. I used to watch them take giant cement mixer trucks up there. That's what the tracks were made for and there's one point where it gets so steep they used to haul the big trucks behind caterpillar-tracked bulldozers. God, they must be fit bastards to have run up there."

They turned the vehicle around and drove back along the wadi to a point where they could see the track leading down from the jebel top.

"It won't take them long to come down from the summit. Wait and see, they'll come flying down that track there."

"We couldn't have dreamed up a better ambush position," said Mills enthusiastically. "No one around. Lots of boulders to give us cover. No means of escape for them. Ideal. Now remember, Brian. Just as we planned it. Leave the shooting to me. And I'll hit them just where we agreed I would. No worries. Now take a Browning and keep me covered, not that there's really any need. Get behind one of those rocks anyway. There'll be a lot of metal flying around and you never know when one is likely to ricochet."

About seven minutes later, just at that delightful time of dawn when the summit crests of the jebels had taken on their first blush of morning pink, Bria, positioned further up the track, signalled their near approach. But Mills had already heard them as they scrambled down the steep mountain track, their trainer shoes scuffing and sliding on the loose stones, and letting out occasional yells of what seemed to be enjoyment from one to the other, no doubt happy that they were on the descent and that the toughest part of their arduous morning routine was nearly over.

Then they came into sight, led by the one who was the tallest of them, the one who had shown that night in the Rani that he was obviously their leader. The last part of their downward run ended about 20 yards before they passed Bria, crouched behind a large boulder, and from there till they passed Mills, similarly positioned, the track was level. They had regrouped in closer running order, but still with the same big man in front.

As soon as the last man passed his hiding spot, Mills leapt out into the middle of the track and, going down on one knee and holding the Steyr rifle tightly to his waist, began firing in a series of short one- and two-second bursts. He emptied one full magazine that way then threw the rifle down, taking the other gun he had strapped over his shoulder and firing it likewise. There were loud yells and screams of pain from each of the five men, their leader barking out what sounded like a series of commands as he fell to the ground wounded.

Bria came running down the track towards Mills, his Browning at the ready, when he saw the five men sprawled on the ground. "How did it go . . . did you get them all?"

"Every single one. And just like we planned. There's at least one bullet in each of their legs or ankles, maybe even their feet, but nowhere else."

Three of them were lying flat on their backs, one was in a sitting position, holding his wounded legs, and the leader was on his knees, shouting both at his men and at Bria and Mills.

"Well, there they are, Brian," said Mills as the two men stood looking at the wounded Spetsnaz. "That's your 1992 Soviet Olympic Gold medal squad . . . for the Paraplegic Games. They should think themselves lucky. Had they been behind the guns, there's no way they would have confined their fire to our legs. That's for sure. Right, let's get out of here before your neighbours over in the flats see what's happened."

They were walking back towards the car when the single shot rang out. It was such a different sound from the crisp, staccato crack of the high-velocity bullets from the automatic rifle which had felled the five Russians just minutes before. This was the old-fashioned sound of a gun going off, loud and lingering, the unmistakable bang of it reverberating round the surrounding jebels like a distant thunderclap.

Mills didn't utter a sound. He just slumped forward and fell face first into the stony path along which they had been walking. Bria ducked low before swinging round with the Browning he was still holding.

It was the one who had been on his knees, the leader, who had the gun. He was struggling to stay in some kind of upright position in order to fire it again. Bria took his time as he aimed his revolver, holding it the way Mills had taught him, both hands on the grip, legs apart to give him a steady stance. Then he fired three quick shots and the man slumped over, mortally wounded.

He could see another one of them, the one who had been in a sitting position, struggling with the little haversack on his back. "Christ, that's right. Two of them always had their haversacks . . . with guns!" He ran quickly up to the man and pulled the bag with the gun from his back, then collected the other gun from the one he had shot. There was no need to do anything further, the others being completely immobile and without weapons.

"Tony . . . Tony," he shouted loudly as he ran back to where his comrade had fallen.

Bria closed his eyes momentarily in a reflex action of both horror and disbelief when he rolled his friend over and saw the huge and still-spreading stain of blood on the left side of his shirt. The bullet had got him in the back under his left shoulder blade and come out through his chest, more than likely having penetrated his heart. He cradled his head in his lap for a few minutes, wiping the dirt from his face.

"Oh Jesus, Tony. Why did it have to be you, mate! Why, why, why, why? And for that bastard Bainbridge. But don't worry. I'll get him. Just like we planned."

He wept for some moments before laying the dead man's head slowly on the ground again. There had been a sheet in the car and he covered him with it, securing it with a ring of small rocks lest it blow away. He also brought his Nikon from the car and began taking photographs of the scene, at the same time emotionally addressing his friend as though he was still living.

"The world is going to know about you, Tony Mills. I'll make sure of that," he said loudly, almost shouting the words and at the same time focusing the camera on the dead and wounded Spetsnaz, taking shot after shot as he circled them. "The Battle of Wadi Duka, Tony. That's what they'll splash it. Every reader in Britain will know about you." He scrambled up on some rocks to get some elevation into his next shots. "You were a hero, Tony Mills. And they're going to know about it. Everyone's going to know about it. The man who beat the Spetsnaz."

Then he walked further away from the scene to get some distance pictures. The more he snapped the more he became emotionally charged by events and began shouting the words even more loudly, continuing to do so when one film had been completed and as he paused to fill his camera with another. "You knew your game, Tony, and by Christ you did it well. But this is my game, son. And you're the greatest story I've ever worked on. Does that sound crazy, Tony? It's what you did, old mate. You did it all, Tony. And you're going to be the most talked-about hero in Britain."

Then the wind-on lever jammed again as another film was completed. He stopped filming at that to look over at the covered body of the young officer. "Christ, Tony. I wish you could hear me, old son. I wish you could hear me."

He stood for a minute and the scene blurred with his tears. Then he wiped his face and ran to the car.

Madinat Emir, where Bainbridge lived, was the best address in the Capital Area. Bria had nicknamed it Toorak, that being the top suburb in Melbourne. It evoked the same sort of class appeal as did Toorak, or T'rak, as they would say it, or any similar suburb anywhere. It was "in" to call it simply ME or Madinat, "out" to call it by the full title Madinat Emir. And always, when those who classified such things had ascertained that you lived in ME, they would want to know which part, not that there were any bad parts, but there were parts which were better than other parts. And the Jalal Mansions part was the very best of ME.

The Jalal Mansions was a collection of handsome, high-amenity villas, stockbroker belt material and built for the highest of the P.D.E. oil company executives. They were on the only hill in Madinat. There was one main access road into the Jalal Mansions Hill. But there was also a smaller unmade road which went to the summit of the rise from the opposite direction. Bria had discovered it on the one and only occasion when the colonel had offered him a drink and he had wanted to avoid the traffic police on his way home to Hamat House. He found the little road again. From its high vantage point he could see the layout of Bainbridge's house and the others around it. He parked the car, slipped the Browning into a hip pocket and set off on foot down the incline lined with prestigious villas.

It was just 6.30 a.m. but with the normal working day in offices, shops and industry commencing at 7.30, most people were up and about. Bainbridge would have been out for his usual morning jog, he thought, and, if he was treating this like a customary working day, would now be at breakfast or in the shower; whatever, he was most certain to be around his house. Thomas, the remaining member of Red Alert and his bodyguard, would be there too. There was also an armed *askar* on the gate of the big villa, but the biggest of houses often had them, more for prestige than for precaution.

Getting access to the rear of the house was easier than he had thought. He simply walked down the hill via a road which ran parallel to the one where Bainbridge lived, then went through the property surrounding the house at the rear of his. It was unfenced and he was able to stroll casually into the bottom end of the colonel's garden where there was a large gazebo cabin beside a barbeque pit and then an ample swimming pool with poolside changing rooms, surrounded by trees and bushes and a sprinklered lawn.

The French doors which led into an informal day-room-cum-lounge were unlocked and he closed the door, ever so slowly and quietly after stepping into the room.

She was standing right in front of him when he turned round again. She was obviously Sri Lankan, wearing the same plain, buttoned cotton knee-length dress they all wore and with her straight, black hair pig-tailed. He closed his eyes for a second, waiting for her to scream.

"Is it Mr Thomas or the colonel you are looking for sir?" she asked with a smile and a matter-of-fact manner as though he had been expected to walk through the French doors.

"Eh . . . actually it's the colonel. Is he home?"

"Yes. Would you like to give me your name so that I can tell him who is here?"

"I'd rather not," he replied. "You see, it's a little surprise visit. It's his birthday, you know."

She smiled and beckoned him to follow. They walked down a long corridor with polished marble floors, off which there were about six or seven rooms, before coming to a door to which she indicated. He nodded a pleasant smile without speaking. As she walked away he took the pistol from his pocket and slipped off the safety catch. Then he opened the door of the room and went inside.

He was surprised at the enormous size of the room, one wall of which was lined with gold-lettered books. At the far end, to the left of the door, a man behind a large, ornately carved desk, slowly lowered a broadsheet English newspaper.

"Do come in, Brian, dear boy. I've been expecting you."

"I'll bet you were, Billy. You knew I'd be here today . . . to kill you," he said, raising the revolver and pointing it at Bainbridge.

"Oh, put that damned thing away, Brian. You haven't a hope in hell of getting out of here. I've got Thomas and other men around the place. How in hell did you get in anyway? But more important, what is this all about?"

"Billy, don't waste stupid words. You know we found out your game. That's why you got my friend Watson done away with, or whatever you did with him. And you knew too I was fast catching on. But everything's not going to plan, is it, Billy? We got your two goons, didn't we? You didn't expect that, did you? And now we've got your men from Razak. They've been blown away. And we nailed the Spetsnaz too. Nothing's worked out, Billy. For the Emir will be safe now."

Bainbridge lost his composure. "You're bluffing, Bria. You wouldn't have got near the ones from Razak. They were guarded. As for the others, you were no match for them. They're not silly amateurs like you. I don't believe a word of what you're saying."

"Then phone your mate Stott and ask him what happened at Wadi Duka this morning when the Spetsnaz were out running. Every one of them was shot. Then ask him if they've managed to identify any of the bodies they took from the house at the Fish Souk that we blew apart before dawn. Go on, Billy. Ask him."

"You cursed interfering fool, Bria. You and your drunken Scottish friend. I was here to do a service for this country and was doing it perfectly till you started your busybodying. This could have been a vastly changed nation as from today. And believe me, it still will be when the new leader takes command."

"You mean to say you think it's still going to happen, Billy? Your Mr Abdullah as the new leader with you as the head of the Army, no doubt, and your comrade-in-arms Stott the chief of police. No chance, Billy. We changed all your plans at dawn this morning. And you're going nowhere now."

"I should have known better than to have trusted someone with your background to come here. The trouble with types like you is you can't keep your noses out of other people's business."

"You should talk, Billy. If there's anyone that applies to it's yourself. What right have you to sit in judgement on a country and its people? You were out to destroy what this man had done here. In less that 20 years he's turned it round from the Dark Ages to the splendid little country it is today. I wish we had some of the morality back in the U.K. that they've got here. Yet you, with the help of a few madmen in a hurry to see their Allah, were going to wreck it all to satisfy your ambitions and the lust for power."

"People who don't understand the ways of Arabia and in particular the Gulf have no right to be here."

"No right! God! And to think that you lectured me not so long after I came that the likes of you were necessary here. What were your words again . . . 'People who know the Gulf and have the Gulf in our hearts'."

"Yes, that's right. And I'll finish it. And will do anything we can to protect it from the people we consider are its enemies. Well, I did consider that their leader had become an enemy. I did consider that it was time for him to go and I did consider that the new leader I was promoting was the best man for the job. It was for that reason and because I did have the interests of the Gulf in my heart that I was doing what I did."

"Then you still had no right. It's not for you or anyone else to interfere in the power of another country."

"There's not a country in this entire Gulf that hasn't people interfering, as you put it, in its future in one way or another. That's what politics are all about."

"But your game wasn't politics, Billy. Your game was profit. You were doing this for Red Alert the company, not for Billy Bainbridge the soldier. And it's the same with all your rivals with their Chief Commissioners and former Army Commanders and the like on the boards to make them look respectable. They're the ugly face of respectability. They're in the power game . . . for money. And when I tell the story of my friend Tony Mills, I'm going to let it be known just what you and your like are up to in places like the Gulf. If Tony's death is to mean anything then it will be the exposure of you lot. And it's because of Tony I'm here to . . . ."

It was the voice—that unmistakable Birmingham voice. Others were there behind him. "Put that gun down, Brian."

"Come to rescue your old commander, Stott?" Bria replied without looking round. "Well, my gun's not moving. Billy here caused the death of my friend today and I've come to square the account."

"Brian," said another voice, repeating his name, "Brian. Don't be foolish, dear boy. Do put your gun down."

"Christ, you David. Not you as well? We thought you might be, but I gave you the credit of the doubt. I thought no. David Anthony wouldn't sell out like them."

"Brian. Please, I don't want to hurt you in any way. You will be all right provided you drop that gun. You have my word on that."

Bria's gun clattered on the floor and as it did two uniformed policemen rushed from behind and went straight past him to grab hold of the colonel, handcuffing his hands in front of him.

David Anthony was smiling when Bria turned round, asking, "What's going on?"

"You got some of it right, Brian. But just some of it. For a start Superintendent Stott here was not involved with Billy Bainbridge. On the contrary, dear fellow, he's been very actively engaged in watching him for months now and he and his men worked tirelessly in getting the evidence we needed to prove our case against our friend here and his Minister, Mr Abdullah, together with two or three others."

Anthony put his arm round Bria's shoulder as they walked through the pleasant courtyard in front of the big villa and past the hapless *askar* (sentry), still standing with his .303 rifle and wondering what was going on about him as the two policemen came out of the house with his former master. Another two policemen were guarding Thomas, also handcuffed.

"I thought it would have been you who was with Major Mills at Wadi Duka this morning. But we weren't a hundred per cent sure until we heard what you told Bainbridge. So the pair of you sorted everything out, as it were."

He nodded in reply and there was a hint of a smile from David Anthony.

They stood on the broad sidewalk outside the house as one of Stott's uniformed sergeants signalled to a fleet of cars standing further up the hill to come down and collect them. As the cars approached, Stott turned to David Anthony. "We'll take Bainbridge and Thomas with us, Colonel. I assume you'll be looking after our Mr Bria?"

"Yes, that's correct, Superintendent. He's in my care."

Stott then saluted smartly and ordered the policemen guarding the two prisoners in the courtyard of the house to bring Bainbridge out first to the waiting cars.

"What's this about you being a colonel, David?" asked Brian.

"Oh, you've a lot to learn about, dear boy. But we can go into every. . . ."

His words were cut short as Bainbridge suddenly lurched forward at the same time as the crack of a single shot came from the direction of the top of the hill. They all ducked, some of the policemen scurrying back into the courtyard of the house again, others jumping behind the waiting cars with guns drawn, looking for a position in which to return fire.

"Oh, fuck," said Anthony in despair as he looked at Bainbridge sprawled in the gutter, a huge exit wound having taken away the top of his forehead. Then he turned quickly to Stott and, without taking any form of cover, calmly issued some commands. "Superintendent! Get your men up that hill as quick as they can. There'll be no more shots from him now so they're quite safe. But they'll need to move quickly."

Bria, who had been crouching by the gates of the house, stood up and looked at the dead Bainbridge and then to Anthony.

"That's another part of the story you didn't know about, dear Brian. It was the sixth man who did that. You thought there were only five Spetsnaz who came. Well, there were six on the mission. Five to perform the usual role of these chaps, creating mayhem and disorder. The sixth was a scavenger, to clean up after the others. Dead men, as you know, tell no tales. And they were leaving no one behind who could ever tell why they had come here. We found his first victim in the early hours of this morning."

"Who was that?"

"Oh, their local contact man here. We had been watching him for some time. A fellow by the name of P. Carl Sabamontes. The name mean anything to you?"

"No."

"Didn't think it would. You would know him by the name we all knew him by . . . Saby."

"Good God . . . our Saby at the Rani?"

"Yes, Brian. Our Saby at the Rani. Bombay Police kindly tipped us off about him when he came. Wisely, the Intelligence fellows here let him stay in the hope he might help them flush out others. But nothing was to happen till the five, hmmm, Dutchmen arrived. That's why they stayed at the Rani."

"He knew Tony and I searched their rooms. That would be why two of them carried guns . . . why Tony got shot. God, Saby a spy!"

"No. Just a contact man. They have them where they think they'll need them."

"How did he die?"

"He was hanged, or perhaps strangled first of all. We found him dangling in a stairway at his flat. We knew then Bainbridge would be immediately vulnerable. By that time your five cripples had been found in Wadi Duka. We fully expected Bainbridge would be dead when we arrived here, hoping like hell he wouldn't be. He could have told us so much. Come on, dear boy. We had better go."

Details from David

IT WAS the first time Bria had been to the area they called The Other Hill. The Hill, as everyone knew, was where they had the headquarters of the Emir's Defence Forces and where Tony Mills had been stationed at the Training Regiment. The Other Hill was much nearer the Capital than that. It was a restricted area on the slopes of the higher jebels which overlooked the Capital and was ringed with security checkpoints, though these were only manned at times of alerts. They were manned that day but their car was quickly waved through on the production of David Anthony's ID card.

Very little was widely known about what went on at The Other Hill. The most that was commonly known was that the people who worked up there were in the nation's security business of one kind or another. As nothing was ever printed or ever mentioned on radio and television about them, the names of the various agencies who operated there were known only to those who worked in them or had some close connection with them.

The Other Hill, in fact, housed the headquarters of the Emirate Internal Security Service, the National Task Force, Emirate Security, and Special Forces, approximates in British terms of MI5, MI6, the Special Branch and the SAS. The TV and radio stations were also on The Other Hill, since they were considered as vital to the security of the nation as the intelligence networks. Both were as vigilantly protected with armed guards and searches on entry.

The road climbed to The Other Hill past the palace which was the home of the Minister of Security and Defence and Bria reflected on Mills' remark about one of his companies being the agents for the Steyr rifles they used. He wondered how much of that profit had gone into this modern-day Windsor with its golden-knobbed domes and fountains which flaunted the ultimate opulence of Arabia . . . water.

Every now and then there were security humps in the road to curb speeding cars. One of these humps was directly outside the main entry gate to the Minister's palace where they could see his retinue of armed *askars* at the gatehouse, an impressive building on its own and capable of passing for a better than average villa at Madinat Emir.

"He's in the richest man in the world ratings, you know," said Anthony.

"Not trying to hide it, is he?" replied Bria, looking through the gate to the acres of lawns that surrounded the imposing palace.

His next-door neighbour also lived in a modern structure that would have rated the term palace, albeit on a much smaller scale. In its grounds was the biggest satellite dish which, Bria said, he had ever seen in anyone's garden. "I'm sure that's even bigger than the one up on Jebel Azraq. And that serves the whole country."

"That's the residence of the Minister of Posts and Telegraphs," Anthony pointed out. "It's his little toy. You see, he likes the worldwide television. And I think he feeds some lines into the Minister's palace next door."

"Worldwide TV!" Bria exclaimed. "He could pick up Mars with that thing. Where are we going anyway?" he asked as they stopped at another police check.

"To my office. It's near the top of The Other Hill."

"So you're not with the Ministry of Culture and Heritage?"

"No . . . another Ministry, actually. Security and Defence. That was my minister's residence we just passed. Splendid fellow. One of The Family, you know. He's the Emir's closest relation. It's always wise to give Security and Defence to someone close like that."

The car stopped at a low, modern building, the same sand colour as the daytime jebels with small, mock watchtowers at either end and the ubiquitous crenellations, which were the hallmark, it appeared, of every architect who designed anything to comply with the directive that new buildings should be of a traditional character; never mind the inappropriateness of the rest of the design, if it had crenellations it would get the stamp of approval. Or so it seemed.

An armed guard at the large, tinted glass doorway smartly saluted as he recognised David Anthony and Bria was led away to a security lodge to be searched and given a plastic-covered name tag.

"They don't miss much in the body check," he remarked when he came out from the room. "Like boarding an El Al airliner. Oh, that just slipped out. I've got that stamp on another passport."

"Janie," said Anthony, to a petite and shapely blonde occupying an ante-room to his office, and presumably his secretary. "Get Rashid to organise some coffee, tea, whatever for our guests and find out if the Inspector has arrived yet with the gentleman he was bringing. If he has I'd like to see them right away."

"Well, I must say, David, whatever you are I'm impressed," said Bria as he walked round the tastefully furnished office with its suite of couches and easy chairs in soft black leather and numerous paintings of Arabic scenes.

"The artwork belongs to me," smiled David. "Splendid fellow at the Khudra Souk deals in them. You can get everything at that souk. Even good information." He smiled at Bria.

The buzzer on one of his four telephones went just at that moment and Anthony answered it saying, "Yes, bring them in now."

"What was that about information at the souk, David?"

"Let's just say we weren't all that many steps behind you."

He was going to ask more, but was interrupted as the secretary came into the room with the two men.

"B-r-i-a-n . . . for Christ sakes, it's really you, Brian," exclaimed the familiar Scottish voice exuberantly as Gordon Watson walked through the door into the big office accompanied by a uniformed police officer.

The two men threw their arms around each other in joy and slapped one another's back repeatedly and laughed together as they made jokes about coming back from the dead and disappearing into thin air.

"Right . . . jokes aside. Where the hell were you anyway?" Bria asked.

"Give you three guesses."

"No good. I'd get them all wrong."

"I was back in Zamakh."

"Oh no! And you can laugh and joke like that?"

"But it was different this time. They had me in what they called protective custody and gave me one of the police officer's billets. All mod cons with television, a houseboy, the best of food. They even stocked the fridge with beer. And all on the house. The only thing was not being able to contact anyone. But David explained things to me and why they had to do what they did and that it wouldn't be for long. So I just enjoyed myself and had a bit of a holiday. It wasn't so bad knowing most of the story as I did, although there are still a few gaps."

"Gaps! You're lucky. I'm totally bewildered by what's happened this morning and in one hell of a state of shock. Gordon, did they tell you about poor Tony?"

"Yes, the Inspector here explained everything . . . about the Fish Souk, about the battle with the Russian special forces. I take it they were our Dutchmen. And about Tony getting it. Hellish, isn't it. Did he . . . you know, suffer?"

"No. The bastard who did it was a marksman. Hit him in the back. I think it went through his heart. He didn't know a thing, poor guy. But what about this protective custody bit for you? How did that come about?"

"I was getting too hot on the trail of both the guys from Razak and the Dutchmen who weren't from Holland."

"Did you know before this morning they weren't Dutch?"

"Of course I did. You think someone from Glasgow doesn't know his Ajax Amsterdams from his Ajax Rotterdams. But the Soviet connection, that was a shock."

"What's the significance of Ajax Amsterdam and Rotterdam?" David Anthony asked.

"Knew that would escape you," Gordon replied. "Ajax Amsterdam, you see, is one of Holland's top football clubs. But that night we first met them at the Rani they said they were supporters of Ajax Rotterdam. There's no such club. They cocked it up. And that's when I knew there was something funny about them and decided to keep up my private detective work before being nabbed by your men in their green Merc."

"And you knew that night at the Rani that they weren't Dutch?"

"That's right, Brian. And I knew you did too. But I didn't say. You thought I was going round the bend over the Razak men at that point and had I said anything more I was sure you would have given up on me. So I said nothing and pretended that I thought they were genuine Dutch fish buyers. Bet they wouldn't have known a herring from a haddie. But tell me. What were all those fancy names you were asking them about? Names of old players or something. I never thought you were much of a football fan."

"You mean Zoetemelk and Kuiper?"

"That's right. Something like that."

"Well, you're right about me not knowing much about football. But I knew it wasn't Ajax Rotterdam. That's when I threw in the two names. They're two of their greatest bike riders. Tour de France guys, you know? And Zoetemelk in particular. He's a living legend. A sort of Botham-Robson-Piggott rolled into one. He's a real institution in Holland and there's not a Dutchman alive, including their expats, who doesn't know of him. When they didn't know, I knew for certain that they were not Dutchmen."

"If only you had said, Brian, we could have gone after them together."

"What . . . and both of us ending up in Zamakh!"

The three men sat together for over two hours, drinking coffee and going over the various parts of the story which to each of them had its discrepancies of one sort or another and, in turn, each held some vital information that was an answer.

"But why wasn't I lifted together with Gordon for your protective custody?"

"Because you weren't in the immediate danger that he was. Not at that time, at least," answered Anthony. "You see, when Billy Bainbridge reported Gordon to Superintendent Stott, we knew that if we hadn't taken action and got him out of the way, Bainbridge would certainly have done so. By other means. And you, Brian, can appreciate just what other means he had at his disposal. Before we did, however, and just to double-check that Gordon here really was the clean chappie we thought he was and not working on behalf of others, we had him followed . . . ."

"The green Mercedes," Watson interrupted.

"Yes, I believe that's what they use. And we also had his house searched. That satisfied Superintendent Stott that all was above board with him and it was then he was taken into custody for his own safety."

"So when did you first learn about it all, David? And by the way, I still don't know about you, except what you said about working for the Ministry of Security and Defence and that you're a colonel."

"Actually, dear chaps, I'm only a colonel of sorts. You see, I work for British Intelligence. I'm not going to say which arm. Just British Intelligence. I'm here on secondment to the Ministry because of my knowledge of the area and the personae concerned and they very kindly gave me the rank of colonel for my stay which is why I was able to get one of those lovely houses at Bait al Bonni. They're for colonels and upwards only."

"And what about the Arabist and culture bug you made out to be?" queried Gordon.

"Well, I'll assume you'll forgive me for taking on other guises. I couldn't very well go around exclaiming, 'David Anthony here, of British Intelligence.' So I took the cover of the Ministry of Culture and Heritage. But an appropriate cover. For I really am an Arabist. And I really am a culture bug, as you put it, Gordon. I love the arts, good food and wines. Good God, yes, I'm all of those things."

"So you must have known about all this before you even came here?"

"That's right. I've been in on this right from the very beginning which was back in January of last year; what's that, about 18 months ago! I had been working for some time on a study of the various movements of some of these security agencies, as they call themselves. After their interference in Ireland, in particular during one of the kidnappings there where they played middle broker, and then when they were mentioned at the Irangate hearings, the Government became more aware and somewhat concerned about them, which was why we were asked to do some reports on their activities. I got involved in what connections they might be having with countries in the Middle East. While I was working on this the young Mr Abdullah came to our attention. He had hired a private detective agency to help him make some kind of appraisal of a few of the companies. The young fellow thought he was being clever operating like he did. But, oh dear, how terribly *ingénu*. The agency he went to is one of our informants. That put us on guard and when his father came over we had him on 24-hour surveillance. We were there when he met Billy at the Dorchester. Always so much more convenient for us when people have regular tables at their favourite restaurants and we wish to do a little piece of eavesdropping."

"You mean their table was bugged, David?"

"Well, I don't use words like that. You should know that, Brian. But we do have chaps with all sorts of electric gadgets these days."

"Would love to have heard the conversation."

"It was quite illuminating. But the main part was that Bainbridge would be coming here and that the Emir was under threat. Her Majesty's Government took the view, and most wisely might I add, that it would be undesirable for there to be any change in the rule of this country. We were on very good terms with His Highness and had offered goodness knows how much technical help and know-how to help him achieve the miracle he has performed here. He was also a good friend of ours in the Gulf and it was our duty to stand by him. Besides, there was sufficient instability in the region without this happening merely to satisfy the ambitious desires of Mr Abdullah. So I was sent out here to make sure it jolly well didn't happen.

And happen it did not. And will not."

"So you used the Thursday Club as a sort of listening post?"

"That was a most fortunate accident, Gordon. If you remember correctly, I was a member before Brian here. Actually I enjoyed the company, and I mean that. It helped me to know and understand the problems of the expatriate worker out here in the 'eighties. But when Brian turned up and it happened that he was actually a member of Bainbridge's staff, well that was a real bonus for me. I make no bones about that."

"But surely Bainbridge must have twigged something was going on when he learned you were here?"

"Of course not, Gordon. He never knew that I was with British Intelligence. We last parted in the Army when I left with the genuine intentions of following my pursuit and studies of the Arab world. As it so happened a contact in Intelligence thought I would be of more service to the Arab cause and my country if I worked with them. They were short of people with an intimate knowledge of the Gulf. So, on that basis, I joined up, as it were. No, Billy never knew or suspected."

"What happened to him in the Army, David? He was always a bit cloudy about that and you didn't fully explain it that time we had dinner together."

"Yes, that was a good night, Brian. But Billy and the Army! Well, they just parted ways, as it were. He was a splendid soldier and had the potential of making it to brigadier. But I'm afraid he began to enjoy the things that some people call the good things in life. You know what I mean. Those clubs and places they have in London. And flippant young girls that hang about them."

"I know plenty of officers who have such pastimes."

"Brian, dear boy, the stories I could tell you about some very senior staff officers and their shenanigans at such places. But the difference between Billy and them was that they could afford it. Billy started financing his capers in a most ungentlemanly fashion."

"You mean he was dipping into the kitty?"

"That's right, Gordon. Dangerous territory when you start mucking around with the mess funds. There were never any charges or anything like that. Everything was repaid in full. But there were the whispers. And whispers don't help when it comes to time for promotion. A much more junior colonel became the next brigadier which disillusioned Billy. And the next thing you know we have Red Alert. I suppose these damn companies are all right up to a point. I mean, it's one thing using their muscular and pretty boys as escorts for these people they call stars nowadays. But it's another when you use your military talents to further someone's ambitions for power in their native land. You can't go playing little Reagans and little Gorbachevs. But that's where the really big money is for them and that's why they're doing it. I do hope the Government acts on them in some way."

"So how much was Billy going to get?"

"His company have already collected a million pounds. And there was to be another million on the assumption of power by Abdullah."

"One thing Tony and I couldn't figure out was the connection between the men from Razak and the Spetsnaz."

"Yes, we too spent a lot of time trying to work that one out. That's why we didn't make any early arrests. And that's why it doubly suited us to have you out of the way during those vital days, Gordon. We thought you might have alerted them to all that we knew. And that would have been most unfortunate. It was essential for us to find the link between the two because only then would we know the full story. We knew that Billy had been having contacts with the Soviets. He was observed both here and in Muscat. So he was some part of their coming. But whether that was at his request or theirs, we're not sure. And we'll probably never know now.

"Of course, there is a connection with them coming here and the war in the Gulf. The Soviets, you see, are anxious to get good connections in Iran. That's where America has missed out in the war. Instead of playing the real neutral as they should have, they backed Iraq. Don't they realise that the war will be over one day? And when it is, their actions will be remembered by the Iranians, the most powerful nation in the entire Gulf. It will take years and many gestures, and I don't mean a cake and a bible, before they will be able to get on some sort of friendly footing with them again. Meanwhile the clever Russians have been building up points on both sides; with the Iranians for their non-interference and with the Arab nations for not flaunting superpower domination in their precious Gulf. Remember, while much of the world knows and thinks of it as the Persian Gulf, to the Arab world it has another name. The Arabian Gulf. So Billy and the Spetsnaz connection will be something we'll just have to theorise on. That's another reason why we would have liked him alive. Curse that damned sixth man."

"How did you know about him?"

"We have agents in Yemen. Even in remote Tamrida on the Socotra Islands. Wonderful place. I've been there. Mountain peaks that would make the needles of the Dolomites look blunt. It's always easier to have agents in places where there is resentment, such as there is there against the Russian presence. And as well as our agents, we also have all this modern technology for picking up signals and conversations. They all played their part. Although, at the end of the day, there's nothing to beat a man on the ground, as Gordon here proved by being the first man to spot them here. We knew they were coming and would be landing somewhere on the coast. But my God, look at the nature of that coastline! Hundreds upon hundreds of miles of emptiness. Submarines and people from them can come and go at their will. As it was, Navy surveillance tracked them to the Abu Dhabi area. The five of them then came down here by car, Gordon witnessing three of them that day he followed the man from the Fish Souk. What a stroke of coincidence that was. But we were on to them fairly soon afterwards, although we did nothing but observe.

"We wanted to know all their movements, who their contacts were here and to see if they would lead us to their sixth man. As it was the first man they led us to, alas, wasn't their sixth man but their seventh man. Saby. Intelligence here had known about him since he arrived in 1986, thanks to the Indian Police and their information about his meeting with a Soviet agent in Bombay a few months before he came here. They could have turned him back, of course, but let him come to see if he could lead us to others here that needed uncovering. He was under surveillance from the moment he arrived, poor beggar."

"A touch of compassion for him there, David?"

"Oh, I've got compassion for him all right. He was an innocent in a way. His records show he was merely a dedicated Communist Party worker in Bombay, humble origins, Kerala and all that. He wouldn't have known he was being set up the way he was. Once they had put him to some kind of use, the chances are they would have exterminated him. As it turned out, they did. People like P. Carl Sabamontes are totally expendable to them. He would have done what he did for a few humble rupees, which would all be sent back to his wife and family and probably he would be keeping parents as well. You know what it's like in India. We knew he was connected with them as soon as they booked into the Rani. Our men observed him on several occasions meeting with them. But we left things as they were for it was that damned sixth man we wanted to find, not the seventh one. The sixth man was the danger as far as we were concerned. You see, we didn't know what his role was going to be. It could have been that he was a jackal, sent to assassinate the Emir while the others created some kind of diversion. But we quickly discounted that. The risks of their being exposed for a deed like that were too great for the Soviets, ever anxious to win more friends in the Gulf. They wouldn't have wanted an Emir-gate on their hands."

"So where *was* the sixth man?" asked Watson.

"That we will never know. But our assumption is that he stayed on in Abu Dhabi awaiting the call to tell him his mission was on. It's only a few hours by road, under an hour by plane. They would have reckoned, you see, that the final success of their mission would be if it was forever a secret. To guarantee that they had to be rid of both Billy and Saby. Which led to the paradox that Billy, although the poor blighter didn't know it, was in much bigger danger than the Emir, the man whose disposal he had been setting up. But by the time we eventually had their game figured, it was too late."

"But that still leaves the role of the faction who wanted to take over a bit of a mystery to me," said Bria. "They were as aware as their leader Mr Abdullah that the men from Razak were Fundamentalists. While they would have died in their attack on the Emir and his party, it would be known in Fundamentalist circles, although not to the populace as a whole, that the new power grouping was giving them some kind of tacit support. Wouldn't that have caused the new Government a whole set of other problems?"

"Of course it may have. But that's not the way they would see it. Mr Abdullah and his cohorts were obviously taking lessons from history, but then don't we all? They assessed the group who were giving him backing. Birds of a feather, as it were. Opportunists to a man. And very wealthy ones at that. Their nearest parallel in history was in the 1924-1933 period in Nazi Germany. It was the ultra-rich there that served as a motivating force for Hitler's movement. Of course they weren't Nazis like he and his brownshirts were. But by aligning themselves with an apparently unstoppable force, they were merely protecting their own wealth. Hitler knew that. The man wasn't a fool. But he needed their backing and he got it. It's exactly the same with Fundamentalism. There are the wealthy in a few countries around the Gulf who would willingly sell out to them. Some have already done so. And that is precisely what Abdullah and his claque were up to. They had considered Fundamentalism was inevitable here and if they were to help it at this stage then their riches would be protected for them and their heirs."

"So what will happen to them now? The firing squad?"

"That would have been the case not so long ago. But not now. There are enough martyrs around without creating any more. So instead they will be banished from all forms of power and social acceptability for the rest of their lives. They will never be able to travel. It will be like virtual house arrest, which isn't too bad when you see some of their houses."

"I know you have both had many surprises today. I've not been without them myself. But the biggest surprise was the discovery of the body of Major Antony Mills this morning beside the wounded and the dead Spetsnaz. You see, we weren't aware of his presence, although we knew someone else was working with Brian."

"I know," said Brian. "That's why I was able to remain undetected these past few days. Only one hero emerges from all this and it was Tony Mills. If it hadn't been for him, Bainbridge's two men would have got me that day at the flat."

"Yes, we wondered about that. It was a bit of a shock for us to find two such experienced soldiers as that dead together. There was someone out there, we thought, with skills that we weren't aware of."

"Well, that was Tony. And it was Tony who masterminded the attack at the Fish Souk and how to get the Spetsnaz."

"Obviously the Emir will now be made aware of the role of Major Mills in all this," said David Anthony.

The men sat quietly reflecting for some moments, Watson ending the silence by bringing their attention to the time. "That's more than two and a half hours we've been sitting here. And do you know, I still haven't found out what happened to my friend Yaqoob? It was his death that really started all this off. Did they ever find out who the killer was?"

"Oh, yes. We knew that right at the start. Another prisoner told the full story but we did nothing because at that stage Bainbridge, through Minister

Mr Abdullah's influence, was making regular visits to Jilida, the long-term
wing at Zamakh. Some kind of arrangement had been made to get the Razak
men there every day. And we wanted to know why and whose influence had
got them the visits."

"So who killed Yaqoob?"

"The leader of the men from Razak."

"The one with the big beard?"

"That's right. He was called Khalfan . . . Said bin Khalfan. He had caught
one of his men gossiping with the Pakistani chap and the silly man had
apparently confessed to having told him something. So that night he slit the
Pakistani's throat."

"Poor Yaqoob," said Watson shaking his head. "What a way to go."

"Khalfan?" queried Bria. "Wasn't there another Khalfan from Razak?"

"Ah, you remember our dinner conversation. Yes, there was another
Khalfan . . . Sheikh Khalfan, one of the famous trio, or infamous if you like,
known as The Three, who were the instigators of the Imam revolt 30 years
ago, a war in which I and Billy Bainbridge were both involved on behalf of
the old Emir. The Three were, and still are, legendary figures, Sheikh Khalfan
being known as the King of the Jebel Ahmar. And the one who killed
Yaqoob Jaffar was his son Said."

"And the sixth man? Was he caught?"

"No, dammit. Clever bugger had it well planned and was quick off his
mark. All we found of him was a spent Soviet-made 7.62 cartridge case.
Probably from a Dragunov sniper's rifle, at least so our ballistic boys say.
He'll be the only one to get a welcome back to his regiment. He did precisely
what was asked of him. The four others with their dead commander were
quickly transferred by the Red Crescent medical people to the custody of the
Soviet Embassy in Abu Dhabi, one in a coffin, four in wheelchairs. The
Russians, of course, are horrendously embarrassed by it all for they've already
embarked on a flurry of diplomatic activity to both hush it up and make
quick amends. They'll be pleading, of course, that it was not ordained from
the supreme command. And more than likely that could be the truth. I'm sure
they are not without their Poindexters and Norths."

At that point David Anthony said he would have to excuse himself as he
had an urgent security meeting to attend in relation to matters arising out of
what they had been discussing. "And you two are both free to go, but with a
proviso. That's in relation to your future here. The news I have for you, and I
hope it doesn't come as too much of a shock, is that while the Government
here is extremely grateful for your help, your vigilance and your courage and
while, in your case, Brian, it's willing to overlook that police car which was
destroyed this morning and its occupants shot at, but fortunately not shot, you
both have to leave the country as soon as possible. I hope you appreciate this
is being done as much in your interests as that of the country. There will be a
variety of people looking for some form of revenge after this. You two,

particularly you, Brian, would certainly figure on their lists. There's always a backlash after something like this. We're on a high-alert at the moment for hi-jacking, for instance, one of the subjects to be discussed at the meeting I'm about to attend. It's something like that which these people might get up to for we're still holding a few prisoners from the attack on the police barracks at Razak."

"So when do we have to go?"

"You've got three days. That means you must leave here by Friday the 20th."

The two men turned to each other and smiled. "Suits me," said Gordon. "In fact, I'll probably be away before then. I'm dying to see Jean and the kids."

"And suits me too," said Brian. "My girlfriend Esther comes back from Jordan on the 19th. I might even talk her into coming with me to London the following day."

"London?" queried Gordon. "I thought you were for Down Under. Getting yourself a new way of life and all that stuff."

"That's right. I was. But not now. A lot of things have changed. Now it's back to London and the old job. Oh, before we go, David, there's one thing I meant to say. Weren't you leaving the arrest of the Spetsnaz and the men from Razak a bit late. I mean, there were only hours to go before the Eid prayer service at the Saghir Mosque. And you still had that sixth man on the loose."

Anthony smiled. "No. There were no worries about what might happen at the Saghir Mosque. You see, the Emir wasn't going to be there. We had changed all his regular plans, and that was one of the first ones we altered. Although as far as the crowds were concerned, they would still be expecting him to be there."

"So where is he?"

Anthony folded back the cuff of his shirt to look at his watch. "As a matter of fact, at this very minute he will be at the midday prayer service in the lovely new mosque at Razak."

"Isn't that the one Abdullah funded in memory of his mother? Cost him a couple of million, they say."

"That's correct. He's in the Abdullah Mosque. Life's just full of ironies. Isn't it?"

Arabia Felix?

IT WAS as though it had all been a dream that afternoon of Tuesday, 17 May, when he returned to his flat for the first time since Bainbridge's two gunmen had come for him. And that had only been three days previously. Only the smell of fresh paint indicated that anything was different. The doors had all been replaced, the outside one, again with a spy-hole, with the same lock number to accept his key. All the walls had been replastered, the terrazzo floor tiles which had been chipped and scraped, renewed. There was even fresh white grouting between the tiles of the vestibule floor, presumably to replace the stain of the blood which had poured from the wounds of the two dead men they had left there.

But then it was no great surprise to him that everything had been restored. That was the way of it at Hamat House — the ultimate address, as they had called it. For the company which owned it could get ten men from India or Pakistan for the price of an average worker's wage in Britain. He reflected on that when he had stood out on the balcony of his big modern lounge two mornings later after having slept or rested most of the time in between, only leaving the flat once to attend Mills' funeral.

He remembered that day, just a year ago, when he had first walked on to that same balcony to look at the morning scene, so exotic compared to what he had just left, and how he had looked forward to learning and appreciating as much as he could about this region they called The Gulf. It was much the same scene that morning as it was now. In fact, it was uncannily identical. Only his mind and its interpretation of what he saw had changed.

It was 7.30 a.m. and just as they did that first morning, and every morning since, the workers would arrive at the flats from their camps on the big black-and-white bus, a slow-moving Indian make called a TATA, shoebox-shaped like buses used to be and with a grinding diesel engine obviously suffering from extreme old age. In the disciplined fashion that was the way with them, they filed from the bus straight to the tasks they had left the night before, their overalls indicating the kind of work they performed, light green for the gardeners, usually Sikhs, scarlet red for the tradesmen, electricians, carpenters and the like, mainly from the north of India, and blue for the odd-jobbers, the sweepers and the polishers, the swimming pool attendants, usually darker-skinned men from further south in India, occasionally Sri Lankan but, as Basil, one of them had told him one day "we will all have to go for the foreman is Indian and he does not like us".

At lunchtime the same bus would return with their tiffin tins, the round, stainless steel containers which serve as the Indian's lunch box, each man being given two, one with rice the other with a thin curry, some days mutton, other days chicken, and every day lukewarm. In the same quiet fashion in which they headed to their work duties every morning, so unlike British or Australian counterparts who would have been noisier, certainly cheerier and would probably have lingered for a smoke and a chat first, these men from the subcontinent accepted their lot for what it was and that, as everyone knew, was better than what they had left in their homelands.

What a charmed life it was now for so many of these Gulf nationals, he thought, as he watched the Indians and Pakistanis go about their labours. Allah had brought them their oil and there was the biggest market of cheap labour right on their doorstep, albeit just over a couple of hours' flying time away. Their country could be among the cleanest and tidiest in the world and they didn't have to lift a hand to make it that way. Even the ones who tended and tidied at the Emir's Palace were men from other lands, yet the ruler himself kept urging "Emiratisation", as they called it, meaning that nationals should be doing the jobs of the expatriates.

He had often wondered if they appreciated the work which these men, these modern-day coolies, did for them and his conclusion had always been that they did not. When he asked Gulf nationals about their attitudes towards them, their response was invariably a shrug of the shoulders and "Well, these boys are there and we give them better money than their own masters". There was not a lot you could reply to that.

If their attitudes to the expatriate workers didn't impress him, there were many things which did, not the least of them the discipline and dignity which prevailed in the country. Of course there was crime, or else there wouldn't be a Zamakh. But there was no obvious crime. And they were fearful, even terrified, that the ways of so many parts of the West could slowly impinge upon their customs. It was for that reason that tourists were barred, except for the recent relaxation of that rule by allowing what they termed "select parties", meaning groups from specialised travel firms in Europe whose customers had to be at least 30 years of age, preferably much older, and willing to pay £2,000 upwards for a ten-day sight-seeing package. That kind of tourist was all right. Keep them to their splendid hotels and their guided bus tours and there would be no problems. The Emirate way of life was sacrosanct and must not be diminished. The Emir had often preached that and so had the leaders of neighbouring states.

He envied their society where one never feared the intruder and where precaution from the felon was unknown; he had remembered how vividly that had struck him when he had first arrived from London and realised he was in a community which was virtually free of the pestilence of crime. But he had often asked since then, was it the discipline and love of Allah which was the reason for their moral rectitude or was it the fearful price paid by the transgressor?

It was only the sensational issues they would hear about in the West, the death of a Princess or the flogging of a British expatriate and the like. But there were the regular reports in the local press, such as the stonings to death and the urgings of the Fundamentalists that in future smaller stones should be used as that made the coming of death more prolonged and the suffering all the greater. Just the week before, in fact, a couple of expatriate workers, Indians, had been found guilty of immoral behaviour by the Sharia Court in Ajman, nearby Emirate, and sentenced to 72 lashes each followed by a year in jail for the man, six months for the woman. Their immoral behaviour? The woman's employer had caught them making love outside his house one night. The man was not the woman's husband. Just a few days before that another Indian was sentenced to have his hand severed at the wrist. He had been convicted of stealing a sum of money from a friend.

He had asked them about that too. Weren't they paying too dearly for the way of life? Was there not a greater fear in their society of those who prevented crimes than of those in his society who perpetrated them? Was this the only way they could have their Arabia Felix? But the answer was always the same. It was right that those who transgressed the laws of Allah should be punished the way they were. It was Sayyid, an office manager at the Ministry, and one of his friends who had said to him with some passion: "We like our life this way. The more freedom you have the more problems you have. A couple of places in the Gulf have tried to be more liberal. All it has caused them is trouble. No. If that's what your freedom, as you call it, means then we don't want it."

There was not a lot he could answer to that either.

The Rani was packed that Thursday night, 19 May. It was the first Thursday night after Ramadan and there was a full turnout of the Thursday-Night Club with the exception of David Anthony who had phoned Bria earlier in the evening to say he would be late and to remind him that neither he nor Gordon should mention to the others about his real role in the country. "It would be terribly indiscreet, dear Bria, if any of the events of the last few days were to be mentioned." Bria had said he understood and assured him the subject would not be raised.

"Have a quiet Ramadan then?" Bria and Watson were asked when they arrived, most of the company not having seen them during the month-long closedown of the bar.

They looked at each other and smiled, Watson answering, "Just like yourselves, boys. Sober and boring. And we'll both have a pint."

"You won't have heard the news about Saby, then?" said Jock Carlin. Before they could reply, he went on, "Saby's dead. Topped himself. They found him in his room the day before yesterday. Poor Saby. Best bloody barman in the business."

Watson and Bria were rescued from having to fabricate any kind of comment by a loudspeaker introduction of a girl pop singer. The others turned to listen to her and that gave Bria and Watson the chance to have a talk together.

"Well, I'm glad they know that much at least about Saby," said Bria. "I was at Tony's funeral yesterday. It's taking me all my time to talk about it even now. I don't recall ever being so emotional at a burial, and I've been to a few. I didn't even know they had a Christian cemetery here. It was like something out of a scene from another century."

The Christian burial ground was in one of the scores of coves which flanked the Capital Area and could only be reached by launch, or in the old days by a donkey track. They had gone in two launches manned by men of the Emir's Navy. One carried the coffin together with the bearer party from Tony's regiment, the other conveyed the small group of mourners.

Despite the early hour, it was well over 100 degrees and the British Ambassador, who was there with the Military Attaché, was wearing a formal lounge suit and sweating profusely but insisted on keeping his jacket on, doubtless, Bria thought, out of respect for the occasion. The commander of Tony's regiment, a national, was there, and so was a captain, an Englishman and Tony's closest Army friend.

The launches went past the cove at Bandar Bahar and that was the only moment that Bria's thoughts were diverted from the sad journey, remembering that happy evening he had spent there with Esther, lying together on the beach making love.

The cemetery at the little cove was only a few paces beyond the high water mark and contained the graves of men who had been mainly seafarers over the last 150 years, but there were some British soldiers there too and former representatives of His and Her Majesties' Governments, or Agents and Residents as they had been called in the days prior to there having been an established Embassy.

"The heat used to affect them woefully," said the Ambassador as they walked together past some of the graves. "Poor blighters would spend their nights wrapped in sheets or blankets with the punka wallah keeping them soaked with a watering can. If the pneumonia didn't get them, the arthritis did."

A bugler played the *Last Post* after the minister, from the only Church of England in the country, said a brief service as they lowered the light cedar coffin into the shallow grave, which was filled in immediately by a couple of Indian labourers. A white cross had already been erected at the head of the grave with his name and rank and the brief inscription: "Killed in Action, Wadi Duka, 17/5/1988." Yet another corner of a foreign field would be forever England.

"So, will all that be in your story when you get back to London?"

"Yes. Everything will be in the story. I've already been on to one of the big agencies and they're handling everything for me. They're meeting me off the plane."

"You have never explained about that, Brian. The going back to London bit. You were so dead against the place until the last couple of weeks. Why the about turn?"

"Oh, I guess I've got over all that. In fact, I know I have. For I can speak about it now. I couldn't before. That night with Tony up on the roof of the spice mill building and also at his billet, we had plenty of time for talking. I don't know, there was something about the guy that made you just want to tell him things. He had such an open and receptive face and despite him being much younger, he was like a father confessor in a way."

"What was it, Brian? Some sort of hang-up from your Vietnam days? The journalists who were here that time Chas and Di were out, they said something about it."

"Yes, it was Vietnam all right. No two mistakes about that. The war of the lonely people. You went as one kind of man, you came back another. It affected even guys like me who weren't there to fight. But I saw them fighting. And I saw them dying. Then there was a very sad incident in which I was involved; we'll skip the details. When I came back, there was no one to talk to about it. That was made painfully clear to me the first time I mentioned the subject. I was in the Stab, that was our pub, with a group from the office and I started talking about it. Then some guy cut in and said, 'But that was nothing. Did you not see that film they had on TV last night about Vietnam?' And then they all started talking about the TV film.

"From that moment on I kept it all to myself. And I suffered for it. The loneliness of the survivor syndrome, they call it. Despite all the other places I was to go to later, none were to affect me like Vietnam did. And instead of getting better, the years made my loneliness worse. Eventually it got so bad that I just didn't want to face up to life as I knew it in London. Everything about the place sickened me. I thought the only way out would be to turn the clock back in some kind of way. I wanted to go back to my home town Bendigo and pretend everything would be just like it was when I left. An Australia of Graham Kennedy, Bert Newton, Panda, Bobby Limb and Dawn Lake, Bob Dyer, Herb Elliott, Russell Mockridge, Percy Cerutty, Sid Patterson, Ron Barassi, Lou Richards, Bill Collins, Albert Namatjira, the Easter Fair, the Thousand, the Moomba. Now there's a string of names and events that don't mean a thing to you. Well, they were my Australia of the early 'sixties. I knew it wasn't like that now but I thought that by going back to Bendigo, somehow I might be able to pick up where I had left off.

"But I'm glad I'm not going now. You can't turn the clock back. Ever. And I was crazy to even try. But that's the way I had gone. Thanks to Tony and talking it all out with him, everything all changed. Sure, I'll go back home one day. But on different terms from what I was going back this time. That's the story, Gordon. It will be easy for me to pick up again in London, especially with this story and set of pictures I have for them."

Their conversation ended abruptly when Steve Powers, the Londoner, intervened. "Are you two having a ferkin' love affair or are you just trying to miss buying a round?" They were sharply back in the world of the Thursday-Night Club.

"I'll get them," said Gordon. "Might as well, for it's my farewell round. The big surprise for all you guys is that Brian and I are leaving the Gulf. I'm off tonight, or 1a.m. in the morning to be precise, and Brian is on a flight tomorrow."

"That was a bit sudden," someone commented.

"Well, a lot can happen in a month," Gordon replied. "Can't it, Brian?"

"Too right," he answered with a shake of his head. "Too bloody right, and especially during Ramadan in the Gulf."

"Yes, and apparently it all happened this Ramadan," came in Geoff Melmouth, apologising for changing the subject and, looking around before speaking again, "but have any of you heard the *big* story?"

"Sounds good," said one.

"Well, you better all get closer," said Melmouth, "for this is not for the ears of any of the dishdashas from Internal Security they send around the bars. The wife's been here for a month and last night she invited a couple of her mates from the bridge club and their menfolk along. One of them is a bloke called Harry Bedwell. He's been up in the house before. He's a copper. Former Scotland Yard and got himself a pretty senior number in the Special Branch here. Plays the colonel bit now. You know, the waxed moustache, the cravat, posh talk and the Range Rover. Taking it home with him, he says. Funny, they all want to take their Range Rovers home when they become when-I-wozzers. Anyway, he never speaks about his work. Just gives you one of those supercilious smiles if you ask him any questions. Well, I pours the good stuff into him, you know one of those Glen somethings? You'd know its name, Jock."

"Aye. Glenda Jackson."

"Lord! A Scotchman with a sense of humour. Anyway, after the other couple left, Harry's tongue loosened up a bit. Been under a lot of pressure recently, he says, and I thought boring, boring, boring and filled his glass up again. Then the story starts to come out. They've just had a big alert on here. And then he lets it out. 'You didn't know we nearly had a coup in the country a couple of days ago.' Apparently, so his story goes, some of the Ayatollah's lads tried to bump off the Emir. But Harry and his boys were one step ahead and bumped them off. How about that?"

Watson caught Bria's eye and there was the trace of a smile and a nod between them.

"But that's not all," Melmouth went on. "After I topped him up with another big one, he reveals there was a group of Ministers all ready to take over from the ruling family. And what had surprised them in the force was that there was quite a lot of backing for the new lot. But I suppose that figures. They're educating people here now and they must be getting sick of all that Emir propaganda they cram into them. Makes you think, doesn't it? You get the impression that everything's all happiness and light and all the time there's guys figuring out a way to change things. I mean, if old Harry's boys hadn't got in there quick, like he said they had, maybe this might have been an even better country for the locals. Yeah . . . makes you think, doesn't it?"

Watson and Bria looked at each other once again. There was no hint of a smile this time.

"Gawd," said Powers. "It really has been some Ramadan. An attempted coup and Brian and Gordon here leaving us."

"What flight are you on?" someone asked Gordon.

"The British Airways night flight."

"What, the one that comes in from Aussie?"

"Same one."

"You won't catch me on that one again," said Bill French. "Done it twice. Full of drunken bloody Aussies staggering about with their green and yellow shorts, bare chests and bush hats. Bet you most of the buggers have never been near the bloody bush. The last time I was on it a group of nationals got on, the women covered in their usual veils and that. There were these Aussie yobs staring and giggling at them. Downright embarrassing it was. Are they all like that out there then, Brian?"

"You've got your yobbos, we've got our larrikins."

"Who's taking you to the airport, Gordon?" Powers asked.

"I'm sharing a taxi with Brian here. His girlfriend is due in on a flight about the same time. Look at him, he can hardly wait."

"What's that about going to the airport tonight?" someone on the fringe of the crowd asked. "You'll have problems, mate. I passed it about half an hour ago and they've got the place ringed with troops and police."

"Could be another one of your mate Harry's coups," said Powers to Melmouth.

"Probably one of their drills," said Marsh. "They're always bleedin' having 'em."

Not long after one of the barmen discreetly signalled to Bria that there was a telephone call for him and he left to take it in the quiet of the reception area.

"It's David here," said the voice. "I'm sorry, dear boy, but I won't be able to make it for Gordon's farewell tonight. But I will try and be at the airport later. Better tell him, though, that he should be there a bit earlier than usual. We have a bit of an emergency on and I've volunteered my services. There's a few points of strategy we have to work out."

"What's the problem, David? Or is it all hush-hush?"

"We've got a hi-jack on our hands. Not all that surprising, really. Frustration over the failure of their martyrs going the way they did coupled with the fact we're still holding prisoners after the Razak police station attack."

"Fundamentalists again?"

"Worse, dear boy. It's Abu Nidal. And, as you'll know, there's just no dealing with them. That's why I'm involved in working out various responses we'll use, if they come here that is."

"Oh, so it's not happening right here?"

"No. Our connection is that it was a flight that was due here. The hijackers have diverted the plane to Damascus believing that the Syrians will be better disposed towards them and perhaps let them make whatever demands they have from there. But it might not be all that simple for the Syrian attitude is not what it used to be with Abu Nidal."

"Which flight was it, David?"

"A Gulf Air one coming down from Amman via Bahrain and going on to Muscat after here. Was due to arrive about midnight."

"Oh God, David. My girlfriend Esther is on that flight. GF 046 isn't it?"

"I'm afraid that's the one, Brian. I am so sorry to hear that. But don't overworry, dear boy. Remember, most of these affairs do have a successful conclusion. Some of them just take time, that's all. And, of course, they can be very trying."

"But you said Abu Nidal, David. They were involved in the Karachi hijack. It was slaughter because they don't give up. Abu Nidal! For Christ's sake, David."

Anthony had no reply to that.

"Brian. Take a note of my office number. If I'm not at the airport, phone me and I'll give you what news there is."

Father of the Struggle

ABU NIDAL is the pseudonym of a middle-aged Palestinian called Sabri al-Banna. It means Father of the Struggle. Abu Nidal has been called the Master Terrorist, more feared even than the one they called Carlos. But the fear is not so much for Nidal the man as Nidal the group. For, as its organisation has many times proclaimed, Abu Nidal is not just about its founder. Abu Nidal is a symbol "which will fight to the end against imperialism and Zionism".

In the early 1960s, Sabri al-Banna, the son of a very wealthy Palestinian family, with some others, including one called Yasser Arafat, formed the group known as al-Fatah, the dominant force in the Palestine Liberation Organisation. But by the early 'seventies, after he had been to terrorist academies in North Korea and China, al-Banna broke with Arafat. The reason? He considered him and his supporters too moderate. He had even heard that some of them were willing to have political dialogue with the Zionists. Thoughts like that were anathema to such a Godfather of the struggle. There was only one way to deal with Zionists. War.

To demonstrate just how ruthless and merciless that war should be, and using all the skills and techniques he had learned in Korea and China, al-Banna and his followers were to prove time and time again they were the ultimate terrorists. Innocents mean little to those in the terrorist trade. "Blame those whom we fight against, not us," is their cry. To Abu Nidal, innocents don't even mean little. They mean nothing.

In the last 12 years they have attacked Arab embassies and hotels in Damascus, Rome, Islamabad and Amman. They've committed assassinations of others in London, Nicosia, Kuwait, Paris, Brussels, Vienna, Warsaw, Madrid and Lisbon. They blew up a Gulf Air flight near Abu Dhabi, killing all aboard. They attacked a tourist hotel in Athens, a café in Rome and kidnapped and claimed the killing of British journalist Alec Collett in Lebanon. They killed 22 worshippers at prayer in a machine-gun attack at an Istanbul synagogue. In a plane hi-jack in September 1986, they took over a Pan Am Jumbo at Karachi Airport with 358 passengers on board and ordered it to be flown to Cyprus where they were to demand the release of prisoners. Pakistani troops, however, ended the hi-jack with the loss of 22 innocent passengers killed during the battle which took place in the big cabin of the plane.

There are no bounds to the ruthlessness of Abu Nidal. And both David

Anthony and Brian Bria knew that.

Gulf Air flight 046, a twin jet Boeing 737, was scheduled that day to leave Amman in Jordan at 3 p.m. (local time) for the seven-hour flight, with a stop at Bahrain, to Emirate, where it was due to arrive at midnight, local time being two hours ahead of Jordan. All 12 first class and 87 economy class seats were full.

As soon as the seat belts sign went out the five men rose from their seats and headed for the rear of the plane, stopping at the last luggage hatch on the left where a big canvas bag was lifted down. It had been placed there by an accomplice in the ground servicing crew at Amman. Quite coolly and calmly, they stood in the middle of the passageway taking weapons from the bag, checking them and affixing magazines before cocking them at the ready and then distributing a number of grenades which they stuffed into pockets.

Landing permission at Damascus was at first refused the English captain of the flight after he had told ground control that his plane had been taken over and that his request was made on the orders of a man who had invaded the flight deck.

"Now tell them we are Abu Nidal and we will detonate this aircraft over the city if they refuse again," ordered the man who was holding a pistol behind the pilot's right ear.

The Syrians had enough experience of Abu Nidal to appreciate that such threats could not be taken lightly. The country had been one of the first victims of Abu Nidal as far back as 1976 when they had attacked the Semiramis Hotel in Damascus, demanding the release of prisoners. After that there were assaults on Syrian embassies in Rome and Islamabad and assassination attempts on their then Foreign Minister Abdel-Salim Khaddam. All this, paradoxically, against one of the most hard-line Arab states.

There was then to be an accommodation between the two, Nidal being given permission to establish offices in the Syrian capital where if you wished any information you merely phoned Damascus 774236 and their spokesman would invariably oblige. There was considerable cooling towards them, however, following the Hindawi case, Nazar Hindawi having been the Arab travelling with a Syrian passport who had given his unsuspecting Irish girlfriend a bomb to carry which was timed to blow up the El Al Jumbo she would be travelling on to Israel from London. Again there was Nidal involvement and because of the world outrage, their offices in Damascus were closed.

Landing permission was granted the hi-jacked plane and Gulf Air flight 046 with its 99 passengers and seven crew who had been bound for Bahrain, Emirate and finally Muscat, touched down at Damascus International Airport, 30 kilometres south-east of the city, just one hour after its take-off from Amman.

Word of the plane's landing and of the presence of the Abu Nidal group on board was picked up within minutes by the sophisticated listening post situated in the Soviet Embassy in Adawi St on the Aleppo Road to the north of the city. The extensive Soviet complex was mainly hidden from sight by a high protective wall, adorned by strategically placed cameras and other electronic devices. Because of events in Emirate, they too had been anticipating some kind of incident and the first inquiry from the Embassy to its agent in the Syrian Air Force Intelligence was to find out the demands of the hi-jackers. He was able to report back to them about half an hour later. That information was immediately relayed to Moscow. Orders had gone to all their embassies in the region to provide immediate notification of any such incidents.

Meanwhile the Gulf Air jet was parked on a perimeter apron of the airport and surrounded by a variety of vehicles, including a mobile stairway truck and buses with detachments of Syrian Special Forces, many of whom had taken part in the ruthless suppression of their own countrymen in the Muslim extremist uprising in Hama six years previously and in which up to 20,000 are estimated to have lost their lives.

"We have the passports of 60 Gulf nationals and Americans," said the voice from the plane on its next call to the airport control tower. "Unless our heroic brothers in Zamakh Prison in Emirate are released, we will kill a hostage every hour." Just to make sure everyone understood, the chilling threat was spoken first of all in Arabic then repeated in English.

Their brothers in Zamakh! That description caused a stir among the intelligence analysts monitoring the transactions between the plane and the Air Force officer taking their calls. Abu Nidal had not proclaimed themselves as such on behalf of any particular Fundamentalist revolutionaries in the past. But their history had shown them to be highly skilful in adapting their cause towards that of the changing policies of their financial backers and also to changing their attitudes towards new ones. Syria had cut their funds. Also, following the emergency Arab League summit meeting in Jordan six months previously, they saw the Gulf Arab countries softening towards Israel by moving closer to Egypt and roundly condemning Iran. Therefore was this a chance to demonstrate that Iran was their new paymaster? As a gesture towards Iran were they manifesting their solidarity with the men from Razak being held in Zamakh?

"May Allah be merciful on us," sighed one of the officers as they discussed the significance of this probability.

There were hurried discussions between the various military attachés representing the countries whose nationals were under threat on the plane, the one from Emirate explaining to them the background to the Razak attack and some of the other moves that had been afoot in his country, although, on instruction from his own Minister of Defence, not mentioning the Soviet involvement. The consensus of the attachés was that the Iran theory was, in fact, the case. Through their Ambassadors, meeting with the Syrian Minister of Defence in his offices in Ommayad Square, they gave their support to the

Syrian line that there should be no compromise with the hi-jackers, whoever their new backers might be, whatever their demands might be. They accepted that this could lead to loss of life but that would be preferable to surrendering to their demands.

As they were nodding in agreement to this conclusion, the meeting was disturbed by a call to the Syrian Minister from the airport. The first victim had been shot and callously thrown from the plane's front door on the apron tarmac.

There was some dissent at the meeting after that. "They will kill everyone on board," said one of the Ambassadors. "We cannot sit it out with them. We must come up with some kind of solution."

Unknown to any of those at the meeting, other people were working on a solution. After another phone call, the Syrian Minister of Defence said he had an urgent summons, though not saying where, and immediately left the room. A dark blue Mercedes, the big top-of-the-range 560 SEL model, sped him the 20 minutes' drive out to the Soviet Embassy where he had been told the Ambassador had an important message from Moscow.

The normal formalities of coffee and pleasantries were dispensed with as the Minister and an aide took their seats at the Ambassador's big desk.

"Our people are very concerned about this affair," said the Ambassador, an olive-skinned Georgian who spoke fluent Arabic. "It may be demonstrated by those who are our enemies that the ones who are prisoners in this Zamakh place have some kind of connection with us. This is not the case and must not be seen to be the case. Nothing must happen to weaken our growing relations with the countries of the Gulf. Effective action must be taken against this group holding the plane. They must all be eliminated."

"But Mr Ambassador. There are over 100 people on board that aeroplane. There could be a slaughter. The Abu Nidal ones have automatics, grenades and explosives."

"They must be eliminated. Quickly. And totally."

It was only a ten-minute drive in the big Mercedes from the Soviet Embassy to the suburb they called Muhajreen, or place of the immigrants. Kurds and others from the north had first settled there, hence its name. But it was a different kind of immigrant that lived there now. For on the pleasant slopes of the hill on which it was situated were the best of houses, many of them the homes of senior diplomats from various nations. The big Merc swished through the gates of the most prestigious establishment on the hill of Muhajreen, the Presidential Palace.

The Ambassador relayed the details of the brief conversation he had with the Soviet representative and the message which had been received from Moscow. The General, seated at his big conference table at which there were also three senior officers, two from the Army and one from the Air Force, scribbled some notes with a slim gold pen as the Minister spoke. He did not consult any of the others when the Minister had finished speaking. Instead he continued staring at the notes he had been making. It was more than half a minute before he broke the silence, looking across the table to the Minister and saying just one word.

"Naffith."

The word meant simply . . . comply.

When the door of the 737 opened once more to eject ignominiously another dead body on the tarmac the Syrian commandos stormed the plane. The gunfire and the muffled explosions inside lasted for about four minutes, coming to an end with the loudest of the explosions from somewhere in the tail section. A deep red flash ran along the small windows of the main cabin like volume indicator lights on some giant stereo player. After that the squads of waiting firemen and ambulance crews flooded on to the smouldering aircraft.

Few of them — and some were hardened veterans who had served in Beirut — had seen anything like it before. The recently refurbished interior in the airline's new colour scheme of soft white, grey and blue pastels was splattered from ceiling to floor with blood. Slumped in their seats and scattered about the passageways were what seemed like countless bodies and pieces of bodies of terrorists, commandos, flight crew and innocent passengers. Six grenades had been detonated and the gunfire between the automatics of the commandos and the Kalashnikovs of the hi-jackers had shredded seats, walls, bulkheads and people before the bomb which had been planted in the rear of the plane went off. Another two similar bombs had been primed further forward in the plane but had failed to explode.

A total of 56 dead were taken from the plane, 41 of them passengers, four flight crew, six commandos and the five terrorists, three of whom had been killed in those horrendous first minutes, the two who had survived being executed on board. The majority of those who survived were wounded, many of them seriously.

The Syrians had complied.

Memories

HE TOOK the news a lot better than he had thought he might. Maybe it was
because he had been prepared for the worst, lying awake as he had been
through the night waiting for the call the sister at the Al Nahdha Hospital said
she would make as soon as she had word about the party of seven nurses who
had gone from there to sit the examination in Amman.

"I'm so very sorry, Mr Bria. So very, very sorry," she had said in an
unmistakably Scottish voice, which seemed to be the trademark of the senior
nurse in the Gulf. "It's been a tragedy for all of us. Esther and four of the girls
were killed outright. The other two are seriously ill in hospital. We are all
deeply shocked for they were lovely girls. Esther in particular was one of the
most popular girls on my staff. It's a terrible business, Mr Bria. Just terrible."

It was just after 6 a.m. and he stood at the big picture window of his
lounge flat looking out over the jebels, their fawn velvet softly contrasting
with the gentle grey-blue of the new day's sky. In that stillness of the early
morning his mind filled with the memories of Esther; that time when he had
spoken to her at the flower shop and felt so gauche about it all and afterwards
so contrite for what he had thought was his middle-age foolishness; the laughs
they had together when he teased her about the sing-song way she spoke and
the misuse of words like "already" and "too much"; that first night they had
made love together under the stars on the beach at Bandar Bahar and the
many moments of similar joy they had shared after that. He had never known
a woman who could make love the way she did, the enraptured way she
would coil into him, and hold him, and caress him, and make her movements
so gently flow with his. And now she was no more.

Maybe if he had believed in God he could understand it all better. He
admired the Christian. He had come to admire the Muslim even more for his
discipline and the strength of his belief. He had wanted many times to believe
too, but couldn't for there were always too many unanswered questions. Like
there were now. Why his Esther? Why their happiness lost forever? Why a
love stilled the way it had? Why God? Why?

The words came back to him, and he couldn't think precisely why he had
remembered them so well, of the man who had spoken so heroically, so
tragically, at the time of the Enniskillen Remembrance Day bomb in
Northern Ireland. He was the father of a young girl, like Esther, a nurse, and
who had held his hand as she died under the rubble of that blown-up
building. When he spoke about it the following day he had said: "Don't ask

me, please, for a purpose. I don't have a purpose. But I know there has to be a plan. If I didn't think that I would commit suicide. It is part of a greater plan and God is good and we shall meet again."

There was something about those Irish people. There were those with the hearts of stone and there were those, like that brave Enniskillen father, with hearts of the purest flesh, from whom the goodness and the strength seemed to shine. And God, how he wished he had some of that strength right now, for nothing, no power that was within him, could relieve the agony that was inside him, the rawness that was a part of him at the loss of Esther.

David Anthony called just before lunch-time. He had heard the news. "We got the casualty lists at Intelligence and I checked with the sister at the hospital. It must be a terrible blow for you, dear boy."

"I'm so glad you called, David. I was getting a bit morose there. Actually I've taken the news better than I thought. When Tony was killed right there in front of me, it sort of paralysed my mind. With Esther I had time to think about it. I didn't give her much of a chance, not with it being Abu Nidal. Did you?"

"To be truthful, no, despite what I might have said to you. And when we learned the Syrians were going to terminate it. Well! So tragic, Brian. So terribly, terribly tragic. So many innocents dying so needlessly. But that's the way of it nowadays. It's the day of the innocent. For years people have been talking and worrying about World War III. Goodness, does no one realise World War III is here and has been for years! World War III is in Ireland and Sri Lanka and the Punjab and Lebanon and the Gaza Strip and the Spanish Basque country and in South America and so many other places. Anyone, anywhere can be a victim, just like those unfortunate people on that aeroplane last night. Like you, Brian, I find it all rather unbearable to think about."

"I find it all just as unbearable, but I can't stop thinking about it. There are so many ifs and buts. If only we hadn't killed the men at the Fish Souk. If only we hadn't taken on the Spetsnaz. If only Gordon hadn't become obsessed with the men from prison. If only. I could go on and on. Both Tony and Esther would be here had we not intervened. And nothing would have happened to the Emir anyway for your people had it planned he wasn't even going to be at the Saghir Mosque. But on top of that they were saying last night at the Rani that had the coup been successful it might have been for the better of the country."

"The story's out then?"

"Yes, they seem to know most of the details. So what's the answer David . . . would it have been for the better or the worse had the coup worked?"

"I'm afraid that was never a consideration to us, dear boy. We had to view it in global terms. It would have been bad for the stability of the region had the Emir been deposed and it would have been very bad if the Soviets had increased their sphere of influence in the Gulf."

"And that was your people's only concern? To hell with what the people might have wanted in this little corner of Arabia. It's what the Super Powers want. That's all that matters, David. Ordinary people matter as little to them as the terrorists and their bombs and bullets. And Tony and I were naïve enough to think we were saving this little country!"

"Don't have any remorse about your participation in events here. You and Tony did the honourable thing. What you didn't appreciate were the ramifications. But I think you do now. Please don't think me callous for saying that the people weren't a consideration when Her Majesty's Government took the action it did to protect the Emir. I care very much for the people of the Gulf. I happen to think they are among some of the most charming people on earth and I'm not ashamed to say that I'd much rather they were under our influence, if they are to be under anyone's influence, that is, than that of the Commissars. Now, how about joining me down at the Rani for a drink."

"Please don't be offended, David, but I'd rather not. I want to remember it for the happy Thursday nights there, not the way I feel today. Besides, there's someone I must go and see. Would you mind dropping me down town?"

"Delighted. I was also planning to run you to the airport tonight, if that's all right."

"There may be someone with me."

"I think the car can cope."

Another Filipina girl came to the door of the flat, the friend who came from Baguio, he presumed.

"Amar has left," she said, unsmiling.

"What do you mean . . . left. Left for the Philippines?"

"I don't know. She didn't say. She just packed her case and said she was going and wouldn't talk about it."

"Did she get the money for the flight?"

"I don't think so. That was being organised by the girls who went to Jordan."

"Are you her friend from Baguio?"

"No. She was with the girls who went to Amman. She is dead too."

"When did Amar leave?"

"About an hour ago."

There was a quick taxi journey to the bus terminal where there were always crowds of villagers from the Interior waiting for one of the big green-and-red German diesels that serviced the country. The airport bus left from the last stance. But there was no bus there, nor was there anyone waiting.

Then he went to the main office of Khamis's the travel agency, to check the flights for Manila. There were two that day, both in the late evening.

He couldn't recall a time in his life when he had felt so alone, so disconsolate, as he did on that taxi ride from Rani back to his flat at Hamat House. It just seemed to be one blow after another and he wondered if he could take any more. Then he thought about being in London the following day. That would help. Yes, he was really looking forward to that now. The Gulf for him wasn't the happy place it had been any more. There were too many sad memories now.

Flat 604 was one of the furthest from the elevators and there was a walk along a long, straight corridor. Its polished marble had been re-polished that morning as it was every morning and the gentle hiss of the air-conditioning vents wafted down their refreshing, cool temperatures. He was about halfway down the bright passageway when he looked up and saw her there, sitting on an upturned suitcase at the door of his flat. His pace quickened and then he ran a little as she stood up and came towards him.

"Amar! Amar . . . darling. God, am I thrilled at seeing you! I thought I had lost you. Lost you forever."

He held her tightly and they kissed. Then she sobbed as she rested her head on him.

"It's all right, darling," he said softly. "Everything will be all right now. We're together you and I."

"Oh, Brian," she said looking up at him, the tears making those large Spanish eyes more lustrous than ever. "I wanted so to come for you this morning when I heard. But it wouldn't have been right. You would have thought I was rushing at you because. . . . Oh my God, the news was terrible. Poor Esther. And my friend from Baguio too. It was because of Esther I didn't come. No . . . no . . . it wouldn't have been right. Not yet, anyway. Not for a long time. But I had to let you know. That's why I came."

"And then where were you going?"

"Back to my employer."

"Not now you're not. You see, Amar, I went for you. And I was thinking the same thing as you . . . that it wouldn't be right. But why shouldn't it be? Why should we have to wait? We need each other you and I. And now we're together, nothing is going to separate us."

They embraced again.

POSTSCRIPT

Postscript

JUST AS Brian Bria had promised his dead friend Tony Mills after the encounter with the Russian Spetsnaz in Wadi Duka, the world did hear about the exploits of the British officer. The story broke in the main evening TV news programmed in Britain on the Saturday evening. Both channels showed some of the still photographs which they said were from a world exclusive story which would be appearing in the biggest-selling of the serious Sunday newspapers the following day. The story was headlined "Soviet SAS men beaten by lone British officer" and occupied a large panel at the top of page one of the newspaper. Inside there were two further pages of pictures and detail.

Other Sunday newspapers picked up the story in their later editions under a variety of headlines, suited to the market in which they sold. They included: "Brave British Major's Desert Duel", "Secret Soviet Troops Gunned by British Officer", . . . "English Hero Saves Desert Ruler" and "ZAPPED! Desert Brit cripples the Soviet SAS".

There were big follow-up stories too in the Monday newspapers with photographs of Tony Mills as a schoolboy and interviews with his mother at their home in Highgate. The big-circulation news magazines in France, Germany, and the United States also gave splash prominence to the Battle of Wadi Duka.

When asked for details of the incident, the Emirate Ministry of Information confirmed that a Major Antony Mills, a contract officer serving with the Emir's Defence Forces, had died on a patrol. "It occurred in an operation which concerned the internal security of the country and no more information will be forthcoming." None was.

In New York, on a routine visit to the United Nations, the Soviet Foreign Minister was pressed for details. He merely smiled in that affable way of his. His only quote was: "I have no knowledge of what you are speaking about."

OTHER TITLES BY THE SAME AUTHOR

FRONTLINE REPORT
A Journalist's Notebook
John Burrowes

This uniquely stimulating book is based upon the true events which took place in three action-packed years of one journalist's life. John Burrowes originally set out to write about his experiences as a reporter in Vietnam, Biafra and Northern Ireland and to tell, for the first time in book form the full tragic story of British soccer's saddest day: the Ibrox disaster of 1971 when sixty-six people died and hundreds more were injured at the New Years Rangers-Celtic match.

John Burrowes flew with the American G.I.s in helicopter raids over Vietnam, witnessed massacres and firing squads in Biafra, and was on the wrong side of both extremes in the Irish Troubles. These experiences moulded a philosophy which was to be tested on his return to his native Glasgow — where, ironically, his first assignment on his recall to a "desk job" was the Ibrox disaster.

ISBN: 0 906391 27 X
Price: £7.95 (cased)
Extent: 196pp

BENNY
The Life and Times of a Fighting Legend
John Burrowes

Benny Lynch was Scotland's greatest boxer and many seriously consider him the greatest fighter produced in Britain. Although he died tragically in 1946, stripped of his glory, the name Benny Lynch lives on. Perhaps no other British sportsman is remembered as well as the little man from the heart of Glasgow's Gorbals.

In *Benny* the true life of the Gorbals is remembered and portrayed as never before: the corner boys, the gangs, the dance halls, the legendary pubs and eating places. For the first time a vivid account of how the bubonic plague swept through the Gorbals is provided. That was just about the time that Benny Lynch's father settled there from Ireland.

Benny is not just a boxing book. It is a slice of the true life of the 1930's, a real social history as remembered by the people who were the contemporaries and ring rivals of Benny Lynch. As such it portrays the colour, the humour, the community fellowship and human tragedy of the depression period in the poverty stricken Gorbals. The book is fully illustrated and contains some rare pictures of both Benny Lynch and scenes of the Gorbals and its characters as they were.

ISBN 0 906391 32 6
Price: £7.95 (cased)
Extent: 224pp

JAMESIE'S PEOPLE
A Gorbals Story
John Burrowes

John Burrowes has followed his best-selling *Benny: The Life and Times of a Fighting Legend* with a hard-hitting novel set in the Glasgow of the same period.

The Nelsons were the best-known family in Glasgow's Gorbals. For Jamesie Nelson, the fighting man of the family, was the hardest of the hard men in that toughest and roughest of areas. They didn't call him "king" or any other menacing nickname — "Jamesie" was enough to spread fear among those who lived in and knew the Gorbals.

The Nelson family experienced all the emotions of Gorbals families in the 1930s and through the years of the Second World War. Jamesie's brother Sammy led one of the first strikes of storeworkers — and was humiliated for it by one of Glasgow's richest merchants. Sammy in turn clawed his way back to become the most successful black-marketeer in wartime Glasgow. He traded with the Americans, founded an empire on bootleg whisky, wheeled and dealed in corruption with the politicians, and came to own one of the city's finest houses.

The Nelsons endured the Gorbals during its worst years. Their story is full of the passion, humour and terrible events that were such a part of everyday life there at the time when that part of the world became stigmatised as "No Mean City". But John Burrowes goes deeper: there is a warmth and an understanding in his novelisation of those traumatic times in the area where he was born.

ISBN: 0 906931 71 7
Price: £9.95 (cased)
Extent: 240pp

INCOMERS
A Glasgow Novel
John Burrowes

They endured life in Glasgow's Gorbals during the worst days of
the thirties and the grim days of the wartime forties. Now the
Nelson family, featured in John Burrowes' earlier successful
novel, *Jamesie's People,* face the heady and hectic days of the
fifties. With the war behind them and rationing and other
restrictions eventually ended. Glasgow geared itself for better and
happier days. The good times were ready to roll. Sammy Nelson
and his niece set out to capitalise on the boom days ahead and
become involved with a new force to arrive in the Glasgow scene,
bringing with it a whole new life to the city — the incomers . . .
migrants from Asia and Europe.

The story of the *Incomers* and the continuing saga of the Nelsons
is full of the same passion and humour which made *Jamesie's
People* such a startling success. Set against a background
of corrupt local government it confronts the ugly and stark face of
racism.

ISBN: 1 85158 32 8
Price: £9.95 (cased)
Extent: 224pp